THAT STREAK OF EBONY

By the same author:

The One They Could Never Catch, The Book Guild, 1991

THAT STREAK OF EBONY

Roger Clarke

The Book Guild Ltd
Sussex, England

This book is a work of fiction. The characters and situations in this story are imaginary. No resemblance is intended between these characters and any real persons, either living or dead.

This book is sold subject to the condition that it shall not, by way of trade or otherwise, be lent, re-sold, hired out, photocopied or held in any retrieval system or otherwise circulated without the publisher's prior consent in any form of binding or cover other than that in which this is published and without a similar condition including this condition being imposed on the subsequent purchaser.

The Book Guild Ltd.
25 High Street,
Lewes, Sussex

First published 1996
© Roger Clarke 1996

Set in Baskerville

Typesetting by Wordset
Hassocks, West Sussex

Printed in Great Britain by
Bookcraft (Bath) Ltd.

A catalogue record for this book is
available from the British Library

ISBN 0 86332 998 5

INTRODUCTION

In the previous book, *The One They Could Never Catch*, Isabelle Reynolds rides her beloved stallion Hurry-On to victory in England and France. She lives at Oakfield Lodge with her father, known as the master, and her brothers Leon and Roger. The master and Leon, who is romantically involved with his distant French cousin Anne-Marie, spend most of the year at the family engineering company in Nigeria. Roger is struggling to qualify as an engineer at London University, and Milly, an Oxford graduate who lives in the village, is coaching him.

Life in the Berkshire village of Winkfield revolves around racing. Even the Vicar, the Reverend Charles Manning, goes to meetings and keeps an eye on the odds. Most evenings are spent in the Milligans' kitchen (Milligan is the bailiff) discussing racing prospects with George Marshall, the local trainer. Another frequent visitor is Mr Buchanan, the Irish owner who specialises in entering previously untried horses which win at long odds.

As the book ends and this one begins, Isabelle and Hurry-On have just won one of the biggest prizes of all: The Gold Cup at Royal Ascot.

1

On the evening of Isabelle's Ascot Gold Cup victory, Milly had just arrived at Oakfield Lodge for the celebrations when she was accosted by Isabelle's father, known as the master.

'Good evening, Milly. Can you spare me a few moments in the study?'

'Certainly, sir.'

He closed the door and offered Milly a seat.

'How are Roger's studies progressing this term?' he enquired.

'A marked improvement on the Easter term, sir.'

'Splendid.'

The master smiled at Milly. 'You will recollect the other evening I wanted to have a word with you and then I had to take a telephone call? Well, it seems that our London office has a vacancy for what we term an "overseas liaison officer". In effect this means acting as a link between our Nigerian trading partners, staff and engineers, and the manufacturers in UK and Europe. I wonder if the post would interest you?'

Milly responded immediately. 'It sounds exciting and challenging, sir.'

'So you accept the idea?'

'Yes, sir.'

'Good. Then Monday morning, if you can travel up to the London office, Miss Evans, our staff chief, will discuss all the formalities with you and establish a starting date.'

Milly stood up. 'Thank you very much, sir.'

'Hopefully you will continue to encourage Roger with his studies,' the master added.

'Of course, sir.'

The interview came as a surprise to Milly, and to Isabelle

and Roger, and they were all pleased with this new turn of events.

'This means, Milly,' Roger said, 'that we can often lunch together in the West End. The College is in Southampton Row, not ten minutes from the Piccadilly office.'

'Miss Evans has been asked to explain all the formalities to me on Monday. Incidentally, dear Isabelle, your father requests your presence in the study now.'

Isabelle left the room quickly.

'Hello, my darling,' he said as she came in. 'What a race! Uncle Bill, the colonel and myself, we saw it all from the enclosure. Congratulations.'

'Thank you, Daddy.'

'Before returning to Lagos next Sunday it will interest me to know more about my lovely and accomplished daughter. We have always been so close to one another, especially since Mummy died. Tell me, have you any personal prospects for the future?'

Isabelle sighed. 'No Daddy, nothing in sight yet.'

'It seems incredible – such a lovely girl, under thirty and no prospects.'

'You forget, Daddy dear, all my boy-friends were killed in action in the last war: Jimmy, Squadron Leader, Fighter Command – with fourteen bandits to his wallet – killed in September 1940, one of the few. Then John sunk in the Mediterranean during the Malta Convoy rescue operation. And Allen, Sergeant Pilot, Bomber Command, after forty-seven trips to Hamburg, Mannheim, Düsseldorf, shot down in 1944. And finally Richard, Parachute Regiment, missing after Arnhem, 1944. Commando.'

It was her father's turn to sigh. 'So it's like that. You are not exactly courting the society of young men.'

'Not really, Daddy dear. To be hurt four times within four years is the signal for prudence. But my faith has kept me going. Those boys died, as your close friends at Mons, Ypres and the Somme died, for future generations. That was especially brought home to me during our night together with Uncle Bill and the colonel, when they recounted the retreat from Mons and the extraordinary military feats of the BEF against the Prussian Guard, the Kaiser's finest troops.'

'But the future, Isabelle?' her father said gently.

Isabelle shrugged. 'No prospect in sight, dear Daddy. On the other hand, my life will be a little more relaxed now that the big race is over. Of one thing you may rest assured, you will be the first to be informed if a prospect ever comes into my life again. You have been so kind and affectionate, dear Daddy, ever since my earliest days.'

'Thank you, my dear. It would give me immense pleasure to know if anything happens when I'm in Lagos.'

Mrs Plant knocked at the door. 'Excuse me, sir, there is a very military man at the door asking for Miss Isabelle.'

'Ask him to come into the study, Mrs Plant,' replied the master.

The visitor came straight to the point. 'My apologies, sir, for this intrusion, but my mission is to speak to Miss Isabelle Reynolds. One of our men captured by the Germans at Arnhem has recently been returned by our intelligence service, from the Russians. His name is Lieutenant-Colonel Sir Richard Cameron, Parachute Regiment, Commando Division. He is in the military hospital at Aldershot, soon to be moved to Reading – he is still very weak, and constantly asks for Miss Isabelle Reynolds.'

The room was going round Isabelle. Her father just caught her as she fainted.

'Good God, just ring that bell please, officer.'

Mrs Plant responded immediately.

'Isabelle has received a pleasant shock,' the master told her. 'Have you some brandy and water?'

'Did you say a pleasant shock, sir?' the visitor enquired.

'Sorry about this, officer. Yes, this is my daughter Isabelle. She was telling me about Sir Richard only this morning. It must be five years since he was captured.'

'Yes sir. It took us time to extricate him from those stupid Russians.'

Isabelle woke up to see herself surrounded by Mrs Plant, her father and the officer in commando uniform.

'So sorry, dear Daddy, that is my first faint ever. I feel better now. But is it true that Richard is alive?'

'Yes, Miss,' the officer assured her. 'But he is still very weak, only released from the intensive care unit yesterday. It took the medical director, the consultants and the surgeon four weeks of coaxing to find out your surname, Miss. Two female nurses are in attendance twenty-four hours. He is only semi-conscious for a short time of the day. However, the consultant is convinced that the mental and physical balance is returning gradually to his war-torn frame, although it may be over a year before he can walk. The consultant asked me in particular miss, whether you have a photograph of yourself, taken near the time you last saw him.'

'Of course, officer.'

Roger, who had just entered the study, was asked to supply the framed photo of Isabelle in his room.

The master turned to the visitor. 'May we offer you a drink, officer?'

'Thank you, sir. A glass of ale will suit admirably.'

'But Daddy, Richard never told me he was from a titled family.'

'Few of us in the ranks, Miss, were ever aware of it either. But the Camerons are an old Scottish family as far as my knowledge goes, Miss.'

'Roger please ask Miss Evans to let me have some information about the family of a Scottish officer called Sir Richard Cameron.'

'No problem, Dad,' said Roger, leaping to the phone.

Ten minutes later Miss Evans replied direct to the master.

'Isabelle, please listen in on the other phone,' he told her.

'The Camerons of Inverness,' said Miss Evans, 'are an ancient Scottish family with French origins. Settled in Scotland four hundred years ago during the French civil wars. According to their solicitors, Sir Richard Cameron the last surviving member is still missing, believed killed at Arnhem in 1944. The elder brother, Lindsay, was killed during the commando raid at Dieppe in 1943 and the younger brother was killed at the raid on St Nazaire in 1944. The father was killed at the Somme in 1916.

'In fact they have been a family of army men for generations, since the fifteen hundreds. Nevertheless, the castle at Inverness remains in splendid condition; twenty-one servants were once in attendance. The estate is vast, mostly woodland. But the family investments are considerable, with large stakes in shipping, steel and heavy engineering. These interests are managed by a group of executive directors. The estate includes eighteen farms. I hope this answers your enquiry, sir.'

'Thank you, Miss Evans.' The master put down the phone and turned to the visitor. 'Officer, did you know that Sir Richard came from a family of army men, going back for the last four hundred years?'

The officer nodded. 'Yes sir, although it had not occurred to me that the association was as long as that.'

'When do you think, officer, it will be possible for me to see Richard?' Isabelle wanted to know.

'Within the next ten days, Miss – as soon as the doctor and the consultant believe the time is right. Meanwhile here is my card. My station is the Medical Coordinator for Army Group B, Reading, Berks.'

'Thank you very much, officer. One last question. Do you know whether your patient has a small scar on the left side of his forehead?'

'The nurses will be asked to establish whether it exists, and you will hear from me tonight.'

After his departure, Isabelle's eyes were filled with tears. Her father drew her close.

'It seems, Daddy, that your question will be answered before departing for Lagos. There may well be a prospect for my future after all.'

'Splendid. Tonight, after the phone call, presumably?'

'Yes, Daddy. Please tell Mrs Plant that if there is a call for me before six pm, to explain that I will be at the church preparing for the flower display tomorrow.'

At six thirty a call came through from the officer. 'Hello, Miss, you are quite correct, the scar is in evidence under the hair. How did it happen?'

'At Twickenham, officer, during the Oxford and Cambridge rugger match before the war.'

'Thank you, Miss.'

'How is Richard today?'

'Making forward strides every hour,' he assured her. 'You will be hearing again from me in ten days' time.'

'Many thanks, officer.' Isabelle said, and hung up.

*

The next day another call came from Army Group B.

'Is Mr Walter Reynolds available?'

'Speaking.'

'One moment, sir. Brigadier Sir Ralf Harding wishes to talk to you.'

'Hello, Mr Reynolds. So sorry to interrupt your morning. Two of my intelligence officers, accompanied by me, would be grateful for half an hour of your time tomorrow morning about eleven am at your home – for security reasons.'

'No problem, Sir Ralf, but why the security?' the master wanted to know.

'The reason is confidentiality,' the brigadier explained. 'Either Richard was dumped at Hamburg or he escaped from the Russians. Fortunately, he was picked up by our intelligence unit, but not without a shoot-out with the KGB. We lost three but they were all killed. We believe that they wanted Richard dead, for reasons best known to themselves. More details later. Meanwhile, it is only fair to ensure that your daughter Isabelle is fully aware of the future risks which may have to be faced during the convalescent period.'

'Thank you, Sir Ralf, for revealing the situation. We look forward to your visit tomorrow at eleven.'

The master immediately convened a family conference, which included Daniel Faure, Anne-Marie, Milly, Mrs Plant and Milligan the bailiff, alerting them to the circumstances surrounding Richard's arrival in the UK.

Isabelle ventured, 'But Daddy, the officer explained that it may be twelve to eighteen months before Richard is able to walk.'

'My darling, tomorrow you will witness the British Secret Service in action. Have patience until then. In fact it is my guess that you are in for a pleasant shock tomorrow.'

'Daddy, you are incomprehensible,' Isabelle protested.

'And you are gorgeous – especially when that brilliant intellect is puzzled.'

The officers arrived on time the following morning, accompanied by an elderly white-haired man with a stoop, who was introduced as the private secretary to the brigadier, a Mr James.

'Good morning, Sir Ralf, you are welcome.'

'What a lovely home!' exclaimed the brigadier. 'It must be a few hundred years old.'

'Three hundred to be exact.'

The brigadier turned to Isabelle. 'Delighted to meet you, Miss Reynolds, and to know of your past association with Richard.'

'How is he, sir?' Isabelle asked anxiously.

'Progressing rapidly, especially since he received your photograph. But we do not want to rush him in his present state. So far he is not ready for the de-briefing. This is where you may be able to help. In about ten days' time we will send a car for you to visit Richard. By then his memory may have returned. In particular we want to know the names of the other British officers in the same camp. You will have to be patient, it will take delicate handling. However, in view of the way you ride winners, we have complete confidence in you. As long as Richard is not too tired after his talks with you we will arrange for a car to pick you up every two or three days until he is able to walk about. Are you happy with this suggestion?'

'Very, sir. But what exactly is wrong with him?'

'He's not suffering much now, physically. It is his memory that has gone. That is why your photograph was so useful. The consultant has expectations – particularly since Richard expressed so much pleasure in seeing the photograph. In fact he keeps it next to his pillow and will not allow the nurses to touch it!'

Addressing the master, the brigadier added, 'So kind of you, Mr Reynolds, to allow me this introduction to your charming daughter.'

'It is a pleasure to be of service to the military, Sir Ralf,' the master responded. 'Quite apart from the news for Isabelle, who has been given quite a lot to think about – especially the future.'

The brigadier took his leave. 'Goodbye, Mr Reynolds. Thank you again, Miss Reynolds, for your cooperation. During my absence the two officers will be at your disposition during every visit to the HQ.'

After their departure Isabelle and her father settled

down to a long chat. Eventually the conversation returned to the brigadier's visit.

'How curious, Isabelle, that Richard evidently remembers you, and no-one else at the HQ. And what about his relations?'

'According to Miss Evans, Daddy, he had none left,' Isabelle reminded him.

Just then Mrs Plant came into the room. 'Excuse me sir, one of the officers on the phone for Isabelle.'

Isabelle went out to take the call.

'Hello, officer.'

'Miss Reynolds? We have just received a visitor from Richard's home in Inverness. She is the elderly head housekeeper, who nursed Richard as a baby. Richard went quite wild with delight and insists that she sees you immediately. We have, therefore, taken the liberty of directing Miss Glenfield to your home.'

'Thank you very much officer, but how will she get here from Reading?'

The officer chuckled. 'Do not worry about that problem. You are about to see a particularly beautiful black and silver chauffeur-driven Rolls-Royce.'

Isabelle hurried back to report the conversation to her father.

'Well Daddy, what a *drame*, as we say in France!'

'At least Richard has recognised his head housekeeper.' He added, 'It is a long time since the description "head housekeeper" has been used in England. It must be an impressive residence.'

'Do you think that we ought to invite her to lunch, after travelling 500 miles from Inverness?'

'Of course, my dear, we will then learn something about Richard's home. But Isabelle, had you no inkling of Richard's background before the war?'

Isabelle searched her memory in vain. 'No Daddy, simply because we met during the early part of the war, before his brothers' deaths. Indeed it is a surprise for me to know about his background now. He never even hinted about the extent of his family fortunes. We had such simple and happy lives together. He was so full of fun – and yet utterly fearless when the need arose.

Her father voiced his concern. 'You realise that Richard may be a cripple for life or even mentally handicapped?'

'Yes, dear Daddy. All this I have considered with care. But the path of my duty is quite clear – you forget that it was Richard who restored my faith.'

Roger was at his bedroom window when the beautiful black and silver Rolls slid into the drive.

'Who on earth is that – and what a car!' Racing down the stairs he all but cannoned into Mrs Plant, who was about to open the front door. 'So sorry Mrs Plant, but there is a gorgeous car in the drive. Who is the visitor?'

'It is the head housekeeper of Isabelle's friend at the hospital,' Mrs Plant informed him. 'Good morning, Miss Glenfield. The master is expecting you. He heard from the military at Reading. I am Mrs Plant.'

'Thank you, Mrs Plant. What a lovely home, and a simply beautiful front garden. I believe Miss Isabelle lives here with her father and family.'

'That is so. Please let me take your raincoat, madam, and come this way.'

After the introductions, Miss Glenfield gladly accepted an invitation to stay for lunch.

'It was a relief to me, Mr Reynolds, to find Richard after all those years of doubt. Since his brothers were killed, most of my time has been devoted to acting as his private secretary. Fortunately, this morning he was able to sign several bank documents in order to establish his authority as the master of the estate farms in Inverness. I have been at the hall for fifty years. Richard was born thirty-three years ago, and Lady Cameron died soon afterwards, so it has been my duty to act as his nurse, guide and mother all these years. He was happy to see me, and appeared to be quite normal on the surface. But it seems that relapses are frequent, and he goes off into a faint without warning. However, the medical officers are most confident, especially after meeting you, Miss Isabelle.'

'But they say it will be a long time before he is able to walk again.'

Miss Glenfield looked sceptical. 'You may not recollect that Richard won a Cambridge blue at rugger and remained in fine physical shape up to Arnhem. It is my opinion that he will recover rapidly.'

'What did he read at Cambridge?' asked the master.

'Applied mathematics and engineering science – with a double first. He also devoted much of his time to golf and classical music. In fact he is an accomplished pianist,' replied Miss Glenfield.

'Incredible,' commented Isabelle. 'So much of this is new to me.'

After lunch, Miss Glenfield prepared to take her leave.

'Are you returning to Inverness tonight, Miss Glenfield?' the master enquired.

'Oh no sir. The family legal advisers are expecting me in London tomorrow morning. A reservation has been made for me at a small hotel in Jermyn Street.' She shook hands with her hosts. 'Richard will be so happy to come and see you in this lovely home, Miss Isabelle.'

'He will be most welcome to stay here whenever he is better,' responded the master.

'That is most kind, Mr Reynolds. Richard loves people and activity. I know he would be delighted to spend some time here during his convalescence.'

A week went by, but no news came from the hospital.

Milly was intrigued when she heard about Richard. 'Applied mathematics and engineering science, a double first at Cambridge! He can give Roger some additional guidance for his studies at Faraday House College, especially now that my future will be centred upon the Piccadilly office.'

'A call for you, Miss Isabelle,' interrupted Mrs Plant.

It was the officer from the military hospital.

'In ten days' time, Mrs Plant, they have invited me to see Richard.' Isabelle reported.

'Bless you, my dear. Evidently there is going to be a lot of activity around here later on in the summer.'

At that moment Leon entered with Anne-Marie on his arm.

'Mrs Plant we thought you ought to be one of the first to know that we are intending to be married.'

As Mrs Plant gave him a kiss, Isabelle kissed Anne-Marie. 'My darling, this is lovely news.'

'Thank you, dear Isabelle, where is your father?'

'Here he is,' replied the master. He had heard Leon's announcement. 'Bless you both,' he said, giving Anne-Marie a warm hug.

'We thought about late October, on my return from Lagos,' said Leon.

'Splendid idea. Incidentally, did you know that we may have a long-term guest in the house by then?'

Leon nodded. 'It was just like you, Dad, to make that kind gesture. Isabelle told me all about it.'

'Since Richard is still officially attached to B Group Airborne Division, they indicated that a full-time nurse will be provided if Richard is able to convalesce here at the lodge.'

'Is that so, Daddy,' said Isabelle. 'Perhaps it is necessary because we are not yet aware of his medical problems. The officer said that sometimes he sleeps twenty-four hours round the clock.'

'Poor devil,' sympathised Leon.

Isabelle was ready and waiting at eleven am on the appointed day when the military car swung into the drive.

'Good morning, officer, how is the patient today?' she asked as she stepped in.

'So excited about your visit that it was difficult to make him eat breakfast,' the officer told her.

Isabelle felt a bit shy and nervous as they entered the large grounds of the hospital. The place seemed vast. After a lengthy walk through long corridors they arrived eventually at number 5A – Richard's room, with its glass inspection window. He was asleep.

'Good,' said the officer. He beckoned to the nurse as they entered Richard's room. 'How long, nurse?'

'About five minutes ago, sir.'

'Give him another five minutes for Miss Reynolds to settle down, but keep in touch with her throughout the visit.'

'Yes sir.'

Richard looked a little thin, but otherwise quite normal. 'Is he able to walk a little more?' asked Isabelle.

'As it happens, he started today, just to the door and back to bed. He will need a stick for some time.'

Isabelle suppressed a tear when she thought of him before the war – now such a wreck of a man. She sat down in a low chair close to the bed-head.

Richard stirred when Isabelle's hand closed over his on the bedsheet. 'God bless you, my dear little friend.'

Isabelle took his hand to her breast and kissed him several times.

'Do you mean to say that you still love this useless broken-down corpse?'

'Don't be silly, Richard. Your progress has been reported to me by the hour, and you are far from a corpse.' To prove her point, she kissed him again.

2

It was three months before Richard was discharged from the Military hospital at Reading. It was a lovely late September afternoon with a slight nip in the air. As the military car entered the drive at Oakfield Lodge a loud cheer went up from several of the farm men and onlookers from the village of Winkfield. The driver was quick to open the door, and saluted as the consultant, followed by the nurse and Richard, with two walking-sticks, moved slowly towards the front door. It was then that a powerful voice from the small crowd shouted, 'Three cheers for our hero from Arnhem ... hip hip hurrah – and congratulations, sir.'

The congratulations were for the award, announced in most of the national press of the Military Cross for the gallant stand made at the bridge at Arnhem in 1944. As the cheers continued Richard turned round and gracefully acknowledged the warmth of the reception.

Isabelle was waiting for them at the front entrance. After an affectionate hug from Richard, Isabelle addressed the consultant.

'The tea has just been made, sir.'

'That sounds a splendid idea, Miss Reynolds, and it will give us the opportunity of explaining some of the take-over notes for the treatment of the patient.'

At that moment in burst Roger and Milly.

'So sorry, Isabelle, we did not know you were in the study.'

'You have both come just in time for there is a little job for you. First of all, Richard, this is my younger brother Roger, and Milly, our friend from the village.'

Richard shook hands, 'I have heard a lot about you, Milly, at the hospital. It seems we have something in common – applied mathematics.'

'Yes, sir, but not quite to your double first standard at Cambridge.'

Richard smiled, 'Those days have long since drifted into the past.'

'Roger,' continued Isabelle, 'will you and Milly take Richard around the farm? In particular he wishes to see Hurry-on.'

'This way, sir. Do take my arm.'

'Thank you, Roger, but it is important for me to use my limbs. The going may be a bit slow at first.'

'Let me lead, sir – this way.'

Addressing Isabelle, the consultant explained that Richard might take about a year to be normally fit, mentally and physically.

'For the first month we wish to leave you with, Marion,' indicating the military nurse.

'That is no problem, sir. We have made arrangements for Marion to be next door to Richard – with radio communication between the two rooms.'

'Excellent. Richard is making progress, and the situation here is quite ideal. For example any little job on the farm will gradually bring back his physical confidence. He can eat anything, drink anything. As the legs return to life, short walks are essential daily – later long walks. It is fortunate that he retains a keen interest in his engineering studies. A whole trunk full of textbooks arrived from his home in Inverness. One last word of caution. Under no circumstance must he be allowed out alone – until the memory tissues are fully recovered. This may take another month, when my next visit is due. Meanwhile Marion will be in touch with me at the hospital in case of need. We have to thank you and your father for this generous gesture. The brigadier will be writing to your father when he returns from West Germany at the end of the month.'

'It will be a privilege and a pleasure for us all to encourage Richard back to normal health, sir,' Isabelle assured him.

'Thank you very much, Miss Reynolds. Goodbye Marion, and good luck with your patient.'

'Thank you, sir.'

As the military car left the drive, Isabelle turned to the nurse. 'Let me show you to your room, Marion. Hunt, the chauffeur, will look after all the luggage.'

Upon opening the bedroom door Marion gave a cry of delight. 'Miss Reynolds, this is luxury. It is such a lovely room. We are not used to this kind of accommodation in the Army. It is all so feminine.'

'Please call me Isabelle.'

'Thank you, Isabelle, I will.'

Marion was shown around the house and introduced to Mrs Plant, who asked questions about the patient's diet.

'No, Mrs Plant, there is no strict diet, in fact the opposite. He eats still so little. It will be more a question of tempting him. I am sure you can provide some special country dishes.'

'All right, my dear. This will be quite a challenge.'

On the way through the kitchen garden Marion explained that Richard was to be officially discharged from the Army at the end of the month, and all his civilian clothes were on their way from Inverness.

Richard soon settled down to the routine life on the farm. In spite of the two walking-sticks, he managed, guided by Milligan, to undertake some light work, and he found time to help Roger with his engineering studies in the evenings. Both Leon and the master were back in Nigeria, and by now it was late October, shortly before the marriage between Leon and Anne-Marie was due to take place. Isabelle and Milligan had made several trips to the Buchanan stables in Northern Ireland, and three of Buchanan's mares had been lodged at Oakfield Lodge since June. One evening a call came through from Buchanan for Isabelle.

'Miss Isabelle, Joe Mercer, my lead jockey has gone sick with lung trouble. He may or may not be ready for the One Thousand Guineas at Newmarket at the end of March. You are formally invited therefore to ride Colleen in the race in June. If you accept the challenge, it will mean that Colleen will be sent to Oakfield Lodge stables in a few days so that you can start training together. How do you feel about this proposal?'

'Mr Buchanan, it will be a privilege. It is most kind of

you to ask me.'

'Not at all, young lady. Already you have proved to be a first-class rider on stayers. Now you must acquire the tricks of riding sprinters.'

'How long is the One Thousand Guineas race?' Isabelle asked.

'One mile, for fillies only,' Buchanan explained. 'Colleen is wintering well and is very fast.'

A week later Colleen arrived at Oakfield Lodge.

'What a beauty,' exclaimed Richard and Mrs Plant together as the filly left the horse box, led by Milligan.

An hour later Isabelle returned from Bracknell and introduced herself to Colleen. They fell in love with one another at once, as Isabelle rubbed her down and prepared her for a short walk around the fields. The next morning, with Isabelle up, they arrived on the Marshall training-ground.

'Good morning, Miss Isabelle – so this is the famous winner of the Coventry Stakes at Royal Ascot. Indeed beautifully proportioned and another jet black, just like Hurry-On.'

'She is so good, Mr Marshall, and so quiet. When do you think we ought to try her out?'

'A walk around for today, and next week my two best sprinters will be ready for a trial run.'

That same evening, during a gathering in Mrs Milligan's kitchen, the general topic of conversation was Colleen. Even the vicar was keenly interested. But there was a surprise visit from Mrs Plant, who came in a hurry from the Lodge.

'So sorry, Mrs Milligan, but a call from Lagos from the master. Leon is on BCA4 flight to London, sick with malaria. We are to arrange to drive him from the airport direct to the Hospital for Tropical Diseases in London. He is due to arrive at six am tomorrow morning.'

'No problem, Mrs Plant,' Isabelle assured the house-keeper. 'Richard and I will organise it immediately. Goodnight, Mrs Milligan. Thank you so much for the evening.'

'Do hope he will be all right, Miss,' Mrs Milligan told her as the visitors left.

Anne-Marie, Isabelle and Richard accompanied Leon to

the London hospital. He was perspiring profusely all the way. Once in the hospital, Leon was treated without delay and slept for seven days without waking. Anne-Marie hardly left the hospital and telephoned every night to Isabelle at the Lodge. After he awoke at the end of the week, the fever left him. He was weak but well. The doctor, however, insisted he stayed in bed for another week until all the dead malaria parasites on the blood slide appeared no more. The doctor advised also that Leon ought to rest at the farm for at least a further six weeks. The marriage therefore was postponed.

The following week Leon was introduced to Richard, who was able now to use only one walking-stick, and had come to visit him at the hospital.

'Hello, Leon. We seem to be both in the same boat, temporarily confined to the sick-bay.'

'Delighted to know you, Richard,' Leon returned. 'Isabelle has told me all about you, and about the recent award. Congratulations.'

'Thank you. Incidentally, it seems that you are concerned with industrial burners and boilers in Nigeria. You may not be aware that before the war it was my task to design them.'

'Great Scot, you are the very man we have been looking for.' Addressing Roger, who had accompanied Richard to the hospital, he added, 'Roger, in my study there are up-to-date service manuals on burners made by the leading manufacturers, namely Hamworthy (British), Saacke (German), Wanson (Belgian and French) and Nu-way (British). Will you please see that Richard has a copy of each immediately.'

'Yes Leon, as soon as we return,' Roger agreed.

'After a few weeks' study of these manuals, Richard, there are one or two problems in Nigeria upon which you may be able to help us.'

'It will give me pleasure, Leon.'

3

From Oakfield Lodge to the Vicarage the walk across the field path usually lasted about twenty minutes, and today Richard was most keen to be included in the next discussion with the vicar on the subject of planetary science. So, still with one walking-stick, the walk lasted half an hour.

'Hello, children,' welcomed the vicar. 'So this must be Richard.'

'It is a pleasure to meet you, Reverend Manning. Thank you very much for including me within the family circle.'

'You must be tired after struggling with that walking-stick along the narrow path across the fields. Come and sit down in this armchair.' The vicar turned to Milly. 'Now Milly, if you care to ring that bell we can all commence to enjoy a cup of tea – this time with teacakes made this morning.'

'What will be the subject today?' asked Roger.

'The mysteries of planetary science.'

The vicar talked at length about these rival theories.

'A great difficulty is posed by the Scriptures,' he concluded. 'Does the incarnation offer salvation to sinners everywhere? The testaments are silent on this subject. My own views, children, are quite clear on this complex issue, which will be revealed at our meeting next Saturday.'

'Thank you very much, sir, for a most enlightening lecture,' responded Richard.

'So glad you found it interesting Richard,' replied the vicar. 'In today's secular climate of scientific thought it is easy to forget the long intellectual history of human attempts to comprehend the starry heavens. As we reach outward with modern instruments it is good to be reminded of the labours of others who, lacking any means of proof, still dared to think seriously about the implications of this question: are we, or are we not, alone? And with that thought, children, it is now necessary to prepare for my Sunday sermon.'

'It was so stimulating, sir. Thank you very much,' said Isabelle.

On the way home Milly asked Roger, 'Are you as bewildered as me?'

'More so, Milly – completely confused, especially about the other worlds. It will be interesting to know how the vicar will conclude the subject.'

The following morning Isabelle, mounted on Colleen, entered the Marshalls' stables, where the riders were already mounted for the trials over the one-mile distance.

'Good morning, Miss,' welcomed Fred, the lead rider. 'These are our best sprinters. At the four-furlong post the second sprinter will take over with a flying start. Is this all clear, Miss.'

'Perfectly, Fred.'

Colleen was lined up with the first sprinter and the flag went down. The race started. Jameson, a three-year colt, was fast during the first two furlongs and managed to hold Colleen neck to neck. But at the end of the half-way mark, four furlongs, Colleen was five lengths in front. It was then that Billy, the second colt, took over with a flying start. But Colleen was by then well in her stride and Billy only held it for one furlong of the second half, after which Colleen drew away to win the mile by twenty lengths.

As the horses came into the paddock Fred expostulated. 'Never seen anything like it, Miss. How right of the critics to describe her as a streak of ebony when she won the Coventry stakes.'

That night in Mrs Milligan's kitchen there was much excitement about the trial. 'According to Mr Marshall, sir, Colleen is the fastest filly on four legs he has ever seen in his racing career in his stable,' Milligan told the vicar.

'What's her price for the One Thousand Guineas?' asked the vicar.

'The current price is ten to one, sir, Dhoti, the Aga Khan's entry is a hot favourite at two to one. There are twenty-nine runners.'

'Splendid, but this trial result must remain confidential.'

*

Early in December Leon began to feel stronger. It was then that Anne-Marie brought back from the office a message from Lagos.

> 'Attention Leon. Shegu due to arrive Monday with problem on combustion, at Lever Brothers, Aba, East Nigeria'.

Richard took it to Leon, who was still in hospital.

'Excellent,' responded Leon, 'We will solve it together, Richard.'

At eight am the Nigerian Airways plane landed at London Airport. Shegu was met by Isabelle and Lander, the chauffeur. The Yoruba Man's six and a half foot figure was easily picked out by Isabelle.

'Good morning, Miss Isabelle,' he greeted her. 'How is the young master Leon?'

'Hello, Shegu. Welcome to England. My brother is still a little weak, but he improves daily.'

At Oakfield Lodge Shegu was introduced to Richard.

'In half an hour Richard will go with you to see Leon in the hospital. That should give you time to prepare your drawings and papers. Meanwhile, you are most welcome to your usual room. How is my dear father?'

'The master is fine, Miss, and asked me to give you this letter.'

On the way to the Hospital for Tropical Diseases Shegu explained briefly the nature of the combustion problem.

As they entered the private ward, they met Anne-Marie and the day-nurse. Leon was sitting up and gave them a warm reception.

'Remember now, gentlemen,' the nurse insisted, 'you only have half an hour. The patient is still in an exhausted state. This is doctor's orders.'

Leon smiled, 'Nurse, when will Kronenbourg beer be allowed instead of this horrible barley water? Four times a day this jug of barley water must be swallowed, Richard,' he explained.

'The doctor will be informed of your request,' concluded the nurse.

'Do you think we can have a small table, nurse to use for our drawings?' Leon requested.

'Certainly, sir.'

In a few minutes two orderlies brought in a suitable table.

'Shegu, it is so good to see you. Richard, we have been through a thousand battles together. Sometimes Shegu has worked three days and nights non-stop.'

Shegu beamed, 'But we do miss you sir – especially now at Lever Brothers, Aba, Nigeria. The problem has beaten us all, and they only have the other 35,000 pound per hour boiler operational – on high-fire non-stop, twenty-four hours a day, seven days a week.'

'Well, Shegu, What is the nature of the problem?' Leon asked.

'In fact there are two problems sir. The first one is a combustion problem.'

'Just a minute, Shegu,' Leon interrupted. 'Lever Brothers, that is natural-gas firing.'

'Correct, sir.'

'There is a clear build-up of carbon at the far end of the furnace, between the first and second passes. Every few days we have to clean it out and it is becoming worse with time. It is not thick but it is widespread.'

'All right Shegu – ready with pen and paper? There is an excess of carbon monoxide gas at the far end of the furnace,' Leon explained. 'This is the reason for the carbon build-up. Now, the solution is simple:

(a) Reduce the primary air by one third of the damper travel. You understand?'

'Yes, sir.'

(b) Reduce the butterfly gas volume at the burner end of the gas train by one, repeat one degree. The dial is marked in degrees from No.1 to No.17.'

'Right, sir.'

'From this drawing, Shegu, you will note that the main furnace tube is long for this size of boiler. The combustion of the natural gas flame takes place much further along the furnace tube than is the case with the oil flame. Now the second problem, Shegu.'

But at that moment the nurse entered. 'Only five minutes

left, gentlemen.'

'Quick, Shegu.'

'It is the T.D.S. of the boiler water, sir. It is 8,000 ppm, and we cannot reduce it.'

'Ready with your pen?'

'Yes, sir.'

The nurse looked worried.

'They must blow down every half-hour for thirty seconds each time until the T.D.S. is reduced to 2,000 ppm. It may take four days and nights, otherwise the boiler will blow up!'

The tall Nigerian bowed. 'Thank you, sir. May God bless you.'

'Gentlemen, the time is up,' urged the nurse.

'Goodbye, Shegu. Expect me back in the front line again in about six weeks.'

'That's the best news this year, sir.' Anne-Marie was left behind with the nurse, who frowned as she took Leon's pulse rate. 'As expected, Miss, it is too high. The patient must relax, and no more visitors for today or tomorrow.'

Leon was already asleep before the nurse returned with a tranquilliser.

There were tears in Anne-Marie's eyes as she kissed Leon on the forehead. 'God bless you, my darling. Let me know, nurse, by phone, in case of need.'

'Do not worry, Miss. The patient is doing well after this attack. Malignant tertian malaria is generally fatal. The doctor has treated the patient with Atabrin, to which he has responded well. Indeed, Dr Manson Bhar is the greatest specialist known for this type of malaria – the deadliest ever known in the world and confined to western Africa.'

In fact the patient was only five days from the point of no return, as Isabelle had read on the bed chart.

'This is what gave western Africa such an evil reputation for deaths without warning, for hundreds of years,' the nurse added. 'Please, Miss, do not worry. Only one request – no more meetings with his engineering friends from Lagos for at least four weeks.'

'Thank you, nurse. I will lay down the law upon my return home tonight. You have been most helpful and encouraging.'

Leon slept for twenty-four hours non-stop – to find Anne Marie by his bedside the next day.

'Have they gone, my darling?' he asked her.

'Twenty-four hours ago!'

'*Pas possible*, Anne-Marie.'

'Yes, my love – and no more talky-talky for you today.'

'Except love talk?' Leon ventured.

'Perhaps.'

4

Upon arriving at Oakfield Lodge Richard met Isabelle and the vicar, and recounted the scene at the hospital.

'Really, Isabelle, it is a most extraordinary situation. Your brother had all the answers to the technical problems raised by Shegu. What a fabulous illustration of front-line work to the developing world, which all took place in the Hospital for Tropical Diseases. 'And Shegu is already on the plane back to Lagos with the solution to the problems.'

'What, already?'

'Oh yes, he returned to the airport immediately from the hospital. Shegu never wastes time – which he always refers to as God's time!'

Richard thought a lot about that experience. What a company – and what a dynamic Nigerian Shegu was!

Two days later a telex came from Shegu at Lever Brothers, Aba, Nigeria.

> *The Chief Engineer, Mr Fugbule, most grateful for solution by Master Leon. All problems resolved. We all wish him a quick recovery. Thank you again for all your help and facilities given during my visit to London. Shegu.'*

The following Saturday afternoon the young people gathered at the Vicarage for the next discussion on planetary science. Soon after returning home they saw Anne-Marie. She had called at the Piccadilly office to collect her things for the weekend, after visiting Leon in hospital that afternoon. It was fortunate she had done so because three telex messages had arrived from Shegu in Lagos. She handed them to Isabelle.

'They are, in fact, for Leon – three technical problems at Mobil Oil, Lagos University Teaching Hospital and Cadbury Nigeria – all in Lagos area. We had better phone the hospital to find out whether Leon is well enough to reply.'

'If they give the green light, Isabelle,' warned Richard, then added, 'let me have the details. Leon has already explained several technical aspects of the burners and the boilers, and I've read the manuals.'

Isabelle telephoned the hospital immediately.

'Not tonight, Miss Reynolds. His pulse is still above normal. It is nine pm and he is about to settle down for the night.'

'Any chance tomorrow, nurse? It is a question of replying to three important technical problems which have arisen in Lagos late this afternoon.'

'I will give you a call about nine thirty tomorrow morning, if he has passed a satisfactory night,' the nurse agreed.

'Thank you very much nurse – good night.' Isabelle put the phone down. 'You heard that, Richard? Here is a copy of the telex. It is rather long, but you will have the time to study the technical details before discussing them with Leon. How are your legs tonight, my darling?'

'One of them is almost back to normal. The other still has a problem: loss of control, but only for a few minutes three or four times during the day. Too early yet to risk driving a car, and it is Saturday night. After dinner let us go to the Milligans' kitchen,' suggested Richard.

'Excellent idea,' Isabelle replied.

At nine-thirty pm Richard, Milly, Roger, Isabelle and Anne-Marie entered Mrs Milligan's kitchen for a little distraction. Little did they know that Buchanan was there already – just arrived from Northern Ireland.

'Miss Isabelle, how lucky to meet you here – in fact, you are the reason for my visit.'

'This is Mr Richard, convalescing after his discharge from the military hospital at Reading. He was captured by the Germans at Arnhem,' Isabelle explained.

'It is a privilege to know you, sir. May God bless you. My boy Frederick was seriously wounded during the raid – some of us believe that Churchill made a mistake to mount that venture. It was too soon.'

'What was his Division?' Richard asked.

'The Parachute Airborne Commando Unit from Army Group B. He was the Sergeant heading the last Airborne Squadron.'

'He did a fine job, Mr Buchanan. He held the rear. I held the front. We nearly brought it off but Monty was unable to arrive in time. Your son may be interested to know that tonight you met his commanding officer in charge of the raiding party.

'You're not Lieutenant-Colonel Sir Richard Cameron!' Buchanan exclaimed. 'Great Scot, Frederick will be so pleased. He thought that you were killed – in fact he saw you go down. He described often to his mother and me how your unit held the front of the bridge. He would be thrilled to meet you again, sir.'

'Well,' interrupted Isabelle, 'your son will not be disappointed. As soon as Richard's other leg improves we will be able to visit together your HQ in Ireland again with Milligan.

'Miss Isabelle, it will give me and my family a great pleasure to meet you all – especially Frederick, who is now managing my stud. He turned to Milligan. 'Boyo, surely this calls for a bottle of the best.'

Mrs Milligan replied, 'Quite right Mr Buchanan – leave it to me.'

It was then that Buchanan noticed Anne-Marie. 'Colleen – as beautiful as ever, Mrs Milligan. We have beauties in Ireland but none to match the French,' he complimented.

Anne-Marie blushed.

Mrs Milligan explained that 'colleen' was common in Ireland for 'darling'.

'Colleen now for a top secret. Do you remember the winner of the Coventry Stakes, this year at Royal Ascot?'

'Yes sir, your Colleen.'

'Exactly. You can back her now for the Derby next year at fifty to one!'

Everybody gasped.

'But Boyo,' explained Milligan. She's a filly – not a chance against the colts including the Aga Khan's unbeaten Dhohbi.'

The Irishman continued, 'That's the big secret. The entry fee was paid up yesterday. First of all let me explain my strategy. The first two classics, the Two Thousand Guineas and the One Thousand Guineas, are run at Newmarket in late March, for colts and fillies respectively. Dhohbi is entered for the Two Thousand Guineas on the Wednesday and Colleen is entered for the One Thousand Guineas on the Friday. Both races are run over the course of one mile. In both cases two of my staff have been instructed to do a double check on the time to complete the course for both runners.

If, therefore, both times coincide, or nearly, then Colleen will challenge Dhohbi in the Derby – which is open to all concerned, whatever sex, for three-year-olds only. Now for one of the reasons of my visit – Colleen has not run since her win at Ascot as a two-year-old, she is priced now at ten to one for the One Thousand Guineas. There are three favourites all at seven to one, so the market is open. But nobody knows of the trials by Miss Isabelle, who gives me weekly reports about the progress made by Colleen.'

'Do you not intend to run her, Mr Buchanan, before the Newmarket meeting?' asked Isabelle.

'Exactly, my dear.' So, Colleen, my advice is simply to place your ante-post bet on Colleen with Ladbrokes on Monday for the One Thousand Guineas run in April.'

'Thank you very much sir, but do you really think she will win?'

'My dear Colleen, do you remember how that Royal Ascot crowd described Colleen when she won the Coventry Stakes in June last year – "that streak of ebony", and so she remains. Even in the sporting press she is so described today – just as Hurry-On was described as "the one they could never catch".'

'Mr Buchanan, it gives me a thrill to know you have such confidence about your beautiful filly. With Roger, we go to see her in the stables every evening before dinner – she is next to Hurry-on.'

The Irishman smiled. 'Now the next reason for my visit. Miss Isabelle, if she runs in the Derby – subject to a satisfactory win for the One Thousand Guineas – will you mount her? Joe Mercer, my lead rider, will not be well enough by June this year.'

'Mr Buchanan, it is always a thrill for me to ride Colleen

at the Marshall stables, but the Derby is run over a mile and a half in public.'

'My dear lady, the way you handled Hurry-On at Royal Ascot in June against those two proven stayers stamped you in the eyes of the racing public as an accomplished artist at the game.'

'You are very kind Mr Buchanan, but this is my first experience with sprinters – and Colleen is fast, very fast,' Isabelle replied.

'It is a little over three months before the Newmarket meeting – please say yes.'

'All right, Mr Buchanan – I hope you will not be disappointed.'

'Bless you, my dear. Now, Boyo, it will give me much pleasure to sample some of that excellent port. To your health, everybody.'

It was another merry evening.

At nine thirty am sharp next morning, Sunday, the nurse telephoned as promised to announce that Leon was well enough to see Richard about the technical problems received from Lagos. Isabelle drove the car as Hunt the chauffeur was off duty.

'Hello, Leon. How are you this morning?' asked Isabelle.

'The doctor was pleased with the slide test this morning,' said the nurse addressing Isabelle. 'There are no more dead malaria parasites in the blood sample.'

'Thank you, nurse. Have we the usual half an hour?'

'No problem, Miss Reynolds,' the nurse assured her.

Richard was already at the table, unfolding the engineering drawings and the schematic oil flow diagrams.

'First of all, Leon, let us take the Lagos University Teaching Hospital. The intravenous fluid solution process plant is out of action because the coil boiler locks out during light-up,' explained Richard.

'How many seconds after closing the Burner switch?' asked Leon.

'Between five and six, according to Shegu,' replied Richard.

'That's a simple solution – ask Shegu to change the photo cell,' said Leon.

'Good. Now for No. 2, Cadbury Nigeria. The Babcock steam boiler fails to light up. Ignition flame seen from the rear inspection glass window is small, blue in colour.'

'Far too much air, Richard,' responded Leon. 'The ignition flame must be half blue, half yellow. The air is reduced by moving the manual control lever about half an inch towards the low fire zero position.'

'Excellent, now for No. 3, Mobil Oil. Power to all low water controls, but no supply after sequence timer and no spare.'

'They must telex L and G in London to send out by courier a new LAL2.1 model sequence timer, which must be fitted by Shegu – there are thirty-one terminals. He must remember not to mix No. 6 with No. 9.'

'Splendid,' replied Richard.

At that moment the nurse re-entered.

'The time is up, Miss Reynolds. Has the patient been able to provide the solution?'

'He has indeed, nurse, most effectively,' Isabelle told her. 'It is most kind of you to arrange this out-of-hours visit.'

On the way back to Oakfield Lodge, Richard expressed admiration for Leon. 'You know, Isabelle, Leon gave another front-line service to Nigeria this morning – from a hospital bed!'

5

The week before Christmas another telex arrived, this time for Isabelle, to announce the arrival of the master the next morning at seven am at No. 2 terminal, London Airport.

'Will you be able to come with me, Roger – Hunt will drive us?'

'Quite free sister – for a six am start presumably.'

It was a dark wet morning when they saw him, accompanied by a porter with some heavy luggage – looking well.

After the usual greetings the master asked, 'How is Leon?'

'The doctor believes that Leon will be able to come home for Christmas,' Isabelle informed him.

'That's a blessing, my dear, and how about Richard?'

'He is only using one walking-stick now, Daddy, and he is improving physically every week. But the Reading Military Hospital insists that Richard completes the convalescence period of twelve months – that is until the end of June next year, Meanwhile, he is so helpful in many ways and has taken a keen interest in Leon's engineering work, apart from helping Milligan in so far as it is possible with only one active leg.'

'And how is Roger?' he asked, looking at Roger.

'Bad news, Dad, just managed a fifty-one per cent pass at the end-of-term exams. It is really tough going. Milly and Richard have been most helpful as my tutors. In fact, Milly is insistent that no time is lost during the three weeks' university vacation which starts today in catching up with work I did not understand during term-time.'

'Good for Milly. Let her know that it will interest me to have her verbal report upon your performance. And Anne-Marie?' the master added.

'As beautiful as ever, Daddy, but so worried about Leon.'

Isabelle told him.

'Tell her not to be. Anyone recovered from malignant tertian malaria never has it again, nor any of the other seven versions of that deadly disease,' the master explained.

'And Milligan – the farmer with my fifty-two pedigree shorthorns?'

'All in excellent condition, Daddy. Milligan remains the main pillar of strength during your absence, and Mrs Milligan's kitchen is still the principal source of entertainment and relaxation during Saturday evenings.'

'And that rogue Buchanan, still a regular visitor to the Milligan's home?'

'He is not a rogue, Daddy,' Isabelle protested. 'We are in business together. Milligan's says that he is the most experienced breeder of bloodstock in Ireland.'

'He would, they are both Irish!'

'Daddy, that's not fair.'

'All right, my darling – you are the best judge. But first a word of caution. My friend the chairman of the course stewards at Royal Ascot informs me that they have their eye on him. He has the extraordinary ability to bring out those long-priced winners at Royal Ascot – some of them never run before!'

'But Daddy, he is shrewd, and plans his attack on Royal Ascot with months of gauging the opposition, and trial runs.'

'Darling, my confidence in you remains at one hundred percent. Lastly, how is Mrs Plant?'

'Looking forward so much to seeing the master, as she referred to you last night.'

Isabelle snuggled under his arm like a child as the BMW purred towards Oakfield Lodge. Within minutes she was fast asleep.

Roger whispered, 'Do you want a rug, Dad?'

'It's all right, my boy. She must have been tired out.'

It was about one hour's drive to Oakfield Lodge and Hunt was an experienced driver who drove only for the comfort of the passengers – never a single jerk.

'Perhaps you are right, my boy,' the master conceded. 'Place the rug gently across her shoulders and over my arm without waking her up.'

Mrs Plant was waiting for them at the front door. Hunt drove so smoothly that Isabelle remained fast asleep when the car slowly came to rest just opposite the door. Mrs Plant was about to cry an audible welcome when the master put his finger to his lips and pointed to the sleeping Isabelle.

'Is she ill?' whispered Mrs Plant.

'No, dear Mrs Plant – just happy. Roger, tell Hunt to wait a moment with unloading while she is brought back to the land of the living.'

Very gently the master squeezed her to his breast, and her eyes flickered. 'Oh Daddy, how wonderful to have you back – no more responsibility, no more tricky decisions to make, the master has returned. But have we arrived already?'

Everyone laughed.

'We were all waiting for you to wake up,' the master told her.

'Daddy, it is shameful of me to sleep like that, instead of preparing a welcome for you.'

Giving her a warm hug, the master replied, 'You are my welcome, darling daughter – so like your mummy.'

'Mrs Plant,' warned Isabelle, 'You must not stand there in the draught. The wind is cold this morning.'

Then came Milligan to welcome home the master.

'Bless you, Milligan. How is it with you and the family?'

'Thank you, sir, we are all very well. But coming from tropical Africa perhaps you do not know that during the last six hours the temperature has dropped twenty degrees Fahrenheit. It is now one degree above freezing and still falling fast.'

'Excellent, Milligan. That is good news. Perhaps we shall enjoy some skating at Christmas time, like last year, with you at full back and me in goal – yes, me, even at eighty- four.'

'It would be great fun, sir, but you ought to take care because of your advancing years.'

'Don't worry Milligan. Black ice will be in my prayers tonight! Mrs Plant will find my ice hockey skates tomorrow. Look at the weather vane over the garage, Milligan – the wind is straight from the east.'

'Welcome home, sir,' Richard greeted him as he entered with walking-stick from the farm gate.

'Thank you, Richard. It seems that you are making progress – only one stick now.'

'Yes sir. Early in January the military want me to walk without it.'

Most of the Sunday morning the master was closeted with Milligan discussing farm matters, planning the ploughing and ditching programme. At ten forty-five the family made their way across the field paths to the Winkfield church. It was the Sunday before Christmas. A prayer of thanks was offered for the return of the master. After the morning service several parishioners came to welcome him back, and so did the vicar.

'Wonderful to see you, Walter – and looking so well,' he said, as they shook hands.

'Dinner at eight thirty? We will break one of those old and crusty hundred-year-old bottles of port. Are you free?'

'You cannot keep me away, Walter.'

During the walk back across the fields ice was seen to be forming on several of the small ponds.

As they entered the farm about twelve thirty, Mrs Milligan was just coming out of the dairy.

'Bless you, sir. Welcome back to England.'

'How happy it makes me to see you again, Mrs Milligan. Sometimes during the Christmas holiday you will find me in your famous kitchen.'

'Any special night, sir?' she asked.

'Yes, Boxing Day night, if that is convenient.'

'It will be an occasion, sir.'

'Now, Mrs Milligan, please ask your husband to accompany you for a glass of sherry, in accordance with the usual Sunday tradition, in my study.'

'That is most kind of you, sir.' Mrs Milligan replied. 'As soon as he is found we will be there.'

As they all assembled for sherry in the study, Richard and Roger declined in favour of draught lager.

'Did you have a comfortable trip, sir?' enquired Mrs Milligan.

'Slept all the way, Mrs Milligan. Night flying suits me.'
'Dare we ask how long you will be with us, sir, before your return to Lagos?'
'The middle of January, Mrs Milligan.'
'Oh no, Daddy,' expostulated Isabelle, 'it's too short.'
He put his arm around her.

The next morning, Monday, the wind was blowing a half gale at minus five, freezing up all exposed water. The severe weather continued for the next five days, after which the lakes nearby, Virginia Water and Englemere were frozen solid with twelve inches of ice. A scratch ice hockey match was immediately arranged between Winkfield and Ascot – made up of local students, boys and girls, farm hands, caddies from Sunningdale and some local retired residents. The game lasted all Friday afternoon until the light failed at four pm.

As anticipated, Milligan was positioned at goal and the master at full back. In fact, Roger and Milly, who proved to be an excellent skater, were perspiring in spite of the freezing wind. Isabelle played an excellent game at centre forward for Winkfield and scored two goals. Gordon Welland and George, the village policeman, scored the two goals for Ascot, making the match a draw – to be continued on Sunday, Christmas Eve, if the cold weather held.

As the family entered Oakfield Lodge via the kitchen door, Mrs Plant enquired, 'Any broken bones, Miss Isabelle?'
'No, Mrs Plant, but so many bruises,' Isabelle answered.
The master then entered the kitchen. 'After an afternoon like that, Mrs Plant, it makes me feel twenty years younger, but it makes me also very hungry. What's for dinner?'
'Roast duck, sir.'
'Mrs Plant, that is the best news of the day – now for my bath and change.'
After his departure upstairs, Isabelle remarked to Mrs Plant, 'Isn't it marvellous that the master remains so fit and well at his age, and is able to join in our game of scratch ice hockey in that freezing wind?'
Reverend Manning and Milly joined the family for

dinner. There was nothing left of the five ducks, and towards the end of the meal Mrs Plant interrupted, 'Excuse me, sir, there is an elderly man in the kitchen who wishes to see you for a few moments. His name is Bill Dodds from Dodds Farm.'

'Mrs Plant, this is a happy occasion. Please ask him to come in. You will not remember perhaps that twenty years ago it was possible for me to help him buy that small holding.'

'Yes sir,' replied Mrs Plant.

'Roger, please bring up that chair next to me,' the master said. Then, as the visitor entered, 'Hello, Bill. Haven't seen you for several years. How are you and the family, are they well?'

'Thank you, sir. We are all well. Please excuse me for interrupting your dinner-party, but it seemed to me that you ought to be warned about an imminent change in the weather, in view of your valuable pedigree shorthorn herd.'

'You mean a sudden thaw, Bill?'

'No sir. It is going to snow long and heavy as it did thirty- five years ago, you may remember.'

'Yes indeed, when you gave us a similar warning. Thank you very much, Bill. When do you anticipate it will start?'

'A little after midnight tonight, sir.'

'Oh dear,' interrupted Isabelle, 'Leon is free to come back tomorrow morning. Perhaps we can fetch him tonight – now.'

'Telephone the hospital, Isabelle,' the master told her. 'If they agree, you and Richard can take the BMW now. It will only take one hour to arrive there and, if he is ready to leave without delay, there will be just sufficient time. It is only ten pm now. 'Ready Richard?'

'No problem, sir.'

'No, Roger, you will be needed to warn Milligan of impending snow. He may want help to protect the stock and prepare for the night's storm.'

Roger departed immediately. Meanwhile, Iabelle announced that the hospital agreed to let Leon leave in about an hour, on condition that he was kept warm.

'Apparently he has been out of bed only for a few hours

each day for the last two days,' explained Isabelle.

'In that case it will be better if Anne-Marie and Milly accompany you. Then they can both keep him warm in the back seat.'

'What a lucky man,' remarked Reverend Manning, turning to Bill Dodds as the children left the room. 'How do you know that, Bill, about the weather?'

'It is difficult to explain, sir, all of a sudden a premonition comes with a change in the sound of the wind. It is pitched high and seems to scream through the trees.'

At that moment Roger returned from the Milligans' kitchen. 'Dad, the snow has started, tiny dry flakes but many of them – just like during Napoleon's retreat from Moscow in 1812.'

'Tell Mrs Plant to put three hot-water bottles in Leon's bed now.'

'Already done, sir, and a fire ready to be started in his bedroom upon arrival,' interrupted Mrs Plant, arriving with a hot cup of soup for Bill Dodds. 'There you are, Mr Dodds. This will keep you warm on your way back to the farm.'

'Thank you very much, Mrs Plant.'

'You reckon it will last several days Bill?' the master enquired.

'Possibly a week, sir.'

'Imagine the chaos,' said Roger.

At that moment Milligan entered.

'So you received my message,' the master observed.

'Yes sir. All precautions are under preparation for a heavy fall.'

'How are you Bill?' asked Milligan.

'Growing older, but feeling younger,' the farmer replied. 'Glad to know that you are prepared for the worst.'

'Let me run you back to your farm before the snow starts to settle,' Milligan offered.

'That's very good of you Milligan. Goodnight, sir. Thank you for the excellent cup of soup, Mrs Plant.'

When they departed it was snowing hard, and how the wind shrieked through the window cracks and rafters of the old mansion. Fires were alight in most of the rooms and a large one was burning anthracite in the study.

After an hour and a half had passed, the master visited Mrs Plant in the kitchen. At the same moment Roger entered by the back door. 'It is blowing now at minus nine, Dad, and everywhere is covered with a white blanket.'

'There is some special broth ready to be heated up for master Leon upon arrival, sir,' the housekeeper told the master.

'Don't you think that you ought to go to bed, Mrs Plant? It is nearly midnight.'

'Oh no, sir. Mr Leon was nursed by me when he was a wee mite and tonight he will be under my care.'

The master smiled.

At the stroke of twelve the BMW was heard in the drive and Isabelle was the first to enter the hall.

'All went well, Daddy, except for a puncture half-way home,' she reported. 'Richard managed to change the wheel in that terrible wind while we kept the engine running. During the last twenty minutes the snow was so thick it was not possible to see more than thirty yards in front of the car. Richard must have some brandy to warm his inside.'

At that moment Richard entered, supporting Leon.

'Hello Dad – still going strong, like Johnnie Walker,' Leon observed.

'Bless you, my boy.' This was said with a warm hug, and then it was Mrs Plant's turn for an affectionate embrace.

'But you are so thin,' she remarked.

'Not surprising, Mrs Plant, when one has to live on gallons of barley water.'

For the last few weeks my dreams have been confined to your roast sirloin of beef and Yorkshire pudding.'

'Yes, but not too much at the start, Mrs Plant. The nurse advised that the liver is still a little delicate,' added Isabelle.

'You must be perished after changing that wheel, Richard, what about a nightcap?' offered the master.

'Thank you, sir. An excellent idea.'

6

The snow storm raged all night and all the next day, until eight pm the following day, Christmas Day. The midday news disclosed that London Airport was closed until further notice. It was also announced that hundreds if not thousands of cars and trailers had been abandoned on the roads. It started snowing again at midday on Boxing Day, by which time it was learned that all Northern Europe was in the grip of a northerly air stream. Nevertheless, it was a memorable lunch attended by Reverend Manning, Mr and Mrs Milligan, Milly and George the village policeman, who was on morning duty, and Leon who insisted on being included; in fact, although still weak he was in splendid form.

The night after arriving from the hospital Leon had slept solid until midday, when he woke to find Mrs Plant with a breakfast tray of eggs and bacon etc.

'Dear Mrs Plant, is it breakfast-time so soon?'

'My dear boy it is midday. Four times you have been visited by me and Anne-Marie since seven thirty this morning. During that time you slept like a child. It warmed my heart to see you so relaxed, and here is Anne Marie to keep you company.'

'My darling, you ought to have woken me up,' he said as she pressed his hand close to her breast.

'Quiet now. Try to eat your lunch,' she replied.

So passed Leon's first day at home. To return now to the Boxing Day lunch.

'How long, Daddy, do you think this cold spell will last?' asked Isabelle.

'My dear child, at your age we used to refer to these cold periods as a "Lorna Doone winter". Sometimes they lasted for three or four weeks. But in the days of Lorna

Doone, the 1667 winter lasted from 15 December to 15 April and wiped out half of the population of Europe and most of the livestock.'

At that moment Roger emerged from the front door. 'Dad, it is over a foot thick already everywhere.'

Indeed, the snowstorm continued until well into the night.

The next morning the sky was clear, but it was accompanied by such a severe frost that loud reports came from some of the oak and elm trees as the bark burst open. In fact, the freezing wind continued for the first ten days into the new year, so that the master had to postpone his return to Lagos. Meanwhile, a happy spirit prevailed throughout the household. Leon gradually recovered his strength and Richard was walking without his crutch. All members of the family were busy clearing paths around the farm, including one to the Milligan's cottage and another across the fields to the parish church. One evening the master, Richard, Leon and the vicar were discussing the future.

'Officially, my discharge from the military hospital is to take place in June, sir,' Richard disclosed. 'Meanwhile, permit me to say that it has been a privilege for me to convalesce in such lovely surroundings. Later on, subject then to no relapse or set-back in my health, it is my intention to ask your blessing on my proposal to marry your daughter Isabelle.'

'My dear boy, you have it already, for it has been evident, since the day of your arrival, that Isabelle has been a different person. But about your future, will you take up a post in the army?'

'No sir, my military activity is over – as has been explained to me by the CO of Army Group B.'

'High time,' interrupted Isabelle, just entering the study. 'Excuse the interruption, Daddy, but Mrs Plant has made this broth for the two invalids.'

'Congratulations, Isabelle my dear,' said Reverend Manning.

'Oh Richard, you have told them?'

'Yes darling, your father asked me about my future plans.'

'Well, Reverend Manning, this calls for a bottle of the

best,' gestured master.

'Leave it to me, Daddy.' With that Iabelle went in search of a bottle of vintage Veuve Clicquot.

'But what do you envisage as an occupation, Richard, from June, then officially discharged,' continued the master.

'That's a subject which it is my intention to explore with you, sir, for there is no-one else for me to turn to after the loss of my two elder brothers. In the Highlands, due to the death of my two brothers during commando raids, the whole estate of ten thousand acres, including eight farms, has been left to me. It has been entailed for the last three hundred years. However, there is a capital cash balance accrued during the last generations amounting to £800,000, which reverts to me as the last of the line.'

'That is a tidy sum, Richard.'

'Yes sir, and here is my proposal. For some time now Leon has been kind enough to explain in detail his work in Nigeria as an engineer. It is meaningful work and it has its attractions. It interests me. My training at Cambridge qualified me as an engineer. It is my desire therefore, to offer my services to your company in Nigeria, as a practical man. Evidently, it is a necessary service. The Nigerians need our know-how as engineers. For me to serve will be a privilege, sir, and I can also make considerable financial investments.'

At that moment came an interruption from Mrs Plant. 'A telegram from Inverness for Mr Richard, sir.'

'Thank you very much, Mrs Plant,' replied Richard.

'We hope all is well, Richard, at your home in Inverness,' ventured the master.

Richard handed the telegram to Isabelle, who in turn handed it to the master.

'Oh Richard, there seems such a lot we don't know about you,' exclaimed Isabelle.

The master read out the telegram. It was from the head housekeeper, Miss Glenfield, Inverness Hall, Scotland.

'The management of the London Philharmonic Society has only just heard of your arrival back from Russia. They are offering you the solo in Beethoven's Piano

Concerto No. 4 at the Albert Hall, London, 30 May. Your contact is Mr G. Jeffrey, Coordinator, London office.
We suppressed your present address as you requested. Warmest regards. Glenfield.'

Isabelle was speechless for a moment. 'Something else, Richard, we don't know about you. When did you last perform for the London Philharmonic?'
'It was June 1939, just before joining the Airborne Division.'
'Oh Richard, what other secrets have you hidden away?'
'Nothing else, my darling,' Richard assured her.
'Are you going to accept,' asked Leon.
'Not having played for ten years, Leon, it is impossible – apart from which there is no piano here.'
'But there is a baby grand in my study,' proposed the vicar.
'Surely, Richard, it is worth a try. This is only January,' responded the master.
Richard hesitated. 'The music fascinates me, sir, but whether it will be possible to perform in public by 30 May is a different matter. Although there is still a full-sized grand piano in my home at Inverness....'
'That settles it,' said Isabelle.
'It is surely worth a try,' ventured the master.
'True, sir, but the Albert Hall will want a firm reply soon either way.'
'But Richard,' interrupted the vicar, 'Why not tell them the truth, namely that you may not be ready for the performance on 30 May. They will then undertake to prepare an understudy to take your place in case of need. Why not draft a letter to that effect now. It can be posted as soon as the weather breaks.'
And so it was agreed that Roger, Milly and Isabelle would travel with Richard by air to Inverness via Glasgow from Heathrow as soon as the weather became warmer – which it did the following week. Anne-Marie insisted upon staying with Leon during his convalescence after leaving the Hospital for Tropical Diseases.
The chauffeur of the black and silver Rolls from Inverness

met them at the airport. 'Welcome back to Scotland, sir,' he said.

'Thank you, Jameson. How is Miss Glenfield?'

'Very well thank you sir, and we are all looking forward to your return home.'

It was a long and beautiful drive to Inverness Hall with the snow everywhere. Mrs Glenfield gave them a warm and affectionate welcome, and for Richard a special hug.

'Where are your crutches, Richard?' she asked, but at that moment in came a whirlwind of wagging tails and barks of joy as three dogs, Lupa, the Irish terrier, Dante, the Labrador and Boozer, the Irish Setter, all leapt at Richard, licking his face, climbing on his shoulders with wild joy as he knelt down to embrace them. Indeed it was a moving scene.

Miss Glenfield's eyes were moist with happiness as she addressed Isabelle. 'Sometimes Richard would start with a sandwich and Thermos of tea laced with a wee dram of twelve-year-old, and cover twenty miles in a day across the mountains with these three dogs. It would be dark when they returned, stimulated with Highland winds, the dogs covered with mud, and Richard soaked to the skin. After a hot bath and Scotch haggis, next to a blazing coal fire, Richard would sometimes play Beethoven sonatas, far into the night, with the dogs fast asleep on the mat, exhausted after their run. It was after one of these day-long walks across the hills with the dogs that Richard played until three am in the morning and woke me up. Immediately, I prepared a cup of his favourite vegetable soup and, after surprise at my interruption, he noticed the late hour and said then, "Nanny" (that was always my name since Richard was a tiny tot), "soon after my new life begins with the commandos at Army Group B next week, an angel will walk into my life." And so it was during May 1940 the name Isabelle began to appear in his letters.'

'Oh Richard,' exclaimed Isabelle, 'you never referred to me as an angel?'

'No, my darling, you were too busy tracking the enemy war planes in the operations-room near Dover at the time.'

'How wonderful,' exclaimed Milly, 'A real romance! But Miss Glenfield, do you mean that Richard spent most of his time at this lovely grand piano?'

'My dear, far into the night – except when after thirty-six holes of golf he would return home exhilarated, but too exhausted to play for long.'

'Extraordinary,' thought Isabelle.

Lovingly Richard fingered the piano. 'It is too long ago, Nanny, and too late to continue with my music connections. My recovery is almost complete and it is time that my energies were devoted to production, not to the arts. My life has been spared and my reason is regained. It is so wonderful to live again and to be home. Indeed, it is my duty to society to give, after my experience with modern war.'

'But you have six months Richard, before your formal release from the medical division of Army Group B. Why not give it a try? After all, consider the pleasure given to the public.'

'Nanny, it cannot be turned on just like a tap.'

'True, Richard, but you are making a rapid recovery, and with the return to normal health your former passion for Beethoven will reassure your mind and restore lost confidence.'

'Miss Glenfield, that is a splendid suggestion,' added Isabelle. 'Richard, here is my proposal. Why not recommence your studies here in these wonderful surroundings, continue your recovery with these lovely dogs, and return to us for the weekends in order to report on the progress with your health and your practice for the possible May concert?'

'What a wonderful idea, Isabelle,' replied Miss Glenfield.

As if Lupa understood the conversation, she jumped onto Isabelle's lap with a bark and licked her cheek.

'Aren't you gorgeous?' said Isabelle, hugging her close.

'You see, Roger, there are too many women directing my action,' Richard laughed.

'You must explain this to Leon. Indeed, it was my intention to devote the next six months to the study of burners and boiler controls, as I mentioned to your father.'

'There will be plenty of time for that,' responded Milly, 'after your final discharge from the Army in June.'

So it was agreed Richard should stay on at Inverness Hall when the other three departed for Oakfield Lodge at the end of the week.

7

Little by little Richard's ability to play returned, and with it the strength to last those twenty mile walks across the wooded hills in the teeming rain and high winds. After he returned late evening, soaked, Miss Glenfield was naturally cross.

'Richard, even the old cap, worn by your father all his life, is soaked through, and the dogs – what a mess in the kitchen!'

'But we love the mess when Richard is here,' interrupted Bessie, the crippled cook. 'It is wonderful to see the new master so well and at home. After all, it is just you and me – the head housekeeper and the cook, instead of the twenty servants before the war.'

Indeed it was a wondrous existence for Richard with the return of life and passion to his battered body and mind – reflected in his passion for Beethoven. Often he entered a small crofter's cottage, where friends of his early youth were enraptured to learn of his experiences in the army and in particular at Arnhem, where he pooled his well-prepared picnic with their more modest fare. It was a different world – his world, the storms, the rain and the high winds of the Highlands.

The same Friday evening, returning about six, soaked as usual, before going back to Oakfield Lodge the next morning, he met Miss Glenfield in the kitchen.

'May God bless you, Nanny,' he said, lifting her up almost to the ceiling. 'Nanny, it's this love thing. Do you approve?'

'We cannot help it, Richard, she is accomplished, and a charming personality – above all, someone to keep your wild emotions under control. For example, just look at you. Soaked as usual. It makes me cross. Suppose you catch pneumonia – your betrothed will never forgive me.

Upstairs with you now, the bath water is steaming hot.'

With a kiss for his housekeeper, he raced upstairs.

The following day, Richard, accompanied by Lupa, travelled by plane to Oakfield Lodge. Lupa took to Isabelle immediately and insisted on monopolising her lap.

'You will have to watch Lupa when she sees the chickens,' Richard warned. 'She believes they are made for her entertainment.'

'Hello Richard,' Leon said as he entered the study.

'How are you, Leon?'

'A bit weak but progressing gradually. Richard, my father would like to have a word with you. He is leaving for Lagos tomorrow.'

They went into the study together.

'Hello, Richard,' welcomed the master. 'You are beginning to fill out at last – keep it up. It will give us all immense pleasure to see you through this Beethoven concert at the end of May.'

'Thank you, sir. By the way, have you thought about my idea of investing in your company with part of my cash inheritance?'

'Indeed yes, Richard. Upon my return to Lagos my proposals about your offer will be put to the board. Within the next few weeks, therefore, you will receive a formal invitation to become a member of our board, in London and Lagos.'

At six am the next morning the master left for Lagos. As Mrs Plant entered the dining-room at breakfast-time with the coffee for the family, she was unable to restrain her tears.

'Dear Mrs Plant,' comforted Isabelle, 'it's not for long. He will be back in April. Remember too, Mrs Plant, that Daddy is still the driving force behind the Nigerian enterprise; besides, Leon has been very ill lately and the Lagos company needs Daddy's guidance more than ever.'

'Yes, Miss Isabelle, but at eighty-four years old!'

'Daddy is remarkably fit, Mrs Plant – as we all witnessed when he was playing ice hockey at Englemere a few weeks ago.'

At that moment the postman arrived with a telegram from Ireland.

'This must be from your Irish friend, Mr Buchanan,' said Mrs Plant, handing it to Isabelle.

It ran as follows:

> Last weekend of January will be staying with Milligans. Look forward to discuss with you strategy for Colleen in Thousand Guineas Race. Very Happy New Year to you all, Buchanan.

The winter months passed too quickly for all concerned, especially for Roger, who was struggling valiantly to keep up with his contemporaries at Faraday House College.

Milly gave him all the usual encouragement. 'You can only do your best, Roger, and don't worry. Life is too short to worry. Some of us are born slow to develop, and some fast like your brother, but we all eventually find our feet firmly on the ground – providing we try to understand the Lord's will.'

Isabelle was now fully occupied with the intensive training for Colleen, who responded gamely to all the urging she applied.

Richard returned regularly every Saturday morning to Oakfield Lodge, and the last Saturday evening of January a meeting took place in Mrs Milligan's kitchen, where the young members of the family and the vicar met, together with Mr Buchanan, who always had a soft spot for Anne-Marie.

'Bless you, Colleen, and how is the invalid, your fiancé?'

'Improving every week, thank you Mr Buchanan – as you see.'

'How is my sister progressing on your Colleen, Mr Buchanan?' Leon asked.

'This is what we will discuss tonight, Mr Leon, Briefly, the answer is encouraging to say the least. Miss Isabelle, you look the picture of radiant health.'

'Thank you, Mr Buchanan. You have to put it down to that lovely filly – so beautiful and so even-tempered. You must come to see her tomorrow morning.'

'Indeed, that is my intention, Miss Isabelle. But first of all let us consider the briefing for the One Thousand Guineas. The strategy is simple. Try to start fast from the gate. Do not look right or left. Let her go flat out from the gate to the post over the Newmarket mile. Colleen will win, of that there is no doubt. She was close to the market favourite at ten to one – even although she has not run since winning the Coventry Stakes at Royal Ascot last year. For the Two Thousand Guineas race over the same mile two days later, the Aga Khan's Dhoti is still the favourite and is bound to win. As I have said, if the time for each race coincides closely then Colleen will run in the Derby in June, against Dhoti.'

'Do you think Colleen will take to the excitement of the Epsom crowd without problems?' ventured Anne-Marie.

'Colleen, she is intelligent, and with your future sister-in-law as my selected jockey, no problems are anticipated. Incidentally, my dear, let me tell you about my runner for the King Stand Stakes – always run as the last race at Royal Ascot. He is called Foray, a five-year-old. The King Stand Stakes is for all ages, but the race is only five furlongs in length – probably the fastest sprinters' race in the racing world. Foray is particularly fast over just that distance – again a jet-black Irish thoroughbred, a massive stallion. He has not run for eighteen months. Indeed it is a gamble. He may just pull it off, with thirty-five runners at the starting tapes. We believe he will win, but only just, in view of the competition from all over Europe.'

'How very exciting, Mr Buchanan. A little prayer will be said for Foray on the day,' replied Anne-Marie.

'Once again, Buchanan,' interrupted Mrs Milligan, 'you will be called before the course stewards if he wins.'

'Not this time, my dear Mavoreen – this was his name for Mrs Milligan – he will not win by a distance, as Hurry-On used to. No, my dear, he will win by a whisker, if at all. Nevertheless, it is worth an Irish gamble for this young and beautiful Colleen.'

Anne-Marie blushed. 'Thank you very much, Mr Buchanan. It will be so exciting, especially for all the ladies at Royal Ascot. How much they will love you, once again, for entering a long-odds winner from such a competitive field, if he wins. Often my friends have asked me "Has Buchanan a runner in this race"?'

'Indeed, you are a great friend of the ladies,' said Mrs Milligan.

'And of the bookmakers,' added Milligan.

8

As the end of March approached excitement was centred on the Newmarket meeting. Colleen was at the pitch of her training, so was Dhoti. It was a dry month, with the usual cold winds from the north. Leon was now fully recovered and was planning to return to Lagos after his marriage to Anne-Marie, in late June.

The day before the meeting, Milligan and Isabelle travelled to Newmarket with Colleen and the stable team from Marshall's stud, including Isabelle's friend Gabrielle from Paris and Anne-Marie.

'What a beautiful Arab grey,' commented Gabrielle as Dhoti paraded with the other contenders for the Two Thousand Guineas event on the Wednesday. There were twenty-five runners in all. The grey was quoted at two to one as a firm favourite. After cantering down to the starting-tapes the flag went up ready for the off.

The sun came out as the flag went down, and the thoroughbreds commenced their race along the famous mile straight. As expected Dhoti was up with the leaders soon after the start – at the same time the special stopwatches, monitored by the Buchanan stable staff, commenced to check the time for the race. At the half-way post Dhoti was five lengths in front of the pack and going well. There seemed to be little hope of any serious competition from the field. As Dhoti went past the post ten lengths in front of four other runners which deadheated for second place, the stopwatches checked the time for the race. One of them was Joe Mercer, the injured lead jockey of the Buchanan stable.

'Well, Jo,' enquired Mr Buchanan as they met in the paddock.

'It was a fast race, sir, only one better time this century.'

Then came the One Thousand Guineas event on the Friday, and again a lovely early spring day. Gabrielle and Anne-Marie were full of praise for the beauty of Colleen as she paraded with the other contenders in the paddock.

'Good luck, Isabelle,' said Gabrielle, as her friend mounted for the canter to the starting-tape.

'What a wonderful sight,' exclaimed Anne-Marie as the twenty-one starters passed the stands.

The loudspeakers announced that the starter's flag was up. At the same time Joe Mercer's finger was on the stopwatch.

'They're off. A few seconds later the announcer added, 'Already one out in front, colours not yet clear, white, green and something – yes, it's the Buchanan colours, that streak of Ebony.'

There was a huge yell of delight from the ladies in the stand, and Milligan smiled.

The announcer continued at the halfway post, 'Colleen is now five lengths in front – and not letting up, still going on as if the devil is behind her.'

As she flashed past the winning-post eight lengths in front of the field, the race crowd gave Isabelle a loud cheer of congratulations, and it was noticed that the new name, that streak of ebony, was checked up on all the betting-boards of the bookmakers.

Joe Mercer's finger released the stopwatch and he walked over to the paddock.

'Well, Joe?' enquired Mr Buchanan.

'Same, sir – not a question of a second difference. Weather conditions same, going unchanged from the Wednesday race.'

Buchanan whistled.

That night in the Milligan's kitchen there was quite a gathering – including the vicar.

'Well, sir,' said Isabelle, addressing Mr Buchanan, 'were your instructions correctly interpreted?'

'Admirably, my dear.'

'But why flat out from start to finish?'

'Simply, my dear, in order to compare the time taken by Dhoti: he explained.

'And?'

'Identical to the second,' replied Mr Buchanan.
'Is that so,' remarked the vicar.
'Well, Boyo,' Buchanan said to Milligan, 'we are going now to make a bid for the Derby.'
'You must be crackers, Mr Buchanan,' commented Mrs Milligan. 'The Derby is half a mile more, and normally only colts compete. The fillies' race is the Oaks on the Friday. Why not let her run in the Oaks, with her own sex? The prize money is considerable and she is bound to win after her performance in the One Thousand Guineas.'
'True, my dear, but Colleen is an exceptional filly. It is rare that any filly has a chance to win the Derby. This one has.'
'You don't think, Mr Buchanan,' enquired the vicar, 'that you are going to push the filly too far?'
'The answer, sir, is simply that we have already tried Colleen over the one and a half mile distance more than once and she performs well.'
'The market rates her chances at ten to one, compared with Dhoti the favourite at two to one for the Derby.'
At that moment a knock on the door.
'That will be George,' said Mrs Milligan.
'Congratulations, Miss Isabelle, a convincing performance,' the village policeman offered.
'Thank you, George.'
'Mrs Milligan, my visit tonight is simply to establish whether or not my shilling ought to be invested on Colleen for the Derby?'
'George, my friend,' interrupted Mr Buchanan, 'it is a gamble at long odds and it is my impression that Colleen's chances are reasonably good, but we are up against the best from the stables of the Aga Khan.'
'All right, Mr Buchanan, so what will be your instructions as owner to me, the jockey, on Derby Day,' prompted Isabelle.
'Miss Isabelle, that is a leading question and, as before, the answer is simple – flat out from start to finish. Even watch the starter's hands as he reaches to pull down the flag – for in this case our enemy is formidable, one of the great flyers of the Aga Khan's stable of Arab greys, There will be no question of five lengths, even one length, indeed,

if she wins at all it will be by a whisker. Apart from Dhoti there are two French challengers, unbeaten so far, but strangers to the English turf. They are known as Verité and Linda – another filly.'

With the finish of the Newmarket meeting, the London season commenced with a brilliant April. Roger once again started the third term of the scholastic year at Faraday House. Milly was hard pushed to guide him during the evenings, and likewise Richard, during his weekend visits from Inverness, spent much time with Roger on the subject of steam distribution and condensate return systems.

During the last Saturday of April Richard arrived a bit later than usual at Oakfield Lodge, while the younger members of the family were still with the vicar at the vicarage. Richard was able therefore to enjoy a welcome cup of tea with Mrs Plant in the kitchen.

'Is it true, Mrs Plant, that Leon and Anne-Marie's marriage will take place after Royal Ascot week?'

'Yes Richard – soon after the master arrives from Lagos,' the housekeeper replied.

'Has Leon fully recovered from malaria?'

'So it seems, Richard, but he is still thin, and without doubt took a beating from that cursed disease. How do you feel about working in Nigeria, after all the good and the bad you have heard about that country?'

'It is going to be a great challenge, Mrs Plant – and, above all, a privilege to serve the master and the Nigerian community.'

Soon afterwards the young people arrived with Reverend Manning, who was invited to stay over for dinner.

'How is the Beethoven concerto progressing, Richard?'

'Much better than expected, sir. The fingers are now back to the flexible movements so necessary with most works of Beethoven. The opportunities for long hours of concentration are limitless, and the piano is now well tuned.'

'Splendid, and when is the first rehearsal?'

'Next week, at the Albert Hall.'

'Make a note of that, Milly, we will attend at least a part of it,' Isabelle said.

'Afraid not, Isabelle. Only performers are allowed at rehearsals.'

The next morning at breakfast Mrs Plant brought in a courier letter for Leon from Lagos, which announced that the master was due to arrive at seven am on the Sunday morning after Royal Ascot.

'May God bless the master,' cried Mrs Plant. 'We must keep a fire in his room day and night a few days before his arrival.' This in spite of the recent warm weather.

Soon after Milly and Roger left for London, a call came through from Richard in Inverness. Isabelle took it.

'How is it shaping, my darling?'

'At two am this morning the whole concerto was completed – non-stop. It was the first time since 1939. More feeling and harmony have been introduced – as an afterthought. Another ten days to go as the Highlands winds whistle through the fir-trees and the melodies of Beethoven impinge on the ear during my long tramps across the rain-drenched hills with those lovely dogs. Sometimes it seems that strange spirits accompany me during those long walks. But the music there – some of the locals refer to it as the "phantom music of the forests" – is spellbinding, another world, my darling, the world of the spirits. A world into which our children will be born – perhaps it is better for me to stop.'

'Oh Richard, *je t'adore*. Try to come early on Saturday and tell me more about your adventures into the spirit world.'

'Perhaps they will disturb you.'

'Oh no, Richard.' Isabelle protested. 'Once the administration and accounts of the farm have been left behind, my mind, body and soul will be lost completely in your spirit world – to be guided by you through the problems of life.'

'To hear you express your thoughts like that makes me impatient for our marriage.'

'But you have not proposed yet,' Isabelle objected.

'My darling, you must be crackers. The army medical experts must be quite certain that my mind and body (they are not interested in the spiritual world) are sound before embarking on a life of creation with thee – 1 June is the last day, after which they have to pronounce me sound in heart and limb, officially. It is then that the formal marriage proposals will be made in writing. Meanwhile, they have been made already in the spirit world between you and me.'

'Oh Richard, do you believe seriously that you will be fit enough to concentrate on the Beethoven concert – for one hour and a half – non-stop?'

'My darling, little do you know me. It is not a question of concentration. The concert will be a living event during which my interpretation of the concerto will be stamped on the minds of the critics and the musical experts. They may not like it – but the audience will be the judge. During the performance my mind will be focused on the winds and the wild heather of the Highlands. My spirit will float simply through the God-given peace of the forests and the fast-flowing rivers. Whether the performance will be considered good, bad or indifferent by the critics are the least of my problems. It is my intention to ensure that the audience will take away an unforgettable memory.

'It is now eleven,' Richard continued. 'My sandwich is ready, together with a wee dram. The rain is teaming down, the wind is strong. Dante, Lupa and Boozer all regard me with keen impatience, they are the most human of dogs. But they know that the twenty-mile tramp is about to commence in spite of my late night work on the concerto. May God bless thee, my darling Isabelle.'

'Goodbye for now, my dearest Richard.'

Indeed it was an unforgettable tramp, and for the first hour the rains never ceased. Many thoughts raced through Richard's mind. Why had his life been spared, at Arnhem and in the hospital? How strange that Isabelle had waited for him and, with such wondrous care and love, had nursed him during the latter part of his recovery at Oakfield Lodge. At least three times he knelt down by three small waterfalls during the tramp to thank the Lord for his unbelievable good fortune. *Hopefully O Lord, my future endeavours in this thy wondrous world will be blessed. Amen.*

As the semi-gale raced through the pines, his thoughts persisted that perhaps the Lord had need of his unsuspected skills at some future date in time. Hardly, he mused – for example, what skills? My legal, medical and administrative skills are non-existent. My practical engineering skills are as yet untested through lack of experience. It was then that a strange voice lifted above the subsiding wind was heard quietly. It murmured simply, 'Have no anxieties, you are spiritually aware.'

The three hunting dogs for some unknown reason clustered around him. The rain had stopped. He caressed them, 'No problems, my beauties, we will enjoy a rest in yonder crofter's hut.' It was empty. Three meaty bones were given to the dogs to chew over during the half hour's rest. The wee dram in the hot flask of strong tea seemed to stimulate his senses. He pondered in silence a lot about his future. It is important for me to have a worthy job, meaningful and acceptable to the Lord and to have the respect of my fellow men,' he thought. Only a single word was heard from the pines in spite of the high winds after the rains. *Patience*!

On that note he enjoyed another swig at the flask of tea laced with twelve-year-old Scotch. He started the great walk back to the Hall through God's country with the three hunting dogs – wild with delight and with apparently unlimited energy. But dear Nanny was alarmed as they all arrived in the kitchen, soaked to the skin, like a sponge, she insisted.

'Dear Richard, you deserve to catch pneumonia tomorrow,' she scolded.

He gave her an affectionate kiss and departed for a hot bath.

The following week was full of preparations for both the concert and the Derby. The concert was due to be performed at eight pm on the Saturday evening before the Derby. Richard arrived on the Friday night with Lupa, Isabelle's favourite.

The vicar came to dinner too.

'We have arranged to include you in the front row, sir, with Leon, Anne-Marie, Roger and Isabelle if you are able to attend,' announced Richard, addressing the vicar.

'That is most handsome of you, Richard. It will give me great pleasure.'

'Good. Leon will drive and we will leave here about six pm,' concluded Isabelle.

Just before they left Oakfield Lodge the next day, a call came through Inverness.

'Hello, Richard. Just to wish you well at the concert and to let you know that I will hear it on the radio.'

'Thank you, Nanny. May God bless you.'

It was a wet evening when the BMW left the drive at Oakfield Lodge en route for the Albert Hall, where a considerable crowd had collected. During the journey to London Isabelle's hand never left Richard's. As the car, driven impeccably by Leon, sped along, Richard thought that to be alive in this fabulous world, with marriage prospects, unique in his experience, stimulated him to great heights.

The Albert Hall was packed and the rain was heavy as they entered the building. In fact the evening was dark early for late May, but it was warm.

With a good luck kiss Isabelle left Richard at the backstage entrance, and during the next half hour the party settled down into their places in the hall.

The concert commenced on time with a Mozart overture. This was followed by the Beethoven Piano Concerto No. 4 in G major, Op. 58. It was a brilliant performance. Isabelle observed, however, that Richard was in a different world, his features were completely relaxed as he executed the various movements with the grace and delicacy of a master player, which held the audience spellbound. Towards the end of the concerto Isabelle noticed also that there was no strain nor sign of exhaustion on his face. On the contrary, he seemed to be completely at ease. At the end of the Rondo vivace movement the applause was thunderous. Indeed, there was a standing ovation amid cries of calls for repetition – so much so that Richard settled down to play two parts of the Beethoven Piano Concerto No. 2, the Allegro and the Rondo Molto allegro. It was a masterful performance – as *The Times* recorded on Monday morning:

> 'Sir Richard Cameron has not lost his touch since playing the same works just before the outbreak of war in 1939.

It was brilliantly executed with the grace and harmony of an experienced player and received an appropriate ovation from a packed house. It is to be hoped we will see more of this popular pianist in the near future.

The next morning, Isabelle was the first up for breakfast when Mrs Plant entered the dining-room with the coffee pot.

'Well Miss Isabelle, there is no need to ask you whether the performance was a success. It was broadcast all over England.'

'Mrs Plant, it was a magnificent performance and the audience was deeply moved to see a wounded soldier execute so well such a classic work. Meanwhile, dear Mrs Plant, please let him sleep till midday.'

9

The Epsom meeting started on the first Tuesday of June – with almost a quarter of a million race-goers from all over the world. The leading events included three races for two-year-olds only, first time out. The Aga Khan stable secured the first three places for all three races. Sound breeding, thought Mr Buchanan. Wednesday arrived with splendid weather – little or no wind and a cloudless sky. The Derby runners commenced the parade round the paddock, including Dhoti a magnificent grey Arab.

Mr Buchanan himself was present at the parade, 'Not too nervous, my dear?' he asked Isabelle.

'That is one trouble never noticed by me, about Isabelle, Mr Buchanan,' responded Gabrielle, who had travelled from Paris to see her great friend run in the Derby. 'Indeed it is my experience that Isabelle bewitches racehorses.'

'You may be right, Miss Gabrielle. There is no doubt that the onlookers are affectionately disposed towards Colleen and her rider.'

After the usual three quarter of an hour's interval for the parade, the runners were mounted and commenced to canter down to the starting-gate. Colleen and Dhoti were positioned at each end of the line of thirty-one runners.

Up went the starters' flag.

'They're off,' blazed the loudspeakers. After a few seconds the announcer recorded that four runners were leading the field, Dhoti in there with one of the French colours – Linda. The third leader is in Mr Buchanan colours, Colleen.' Approaching Tattenham Corner, the four leaders were still running neck to neck – all going at a rare pace. Coming into the six furlong straight from Tattenham Corner there was not a whisker between them, and the crowd was crazy with excitement.

'How is it with Colleen, Milligan?' ventured the vicar.

'Difficult to say, sir, except that she is fully extended, but so is Dhoti, whose jockey is head down, exerting every ounce, yet not using the whip.'

'One furlong from home,' came from the loudspeaker, 'and all the four runners level.

'Indeed an exceptional race,' commented Milligan. 'Now half a furlong from the post and still nothing between them. Photo cameras are prepared for a very close finish. 'Wait a slight change has occurred, Dhoti and Colleen have both inched in front, at least as seen from the stands.'

Yet past the post all seemed to be in line. Up went the flag for a photo finish.

This meant a delay of five minutes. As the flag was pulled down, the winners, Colleen and Dhoti, dead-heated for first place as both French runners dead-heated for a second place – a short head behind the leaders.

A loud cheer went up from those who had backed the winners.

'Well, Milligan,' continued the vicar, 'all three classic runners are entered for the Queen Mary Stakes at Royal Ascot, presumably – including Colleen – over the same distance?'

'Correct, sir.'

A big crowd gathered in Mrs Milligan's kitchen. It was a hot evening and the draught beer went down by the gallon. Milligan was in close conversation with the vicar, Leon and Anne-Marie, when in came Isabelle, looking well after a bath and change following the race. A loud cheer of congratulations arose above the chatter as Mrs Milligan gave her a warm hug, followed by an affectionate kiss from Anne-Marie.

'How do you feel, sister, after that splendid effort?'

'Leon, it took me a full five minutes to recover at the end of the race – which is simply an endurance test from start to finish.'

It was at that moment that Mr Buchanan arrived. He gave Isabelle a warm hug. 'What a lass, and Colleen, how did she perform?'

'Mr Buchanan, dear Colleen gave every ounce of her

ability to race against incredible odds, but surely never again.'

'Only one more race for Colleen – the Queen Mary Stakes at Royal Ascot. All the Derby horses are entered, including Dhoti and a stranger from the USA – unbeaten on their hard-going tracks,' the Irishman explained.

'But Mr Buchanan, Colleen was fully extended,' Isabelle objected. 'Do you really believe she can hold that field at Royal Ascot?'

'Yes, my dear. First of all, the course at Royal Ascot is flat for much of the way and slight uphill for the last five furlongs – a factor not favouring the long legs of Dhoti. Secondly, it was revealed after the race that Dhoti likewise took a beating. He was fully extended too. Thirdly, the times were a record for the race. The Queen Mary Stakes therefore is going to be the deciding one and a half mile classic race of the century.'

'Well, Mr Buchanan, so long as it is the last for that lovely filly that streak of ebony!' Isabelle agreed.

'No problem, my dear. It is a promise.'

'Miss Evans telephoned through to Mrs Plant with a message for you, Mr Buchanan.

It says "At six pm this evening Colleen was marked up as favourite for the Queen Mary Stakes at evens. Dhoti, Verité and Linda are all second favourites at three to one".'

'Fancy, a red-hot favourite – my darling Colleen.'

Then came a loud knock at the front door, just as Roger and Milly came in from the garden gate.

'Mrs Milligan, there is a beautiful Rolls-Royce outside your farm gate – but no one is inside,' added Milly.

'Roger, please see who it is.'

An impressive chauffeur addressed Roger. 'My master's compliments to Mr Buchanan. Is it true that he's staying here?'

'Yes indeed,' replied Roger.

'Good. Will you please ensure that this envelope is placed in his hands immediately?'

'Thank you. It will be done at once.'

The chauffeur bowed and left.

'One guess,' said Mrs Milligan.

'Dead right,' said Mr Buchanan revealing the Aga Khan's

crest on the back of the envelope – HRH AGA KHAN. He read aloud: 'Dear Sir, My congratulations upon the performance of your Colleen this afternoon at the Epsom Derby – and especially upon the performance of your distinguished rider. My offer this time is simply £500,000 cash for Colleen which remains open until the day before the Queen Mary Stakes at Royal Ascot. With my respects and best wishes. HRH Aga Khan.'

All eyes on Mr Buchanan were asking the same question.

'Do not worry, my friends,' he assured them. 'Colleen was made for love not money.'

Isabelle gave him a kiss.

'Did you doubt me, my dear?'

'No, Mr Buchanan, but you do make us work hard.'

It was late when the party broke up, and upon arriving back at Oakfield Lodge Isabelle and Leon went to say goodnight to Colleen, who had recently been rubbed down for the night by Milligan.

'What a beauty you are, my darling,' said Isabelle with a kiss on his nose.

The evening before the Royal Ascot week was a busy time for Mrs Milligan. The large oak-beamed kitchen was filled with visitors by nine pm, including Mr Buchanan.

As Anne-Marie and Isabelle entered with Gabrielle and Milly, Mrs Milligan was struck with the beauty of the scene: four lovely people gracing her thousand-year-old kitchen. 'Why is it that my ancestors never told me that the French produced such beautiful women, Mavoreen,' Buchanan said, addressing Mrs Milligan by his favourite name for her.

'Alas, Mr Milligan, fifty years ago so few travellers plied between Ireland and the fair land of France.'

'Tell me, Colleen' – his fancy for Anne-Marie – 'from which part of France does your family come?'

At this question her hand searched for Leon, standing close by. 'What is left of it, sir. I live in the Bordeaux area of France.'

'Your answer invites the question why? Was it for example due to a famine of potatoes such as we had in Ireland not so long ago?'

'No sir, something worse – a revolution, when ninety percent of the French aristocracy was wiped out. My ancestors were guillotined in Paris in 1799 and their estates confiscated – a part of which was restored after the country became stabilised with the advent of the Emperor Napoleon.'

'You are an advocate of Napoleon?'

'Oh yes, sir. The Emperor was the forerunner of democracy throughout the world.'

'How very interesting,' interrupted the vicar. 'Evidently you are a student of European politics.'

'Oh no, Reverend Manning, only that part of French history which is so fascinating and so full of violent change for the better.'

'Incidentally, we look forward to your mother's visit for the wedding,' interrupted Isabelle.

'She telephoned this morning,' replied Anne-Marie, and is keenly interested to see you all. It will be her first visit to England.'

The Queen Mary Stakes was run on the Wednesday. It was a field of twenty-five. During the parade the runners made a great impression. Dhoti, the Arab grey thoroughbred, was looking superb, but for sheer beauty Colleen was exceptional. Gabrielle gave a warm hug to Isabelle before the riders proceeded to canter down to the starting-post. It was a beautiful afternoon as the runners lined up for the start of the race.

'They're off,' announced the loudspeaker. 'Several off to a flying start and at least five all in line after the first two furlongs. Dhoti is in there with the two French challengers and the new American challenger. The other runner, on the far side, is carrying the Buchanan colours, evidently Colleen. This was followed by cries of joy from the ladies as usual.

'Approaching the half-way post there is nothing to divide the five leaders,' continued the announcer. 'They all seem to be fully extended and moving fast, approaching now the famous Ascot five-furlong straight, yet still nothing to chose between the leaders – now five lengths in front of the field. Half-way up the straight the new American challenger is drawing ahead, but his effort is premature, especially before that well-known slope to the winning-post. Both Dhoti and Colleen are overhauling it a furlong from home. It has now become a race of the two rivals fully extended. Even at the winning-post it is impossible to divide them.'

As the photo-finish flag went up there was a hushed ten minutes' interval. Colleen, it was announced, had won by a very short head, which was acknowledged with loud cries of congratulations both for Colleen and her rider.

Gabrielle was the first to welcome Isabelle in the paddock. 'You really are a wonder, Isabelle. You have proved to the racing world your ability as a leading rider of stayers and now sprinters.'

'But never again, dear Gabrielle. It is too exhausting. My future mounts will be confined to three miles and over – no more sprint races for me.'

'That may be so, my darling,' interrupted Richard, 'but it seems to me that your racing programme will have to give way to the marriage stakes in the near future. My medical clearance has come through at last from Reading. But first of all, my warmest congratulations.'

'Turning round, she saw Richard, full of expectations. 'My darling,' she cried, and rushed into his arms, 'this is the best news of all.'

Richard was introduced to Gabrielle.

'Is it true that you are to compete with Buchanan's Hurricane for the Gold Cup?'

'Yes Richard – after which it will be time for my retirement also. Daniel Faure made his formal proposal of marriage to me last night in Paris and he has been accepted.'

'Oh Gabrielle – how wonderful! That has made my day,' Isabelle gave her a warm hug.

'It sounds to me,' said Mr Buchanan, overhearing, 'that tonight champagne will be flowing in many directions. Congratulations, my dear, both upon your engagement to Richard and for winning the Queen Mary Stakes on Colleen. And dear Miss Gabrielle, my congratulations upon your own engagement to Monsieur Faure.'

'Thank you very much, Mr Buchanan.'

'So, Miss Gabrielle, this will be the last time we compete together for the Gold Cup?'

'Indeed, Mr Buchanan, it will be the final issue between Irish and French thoroughbreds. If we can hold you even to a dead-heat, honours will be satisfied. Irish thoroughbred stayers are famous the world over. In France it is rare to find a three-miler to compete at Royal Ascot. However, in this case our confidence in the Cobler is believed to be justified by most racing circles in France. May the best horse win, Mr Buchanan.'

With the announcements of two additional engagements, Mrs Milligan's kitchen that evening was the meeting-place of many local friends, who came to congratulate Isabelle and Gabrielle. Indeed it was a happy moment for Mrs Milligan when the vicar escorted them from Oakfield Lodge after dinner, with Milly and Anne-Marie. They met George, the local policeman, Mr Buchanan, Mr Marshall and dear Belcher, the head gardener at the Lodge.

Mrs Milligan greeted them. 'God bless you, my dear, and congratulations upon your success over Dhoti.'

'You remember my friend Gabrielle, Mrs Milligan?' Isabelle asked.

'Indeed yes, Miss. Congratulations, my dear, and may you win tomorrow.'

'Very unusual for me to bet against a Buchanan entry at Royal Ascot, Miss Isabelle,' interupted Belcher, 'but my wife suggested that we ought to invest our five shillings on the Cobler, your friend's mount.'

'Thank you, Belcher, the Cobler will do its best to justify your confidence,' responded Gabrielle. 'At tonight's call-over they were both quoted at evens and the other entries were priced at fifteen to one. The bookmakers seem to think that it will be a two-horse race,' commented Mr Marshall.

10

The papers the next morning highlighted the great race, in particular the splendid record of last year's winner Hurry-On, 'the one they could never catch'.

As Anne-Marie and Gabrielle met Isabelle for breakfast, Milly and Roger were just about to leave for London, but not before giving an encouraging kiss to Gabrielle.

'Good luck, Gabrielle.'

'Thank you very much. The Cobler will do his best.'

'For the first time in two years my role on this Gold Cup Day will be that of a spectator,' observed Isabelle.

'Excuse me, Miss,' interrupted Mrs Plant, 'several reporters wish to take photos of Hurry-On.'

'Don't worry, Mrs Plant, Milligan is expecting them. They all wish to highlight the history of that great slayer, and why not?'

A moment later Mrs Plant announced the arrival of Mr Buchanan.

'You are most welcome Mr Buchanan to our family breakfast,' Isabelle told him.

'Thank you, my dear. Just a large cup of coffee will suit me to the ground.'

'Everything is in order – no problem except that the stable lad reported Hurricane had a slight attack of coughing in the night. But Hurricane was sleeping until an hour ago. So hopefully he will be well enough for the race at three twenty this afternoon.' He turned to Anne-Marie. 'Colleen, what a picture you make on this beautiful June morning! By the way, do you remember earlier this year when you were told about my entry for the King Stand Stakes on Friday, the last day of Royal Ascot – Foray, the fastest five-year-old Ireland has ever produced? Well, now he is still fifty to one. He has a gambler's chance in the races.'

'Thank you very much, Mr Buchanan. My bet will be placed this morning. Good luck this afternoon, Mr Buchanan,' she added as he left Oakfield Lodge for the course.

The course was packed with a quarter of a million race-goers on that lovely afternoon. Both the Cobler and Hurricane cantered down together to the starting gate. In all there were twenty runners for this important event in what is known as 'Ladies Day' at Royal Ascot, the Gold Cup.

Isabelle, the vicar and Milligan watched the race from the stands.

'They're off,' came the announcement from the loudspeakers. 'It is a fast pace for the start of such a long race. Both favourites are up with the leaders. At the quarter-mile post Hurricane is just in front of the Cobler, but both runners are already drawing away from the field. Approaching the halfway post the two leaders are now four lengths in front of the field, and increasing the pace. Hurricane is now half a length in front of the Cobler.'

'What do you think, Milligan?' asked the vicar.

'They are in a class by themselves, sir. It is difficult to predict the result at this stage. They are both racing at a rare pace.'

'A mile from the winning-post,' continued the announcer, 'and both the leaders are now neck and neck – four furlongs from the winning-post and the leaders are now ten lengths in front of the pack. Now two furlongs from the post and both runners are fully extended and still running neck and neck. A hundred yards from the winning-post and still nothing to divide them.'

The excited crowd cheered as the runners flashed past the winning-post for a photo finish. In five minutes the result was announced – a dead heat! A roar of approval was heard throughout the course, and then someone in the crowd at Tattersalls shouted, 'The ghost of Hurry-On, the one they could never catch.' Another roar of approval!

Isabelle's eyes were moist with tears.

'Use my handkerchief, Miss,' offered Milligan.

'Silly of me, Milligan, please excuse this burst of emotion. Do you remember long ago how we managed to bring Hurry-On to Oakfield Lodge, and the stormy crossing from Ireland?'

'Yes, Miss – an unforgettable memory, but now we must go to congratulate your friend Miss Gabrielle in the paddock.'

Gabrielle was exhausted.

'Congratulations, my dear Gabrielle.' Isabelle said warmly.

'Oh Isabelle, as the crowd expressed it so well: "the ghost of Hurry-On". But that is my last race. It is too much to ask of us females, as you said after the Queen Mary Stakes.'

'Well done, Miss Gabrielle,' interrupted Mr Buchanan. 'But it will be a great loss to the racing world to lose you and Miss Isabelle two of their finest active supporters of the turf, as owners I've ever known in my sixty years of racing experience.'

'You are very kind, Mr Buchanan, and yet if we retire from activity on the turf, at least we will continue our regular meetings at Royal Ascot and enjoy the thrill of those long-price winners of yours.'

'In answer to that, dear Miss Isabelle, why not have a flutter on Foray, our entry for the last race at Royal Ascot tomorrow. He is still fifty to one.'

That night a steady rain set in, but it was very warm and thundery with little or no wind. By the time Roger and Anne-Marie arrived from London about seven pm the rain was steady and heavy. Mrs Plant was preparing the dinner for Gabrielle, the vicar and Daniel Faure, who had just arrived from St Cloud near Paris. After giving a warm hug to Mrs Plant, Roger asked about the result of the race.

'Bravo Gabrielle – so she held off Hurricane to a draw, honour satisfied,' responded Roger.

'Mrs Plant, tomorrow is the last day,' prompted Anne-Marie. 'And information has come my way that the winner of the King Stand Stakes will be high priced.'

'That is obvious, my dear Anne-Marie. There are thirty-one runners and it will be an open race. The field is quoted at fifteen to one, there are nine favourites at that price, but some are fifty to one.'

'That is what my information is all about – but it is top secret.'

'What is the horse's name?' asked Mrs Plant.

'Foray, Mrs Plant.'

'But that is Buchanan's entry. He said nothing about it to me,' grumbled Roger. 'And he,' added Roger, 'he has not run for over a year, so if he wins Mr Buchanan will be in trouble with the stewards.'

During dinner the subject was again raised. Both Gabrielle and the vicar were interested.

'It is true, Gabrielle,' ventured the vicar. 'Foray pulled up lame after winning a major handicap race at York a year ago last October. It was a fast run five-furlong race.'

'That settles it,' replied Gabrielle. 'If Buchanan is trying, it could be a race worth watching.'

It was late when Leon drove the vicar back to the vicarage and the great rains continued heavier than ever. After delivering the vicar, Leon returned to find Anne-Marie waiting for him in the hall.

'My darling, it is eleven-thirty, time young brides-to-be are safely in bed.'

'It is true, my dearest, but my day starts before yours and, since you came in rather late for dinner, you missed the early topic of news.'

'And what was that?'

'Tomorrow's last race at Royal Ascot – the King Stand Stakes. Do you wish to try your luck on a fifty-to-one chance?'

'*Tu es adorable.* You are my fifty-to-one winner,' with which he gave Anne-Marie an affectionate hug.

'*Tu es irrésistible.*'

With another hug they went to their respective rooms.

All night it continued to rain and not until noon the next day did it begin to ease off. But the weather remained warm as the Ascot traffic started to build up. It was an unforgettable day, in spite of the rain which continued well into the afternoon. Eventually the twenty-one runners were paraded in the paddock. Foray was a magnificent black stallion with white feet.

'Milligan, he must be over seventeen hands,' ventured Isabelle.

'According to the records, Miss, Foray is seventeen and a half, and built for speed. Just look at the depth of that chest.'

At that moment the vicar joined the party.

'He has dropped to forty to one,' replied Milligan in answer to his question.

'What a magnificent stallion,' commented Gabrielle, arm in arm with Isabelle.

'But look at the three Arab-bred stallions,' observed Roger. 'Superb thoroughbreds, each with an impressive sprint record this season, and they are all amongst the eight favourites for this open race.'

The bell sounded and the runners were mounted prior to their canter towards the starting gate. But it continued to rain and the paddock became sticky with mud. From the stands they watched the runners line up for the last race at Royal Ascot that season. The sky was heavy and the light poor, so after the off signal was given it was difficult for the announcer to distinguish the colours.

'One only was slightly left at the start,' said the announcer. 'Not possible to distinguish its colours yet, it is on the stand side of the course.' (The stand side at Royal Ascot is slightly higher than the rail side – a significant feature in wet weather.) The announcer continued, 'At least thirteen runners are all in line. The one left a little at the start is Foray, in the colours of Buchanan. He was left two lengths but is making up – in spite of the teeming rain and the fast pace. Foray is now one length behind the thirteen leaders.' The ladies went crazy with delight. 'Now half-way from the winning-post and the leaders are down to nine, including all three Arab-bred runners. Foray is now half a length behind the leaders.'

'Well, Milligan, how is Foray performing?' asked the vicar.

'He is going fast, sir, fully extended – and most fortunate of all he has kept to the stand side of the course, where it is less muddy than the rail side, after a full week of racing. In my opinion, with that advantage under these appalling conditions, he may win.'

The announcer continued, 'Now one furlong from the winning-post. The three Arab-bred stallions have moved to the front with three others in colours not possible to identify in this weather, but Foray is now only a head-length behind the leaders.' Loud cheers from the crowd. 'Fifty yards from the winning-post and all six leaders are fully extended – but Foray on the stand side is now level with the leaders.' More cheers from the stands.

As the leading runners swept past the post, Foray was announced as the winner by half a length but, at the same time, the enquiry flag was hoisted. Buchanan had to see the steward. 'What was the reason for Foray's absence from racing for the last eighteen months?'

'The vet certificates are here, gentleman. He was pronounced fit six months ago,' Buchanan responded.

'May we keep these for a few days?'

'Certainly, gentlemen.'

'Thank you, Mr Buchanan, and congratulations.'

The clearance flag was immediately hoisted amid shouts and cheers from Foray's backers.

'Fifty to one,' exclaimed Anne-Marie that night at the party in Mrs Milligan's kitchen. 'How much will be paid on £5 investment, Mrs Milligan?'

'My dear, that is £250 – a small fortune plus your stake.'

'What's all this?' said Leon. 'A small fortune?'

'None of your business. Perhaps my winnings concern a present for a particular man.'

'Ah – a man. Who can that be?' Leon teased.

11

On Sunday morning, early, Roger and Isabelle started for London Airport in the teeming rain to meet the master.

'Hello, Daddy,' called Isabelle, as the master left the Customs area.

'Well, my child, you have never looked so well and so lovely. Perhaps it is something to do with your engagement to Richard? Is all well on that front?'

'Oh yes, Daddy – a week on Saturday it's our wedding day.'

'You have grown up far too quickly. But life must go on, as the French express it, *les années passent.*'

'How are you, Roger? Are you winning the struggle with your studies?'

'It is so good to see you, Dad. Yes, with the help of Milly and Richard, there is clear progress on most subjects. The summer vacation has just commenced and the work programme for the next two and a half months in London with Mr Anido, my tutor, has just started. Still another two years to go. But it needs all my close attention seven days a week – if I am ever to gain a diploma.'

'We are all behind you in this first great effort of your life. Do not give up. Remember the Reynolds of Yorkshire always went down fighting to the end if necessary. You will succeed. There is no doubt about it in my mind – simply because you have the will to win through.'

As on previous home-comings from Nigeria, there was much excitement at Oakfield Lodge. Mrs Plant was thrilled as usual, especially as the master brought back from Kano, Northern Nigeria, an embroidered Hausa bag of local leather.

'Thank you very much, Master. It even has my initials on it. Bless you, sir.'

'How are you, Mrs Plant? It seems to me that you continue to thrive.'

'Oh yes, sir, especially with all the young people around and three marriages soon to boot!'

'Three?' the master exclaimed.

'Yes sir, Isabelle's friend Gabrielle expressed her desire to be married by Reverend Manning at the local parish on the same day as Mr Leon and Anne-Marie and Mr Richard and Isabelle.

'To whom?'

'To Monsieur Daniel Faure – you will remember his visit to see Hurry-On last year.'

'But how do you feel, Mrs Plant, about coping with this activity at your age?'

The housekeeper smiled. 'No problem sir. Indeed it makes me feel young again, and Miss Isabelle has already engaged several friends from the village who are thrilled to come and help me in the kitchen.'

'Don't you think that a professional team from London ought to manage the domestic arrangements, to prepare tables with food, and receive guests?'

'Oh no, sir. This is to be a village affair and everyone is looking forward so much to come and contribute to the occasion.'

'Very well, Mrs Plant – so long as you do not lose any sleep during the festivities.'

Preparations for the triple wedding commenced immediately. Richard arrived from Inverness in time for dinner, having made detailed arrangements at the old castle for the reception of Isabelle, Roger and Milly after the triple wedding.

Leon and Anne-Marie intended to stay somewhere on the Adriatic Coast of Italy for their honeymoon. Gabrielle and Daniel decided to stay in a small village near Gistard in the Savoy Alps. Richard suggested the Cotswolds to Isabelle.

The master spent much time with Milligan on farm matters during the weekend and the country house buzzed with activity. As usual the master invited the vicar to come to the dinner party on Sunday evening with some of his wartime friends, including Uncle Bill.

'Hello, Leon,' said Uncle Bill. 'Fully recovered now from your setback with Malaria?'

'Thank Heaven, Uncle Bill. It was a rough experience.'

'When do you return to Lagos?'

'About four weeks after our marriage, and later on Anne-Marie will join me at our new residence on the Victoria Island, Lagos.'

'Well, Walter, you look remarkably well. Were you satisfied with your endeavours during the last tour?

'The answer to your question is "yes". Our company is developing well after the four years of economic stagnation caused by the recession in the crude-oil trade worldwide. Leon was doing remarkably well up to the time when we had to send him home with malaria, under competitive conditions too, especially from the Germans.

The old soldiers of the 1914 vintage were keenly interested to press Richard on his experience at Arnhem. Answering questions by Uncle Bill and Colonel Mackleton, Chairman of the Stewards Committee at Royal Ascot,' Richard replied 'A part of Montgomery's first army was diverted to the right flank in order to assist the Americans, who had met stiff resistance. Then Montgomery's leading divisions were never able to link up with the airborne parachute commandos – although they made gallant attempts to do so. On the bridge, therefore, we were simply outnumbered and the Germans attacked from both ends. Half the division was wiped out. Fifteen hundred in all, half Polish and half British.'

'Incredible,' remarked Maclekon. 'That compares well with several battles in 1914, when ninety percent of the contemptibles were killed or wounded.'

'And afterwards?' prompted Uncle Bill.

'We became prisoners of war until the Russians overran the camp. It was a surprise to us that we were not returned to the UK, although most of us were returned six months later. But no reasons were given for my detention, perhaps they wanted to use me in some way. However, one night, to my surprise, my sleep was disturbed by a British officer, who gave me five minutes to prepare for a night journey on foot. After a night spent in a deserted farmhouse, the British officer asked me to wait for him while he went in search of help, because of my wounds sustained during the fighting on the bridge. An hour later a small group of Russians entered the house and during the third-degree process my thinking ability faded out. Upon regaining consciousness shots were heard, dead Russians were lying on the floor, and then some officers entered the room with a few British commandos. They carried me to a Jeep – after which my mind became a blank until awaking in the Reading military hospital, except for a short period later on in the night.'

'Do you remember the name of the British officer, Richard?' asked Colonel Maclekon.

'No, sir.' They asked me the same question at the hospital and brought several photographs for identifications, without success. But the face was unforgettable – handsome and full of encouragement for my predicament. He had a deep voice, his sub-machine gun was still smoking, and he expressed himself with the authority of a leader used to a cutting-out operation,' he concluded. 'He just said, "So much for the KGB – come, we have no time to lose". After that my mental faculties failed again, but that extraordinary spirit which seemed to radiate from his eyes was often close to me during the early days of my convalescence. His last words to me were simply: "You are now on your first step back to civilisation – take courage, England in the future will badly need men like you. *Au revoir*".'

The vicar was impressed. 'And you have no idea of his identity?'

'None, sir.'

'Would you recognise him from a photograph?' questioned the Colonel.

'Oh certainly, sir.'

'In that case, in due course, we may be able to accommodate you.'

Isabelle was moved. 'You may not be aware, Colonel, that Richard was officially discharged from the military authority at Reading only a few weeks ago.'

'Do not worry my dear, it is not my intention to upset Richard about my interest in his experience, but it happens that the British officer described bears a close resemblance to my missing son.'

The party was intensely surprised.

'Have you a photograph of your son?' asked the vicar.

'Yes indeed. Will it upset you to see it now, Richard?'

Richard's hand gripped his wine glass. 'He saved my life, sir. No it will not upset me.'

The Colonel drew out a photograph from his pocket.

Richard's hand shook as he took the photograph. Within seconds he recognised the commando with the smoking sub-machine gun.

'Without doubt it is the same person.'

'You are quite sure?'

'No doubt at all, sir – the powerful shoulders, and the penetrating eyes.'

'When did you last hear from him?' asked the vicar.

'Over two years ago. He was on the Russian border with Germany – engaged like many upon a special military mission, concerned with line of demarcation between Russia and the Allies,' Richard remembered, then added, 'Excuse me, sir. It has just come to my mind, at long last, the curious message your son enjoined me to give to the commanding officer upon my return to the UK.

Thank God my memory has now fully recovered.'

'Well, Richard, what was the message?'

'In fact, sir, it was hardly a message. Your son urged me, quite simply, to take my army boots to the group officer of my Division. He was most earnest about it.'

The Colonel was keenly interested. 'During your convalescence in this lovely home did your group officer ever caution you about security for your safety?'

'Yes,' answered Isabelle. 'They were most emphatic that our premises must be made doubly secure and that Richard must never be allowed out alone – but we thought that his caution was due to Richard's loss of memory.'

'You are partly right, my dear. But do you remember the names of the officers at Reading who were in charge of Richard's movements?'

'Yes indeed, sir. Their names rank and numbers are in our private book.'

'Good – now, since the situation is urgent, is it possible to phone them immediately?'

Within a few minutes three officers were on their way to Oakfield Lodge. Colonel William Maclekon was recognised at once.

'Good evening sir. We have been waiting for this communication for twelve months.'

'Isabelle explained to Richard that all his army kit was stored next to her room upstairs. Immediately his uniform and the precious boots were located.

Again Richard ejaculated, 'Thank heaven my memory has returned. Here, officer, are the very boots which it was my duty to hand over to you.'

Addressing Isabelle, the officer asked for a strong carving-knife. When this was procured he applied it to the right-hand sole, and to the amazement of the assembly a thick wad of paper was extracted from the sole of the boot.

'This is the hand-drawn map which we have been expecting for the last twelve months,' explained the commanding officer. 'We are most grateful to you, Miss Isabelle, for your call.'

'You must thank Colonel Maclekon for triggering off the whole exercise, officer,' replied Isabelle.

Turning to the Colonel, the commanding officer added, 'Once again you have guided us upon the right track. Will you be staying here for the night, sir?'

'Oh yes, officer, the full weekend.'

'Good, tomorrow morning we may have some news for you – about your son. Goodnight Miss Isabelle, and again thank you, sir.'

There was much discussion about the incident which continued well into the night. As the vicar was driven back to the Vicarage by Richard and Isabelle at midnight, he was reminded about the meeting with him at the Vicarage the following Saturday afternoon.

'What will be the subject, sir?'

'That is quite simply answered: how the solar system was originally formed about 4.8 billion years ago.'

'Fascinating,' replied Richard. 'We will look forward to it.'

As they drove back to Oakfield Lodge a discussion started, 'Richard, it gave me a shock to hear the Colonel press you with those unpleasant memories about your experience with KGB.'

'Do not worry, my darling, it is all over now. Besides, his questions prompted a recovery of my memory. Indeed, it has been a blessing to be able to assist him to identify his son.

Isabelle was resting her head upon his shoulder as the car entered the drive at Oakfield Lodge. 'If only this moment would continue for ever.'

'Within a few weeks, my darling, it will continue to eternity. You are worried about something?'

'Not with you close to me, Richard. It is the future which is so unknown, during those years of separation after your joining up with the Airborne Division my spiritual life received a shock. It has now recovered – but what next? It is only when you are close that it is possible for me to enter into the spirit world.'

'Where is your faith now, my darling? This is not our world. The Lord can count upon me for help anywhere, any time. He needs helpers of all kinds, great and small, just like you, everywhere, particularly in Nigeria. Some helpers are in humble occupations, others are in exalted positions. We must listen for His requests at all times every hour of the day, during our blessed life – if we are ever to experience a full and rewarding existence here on this fabulous earth.'

'Are you sure of these things, Richard?'

'Bless you, my precious, of course.'

Richard sighed. The car had stopped in the drive. It was a warm night.

'But Richard, the future – our future, you in Nigeria a partner with Leon, the climate there is only for the strong. You are strong, but not me, with our future little ones.'

'You will not stay in Lagos one day more than is necessary, my darling. We may be separated for a few months at any one time. But consider your father and mother, away back in the early days your parents were sometimes separated for eleven months. It was a great sacrifice. But your father opened up the west coast of Africa to European industry. It was an immense responsibility. Most women are not able to stand such absences from their spouse. But your father and mother were

Yorkshire bred – perhaps the toughest and most virile race on Earth. They won through and enjoyed considerable privileges later on during their life on this earth. It is not what you acquire or possess in this world, Isabelle, what counts most is our own creative ability. The Lord provides us with the challenge. Take Roger, for example, and his conflict at Faraday House. The Lord supplies us with the tools, the product is then left to our creative imagination to respond to the challenge. Your dear father started life with a five-pound note, likewise Uncle Bill. They both became wealthy men, due entirely to their creative ability, for they started their industrial activity in West Africa with little or no intellectual background – indeed, according to most accounts, their success was due to Yorkshire wit, and a strong liver! And what is more remarkable compared with the present-day domestic problems of married couples, was their faith which held for many years of happy married life, until your mother passed from this Earth. Evidently, my darling Isabelle, you emanate from a thoroughbred stable.'

This caused quite a laugh from Isabelle. 'Giant black stallion, you mean. Perhaps, Richard, provided that our progeny are blessed with your fabulous black eyes!'

'For example,' Richard continued, 'take this beautiful home, impeccably kept – not inherited like my small castle, draughty and in need of much repair, perhaps a saddle round my neck, although a haven of spiritual rest for me – but this 500-acre estate, earned by your father following the physical and moral risks during his splendid efforts in Nigeria from the early days and the sacrifices made by several separations from your dear mother over the years. Privilege is responsibility, my darling – your father certainly earned all his privileges. What is more important, he was blessed also with complete harmony amongst all his staff at the farm and at the office in London, and that is priceless whether in a big industry or a small community – a blessing only sent from Heaven to those who merit it. Indeed it is the womenfolk that made England what it is today, in my opinion – the really brave ones who see their menfolk go down to the sea in ships and contribute their skills and knowledge to the needs of the semi-illiterate world. Sorry to labour this issue, my darling, but it is simple for me to understand how your father was motivated – it was from God in heaven. There are great risks about going overseas – moral and physical. Your father and dear mother overcame all these problems. You and I are going to emulate them, and build from where they left off. Now, my darling, don't you think that it is your bedtime? It is one am and the rain has restarted.'

12

The Friday night before the weddings a dance was held in the large hall at Oakfield Lodge. It was a great occasion. Everyone on the farm was invited, also the Marshalls, Reverend Manning, George and his wife, and relatives of the Faure family in France. The girls were beautifully turned out, especially Anne-Marie and some of her friends from France. The young girls from the village of Winkfield were particularly lovely, gay and lively. Several of them were helping Mrs Plant, who insisted that Anne-Marie this night, together with Isabelle, must attend to the reception of their guests. It was a buffet dinner, always the better solution on those occasions. A string orchestra was hired from London and at six pm the guests from France began to arrive.

'*Par ici, maman,*' exclaimed Anne-Marie. '*D'abord, permette-moi de présenter cousine Isabelle.*'

'*Avec Plaisir,*' she replied, giving Isabelle a kiss.

'*Et maintenant, monsieur le père d'Isabelle.*'

'*Enchanté, madame. Est-ce qu'il est passé bien, votre voyage?*'

'*Oui, monsieur. Mais c'est un privilège d'assister au marriage de Leon et ma fille dans cette maison adorable.*'

'*Voilà, Tante Henriette, mon frère Roger,*' Isabelle introduced.

'*Enchanté, Tante Henriette.*'

After all the introductions the guests were shown to their rooms by Roger, in the French style, and, after the arrival of the guests from the farms, the festivities commenced.

They danced well into the night after a sumptuous buffet dinner. The celebrations continued on the Saturday evening before the triple marriage on the following Saturday. Richard and Roger were in great form on the dance floor with Gabrielle, Isabelle and the three village girls, Ginger,

Lucie and Lydia, who came to help Mrs Plant. In fact, the three village girls had almost grown up now. They had known Roger all his life, and altogether the five young ladies enjoyed a lively evening with the boys, giving a splendid display of the old-time dances such as the quadrille, veleta and the keelrow – much to the delight of Colonel Maclekon, Uncle Bill and the master. Henriette and the French visitors were also impressed and in particular Anne-Marie was thrilled with the evening.

The day of the triple marriage was a busy time for all at Oakfield Lodge. At eleven am the service in the village church commenced. People from miles around arrived for this special occasion. The congregation was in fine voice and Reverend Manning conducted the solemnisation of Matrimony with such grace, it was recalled for many years later by the three couples.

'Wilt thou have this woman to thy wedded wife, to live together after God's ordinance in the holy estate of Matrimony? Wilt thou love her, comfort her, honour her and keep her in sickness and health, and forsaking all other, keep thee only unto her, as long as ye both shall live?'

'I will.'

'Wilt thou have this man to thy wedded husband, to live together....'

Indeed a solemn occasion. Marriage is a serious business.

The short address by Reverend Manning then followed.

'My children, you are privileged this day to be united under the blessing of the Lord in this village church from where many of the Reynolds family have gone down to the sea in ships to earn their living overseas leaving behind their loved ones, to work in equatorial Nigeria. The great risks encountered and with loved ones far from home all takes a lot of courage. It is said that privilege is responsibility – how true that is of those overseas adventurers, three generations of the Reynolds family at Oakfield Lodge, another member of which is united in marriage this very day. Indeed, it is well for our little village community to be able to support them and to give them the essential service necessary for their needs overseas.'

Soon after the triple marriage service a considerable

reception was organised at Oakfield Lodge, not only for the principal families, but also for several friends in the village and the outlying farms, known to Isabelle from early youth. It was during this reception that Roger was discussing with Isabelle an invitation from the Old Boys Association to play in a cricket match before the end of the summer term at Abingdon.

'Are you free, Roger, for the last Saturday of the term? It will be a two-day match,' enquired Isabelle.

'What about accommodation? Perhaps it will be possible for me to stay with Bill Bevor and his wife Germaine. I'll have a word with them tomorrow on the phone. Apparently Abingdon has a strong team this season, unbeaten with only Magdalen to play today.'

'Please, Roger, let me ask Richard.'

He was in conversation with Milly and Anne-Marie. All three approached, and Milly noticed that Roger was a little thinner – due no doubt to his studies.

'My darling, some dear friends, old associates from Abingdon, have invited me to attend the last cricket match – Old Boys against the Masters with the First Eleven. Roger, it seems, is also in demand by the Old Boys. It will be the weekend after our honeymoon. Will it be proper?'

Everyone laughed.

'You are gorgeous,' replied Richard.

Isabelle blushed. 'Well, marriage is a bit new to me. It is only right that the husband is consulted.'

'Quite right, Isabelle,' responded Uncle Bill.

'It is the same weekend as the Army Group B needs me for final debriefing – so please do not worry about your visit to Abingdon for the cricket match.'

'Splendid,' responded Isabelle. 'This means, Roger, that I am free to watch you play for the Old Boys team.'

'No problem, Isabelle, except that it is two years since I held a cricket bat in my hands. Also it will be recollected that some of the masters are old cricket blues at Oxford – our opposition.'

'True, Roger, but within the next three weeks the local village cricket eleven will be able to bring you up to scratch.'

'Of course,' interrupted Milly. 'Leave this to me, Isabelle. May it be possible to include me in the invitation to

Abingdon?'

'It goes without saying, Milly – especially if you can exert pressure upon Roger to practise every evening on the village green.'

So it was all settled.

The newly married couples eventually departed, Richard and Isabelle for Gloucestershire, Gabrielle and Daniel for the Savoy Alps and Leon and Anne-Marie for Italy.

For the first fortnight Richard and Isabelle stayed at a lovely quiet inn in the village of Lower Slaughter in the Cotswolds. It was a fabulous experience for both – learning to love one another. They often passed a few moments in the local village church, where Isabelle asked for guidance about their future.

It was a lovely warm night as they wandered into the village hall, where Richard noticed a piano. Then without warning he sat down and started to play Chopin's four favourite nocturnes in E minor and C sharp minor at seven pm. All the windows of the local houses were open, and within half an hour several people gathered around the village hall. Isabelle never forgot that June night. The fragrance of the country flowers was everywhere, under a clear evening sky. She was sitting on a gatepost next to a field close to the hall, lost in Chopin nocturnes, when suddenly she realised there must be fifty people, listening discreetly and quietly to the classic notes of Chopin, played by a virtuoso. Isabelle was well dressed, ready for dinner at the tavern. A young man, with a young female companion approached her on the gatepost. He was in a dinner jacket. In a low voice not to interrupt Chopin he asked, 'Excuse me, madame, are you by chance acquainted with the accomplished pianist?'

'Yes, I am. It is most irregular to be sure, but he will be asked to stop if the community is disturbed.'

'On the contrary, madame, the community is most enchanted and wishes this open-air concert to continue far into the night,' the young man insisted.

'It is well known that artists do not like to be disturbed,' ventured his lady-friend, 'but may we know who he is?' she asked.

'He is my husband. We were married a week ago, and are now enjoying our honeymoon in this lovely part of England.'

'Please, madame, my apologies for such an intrusion.' she offered.

'Don't worry, Richard is an extrovert and loves people. He will be happy to meet all the members of your village during our stay at the Woodcock.'

Meanwhile, Richard was playing with all his energy and the audience was enchanted.

'May we know his name, madame?'

'Yes, of course. My husband's name is Cameron.'

'Got it,' interrupted the gentleman. 'You mean Sir Richard Cameron, the famous pianist who played the Beethoven 4th Piano Concerto six months ago at the Albert Hall?'

'Yes, sir.'

'So you are Lady Cameron?'

'Yes, I am.'

'You are most welcome to our little village. Is there anything that your husband would like at the end of his superb rendering of Chopin, in spite of the village piano?'

'You are most kind, sir,' Isabelle answered. 'Within a few minutes he will be happy to reply to your question.'

Sure enough, Richard stopped and was surprised to see all the local village people, grateful for his impromptu performance. They clapped and asked for encores.

'How do you do, sir, my name is Rankin,' said the young man.

'A pleasure,' responded Richard. 'Any relation to the Rankin family in Sheffield?'

'The grandson, sir, of the late Lord Rankin, who passed away ten years ago at the age of ninety-five. My name, is John, and I'm the third in succession.'

'Splendid, so now you have taken over the helm?'

'Not quite, sir. My brother and I, we try to carry on the tradition of over a hundred years. We manage, but competition is intense from the world over, but for the moment we survive. My wife Batina comes from Germany, but was brought up in these parts. We escape here at weekends during the summer months, from the factories in the north.'

Isabelle was introduced. It seemed that John and Richard were about the same age, and Batina was an elegant brunette full of grace and charm.

'Several people are keen to have informal talks with you, Richard, just for a short while. Will you let me introduce you to a few of the musical ones as a little distraction this evening, at my home. It is only a hundred yards from this spot.'

'It is most kind of you, John.' Richard then turned to Batina. 'Unfortunately, my German is limited. Nevertheless it gives me pleasure to know a German national, whose people have produced such fabulous music for centuries past.'

She responded, 'Your concert this evening, sir, thrilled me, for we have great regard for Chopin in Germany. Your rendering was exquisite, in spite of the piano in the schoolroom.'

'Madame, you have made my day – excuse the American expression.'

'Please call me Batina, since you and my husband have become so well acquainted.'

'Quite right,' expostulated John.

'Excuse me, John, our retired local pianist from France would be grateful for a few words with Sir Richard.'

'Of course, my dear, ask Gaston to come forward.'

'*Enchanté monsieur*,' he said to Richard. 'It is only a simple question, sir. Most of my life has been associated with the music world, yet in spite of the defects of the schoolroom piano you managed to produce a spirit of grace and harmony tonight which seemed to come from another world. Naturally, it intrigues me to know how you manage to convey such an impression to an old man like me.'

Richard was slightly embarrassed. Several people were gathered around the gatepost. The July evening was exquisite, with a clear late evening sky and no wind. Isabelle thought, *This is heaven*. The bees were going to their homes and all was at peace with the world – and Richard was content to answer the questions raised by John's old friend.

'It is difficult for me to express, sir. Nevertheless, the only explanation I can offer is based upon my own reckless weakness – often criticised by my contemporaries. It is simply that my playing has to reflect the spirit of the composer – inspired from Heaven. Most professionals place their performance on the formal composition, considered as the higher priority by the piano perfectionists, without any knowledge of the spirit world. Perhaps, *monsieur*, that answers your question.'

'Indeed, sir, it does – and far more clearly than you may understand, for you have revealed to me – even at my age – why my work lacked the applause I witnessed during your broadcast concert from the Albert Hall.' Monsieur Gaston continued, 'Do you believe that Chopin and Beethoven were truly inspired from Heaven?'

'No doubt about that, Monsieur Gaston, and several others such as Mozart and Brahms also.'

'But how were they able to compose such works? And why were so few composers able to emulate them?'

'The answer to that question, Monsieur Gaston, also needs reflection. It is only possible for me to give you my own interpretation. In the days up to the nineteenth century, men were able to devote themselves full time for several hours daily, without any interruption, which is our main problem now in this twentieth century. Take for example Handel. He wrote the *Messiah* in fourteen days, living on glasses of milk and nothing else – no interruptions – and what a spiritual contribution he made to the world. Does that example help you to the solution?'

'Thank you so much, *monsieur*. You have revealed to me the significance of the spirit world and its application to music. Would it be indiscreet to ask when you became so spiritually aware?' he added.

'Not at all, Monsieur Gaston. At the age of nineteen on my father's estate in Inverness, after leaving public school, in one of the fields where the herds were grazing during a cold February morning, I made a prayer to God in Heaven. Two supplications were requested. For marriage my request was for a beautiful girl, intelligent and affectionate. In front of you, Monsieur Gaston, you have the answer to that prayer!'

'And the second, *monsieur*?' prompted Monsieur Gaston.

'Very simple – but not yet answered – the respect of my

fellow men.'

'There seems to be no problem there, *monsieur*.'

'No, Monsieur Gaston, not yet, but my mature life is about to commence with this lovely girl by my side. Within the next ten days of this honeymoon we will try to work out what the Lord wants for me in this world – His world – and then we will plan and act.'

'Bless you both,' said Gaston.

Batina interrupted, 'John, perhaps we had better retire now to the house verandah and watch the sunset with our new friends and our old friends.'

'Quite right, my dear.'

Batina, who was also well informed about the works of the composers mentioned during the discussion, asked Richard from where he received his inspiration, once they were all seated on the verandah.

'You may not understand my answer to your question Batina,' Richard warned her.

John interrupted, 'We must not tax too much Richard with these spiritual and philosophical questions, my dear. After all, this is his honeymoon.'

'Do not worry, Batina,' responded Isabelle. 'It is a pleasure for Richard to have this opportunity to talk to you all. He loves people and wants to understand their views.'

'You are very kind, Isabelle, but his subject of inspiration does interest me as much, as it does dear Monsieur Gaston and our friends.'

Then John asked Richard, 'Please do not hesitate to tell me when you both feel too exhausted with all these questions, for my car is at your disposal at any time. There seem to be many here who wish to converse with you.'

'Do not be concerned, John, it is always such a desirable distraction to meet the outer world during this honeymoon, especially for short enchanting periods like this evening, but Batina has asked me a pertinent question. It is possible that my answer may give her satisfaction. Now, Batina, in answer to your question – first of all, have you a drink ready in case of need?'

'Yes, Richard, and here is your Ballantines finest and Perrier.'

'Thank you very much, Batina. Now try to imagine the rain-drenched Highlands, near Inverness in Scotland, for years my home. It is walking through the glens and forests during the day when the inspiration becomes apparent, with the wind and the rain – perhaps even a little sunshine. For example, several times it occurs to me that a particular work by Beethoven or Chopin must be presented and interpreted in ways far different from the versions generally heard. Now my darling,' he addressed Isabelle, 'perhaps it is time for us to leave for our host at the hotel – he has prepared a special nuptial dinner.'

Many questions were asked by several others about Richards' music career and spiritual experience in the Highlands. What a heavenly evening, thought Isabelle, to see the sunset and Richard so happy to talk and answer questions. Honeymoons, she decided, are to be enjoyed externally by others, apart by ourselves privately at the hotel.

Every evening Isabelle went to the local village church to thank God for the harmony of her wonderful experience with Richard and several quiet evenings were also spent with Batina, John and his friends at their homes or on John's verandah.

Each night for both their new intimacy was exquisite, and blessed by Heaven.

The evening before their return to the Hall at Inverness, John and Batina gave a quiet buffet party and invited several of their friends. It was a happy gathering. Richard was much in demand, always surrounded by many musical enthusiasts of the great classics, and was able to give them an impromptu concert of works by Brahms, Chopin and Beethoven.

'Your husband seems to be at home, Isabelle, with all our local friends,' observed Batina.

'It is so kind of you and your husband to give us this farewell party,' Isabelle responded.

13

The next day at seven am they left Lower Slaughter for London Airport in a hired car.

It was a turbulent flight to Glasgow, but a little better to Inverness, where the chauffeur met them at the airport in the black and silver Rolls. Miss Glenfield was overwhelmed to see them as they arrived at the great hall.

'Nanny, you have lost weight,' commented Richard as he gave her a warm embrace.

'Due, no doubt, to all my anxieties about your adventures in Lower Slaughter with this lovely bride at your side – whether you were keeping dry after the great rains of the Highlands.'

'Dear Nanny, you are gorgeous.'

It was then that the three dogs entered the hall, Boozer, Lupa and Dante. It was like an earthquake. Lupa made tracks for Isabelle and settled herself in her lap.

Nanny continued: 'You are both arranged in the main bedroom where a fire is lit already, and your dinner will be ready in the library with a fire at eight pm as usual. This will give time for Miss Isabelle to become acquainted with the surroundings.'

Richard responded: 'We are only here for a week, Nanny, before we leave for Oakfield Lodge – then Isabelle for Abingdon and me for the final debriefing at Reading Army Group B.'

Isabelle was taking in the measure of the responsibility as mistress of the Hall. It is vast, she thought, and very ancient. It was well run by Nanny, but draughty, without central heating. There was a dampness everywhere – except where there were fires.

After a dinner of excellent food they both settled down on the carpet by the fire to discuss their future.

'My darling, these small Highland fortresses are out of date. This one can be updated at a cost, but is it worth it? This is the twentieth century and my future activity is to be centred in Nigeria. We have our life to plan after the few immediate duties we must perform. Consider first the children to be.'

'Dear Richard, your heritage is here. What a fabulous tradition. The children must be linked closely with it in a family background of very brave men – you and your brothers – your spirit is rooted in the Highlands.'

'And yours, my darling is rooted to Oakfield Lodge – in a far more civilised community. Indeed, if my life work is to be devoted to industry in Nigeria, it is essential that you are close to those you love and with whom you have been associated in Winkfield. Your mother passed away eight years ago. Your father is devoted to his work in Nigeria, and loves his farm, but how empty Oakfield Lodge will seem without you upon his biannual return to England. Leon and Anne-Marie have established themselves in a beautiful home not far from Oakfield Lodge. Consider the delight it will give Mrs Plant to see our little ones around the farm. The Hall here in Inverness is a symbol of the past far removed now from the essentials of modern living for a young couple newly married. No, my darling, we must be practical. Newly-weds naturally gravitate towards a home of their own – away from it all, but there is also another direction in our case. My nearest relatives have passed away. After seven years of absence from Inverness my position there is that of a stranger. This other direction, dear Isabelle, is quite simply to establish for ourselves a home somewhere near Oakfield Lodge, where all your loved ones remain, so that when I am in Nigeria it will ease my spirit to know that you are close to your dear Mrs Plant.'

Isabelle gave him an affectionate hug. 'Your logic, Richard, makes sense – under the circumstances.'

So it was decided to seek a place near Oakfield Lodge.

'Perhaps, darling, our children may pass their holidays in this little Scottish fortress,' she added.

He returned Isabelle's affectionate hug and drew her close. 'Of course, my darling. It has occurred to me that the Hall may be completely modernised and made into a tourist attraction with fourteen bedrooms, all with bathrooms, and updated reception and kitchens. Also with outside facilities next to the large, lake – swimming and pleasure boats for holiday-makers and bird-watchers.'

'Richard, what a wonderful idea.'

They prepared for their first night at the Hall. Isabelle was thrilled to see the portraits and paintings of his famous ancestors, some were recent, with the Military Cross pinned next to the portraits of his brothers killed in action in 1943, together with an award to his father in a famous painting *Over the Top at the Somme, 1916.*

Isabelle thought a lot that night as she heard Richard breathing deeply by her side after their busy day. This is indeed a distinguished family, may our children emulate their brave ancestors, was her prayer before she snuggled close to Richard for a night never to be forgotten.

It was ten-thirty am when Miss Glenfield ventured into their bedroom. They were still asleep in one another's arms. Discreetly, she prepared and made up the fire, then was about to depart when Isabelle opened her eyes wide and smiled.

'Dear Nanny, thank you.'

Nanny whispered, 'It is cold in this room in the early morning without heating. In ten minutes I will bring you a tray of tea or coffee with sugar and milk. Will Richard by awake by then?'

'Yes Nanny – a large bowl of coffee please for both, with a little sugar, fruit and hot milk,' she whispered.

The fire was burning merrily when Miss Glenfield returned with two assistants, loaded with trays of all the joys of newly-weds – a French breakfast in bed together. Richard was still asleep.

She smiled at him. Softly she murmured, 'Precious, it's morning.'

He clasped his hand upon her lovely breasts. 'What a night to be remembered, my darling.'

Isabelle smiled. 'Do you feel ready for steaming coffee after a quick wash in the bathroom?'

'Of course.'

In a few minutes Richard was back in bed with the tray

on his lap.

'Isabelle, *tu es adorable.*'

Isabelle was happy. She asked, 'Darling, how many children?'

He replied, 'At least twenty.'

An hour later their entry to the main hall was quite a sensation. Lupa bounded again into Isabelle's lap and she hugged her close. The other hunters were waiting for instructions. It was a fine morning. Richard decided to introduce Isabelle to the village people, who were delighted.

Time passed and decisions had to be made soon about their return to the South.

One night before going to sleep Isabelle remarked: 'Do you really mean twenty children, Richard?'

He drew her close. 'No, it was a mistake, it would satisfy me to have a hundred!'

'Oh Richard, do you love me so much?'

'My darling, whether one or a hundred – *tu es toujours adorable.*'

Isabelle slept, so full of peace in his arms.

Once again at ten-thirty am Miss Glenfield entered the bedroom to make up the fire. They were still asleep when she left, but she prepared the breakfast nevertheless – for half an hour later.

Isabelle thought, *if only these moments could last for ever*, as she awoke to see the fire blazing in the chimney, and heard the birds in the trees just outside the open window. Richard insisted that the Highland air was health-giving, so the windows were always open at night, south or north. Isabelle decided that so long as his body was close, no pyjamas, whether snow, storm or hurricanes off Cape Finisterre, she was safe!

Their return to Oakfield Lodge a week later was a happy occasion. It was Saturday, and Roger and Milly gave them a warm welcome.

'Dearest Isabelle, everyone misses you, especially me before bedtime – my usual good-night kiss,' complained Roger.

'What about Milly, now she's resident? Surely you reserve an affectionate good night for her.'

'True, Isabelle, but it is important for both of us to keep our passions under control.'

'Good boy, Roger. So, next Saturday we will all go to Abingdon for the cricket match and see my dear friend Matron. Did you arrange the accommodation?'

'Yes, Isabelle, you will be able to sleep in the sanatorium in the next room to Matron, and Bill Bevor will accommodate me and Milly.'

'You were always one of his favourites, Roger.'

So Isabelle and Richard settled down again to the sounds and movements of the farm at Oakfield Lodge. The wind rustled through the pine-trees clustered at the entrance drive during the warm July evenings before they retired to their double bed.

Isabelle was surprised one night to receive no reply to a question. He was writing music on a piece of white paper by the window in failing light – very preoccupied. She peeped over his shoulder. His writing was confined to music symbols, sharps and flats on a rough score, but he continued at a concentrated rate – listening now and again at the wind through the pine-trees, and making immediate notes as the western sky became a blaze of colour. This concentration went on for an hour. She hardly breathed. It was dusk outside the window, but he seemed to be particularly interested in the noise of the wind. Suddenly he looked up at Isabelle's frightened face.

'My darling, come here.' He gave her an affectionate hug. 'Firstly, my grateful thanks for not interrupting me during those moments of inspiration.'

'But what is it all about, Richard?'

'Quite simply, my darling, it is about the interpretation of Brahms Piano Concerto No. 2 and Chopin's Concerto for Piano No. 2. The producers wrote to me just before our honeymoon in Lower Slaughter.'

'Did they ask you to rewrite it?'

'You flatter me, precious. No, they requested me to give them my interpretation of those works at the Albert Hall at the end of August.'

'And?'

'I explained that now, with my marriage, this was not possible.'

'Richard, you must be mad – why?'

'Simply because my duties as a husband, newly wed, may not give me sufficient time.'

Isabelle said, 'You must tell them that your dear wife is most happy for you to accept their invitation to play at their concert.'

'Are you serious?'

Dear Richard, you really do need looking after, she thought.

'Richard, it is evident that you have a precious gift. Do not throw it away, my darling. Count me in with you all along the line. It is simply that you are such a continual source of wonder to me – full of surprises.'

That night she cradled with her arms the head of her ex-commando – an Arnhem hero – and slept until dawn.

14

It was Friday afternoon when Richard left for Reading – his last visit to Army Group B – and Milly, Isabelle and Roger for Abingdon. Roger was so thrilled to be back at school again. It was a late warm July afternoon. The Head of School was interested to learn about his early struggles at Faraday House, likewise Alston, the sports master.

'Do not worry, Roger,' said the Head, 'it is simply a question of being a late starter academically, but your achievements physically are well known: the mile open you won two years running, the half-mile open when you were only fifteen years old – a record since 1563 – and at the famous Duke of York's camp of four hundred, half young men from factories and half from senior boys from public schools, you came third in the three and a half mile road race and again your rugger and cricket records. Roger, the school and the masters are a little worried about your competiton tomorrow; nevertheless, we are all thrilled to know that you can play – in fact, several cricket enthusiasts still remember those off-side drives of yours, and have come here from Oxford and far off to watch the match!'

'Thank you, sir. You give me encouragement about my future to pass the finals at Faraday House.'

'Hello, Isabelle,' said the Head, as Milly and Isabelle appeared with Matron on the lawn.

'It makes me so happy to be here again, sir, with the Old Boys', observed Isabelle.

'How is Leon – one of our brilliant students of the past?'

'Doing very well in Nigeria, sir.'

Before they settled down for the night, Isabelle and Matron had a long talk about Isabelle's successes in the racing world, and her recent marriage.

After a memorable evening with the French master Bill

Bevor, and his charming wife Germaine, Roger left his little car outside the cottage ready for an early morning start at six-thirty for the bathing-place on the little island in the Thames, the other side of Town. At six am the next morning he joined the group of about fifteen boys, all on bicycles (sometimes, three boys on one cycle and some machines with only one pedal!). The car was not able to travel along the tow-path, so Roger was delighted to accept a lift on the back of the cycle ridden by Jim Lee, prefect in charge. The ferryman was ready for the party. He was delighted to meet an Old Boy, Roger.

'We all miss you, sir. For eight summers you never failed to turn up, often in charge of the bathing party from late April to late July.'

'Indeed, Jameson, they were halcyon days. What is the temperature of the water this morning?'

'About sixty-eight degrees Fahrenheit.'

'Gorgeous,' responded Roger. 'Do you remember that sometimes in late April it was only forty-seven?. When is Sergeant Eyre due to arrive?'

'In a few minutes, sir, but with you here permission to dive in may be given immediately!'

Roger was so thrilled. This was the Lord's world, nature at its best, midsummer, with cloudless sky, the sun fast evaporating the dew, no wind, and fifteen half-naked bodies all eager to await permission from Roger to dive in.

'Ready, my friends, as this springboard is taken by me, in you all go each off your own springboard, in and out six times, no delay.'

This was an emotional moment for Roger. Ten diving-boards reverberated as those fast running dives were taken from the base to the water, which was thirty-five feet deep. Roger flew through the air with a superb swallow dive, followed by all the others with either swallow dives or jack knife dives. The noise of the springboards was deafening as the divers endeavoured to pick up a small stone from the bottom of the Thames to show their ability to deep-dive.

Sergeant Eyre was surprised and delighted to meet Roger. 'We still miss you, sir, Wibbo and me often talk about you far into the night and all your adventures at Abingdon during your unforgettable eight turbulent years at the school. Never a dull moment! Do you remember the days of Mercury, your father's horse, who won six times in succession and won my little Austin seven for me!'

'How well remembered, Sergeant. That was many years ago. My principal memory of you was how you installed a fighting spirit into us during those OTC parades. Indeed, during one occasion you told us, 'Never seen such a rabble since preparing the raw recruits to replace those brave fighting veterans lost at Mons and first Ypres!' After that we rallied.'

After six more leisurely dives Roger was ready to return to the french master's cottage for breakfast.

'Sarge, please remember me to Wibbo, if he is not on duty tonight. Once he nearly caught me out about the mystery of the keys. We made duplicates in the workshops! Jim Lee, it seems will be able to take you back to your car on his cycle. Do you know that he will be playing against you today? Indeed, our distinguished bowler is very fast, the terror of Magdalene College team, according to gossip. Unfortunately for you, he may give the Old Boys a trouncing.'

'Evidently, Sergeant, a man worthy of my steel.'

They parted company. Many years later in the deep bush of equatorial Southern Nigeria, Roger recalled those fabulous moments.

At ten-thirty the match started. Alston, the sports master, was advising the school Cricket Captain.

'Roger Reynolds is a well-known hand at off-sides drives, captain. It is important, therefore, that you have some able field hands on that side and some fast bowlers to frustrate him.'

'No problem, sir, we will post two extra men on that side to guard the pavilion side boundary.'

George, the old Head Boy of many years ago, and Buster, who became a county player, were selected to open the batting after the Abingdon team had notched up 210 runs all out on the Saturday.

George and another Old Boy opened the batting on Sunday morning, after Communion in the school chapel. The three fast bowlers, all young and aggressive, soon despatched one Old Boy for a duck – to the applause of the school supporters. Next came Baxter, an old friend of Roger to face the fast bowlers. He played it steady and took his time to take their measure.

Unfortunately George, out of practice, was clean bowled for fifty runs at eleven am. Then Roger entered the field. As the first fast ball was hurled from the young Abingdon bowler, Roger sent it for a magnificent off drive through the pavilion! The crowd gasped. The second ball was likewise despatched, but this time smashed all the crockery for a mid-morning tea-break in the pavilion. The Abingdon captain delegated the entire field hands to the off-side; the young fast bowler was furious, and sent the next ball on Roger's leg side. He despatched it for a magnificent six across the road near the lodge. The crowd was amazed and cheered.

One older man from Oxford remarked to the sports master and George, who had recovered from his swift dismissal, 'Who is that man Reynolds who is knocking our fast bowlers about? Is it the same Reynolds that played for Abingdon against Magdalen College and Wellington a few years ago?'

'Yes, sir,' responded Bill Bevor, who had just joined the party.

'Thank you,' replied the stranger. 'What a shame he never went to Oxford afterwards.'

'True,' interrupted Isabelle, who was listening with Matron a few yards away. 'Unfortunately, my brother was not bright academically, sir, so he had to be content with London University.'

'At least, Miss, your brother still remembers those off-side drives which gave us all much entertainment. Allow me to introduce myself. William Baxter, father of the young man who is currently partnering your brother.'

'My name is Isabelle, sir, guide and mentor to my young brother since our mother died.'

'Indeed a pleasure to know you, Miss Isabelle. It seems that our young ones are upsetting the opposing Abingdon Bowlers.'

Isabelle wandered off with Matron, who was called away suddenly to attend to a minor accident. So Isabelle walked towards the main school entrance between the beautiful oak trees, but had to stop without warning as one of Rogers' off drives just missed her. She smiled, and came without warning to find Milly alone. There were tears in her eyes. Oh dear, what has happened to Milly, she thought.

'Hello, Isabelle. Come and sit down on the grass with me,' Milly invited.

'But Milly, there is something wrong?'

'Dearest Isabelle no – nothing is wrong except my feelings for your brother, now he is free from his studies and at last in his element, enjoying a fabulous innings of cricket. It is silly of me to be like this, but his happiness is also mine.'

'You are in love with him?' Isabelle guessed.

'Yes Isabelle – who isn't?'

'But by that I meant you in particular.'

'It is true, Isabelle, and I can't help it. Hence the tears of joy to see him so happy.'

Isabelle offered, 'Would you like me to drop a hint about your feeling for him?'

'Please no, dear Isabelle,' Milly protested. 'Young men are so immature they must find their own way around in the intricate society of women. Besides, he is so thoughtful and kind to everyone around him, especially to me, but the subject of love is unknown to him – we must not interrupt that process which the Lord will reveal to him in due course. After all, there are many young attractive eligible girls around here this afternoon, and several from Lady Margaret Hall are coming for the dance tonight. Are you going to dance, Isabelle?'

'Yes, George asked to be his partner last week. So you will partner Roger?' asked Isabelle.

'Correct. It ought to be a great success, the last weekend of term.'

At that moment Roger hit a terrific six across the road to the lower field and held up his bat to the applause of the field. Milly's handkerchief went up to her eyes to wipe the tears.

There was more applause as Baxter hit a six to the leg boundary. At the break for lunch Roger and Baxter were not out. Roger was 70 runs up and Baxter 50 – a total of 150, sixty short of the school sides total.

It was a merry, informal lunch buffet, players and visitors mixing together.

Mr Baxter, the father, approached Roger and George. 'So you have not lost your touch, young man, since I last saw you on this same pitch against Magdalen College.

'Thank you very much sir, but without training my stamina this afternoon may well evaporate.'

'That may be. It is understandable, but what pleasure you have given to so many here this afternoon with my son John.'

The afternoon recommenced in earnest. Baxter was clean bowled about four pm, leaving the Old Boys with 190. The next four Old Boys were all out for only five runs. The situation became critical when Roger and the last Old Boy brought up the score to 200 runs at five fifteen pm, with only a quarter of an hour to go and Roger's stamina running out. The fast bowlers were in their element. The next over they faced Roger, who was ready for them – crash! Another off-side drive to the pavilion for a four. Once again the furious bowler hurled another ball, this time on the leg side, which Roger despatched again for a magnificent six across the road of the lower field. General applause greeted this stroke. The score was now 210, equal with the school eleven. The third ball of the over was hurled at Roger, who once again played a magnificent off-side drive to the boundary, near where Milly was walking with Isabelle. But Smithers, an able young fielder, leaped at it just as the ball was about to cross the boundary, and caught it. It was a fine bit of fielding and raised much applause from the visitors. So the match ended in a draw.

Roger was relieved, for his energy was running out due to lack of training. Nevertheless, he had made 98 and was greeted with a tremendous ovation upon arriving at the pavilion. Youngsters wanted his autograph and the older visitors congratulated him on the rich entertainment they had received during the two-day match. As one elderly visitor from Cambridge remarked in front of Milly and Isabelle: 'Never seen anything like it since Abingdon was in the Public Schools Finals. There was a young chap called Reynolds who landed brilliant off-side drives such as those seen today – they were devastating and placed Abingdon at the top of the league that season.'

George responded, 'Sir, you will be interested to know that our friend here is one and the same man – now an Old Boy.'

The old man was overwhelmed. He gave Roger a warm handshake. 'Was it not possible, sir,' he asked Roger, 'to enter into county cricket?'

Isabelle replied, 'My brother, sir goes to London University, where the game is not followed with great enthusiasm.'

'What a shame, madam. Nevertheless, it made my day to see those off-side drives again during this match – indeed a most entertaining day.'

The evening progressed and the buffet dinner and dance given to the Old Boys and their friends began in the main hall of the school. It was a great success. Roger was much in demand and danced a lot – until he realised that his sister was not present. Just then Isabelle entered the hall with Milly and Matron.

'Darling sister of mine, you have been hiding from me – come, it is a valeta,' he insisted.

'No thank you, Roger. My ankle was injured in a fall earlier in the evening. Matron has most kindly bandaged it.'

Roger looked at Milly. Without a word they entered the dance floor, but just a second before Isabelle left, Milly whispered one word to Isabelle: 'Liar.'

Roger and Milly danced close.

'How does it feel to be the hero of the match?' Milly asked.

'Nothing compared to the feeling of your lovely body next to mine.'

'Roger!'

'Are you shocked, dear Milly?'

She did not reply. They continued to dance and in silence. She matched his movements to perfection – tangos, waltzes and valetas. That strong forearm – responsible for so many off-side boundaries to the pavilion – held her for a second or two a little more tight than was usual. She looked up into his face and smiled.

'Tell me, Milly, do you know much about this business of love?'

'No, not a lot, except that our village friend Reverend Manning insists that it comes from God in Heaven,' she answered.

'But Milly, in the last few years you have become a truly lovely girl – many of those boys tonight are waiting to dance with you. Do you mean that you have never received a formal proposal? Please excuse my impertinence, but we have been such intimate friends during these last few years, and have had such fun on the ice in the winter at Virginia Water, and in the countryside in the summer, especially at Sunningdale Golf Course.'

'In answer to your question, Roger – yes dozens!'

Meanwhile Isabelle smiled. At last those two were on the dance floor together in one another's arms. It was a memorable evening. Their dancing was watched and admired by many.

Before retiring to the home of Bill Bevor, Roger expressed his pleasure to Isabelle. 'Sister of mine, it was heaven to dance with Milly. Her body was so warm next to mine, and she was so ready to understand my every movement on the dance floor – if only it could have lasted for another hour.'

'Never mind. It seems to me that your love life is soon to begin,' Isabelle laughed.

'My love life, sister – yes, it seems to evoke in me strange emotions, but it is difficult to analyse or control or to quantify mathematically. Is this normal?'

'Love is sacred, treasure it if ever you have the privilege of its experience. It is a powerful force. Travel with it, but use your own intuition – do not try to reason with love, because it comes from the spirit world! Sleep well.'

Roger said good night to Milly. 'We have a lot to discuss tomorrow, on the way back to Oakfield Lodge,' he added.

'Indeed on what?'

'Love, Milly!'

Milly met Isabelle and Matron in her room before retiring.

Isabelle remarked: 'Milly, you looked flushed.'

'Dearest Isabelle, your brother has declared himself – with all the dynamism of his off-side drives at the cricket match this afternoon. He frightens me.'

'Tell him so, and he will calm down. You must be firm

or else you will have babies born out of wedlock – a stigma which will persist throughout the life of the child.'

'You are right, Isabelle.'

'But why not contemplate marriage sooner?' Matron interrupted.

Remembering Richard's thoughts on this subject, Isabelle replied: 'No, Matron, far too young, uncertain and immature. It would be unfair on Milly and the Oakfield Lodge standards. Roger must concentrate on his studies, the only time in his life to secure a degree – instead of a young man's anxieties about premature marriage and helping with the nappies. Richard went through the war, nearly lost his life at Arnhem and has now recovered, a fully mature young man, thoughtful, kind and considerate. We are completely united now ready together to await the Lord's will for us on this Earth, but to reach that stage needed patience and faith. This is why my advice to Milly and Roger is simply to have patience if this union is to mature into lasting marriage eventually.'

Milly replied, 'But he was so passionate tonight as we parted. He said that he wanted to eat me and squeezed me breathless.'

'The cannibal!' ejaculated Isabelle.

Everyone laughed.

'Seriously, Milly, you are in a position, difficult without doubt, to contain those passions of young Roger; also in a unique position to channel them into a lasting union.'

Matron replied, 'True Isabelle, but meanwhile both Roger and Milly may find other partners.'

'Of course, Matron, but what a test of their fidelity to one another. Richard and I had to wait for seven years!'

'You are quite right, Isabelle,' responded Milly. 'But it will take some negotiating, given his passions tonight.'

Isabelle replied, 'Of course, Milly, but the stakes are high. everyone around Oakfield Lodge would be so happy to see you both united. Again, my counsel is simply to let Roger prove himself at his studies. This is most important for his self-respect in society later in his life.'

'Dearest Isabelle, I see that in future it will be necessary to keep in check that strong forearm – much in evidence in the cricket match – from squeezing the life out of me!'

15

They departed for Oakfield Lodge the next day, but just before Isabelle left she revealed to Matron that she was going to have a baby.

'Bless you, my child,' Matron said, giving her an affectionate kiss.

'Isabelle,' cried Milly, 'is this really official news, so soon after the honeymoon?'

'No Milly – not yet. Even Richard who will be telephoning Oakfield Lodge tonight, does not know. In fact, no-one but this little circle.'

'But how are you so sure?'

'Dear Milly, the spiritual experience – apart from the physical cycle change. It is so uplifting. The Lord is in his Heaven and all on this Earth is bliss!'

Matron smiled. 'Take care on the drive home?'

'You are lovely, Matron,' Isabelle answered. 'The morning before my arrival here I mounted Hurry-on, in his retirement, and away he galloped into the Marshalls' training-grounds for an exhilarating twenty minutes. That massive stallion is so affectionate and understanding, it is my impression that he knows my condition because of the care and attention given to me throughout the morning gallop. So do not worry, dearest Matron, if the stallion was mounted yesterday for its morning exercise, nor about my drive home, even with the future generation inside me, for I know I will be safe as the Bank of England!'

'What was that about the Bank of England?' said George as he approached the car with Roger before their departure.

'It is top secret,' responded Matron. 'Not for publication at this stage.'

George, the former Head Boy, was a mature young man.

He realized immediately the significance of Matron's remark and approached Isabelle. 'My warmest congratulations, my dear Isabelle,' he said and gave her an affectionate embrace. 'May God bless you.'

'Thank you, George, my old friend. How is the world treating you?'

'Still in the Colonial Service, Isabelle, but it seems to me this life is too short.'

'Are you married?'

'Oh yes, but the children are too young to be left without supervision, hence my appearance alone today. Are you sure you will be able to drive back to the Lodge without problems? It would be a pleasure to drive you.'

Isabelle smiled. 'No thank you, dear George. You are as gallant as ever – true public school style.'

Matron made a last request. 'Darling Isabelle, please – no more gallops on Hurry-On before the birth of your off-spring.'

'No problem, Matron, the exercise will be reduced to a gentle trot until the arrival of the future generation.'

Just before their departure Milly gave Matron an affectionate hug, to which Matron responded. 'Take care of him, Milly.'

Matron was content, but she had a tear in her eyes as she and George watched the departure of the car for Oakfield Lodge.

Poor Roger was puzzled. 'Dear sister, that conversation with Matron and George was a little over my head.'

'Roger, you are the essence of innocence,' said Isabelle.

'What conversation, Roger?' responded Milly.

'The one about the Bank of England,' replied Roger. 'In my opinion it is not all that solid.'

Innocence, thought Milly, and gave a steady look at Isabelle, who was driving. Milly was as quick as George. So that was the situation. May The Lord bless her, she thought. 'My felicitations, dearest Isabelle,' she said aloud.

Isabelle smiled and put her finger to her lips. Roger was intrigued – something was going on.

Upon arriving at Oakfield Lodge Mrs Plant gave them all a welcome and pointedly asked. 'How is the Lady Cameron?'

'The Lady Cameron,' responded Isabelle in a whisper, 'is in production.'

'Bless you, but does Richard know? He has telephoned six times today.'

'No, Mrs Plant, but his next call will be a long one.'

Meanwhile, poor Roger remained puzzled until Milly explained.

'It is normal for the husband to be the first to know that his wife is going to have a baby.'

'What!' ejaculated Roger. 'It is me who ought to be the first as the only male responsible for her immediate welfare.'

'Do not be angry, Roger – your sister was not sure until this morning. Hence her talk with Matron.'

'The ways of women, Milly, will remain for me a complete mystery for ever and ever. So my title will soon be "Uncle Roger" – at my age!'

'Long may it be so, Roger, for uncles are precious to nephews and nieces.'

'But Milly, I am concerned about the morning gallops and driving the car. Next week my driving-test will be a high priority.'

'Calm down, Roger, and remember that the husband does not know yet. There goes the telephone – it may be Richard.'

It was.

'Darling Richard.' Isabelle tenderly gave him the good news.

'Darling, how wonderful,' responded Richard. 'Please take great care.'

'Do not worry. Hurry-On knows also! He is tender and careful with me every morning.'

'*Tu es impossible.* Do you mean to tell me that giant stallion is en rapport with your pregnancy?'

'My darling, of course – right from the start when we took him in from the wilds of the Irish moors, until he became the one they could never catch, famous throughout the racing world. Every night he expects a visit from me with the usual sugar lumps, as he rubs his nose on my neck.'

'You are making me jealous.'

'Dear Richard, you also make me jealous sometimes

when all those music fans of yours crave your time and indulgence. Incidentally, the Albert Hall has booked you for Beethoven, Chopin and Brahms piano concertos towards the end of October. Are you happy with their offer?'

'Only if you are, my darling. It means two months' preparation with my grand piano in Inverness, and only weekends with you at Oakfield Lodge. Now, it is time you settled down for the evening. Have you thought of a name?'

'Dearest Richard, it will be the names, not one.'

'Good God! Are you sure?'

'Well, it's just an intuition.'

'For the sake of Heaven, do take care, and see Dr Loretz immediately.'

They concluded with an affectionate good night over the telephone.

'Where is Roger?' asked Isabelle, entering the dining-room.

Roger was found in the study, alone by the fire, meditating.

'Darling Roger, give me your hands. Do you know that our love for one another is stronger than ever?'

'Stronger than when our mother died?'

'Oh dear, of course, Roger.'

'The trouble with me, dear sister, is this growing-up period – if only the world, my world, could stay still for just a little time for me to grow up more slowly.'

She gave him an affectionate hug. 'Dearest brother of mine, will you trust me?'

'You know I will as always.'

'Well then, even now I'm married and loved by a wonderful husband, I will have deep concern as always for my young brother, who has a great future in this world.'

'Do you really think so, seriously?' Roger asked. 'Why?'

'Many reasons. One, you are a committed Christian. Two, an athlete. Three, striving at your studies with your more academically advantaged contemporaries at Faraday House. Four, Yorkshire bred. Five, your heart of gold.'

'A little while ago my road was to oblivion.'

'Roger, you must never say that again – promise me, your sister. But why this depression?'

'It is something new to me. Perhaps it is because you are

moving away from me, leaving me with no sister and no mother.'

Isabelle could have hugged him close. 'But Roger, for the next several months, at least while Richard is arranging to build our new home close by, I will be in my usual room here.'

'And you will still come to say good night?'

Isabelle gave him another affectionate embrace. 'Dearest Roger, that is a promise – every night as usual.'

Meanwhile, Richard was exerting all his sensitive energy into his piano practice at Inverness. At the same time Isabelle had received confirmation that their new friends, Sir John Rankin and his wife at Lower Slaughter, were able to accept the invitation to attend the concert at the Albert Hall towards the end of October, together with their friend the French pianist Jean Gaston from their village. Isabelle remembered the short interlude on the schoolroom piano during the warm midsummer night – and sitting on a gatepost in evening dress as the sun was beginning to sink low.

Eventually the day arrived for the concert. Isabelle was so happy to be able to accommodate John and Batina for a few nights, together with Jean Gaston. Indeed, it proved to be a memorable occasion. Just before their departure for the Albert Hall Isabelle left a note for Roger, who was still in London: '*Will not forget you tonight however late.*'

It was six thirty pm when the party arrived at the Albert Hall in London. Isabelle was surprised to see such a large crowd. The women were dressed in style for the occasion – elegance was the order of the night evidently. Why? When suddenly a royal party was given priority to enter the hall it became clear. Isabelle was thrilled, likewise Batina. Richard was interested. It seemed that royalty were keen to hear the music of the spirits usually experienced by him in the Highlands from the high winds. So they shall! He thought. At least my interpretation, that of a true Scot!'

What a performance! The first part was devoted to Beethoven. The Piano Concerto No. 4 was followed by No. 5, 'The Emperor'. The audience was thrilled and deeply moved.

Then there was a short interval of twenty minutes when Isabelle and Batina enjoyed a glass of champagne with Sir John, in the lounge bar. The next part of the programme featured Chopin's Piano Concerto No, 2. It was a delicate and intimate interpretation. The audience was most responsive, and expressed their appreciation with appropriate applause. Then came, after another short interval, the Brahms Piano Concerto, which was also received with wonder by the audience.

The audience was so moved that at the end of the concert the standing ovation continued for several minutes – to the embarrassment of Richard, who was still in imagination listening to the storms and winds of the Highlands.

A little note (with a royal stamp marked '*Strictly Private*') was waiting for him in his dressing-room as he retired, covered in perspiration and exhausted. It read: '*Thank you Sir Richard, for a lovely evening – most sincerely*' and was signed '*HRH*'.

Richard was so pleased to receive this encouragement. So the royalty approve! He thought. What a night!

After a few minutes, the steward announced the arrival of two visitors backstage. It was the conductor, Sir William Blake, and the French pianist from Lower Slaughter.

'My warmest congratulations, Sir Richard,' offered the conductor. 'Indeed an impressive performance, and before royalty! It is my impression, as the conductor, that we were in complete rapport.'

'Indeed, Sir William, your command of the orchestra reflected my innermost spiritual intuition during the interpretation of all three works. Thank you again most cordially for your guidance throughout the concert.

'Incidentally,' the conductor said, 'you are acquainted, apparently, with my friend Monsieur Gaston, long since retired from the Paris Conservatoire.'

'Of course. did you enjoy the concert, Monsieur Gaston?'

'Sir Richard, for me it was Heaven, but still it remains a mystery as to how you ever manage to convey such an uplifting effect to each of the four works. My congratulations.'

It was at this moment that Isabelle, Batina and John entered the dressing-room. Isabelle went straight into his arms and whispered with admiration. 'Darling it was wonderful.'

'Careful now, remember that you are in production.'

Everyone laughed and Isabelle blushed.

Batina added her congratulations. 'Never has any major orchestra in Germany been in such harmony as with the soloist this evening.' She gave him a kiss on both cheeks.

'If you are not too tired, Isabelle, John and Batina have asked us all to dinner at the Savoy, with Sir William, his wife Jacqueline and Monsieur Gaston,' Richard explained.

'Are you happy about that, my darling? Good. Let us hope that they have Highland grouse on the menu.'

Isabelle indicated to Batina that, for a change, Richard was hungry, and grouse was a favourite meal.

'No problem, Isabelle – it has been ordered already.'

What a splendid evening at the Savoy. Monsieur Gaston expounded upon his early married life in the Latin Quarter of Paris, to the considerable amusement of the company.

Sir William, however, was more concerned with Richard's future. 'It is my opinion, Sir Richard, that you have a greater future in the life of music in Europe than in the life you contemplate as an engineer in Nigeria.'

'Sir William, that is a subject on which my heart is daily pondering. All that is needed is God's guidance soon, for time is never on the side of us mortals!'

Sir William's wife, Jacqueline, was also an able pianist. French-born and devoted to Chopin, she was as elegant as most French women learn to be. Isabelle was interested to learn that they had a flat on the Ile St Louis in Paris.

'You and Richard will be most welcome to stay with us during your next visit to Paris,' she offered.

'That is most kind of you, Jacqueline. In fact, Richard is keen to perform at the famous Conservatoire de Paris one day.'

'Indeed, then please leave the matter in my hands, Isabelle.'

When the subject of this discussion was revealed to Richard in the car on the way back to Oakfield Lodge, at midnight, with John, Batina and Monsieur Gaston, he was moved.

'Was she serious, my darling?'

'Yes Richard – without any doubt.'

On Arrival at Oakfield Lodge they departed to their various rooms at one thirty am. Isabelle quietly went into Roger's room, and knelt down by his bed to say her evening prayer and to thank the Lord for such a successful evening at the Albert Hall.

To her surprise Roger's eyes opened as she finished her prayer. *'Alors, tu es arrivée!'* He said in French.

'Yes, dear brother – no problem?'

'None, except that it is difficult for me to imagine you living far away from me. Tonight you were missed.'

'Now, I am here true to my promise, just a little late, to say good night. By the time our new home is completed you will have found someone who loves you very much.'

'Do you really think so? Who?'

'That will be revealed to you in God's time, but soon.'

With that she gave him a warm hug. His eyes closed with a smile before she left his bedroom.

Richard was about to jump into their double bed, when Isabelle entered.

'So sorry, Richard.'

'Do not worry, my darling. Your love is wanted everywhere, from the retired Hurry-On to Roger.'

'And now, my dearest Richard, please be in my arms tonight.' It was another night to remember, before Richard's departure for Nigeria. His decision was made.

16

The twins were born six months later – a boy first, then a girl. It was paradise for Mrs Plant.

'But doctor, it will be too much for the breasts of the mother – two wee bairns at once!' She protested.

'No,' responded the German doctor Loretz, an old friend of the family.

'The mother's breasts are developed to cope with this situation. Besides, it is most important that the babies are breast fed in order to receive the natural protection from the mother's milk against all the living organisms in the air.'

Later, Isabelle remarked to Milly, as they wandered into the kitchen from the garden during a mid-November morning, 'Dear Mrs Plant it is the last important lap of her life has just begun with the wee bairns at seventy years of age.'

Meanwhile the little bloodstock breeding establishment at Oakfield Lodge – formed by the liaison between the Buchanan family and the Faure family and Isabelle with Hurry-On – was progressing. Mares from the Buchanan stable foaled two young colts during the first twelve months – both black from top to tail. They were difficult to control at first, as if they had both come from the desolate windswept moors of remote Ireland, thought Isabelle – just like their sire Hurry-On.

Not an evening passed without Isabelle spending several minutes with Hurry-On in a special stable with Dobin the fourteen-year-old retired mare. One particularly windy and wet night in December, Isabelle noticed that his ears flapped often trying to understand his mistress now with two babies in her arms. Hurry-On was interested and with considerable tenderness, considering his fighting strength, nudged his nose onto the cheeks of the two babies. Isabelle was so touched that for a further twenty minutes she continued her talk with the stallion.

Mrs Plant then approached. 'Miss Isabelle, what a delay for supper-time for the wee bairns!'

'Dear Mrs Plant, do look please. These little hands so enjoyed stroking Hurry-On's nose and he loved it!'

'Miss Isabelle, it makes a lovely picture, but the nurse will be after me unless the little ones come in soon out of this gale.'

As the babies left in the arms of Mrs Plant, Isabelle remained with Hurry-On, caressing his nose. 'Never forget my darling you are, the one they could never catch,' she told him.

Hurry-On understood and stamped his feet.

'*A demain*,' Isabelle said to the stallion before leaving.

The three village girls, Lucie, Ginger and Lydia, who were all about the same age as Milly and Roger, were often at church together for the early morning Sunday service. Two of them, Ginger and Lydia, worked at the Marshall training-stables and had acquired a sound knowledge of mounting and breaking in of young colts, for eventual racing on the flat. Often they came to the lodge to help out Mrs Plant. One day Isabelle asked them whether they would have time to teach the twins about riding.

'Of course, Miss Isabelle, it will be a delight – especially the children of such a world-famous rider and winner of the Gold Cup at Royal Ascot – and the Derby.

Much later, the two young colts by Hurry-On were entered for the races exclusively for two-years-old at Newmarket and Epsom. At Newmarket the experience proved to be a disaster. They threw their jockeys! Even before the off. 'At least,' said Milligan, 'They will still qualify for the two-year-olds' first time out at Epsom, by the rules of the racing calendar.'

That night in the Milligan's kitchen, the vicar expostulated. Isabelle was concerned. Milligan and the manager of the Marshall stable, Mr George Marshall were trying to find the solution to the problem of the Newmarket reverse.

'Perhaps, Mr Marshall, we ought to postpone the programme for another year,' suggested Milligan.

Isabelle smiled and interrupted, 'They are so wild, just

like their sire. No, Mr Marshall, my suggestion is worth a try. You have two new riders, recently qualified to ride under the Jockey Club rules, Ginger and Lydia, both from the village and intimate with the two young colts under discussion. It is my impression that they are the answer to the Epsom programme for unknown two-year-olds next year.'

The vicar added, 'Isabelle may well have a point. For the last four decades, Mr Marshall, it has been a delight for me to witness the two-year-olds' first time out at the Epsom Spring Meeting. It is not the horse, however fast and untamed, it is the jockey who counts because it is a question of their ability to control those wild youngsters. They can be very sensitive in a race crowd and the rider has to be particularly masterful.

'Well said, Reverend,' commented Milligan. 'That is also my experience.'

'Are you confident, Isabelle, that my young riders can master these massive wild black Irish colts?'

'Yes, Mr Marshall.'

The vicar asked Marshall, 'What do you think, George?'

'During the last few years sir, Isabelle has often surprised me by her judgement about these problems. Indeed if, she can give me a satisfactory written report upon the physical ability of those youngsters to handle and control the two young giant colts, there will be no problems. It must be recalled, sir, that the two young colts are very strong and very new to the racecourse crowd. In any case, the report will be necessary for the Epsom stewards in case of accidents.'

Isabelle interposed, 'Mr Marshall, I will submit to you the required report, within the next three weeks after some severe trials on your grounds with the two youngsters up.'

The next morning Isbelle was engaged in a long discussion with Ginger and Lydia. Both youngsters were overwhelmed with the propoals.

'Do you both feel physically strong enough to master those wild colts in front of the race crowd?' Isabelle asked. 'You must remember that the Epsom Spring Meeting is a testing-ground for two-year-olds from all over the racing world. Reverend Manning told us yesterday that it is quite an entertainment to see these races, usually short distances of five furlongs only for the first time out. They zigzag all over the course, however capable the rider, they bump and bore, they do everything wrong – even crash into one another – but the racing experts are able to discriminate from the stands those runners who are promising for the future. However, the success of the two-year-olds depends so much on the experience of the jockeys – you girls. Do you understand the importance of these future trials, and do you feel that you have had sufficient experience, both of you?'

'Yes, Miss Isabelle, although we have not yet been on an international public course such as Epsom. Nevertheless, the colts know us well. They are very strong, and responsive to us,' Ginger replied. Lydia nodded.

Isabelle replied, 'Very well, tomorrow will you arrange with Mr Marshall for a trial run any time next week for a five-furlong sprint – under heavy wet conditions if possible – for both colts. And do not be afraid to hold them in on a tight rein, in case of need. Are you truly strong enough to do that?'

'Oh yes, and thank you again, Miss Isabelle, for such an opportunity.'

That night with Milligan in the kitchen Isabelle confirmed, 'Those girls can manage, Milligan.'

'Are you sure, Miss? The colts are wild, so headstrong and eager to break the rules.'

'Do not worry, Milligan, I will watch the trials, mounted on their father, Hurry-On.'

The trials were to begin a week later. Meanwhile, life around Oakfield Lodge settled down to its normal spring routine on the farm, with the master Leon and Richard away in Nigeria.

17

It was the middle of the second month of the summer term, towards the end of the fourth scholastic year for Roger at Faraday House – one more year to go. During his evening walk around the square, about two miles at six pm, he decided to slip into St Mary's village church for a brief communication with the Holy Spirit world, as he described it – specifically to ask for some encouragement during the year-end exams to start mid-June, just before the Royal Ascot meeting. The church interior was quite dark at that hour compared with the bright May sunset. Upon rising from the interlude with his spirit world, Roger discovered that he was not alone. The lady was veiled. Roger was intrigued. Must be someone local, retired perhaps, he thought. No, to his considerable surprise she proved to be the third of the trio, Lucie, Ginger and Lydia.

Roger hesitated, not wishing to startle her thoughts. However, since she left the church about the same time as Roger, he ventured an approach.

'Lucie, this is a surprise meeting, and it gives me the opportunity to talk to you about Ginger and Lydia, now they are qualified to ride at Epsom and Ascot.'

Lucie was a withdrawn character and little noticed locally, except for her charm and growing beauty – indeed youth at its most dazzling.

Roger was entranced, 'Permit me to invite you to a short interlude in the saloon bar of the White Hart opposite, for a long cool drink during this rather hot and sticky evening,' he said ceremoniously.

'Why, Mr Roger?'

'Good question, Lucie. One, because it is important for me to meet people during interludes from my studies, as advised by Doctor Loretz. Two, because you are well known to the Reynolds family at the Lodge. Three, because it interests me to know how your friends Ginger and Lydia are progressing with our wild two-year-olds. Four, because rarely have I seen such a beautiful young lady locally.'

Lucie was about to depart, this was dangerous talk.

'So please, Lucie, do not go. It is such a lovely evening and a Heaven-sent distraction for me to meet the outside world.'

'Mr Roger, you forget our station.'

Roger could have sworn. He suppressed his emotions, but she was right – to be seen in a local inn with Lucie might seem improper.

'Very well, will you come to the Lodge as my guest for an hour?'

'It is most kind of you, Mr Roger, and your generous thought is appreciated. Instead perhaps you may wish to accompany me back home to the village,' Lucie suggested.

Roger was pleased at least in as far as it meant a little progress – and he was indeed intrigued by her grace, tears and beauty. She must be about twenty by now, he thought. Besides, he remained most intrigued by the wet tears on her veil as she finished her meditation at St Mary's church, the moment when he first noticed her in the shade of the failing May evening.

'Are you pursuing any particular course of studies?' he asked with trepidation. She did not reply immediately. He sensed her embarrassment, adding, 'Forgive me if the question is uncalled for, Lucie.'

'My apologies, Mr Roger, for the hesitation to answer your quite natural question. This morning I received a letter from Girton College, Cambridge, advising me that I had been awarded an exhibition for my paper. Hence the reason for my visit to St Mary's church tonight to give thanks. Apart from my mother, no one knows it yet except you!'

'My warmest congratulations Lucie. It will cause quite a sensation in our little village. What are the subjects you intend to follow at Cambridge?'

'Physics, chemistry and planetary science – or possibly medicine. I am especially interested in the research of obscure diseases without any known cure, for example the deadly sleeping-sickness in Nigeria, caused by the tsetse fly.'

'Fantastic!' exploded Roger. 'The very subjects recommended for the future by all the educational pundits. But how on Earth did you manage to reach such a high standard?'

'The Windsor High School for girls granted me a scholarship, following the death of my grandfather in the Navy during the defence of Malta in 1943, my father died two years later also in the Navy. Every morning at seven thirty am the local bus takes me almost to the door of the school, likewise at four thirty pm there is a return bus, although sometimes during the winter there are problems – it is seven miles from the village to Windsor. In consequence a seven-mile walk through the snow was necessary when the bus failed to arrive.'

'Were you not afraid?'

'No, Mr Roger. The journey on foot took me two hours. Physically exhausted, yes, but during those lovely walks I heard a strange heavenly music – a sort of phantom music – which has always interested me. No, never afraid, It was Mummy who was anxious!'

'Are you spiritually motivated, Lucie, or do you have musical talents?' asked Roger.

'Classical music is a passion, especially Brahms, Chopin and Haydn. But we have never been able to afford a piano in the little cottage. In answer to your first question, this will take time, meanwhile the answer is yes – deeply! One of the Roman Catholic teachers at school was most encouraging and coached me for the final entrance exam to Cambridge. There are only a few more weeks to go before the end of term. Then in September my five-year course starts in Cambridge.'

'Dear Lucie, this is truly amazing news.'

They were approaching Lucie's home and found her mother in the garden in a deck-chair, knitting.

'Please do come in Mr Roger,' Lucie's mother invited, 'just for a few minutes and enjoy some chilled beer, for it is warm this evening.'

'Most kind of you, Mrs Arnold, and gladly accepted. You must be pleased with Lucie's efforts after the news received this morning.'

'Mr Roger, it beats me. Except that her father was an able industrial chemist and Lucie has access to his works and technical literture. Perhaps that is the reason for her enthusiasm.'

By now Lucie had returned from her room after a brush-up and she came into the garden to sit next to her mother. Now at ease, she had a radiant innocence. In fact, she ventured a few questions. Roger was entranced.

'How are your studies progressing, Mr Roger, at Faraday House?'

How interesting, thought Roger, the whole village is aware of my struggles at college.

'The terminal exams for the fourth year are due to commence in four weeks' time – mid-June – Lucie.'

'And are you sanguine about your prospects, Mr Roger?'

'The papers for the exam take ten days to complete. There are so many of them during that period, it is not possible for me to be optimistic – at this stage. The course, however, over five and a half years, is thorough. It gives us an introduction to several subjects important to intending engineers. For example, strength of materials, hydraulics, industrial physics, chemistry, electrical transmission and distribution, power generation, radio communication, drawing-office practice, mechanical engineering, heat engines and finally the study of steam, and its distribution.'

'Quite a menu,' smiled Lucie.

'Indeed. An agreeable menu for those who are born quick to grasp. Unlike me, for example. I am slow to develop and still struggling. Yet you with your brain will experience no such problems.'

So they settled down in the little garden to a simple happy talk about the future.

'How is Lucie able to afford all the necessary expenses of a life at Girton College, Mrs Arnold?'

'A good question, Mr Roger. Briefly, the Navy looks after its sailors.'

So it is as simple as that in the Navy – marvellous, thought Roger.

'Quite right too. But, Lucie, the cost of the social life?'

'Mr Roger, that will be based upon my allowance – to

be carefully observed according to the Naval HQ and Whitehall. To me it seems abundant. They seem to have thought of everything – what a fabulous service.'

A few days later Lucie received a letter from the Master, enclosing a cheque for £500.

> 'Dear Lucie. first our congratulations upon your entry to Cambridge. Second: as a well-known friend of my family since you were a tiny tot, it gives us all a particular pleasure to learn from my son Roger that you have won a place at Girton College, which has one of the highest standards for university girls in England. It will make us all particularly happy if you will accept the enclosed gesture of our appreciation for your past kindness to us and to dear Mrs Plant, with whom you have worked so often and so late, after many of the racing celebrations held in our dining-room in past years. With our very best wishes for your new venture in Cambridge. May the Lord bless you. Affectionately, Walter Reynolds.'

This news travelled like wildfire for miles around Ascot, Winkfield and Bracknell. A note from Mrs Arnold to Roger a few days later arrived by hand as he was grappling with a problem on friction (a vital study for young engineers concerned with mechanical engineering).

> 'Dear Mr Roger, Lucie is so overwhelmed with the great kindness of your father that she has gone off her food and will not eat until she has calmed down. Please therefore come for a glass of cold, home-brewed beer, and try to encourage her to see sense.
> Sincerely, Mrs Arnold.'

Roger responded:

> 'Coming this evening, Mrs Arnold, at seven pm for that excellent glass of beer – and to resolve problems.
> Sincerely, Roger.

Lucie looked troubled on Roger's arrival at the little cottage. 'Excuse me a moment, Mr Roger.'

Mrs Arnold received him while Lucie departed upstairs to tidy up; evidently she had been crying. Roger was puzzled. An exquisite young girl in tears – may the Lord guide me, he thought.

'Mr Roger, the child is stupid. She is unable to accept the cheque.'

'Why?' Roger asked.

'That, Mr Roger, is my reason for the SOS sent to you this morning. There is something on her mind which is not easy for me to understand. All she says is, "It is not right, Mummy. They are kind and charitable people and loved throughout the land, but £500 is a large sum – too large for a present to give an insignificant girl about to enter Cambridge on her own merit".'

It came home to Roger then that Lucie was a proud young lady.

'Lucie, it gives me pleasure to see you again tonight,' Roger told her when she returned.

'Presumably it was Mummy who has asked you to come this evening because of my inability to accept such a large present from a comparative stranger and from a class far above our station.'

'Splendid Lucie, now we have the nub of the problem – as my lecturer on mathmatics likes to describe it. First of all the facts: Yes, indeed it was your mother who most kindly asked me to come tonight in order to talk to you as a personal friend about your problem with the cheque.'

'It is not a problem, Mr Roger – it is simply not accepted!'

'Dear Lucie, all I ask of you is a hearing of the case for the defence.'

For the first time there was a flicker of a smile on her lovely features – God, thought Roger, what an entrancing beauty!

'Proceed,' she murmured.

'Keep your mind on the immediate business, said a sharp voice to Roger in his head! Now he realized that he was conversing with a young woman who had recently qualified for an exhibition to Cambridge University. With an able brain she was already spiritually mature for her age.

'Gifts of cheques are a subject a little outside my experience,' Roger began. 'Although once long ago it was explained to me that the giver is equally happy as the receiver – perhaps I read this in the Bible somewhere. Since early days with your friends Ginger and Lydia you have been a household name at the Lodge. It is quite natural therefore for the head of our household to respond to your extraordinary success in winning an exhibition to Girton College. We are all so pleased for you, and for your mother, who must be as delighted as we are.'

'Your sentiments, Mr Roger, are well taken and appreciated, but that is not quite the subject at issue.'

God, if only my spiritual instincts would surface in this sea of legal principles, thought Roger. 'How right you are, Lucie,' he continued. 'Evidently it is the sum which conflicts with your sound sense of balance. For example, a five-pound note might have been welcome and not caused distress.'

'Go on.'

Poor Roger was beginning to perspire in the garden. It was a warm night. Mrs Arnold was sympathetic.

'Another glass, Mr Roger, of our beer?'

'Most willingly, Mrs Arnold, thank you very much.'

'It is not so much surprise and embarrassment, Mr Roger,' Lucie explained. 'The cheque is a large one by our simple standards. The exhibition carries an allowance of four and half years, plus all food and accommodation in college. My future outgoings are unknown. Without a father or relative to help in case of need, my cash problems across this ocean of life are unpredictable – at my young age.'

'Precisely, Lucie – hence the reason for this gesture from my own father.'

She smiled again, just a little.

'May it be possible, Lucie, to compromise? Suppose you responded by accepting the cheque on the basis of a temporary loan of indefinite duration.'

This time she almost melted with a smile of warmth. 'Really, Mr Roger,' added her mother, 'you may have your struggles at Faraday House academically, but without doubt one day you will become a brilliant negotiator.'

In fact he did in Nigeria – another story.

Until then Lucie had said little. Roger was encouraged.

'Perhaps you would like me to help you with your reply to my father, based upon our discussion tonight.'

She looked up – as beautiful as ever in the garden twilight. 'Subject, to the elimination of the last part of your suggestion of "indefinite duration".'

Roger breathed again.

'Please do not go away from this little cottage tonight, Mr Roger, without the knowledge that my mother and I are both extremely grateful to your father for his magnanimous gesture to one simple village girl virtually unknown to him except for the happy past occasions when helping Mrs Plant in the kitchen. Although we saw little of your father, yet from my earliest years I understood how loved and respected he was in the village. So, it would be highly improper of me to reject such a kind and generous gesture. The sum itself is overwhelming, and as a young inexperienced girl of twenty, brought up in the strict discipline of the Roman Catholic Church, it will be necessary for me to commune with the Holy Virgin Mary in order to establish my further course of action. So far no response to my prayers, but you have helped me this evening to clear the air.'

'Mr Roger,' interrupted Mrs Arnold, 'one more for the road?'

'Willingly, Mrs Arnold,' responded Roger with perspiration.

'Mr Roger, may we leave this issue for twenty-four hours to give me time to reflect?' Lucie requested. 'Subject to your return tomorrow evening at the same time for further clarification, do you accept?'

'Of course, Lucie.'

Roger returned to the Lodge a wet rag – Mrs Plant's description – especially after four pints of home-brewed beer! It was nine pm. Milly was fast asleep but Isabelle was free, writing letters in the study.

'Hello, Roger, my thought was that you were lost.'

'Can you give me half an hour now -- my mind is temporarily unhinged!'

Evidently an argument with Reverend Manning, Isabelle supposed.

'My voice is hoarse after a difficult discussion on principle with Lucie.'

Isabelle was startled. 'Have you fallen for her?'

'Of course not!' Roger protested. 'Now listen, Isabelle, you are a dear sister, bear with me after a particular difficult hour in the garden, with her mother in sympathy with me.'

'Mothers usually are, dear boy. Please continue, and my apologies for the interruption.'

'A situation was presented to me which taxed my ability to understand,' continued Roger.

'So, she is not going to have a baby and she has not proposed.'

'Isabelle you are making fun of me – it is not kind. She does not wish to accept the cheque of £500 from Daddy,' Roger explained, and recounted his conversation with Lucie.

This time Isabelle stopped in her tracks – her astute, fertile mind began to accelerate into action.

'Your course of action is quite clear, Roger. She sounds like a young lady of high principles – just what England needs. Indeed, to have leaped all those hurdles, moral and spiritual, before entering Girton College is no small feat. Have you pencil, and paper – good, now make notes for your next interview tomorrow evening with this intellectual beauty.

'First of all, the exhibition award seems a lot to the innocent young lady from our village. It is not enough for Cambridge!'

'Second, Girton College has produced in the past several most able young ladies who have achieved important positions. For someone who wishes to succeed, a smart appearance is essential in front of the directors of industry or those of the Civil Services at Whitehall, so as time goes on she must be appropriately groomed and satisfactorily made up.

'Third, she may well prefer to become a school teacher and spend all her life in our local village school – in which case her expenses will be negligible.'

'Dearest Isabelle, thank God for you. Tomorrow at seven pm it will be battle time again for me – with additional troops. Bless you, good night.'

Roger was too tired for dinner, so he went to bed early,

but as usual he requested Isabelle, who kept late hours, to come and kiss him good night. She did at midnight, when he was fast asleep and said her prayers by his bedside as usual.

At seven pm the next day Roger returned with haste to the little cottage. Lucie was made up – to the very slightest degree – nevertheless her natural beauty was startling to Roger, who was once again overwhelmed with her innocence and youthful charm.

'Have you come with a solution, Mr Roger, to my seeming predicament?'

'Possibly dear Lucie.' Then Roger expounded upon the facts of life as pronounced by Isabelle rather harshly the previous night.

Lucie remained silent.

'Problem, Lucie?'

'No Mr Roger, nothing urgent, but your revelations have disturbed my equanimity!'

'Dear Lucie, your remarkable achievement has shaken the village. An unusual future is now open to you, with two principal options. When receiving the news last week for example what were your own thoughts about the future?'

Lucie blushed. She murmured, 'First of all, Mr Roger, the degree must be gained.'

'There is little doubt about that,' responded Roger.

She continued, 'In Windsor there is to be a technical college for engineering science.'

'And you intend eventually to teach?'

'Yes, for the rest of my life.'

'What about research in manufacturing. That is a second option,' Roger explained.

'Who will be interested in a bluestocking – a teacher with no experience in the manufacturing industry?' Besides, being a teacher will give me peace on earth, security for my dear mother and spiritual satisfaction, here in this little village, my birthplace.'

Lucie pressed his hand warmly as he departed, and added, 'Perhaps, Mr Roger, we really are *en rapport*.'

After an evening walk of one hour through the quiet country lanes in the early summer with strange thoughts and the intoxicating scent of the wild flowers as they were about to fold in for their summer night slumber. He entered the Lodge in time for dinner, but only Isabelle was present.

'At last,' remonstrated Mrs Plant. 'Apparently the young master suffers from moonlighting. A few purgatives tonight and he will feel better tomorrow morning!'

Roger was still unhinged with the beauty of Lucie and only smiled at Mrs Plant. 'Dear Mrs Plant, you mean well. What is on the menu tonight?'

'First, Roger,' interrupted Isabelle, 'what was the result of your visit tonight?'

'Cold as ice at the start, but she requested me to drive her to Girton College in mid-September, which I willingly accepted.'

'So, Roger, you fell for her?'

'Not in the least, dear sister. My emotions about Lucie have not yet been worked out – besides, my relations with Milly are happy and stablised under the conditions you and Matron laid down at Abingdon.'

'So Roger the knight errant, in quest of adventure, returns here satisfied with the evening's experience.'

'Sometimes, dear sister, it is difficult for me to know what side you are on.'

Isabelle smiled. 'My dear brother, you are gorgeous, equally as lovely and innocent as the goddess you met tonight!'

Roger was unable to return the next day because of a call from his tutor in London to discuss the three months' holiday revision programme for the next scholastic year.

18

Milly was away for a month in France on holiday with distant cousins. The master and Leon were back in Lagos. Isabelle was busy with the twins and supervising the training of Lydia and Ginger as jockeys for the two young colts born to Hurry-On. Roger was tired early evening when he arrived back from his studies with Mr Anido, the tutor in Earls Court. Even so, before a late dinner at eight thirty he often roamed the lanes of Winkfield relaxing his mind after the intensive technical instructions given by his tutor. He marvelled at the activities of the Cox family working in the fields opposite Oakfield Lodge farm during the corn harvest. One evening, at eight pm late August when the huge red sun on the horizon was sinking, he observed that even the little tots about eight years of age were still helpng the farm hands and their master. This is production at its best, thought Roger – and indeed is well worthy. Roger dwelt on this unforgettable picture, and as the sun went down and his walk coincided with a corner of their land through a right-of-way path, he met Mr Cox.

'Hello, Roger, you are more than welcome. Come share with me a tankard of home brew.'

'Willingly, Mr Cox. Congratulations upon the success of your harvest. It seems to me that all has been gathering in during this great heatwave. It was 97 degrees at three pm by the thermometer in the kitchen garden at Oakfield Lodge – according to our gardener Belsher.'

'You do not surprise me, Roger. Here is your pint.'

'To your excellent health, sir,' proposed Roger.

His wife then entered, 'Mr Roger, you must excuse me for not being presentable without warning.'

'This is how it should be in these busy harvest times. To drink a draught with your husband – our neighbour – at the end of the harvest gives me immense pleasure.'

'Won't you stay for a little celebration supper, please?'

Roger was so touched that he accepted. 'On condition, that you agree to my help with the washing-up.'

She laughed.

'Mr Roger, it will be quite a sensational story in the village that you helped me with the washing up.'

So they enjoyed a merry evening after the three little ones were safely tucked up in bed.

Mr Cox enquired, 'Do you still have difficulties with your studies at Faraday House?'

'Yes, indeed. However, there is light on the horizon, for the current holiday programme is now well under way. The London tutor is hard at it coaching me three times weekly – to be ready for the Christmas term, starting September. Since it is now rather late, may it be possible to use your phone, Mr Cox?' Roger added.

When he had told Mrs Plant of his plans for dinner, Roger asked Mr Cox, 'What are the current prospects for the harvest?'

'Excellent, Mr Roger,' the farmer replied. 'Only one more field of oats to be gathered in tomorrow. The three barley fields were completed this week. The kale fields were late starting and will not be in production as feed until late October, the yields, however, show promise. So to conclude we have been blessed for our endeavours this harvest. Likewise the fruit trees show prolific yields.'

'What about my favourite Comice pears?'

'No problem, you will receive your usual supply late November.'

'You have made my day, Mr Cox.'

It was eleven thirty when he entered Oakfield Lodge on this warm night. He went to the stables to say good night to Hurry-On and the two jet-black twins. Hurry-On was delighted with the midnight visitor, who offered a few sugar lumps taken from Mrs Cox's table. Roger did not disturb the colts. For some minutes he talked to Hurry-On, unbeaten all those years, the one they could never catch, with his sister Isabelle as his mount. The stallion pricked up his ears as if to try and understand when he heard the name Isabelle. Roger stayed some time with

Hurry-On, often cupping the horse's nose in his hands.

The Lodge was silent as he made his way to his bedroom. Isabelle was still out. It was dark now on this late very warm August night. Roger sat by his window and was full of wonder about the Lord's creation. Those dear Cox people – how very kind to invite me to their table, after the sweat of the harvest work from early morning, he thought. He was about to prepare for bed when he noticed a letter on his pillow. On the top of the envelope was a note from Isabelle, which said:
'Be good. Will be rather late tonight – one am. Lots of sweet dreams. Your loving sister, Isabelle'.

The other letter, however, was sealed. On the front Mrs Plant had written: '*Just arrived by hand, 10 pm.*' On the reverse of the envelope was written: '*From Lucie!*'

Well, well, thought Roger, as he opened it and read:

> 'Dear Mr Roger, Just a note to thank you cordially for the offer to drive me to Girton College, Cambridge on 15 September. Also to thank you for your indulgent responses to my many questions.... Hopefully, we may remain firm friends – in spite of the divide!'
> Affectionately, Lucie.'

Roger was somewhat stunned. So it was still the divide. Isabelle had not yet returned. He walked slowly about his bedroom. Lucie was a beauty, totally innocent about the wicked world, but had an able brain. Roger had strange sensations. The advice often given by Isabelle not to become involved before achieving a degree returned to him, and what about Milly with an honours degree already from Oxford? Who was Lucie – just a local village girl? Nevertheless educated, refined and after another few years, what then? Those delicate and beautifully formed features were not English; the downy delicately smooth skin, black eyes and raven dark curly tresses disturbed him. From what country did she emanate? Only her mother would know. It was two am when his head at last met the pillow with that angelic veiled face in his thoughts. Then delicious dreams, and at three am Isabelle came to kiss him good night, to find only a sheet for cover as the air became cooler. After a short prayer by his bedside she pulled a lightweight blanket over his middle as before. 'May God bless you, my darling brother,' she murmured.

Next morning Mrs Plant had two notes to read in the kitchen – *'Dear Mrs Plant, after the harvest festival feast at the Cox's farm last night, will not be down before eleven am. Mr Roger.'* And, *'Dear Mrs Plant, After the party with the Marshalls last night, do not expect me before twelve midday.'*

Well, thought Mrs Plant, this is indeed the harvest period.

Unfortunately, Roger was kept to a rigorous programme of studies for the next fourteen days returning every evening at eight pm from Earls Court, mentally and physically flaked.

Meanwhile Ginger and Lydia, were training under the keen eye of Isabelle at the Marshall stables. They were instructed in all the different problems as mounts to the hardly yet broken in colts. There was speculation whether those two young black 16½-hand stallions were now destined to become stayers or sprinters, both bred from the famous mare of the Buchanan stable Colleen and the unbeaten stayer Hurry-On.

Isabelle loved them and each night went to see them with a few sugar lumps. Indeed, they were massive stallions for their young age and still wild. Both Ginger and Lydia had been thrown often on the soft ground during the early breaking-in period. Fortunately, the village girls were tough – and this was routine when holding in the bit in order to contain their immense strength. Often Isabelle was questioned by the stud manager whether the girls were strong enough in the forearm. They both insisted that they could manage. So it was agreed with Marshalls that both stallions, now christened Onward and Ebony, were to be entered for the Epsom Stakes for first time out for two-year-olds only. The race was always run early in April, and they were duly entered for the following year.

It was now mid-September and time for Lucie to depart for Cambridge. Roger was invited for the evening before the departure by Mrs Arnold. Again it was a delightful September evening, still warm enough to sit in the garden. Lucie was still fully employed making preparations.

'Delighted to see you again, Mr Roger,' Mrs Arnold greeted him. 'Lucie is a little nervous about the new life amongst the "gentry".'

Roger had difficulty to suppress a smile. 'Do not worry, Mrs Arnold. My presence will be there as the guardian nominated by her mother during the introduction to the Registrar.'

'Splendid, Mr Roger. Lucie will be relieved.'

She was, and began to venture a smile for Roger.

What a beauty, thought Roger, as his brains began to float around his head.

'Please do not worry, Lucie, the formalities will be quite routine and you will not be left stranded because it will be my job to ensure that you are safely accepted into your new home. But remember to telephone your mother from the college to the post office opposite the cottage. They are on duty all night for Oakfield Lodge, especially for calls from Nigeria.'

'Thank you, Mr Roger, very much.' As she returned again to her preparations, Roger seized the opportunity.

'Mrs Arnold, what are Lucie's origins?'

This question startled Mrs Arnold. 'Why do you want to know that, Mr Roger?'

'Her colouring intrigues me, also the miniature of a beautiful young girl she wears around her neck.'

Mrs Arnold smiled. 'You must take care, Mr Roger, Lucie is highly emotional about the miniature, which displays, quite simply, St Agnes who was martyred as a virgin in Rome at twelve years of age and buried in AD 305, for refusing to marry a Roman aristocrat. She was tortured unto death – and held out because her belief was that she belonged to Christ. Ever since, many ghosts walk on St Agnes Eve, in late December! Not being a Roman Catholic, you are not aware of St Agnes, Mr Roger?'

'That is true, Mrs Arnold. Lucie's origin presumably is Italian.'

'More than just an Italian, Mr Roger. She is in fact the last member of an old aristocratic family from Florence. The necklace and the miniature are priceless, the necklace may look like glass, but in fact the stones are diamonds. Later on in the autumn, Mr Roger, you will learn more about her mystery.' This was said just as Lucie entered.

'What mystery, Mummy?'

'Nothing special, Lucie darling, except for how the teachers at Windsor managed to help you win a place at Cambridge.'

'The sisters were so kind, Mummy, during all those years. In fact, one of them told me that my natural gift was for Italian, and it was one of the subjects which impressed the board at my entry exam for Girton.'

'Well, Lucie, will you be ready, books and pens, tomorrow at two pm?'

She smiled – God what a smile, the very sun shone from those black Italian eyes, yet it was raining now after a balmy day.

Lucie was ready on time as Roger drove up to the cottage in his father's BMW. She was frightened.

'Mr Roger is this correct? To arrive in a BMW they will have a false impression of my humble background.'

'Dear Lucie, my strategy is simply to impress the Reception Registrar and the carriers that you are someone to be respected, and therefore that you expect at least a modicum of service from the staff.'

'Is it really necessary, Mr Roger? Perhaps you can drop me at a taxi station.'

Roger continued, 'Dear Lucie, if you ever want service from staff in this world, it is necessary to impress, and that is just my intention.'

Mrs Arnold was amused and intervened. 'He is right, Lucie, Remember it will be a new role of people for you, all strangers just as diffident as you. Mr Roger also will surely agree with me that you should not accept any invitations to parties or groups of students until you have been able to assess their characters. Basically, Lucie, you cannot go far wrong by attending daily at the College Chapel and resorting to your regular morning prayers.'

There were no problems. As anticipated, Lucie was welcomed by everybody. At the moment of departure in front of several hauliers and carriers Lucie expressed her appreciation.

'Mr Roger, it is difficult for me to know how to thank

you for your kindness to me – a remote village girl. This is the only gesture to come to my mind.' And she kissed him. He nearly swooned!

'Courage, Lucie.'

Roger left his card and address with the Registrar. 'Just in case of problems, madam, you are invited to call me at this address any time.'

The same evening Roger returned to the cottage after the long drive from Cambridge.

'Everything is fine, Mrs Arnold. She was well received,' he reported. 'May we continue the subject of her origin Mrs Arnold?'

'Of course, but it is highly confidential. Are you interested in Lucie?'

'Mrs Arnold, who is not?'

'That is not the answer to my question, Mr Roger.'

Roger remained silent.

'Well, Lucie comes from an ancient Italian family in Florence. She is not my baby. Her parents were killed by the Italian dictatorship under Mussolini. It was left to me to keep her save in this cottage. Mr Roger, she is a high-born young Italian lady.'

Roger was aghast! But it made sense. 'How do you mean "left to you"?' he enquired.

'It is a long story. After your journey through the rain from Cambridge perhaps you may prefer to resume this discussion tomorrow evening?'

Indeed, Roger felt tired. 'Splendid suggestion Mrs Arnold, about the same time? There is, however, just one question. Has Lucie reason to be troubled in any way – about her prospects at Girton College?'

'Why?'

'It was during my usual fifty-minute evening walk before dinner round the square with the dogs last Friday when, as often before I spent a few minutes in St Mary's church. In the September light at that time of the day, the church was quite dark inside, so it was not until I was about to leave that I noticed Lucie in a remote corner of the church known as the Holy Virgin Chapel. She also was about to leave. It so happened that, again, she was wearing her veil. But she was bathing her eyes as if to dry unseen tears. In fact, it was evident to me that tears had been flowing for some time beforehand – the veil was wet. It was an embarrassing moment, Mrs Arnold. This was not like the Lucie known to me. Also it was a delicate moment, hence with discretion no questions were asked – I simply offered my hand during the short walk to your cottage. Her reply was simply to shake her head and smile, no words, and she left for the cottage. Indeed a silent rendezvous, Mrs Arnold; the dear girl has some emotional problem.'

'The Roman Catholic religion is unknown to me,' said Mrs Arnold. 'Perhaps her emotional problem is really spiritual. However, her principal passion is centred upon the piano across the road next to the village post office. The elderly lady who lives there alone has a baby grand. Lucie is always welcome to play on it. In fact, with the window open during the warm summer evenings, Lucie has given many impromptu concerts to the delight of the local people.'

Lucie is indeed a young lady of many surprises,' Roger thought.

Isabelle did not return before one am, but as usual she crept quietly into Roger's room. He was just asleep. The night was not so warm as in August. She ensured that he was warm enough after saying her prayers beside his bed, and gave him the lightest kiss. 'May the Lord bless you dear brother of mine.'

Then she visited the twins, likewise fast asleep, in the dressing-room adjacent to her bedroom. Again she thanked her creator for the blessings of the day.

Roger arrived back from town the next evening too late to see Mrs Arnold. His tutor Mr Anido kept him from eleven am to five thirty pm; it was one the last few days before term started. The three months' summer holiday programme was about complete. The following Monday it was battle time for Roger. So an appropriate note was sent off to Mrs Arnold to postpone their next discussion until Saturday.

19

A minor crisis had occurred at the Marshall's stables. Without doubt Ebony was now established as a sprinter; Onward, however, was proving to be a difficult stallion to break in. After throwing Fred, one of Marshall's riders, he promptly threw Lydia – who was still under training. Indeed, she was a little frightened about him. Isabelle was then called in. Fred was not happy.

'We cannot get any sense out of him, Miss. It is my opinion that he ought to go to the knacker's yard – no one can manage him.'

'Understood, Fred. Will you please arrange to bring him over to the Oakfield Lodge stables tomorrow at eight am? Ask for me or for Mr Milligan. We will then undergo some physiological exercises and some breaking-in procedures.'

'No problem, Miss – you succeeded before with Hurry-On. It will interest all of us to see whether also you can manage Onward. He is dangerous. Mind he is very strong, obstinate and bone-headed.'

Isabelle smiled. 'Do not worry, Fred. This is the sort of patient down my street or, if you like, close to my heart.'

The next morning, it was action stations for a difficult customer. Milligan was ready, awaiting instruction from Isabelle.

'Good morning, Milligan. It seems, that no one in the Marshall Stables can civilise Onward. So we will try to show the professionals a few tricks of their trade. First of all, tether Onward firmly to his stable door, near to his sire Hurry-On. Then bring Dobin, the hack, to me. Finally, ask Mrs Plant for a small bag of sugar lumps. Now, Ginger, take careful note of my methods – which are not the established rule for the breaking-in of a difficult young stallion.'

The mighty Hurry-On, the sire, was looking on with keen interest and was delighted to see Dobin again. Meanwhile Onward, the rogue horse, as he was christened by the Marshall Stables, became interested in the activity. Isabelle had Milligan lead Onward out into the rain and wind to allow him to become acquainted with his new surroundings.

Onward was still ready to lash out without warning, as both Milligan and Isabelle saw. Eventually Dobin and Onward were in front of Isabelle, she offered a lump of sugar to Dobin, who accepted it with much enthusiasm, noticed keenly by Onward. The sugar was then offered to Onward on the flat of Isabelle's hand – only one lump. Horses are intelligent. After Isabelle offered another hand with two lumps, Onward seemed to relax, and Isabelle started to talk to him – with Ginger close by. His ears started to flicker in order to try and understand this human creature. It was then that Ginger was asked also to offer two lumps of sugar to the mighty young stallion. Onward began to enjoy himself and felt at ease with these gestures.

'Milligan, you may release him from the stable and he will be led by me and Ginger for a walk around the upper field. Onward must become used to Ginger's scent, and mine, if we are ever to become friends.'

After five minutes without problems, Isabelle asked Milligan to saddle Onward.

'But Miss, he has such a wild reputation at the Marshall Stables.'

Isabelle smiled. 'Do not worry, Milligan. Onward and I have made contact!'

'But,' stammered Milligan, 'he can be violent, Miss!'

Isabelle then mounted Onward. Milligan was so worried because Isabelle had produced two lovely babies two years ago to Richard and perhaps....

'First keep an eye on Ginger, Milligan, because she will be the future jockey for Onward.'

'Yes, Miss. Hopefully you will not go too far with him.'

Isabelle smiled. This was just like the breaking-in of Hurry-On all over again. After several small circular walks she called to Ginger, 'Now Ginger, we will stop next to you, so be ready with a sugar lump, and pat his nose.'

Isabelle felt his muscles quiver as she held him in on a tight rein. She knew by feminine intuition that he was dying to get away into those long meadows. How young, strong and virile he felt.

'Now Ginger, open the gate or he will attempt to jump it.'

This done, Isabelle instructed Ginger to watch the next step. 'I will take him the two-furlong length of the field several times before you mount him, possibly several times again.'

'No problems, Miss,' Ginger smiled with joy. Indeed she was just as keen to master this giant stallion.

Once through the gate, Isabelle went forward and then released the bit. 'Now, my darling, race!'

He did just that, with relish, on the soft going of the field. At the two-furlong limit he turned to race back. 'Faster my darling, faster.' Onward received the communication by instinct and strained every muscle. Finally, after four laps he arived at the gate, Milligan was ready to help Isabelle dismount, but now she urged the stallion for another round. 'Faster, faster, my darling.' Onward was now in his element. It was not until the end of the fourth round that Isabelle stopped Onward and dismounted at the gate.

'Now, Ginger, off you go – just use the words "Faster, my darling" and observe how he responds. Another two rounds will tire him out. It will be an exercise he will not forget and at the same time you will acquire the intimacy with him which is so necessary for confidence.'

It was another four circuits in heavy rain before Ginger dismounted in the rain, completely exhilarated. Onward was hot and steaming all over, but Isabelle noted how content he was to be led to his stable with fresh straw, and to be rubbed down by Ginger, who was no longer nervous of her charge. Onward was now docile and, in fact, very happy.

'You see, Milligan, these difficult and highly strung stallions need love, nothing more nor less. They are extremely intelligent and respond rapidly to care and attention to their needs.'

'It is only you, Miss, who has the extraordinary ability to transmit it, as I witnessed when first Hurry-On was brought over from Ireland.'

For the next few months Milligan, Onward will be lodged here with Ebony,' Isabelle explained, 'and every day Ginger can mount him for a similar run in the two-furlong meadow, whatever the weather – except frost or hard ground. That stallion enjoys soft going. Then, at the start of the flat-racing season, race trials will commence at the Marshall Stables. Meanwhile, my compliments to Fred at the Marshall Stables,' she added. 'Onward is not ready yet for the knacker's yard and never will be!'

'Yes, Miss.'

Next day it was the turn of Ginger's friend Lydia to mount Ebony.

'Good morning, Lydia. What is Fred's report on Ebony?'

'Good morning, Miss. Fred asked me to tell you that Ebony is very fast but fails to keep in a straight line.'

'Dear Fred, that is the job of the rider not the horse,' Isabelle exclaimed.

'He has tried, Miss, but he complains that Ebony is the very devil to hold on the track, otherwise Ebony seems to be more placid in the yard compared with Onward, who he complains is stubborn as a mule.'

'Are you nervous about mounting Ebony?'

Lydia shook her head. 'Oh no Miss, if only he can keep me on his back during those unpredictable swerves.'

'Lydia, that is the art of the rider – you will observe for yourself that the classic five-furlongs are an instructive lesson in horsemanship. The young stallions are all over the course and the jockeys have a devil's own job trying to keep them in order. Indeed it is always the experienced jockey who wins those particular races. In consequence, given this situation, do you feel that you can control that giant, with the excited race crowd in the background?'

'Of course, Miss, at least Fred says that my forearms are strong enough, for he believes that the key to the art is in the wrist and forearm.'

All through the early weeks of the following year Lydia became more acquainted with Ebony on the training ground in the Marshall Stables. Early March Fred staged a race with two of their front-rate two-year-olds, over five furlongs. The sprinters, both last season winners, were given a two-length start. It was a big advantage.

The flag went up. Lydia felt the muscles of Ebony quiver for action never so far experienced. He went like the wind, as she explained afterwards to Isabelle. Ebony arrived five lengths in front of last year's sprint winners. This was news for the Milligan kitchen that night.

Several of the locals were there, including the vicar and Mr Marshall.

'So Lydia, you have an exceptional charge on your hands,' the vicar said.

'Thoroughbreds, Reverend, usually breed true. Evidently Ebony takes after Colleen. Buchanan will be happy.' He was. The telephone rang from Ireland. Mrs Milligan answered.

'Mavoreen, is it true that one of my children, from my own Colleen, has impressed the local public at the trials this afternoon.'

'News travels fast, Mr Buchanan. Yes it is true, he was fast, very fast according to George Marshall.'

'Good, now we must do some quiet planning to please the ladies at Royal Ascot!'

'No tricks, Mr Buchanan, or they will lock you up,' responded Mrs Milligan.

'My dear Mavoreen, you are gorgeous. Leave the planning to your dear husband and me. Between us we will present a two-year-old sprinter not to be forgotten in racing history.' And they did.

'Do be careful, Mr Buchanan, the whole racing world is aware of your long-odds winners at Royal Ascot. The stewards will examine with minute care every entry, and check its history and birthday. We do not want to see you languishing in goal, on bread and water for misdemeanours.'

Buchanan was highly amused. 'My dear Mavoreen, a message for your dear husband before this call ends. What a lucky man to have such a devoted red-headed mate. Before the early Spring Meeting at Epsom please keep my bed warm in your lovely cottage.'

'No problem, Mr Buchanan. You are always welcome here. With love from all of us, good night.'

The vicar asked, 'Do you intend to enter Ebony for the

Epsom Down Stakes for two-year-olds early April?'

'Yes, Reverend Manning,' Isabelle replied. 'So far there are fifty runners on the list. by early April this will be reduced to twenty at most. The Aga Khan has four runners, all Arab-bred. After that, the Newmarket Stakes for two-year-olds, only, at the end of April. If successful, Reverend Manning, the next year it will be the three-year-old stakes at Royal Ascot.

'Dear young lady,' the vicar addressed Isabelle. 'You do still have ambitions then?'

'Oh yes, Reverend Manning, especially for my two babies bred from Ireland, Onward and Ebony.'

20

Eventually came the Spring Meeting at Epsom. The weather was cold as usual, blowing a north-easter so typical at that time of the year. But Ebony was full of the joys of a young two-year-old. The field of thirty cantered up to the start of the Epsom Stakes on this cold but sunny afternoon.

'Well Milligan,' said the vicar, 'it may remain a bright day in spite of the keen wind.'

The race started and they listened to the loudspeaker commentary.

'It is difficult to distinguish between the colours at this stage, and the two-year-olds are not keeping to a straight run. However, there are two in the colours of the Aga Khan in front. Only one of the runners was a late starter, left five lengths behind. The name is Ebony ridden by a female jockey known as Lydia, wearing the Buchanan colours. The black is making up lost ground fast. The Arabs, now three of them, are all racing neck and neck a full length in front of the field. But Ebony is coming through now at a devastating pace and ridden in masterful style – evidently a highly experienced jockey,' continued the announcer, 'although the name is new to me. The runners have just passed the half-way posts, the three Arabs are still in the lead and their pace is impressive because the field is now five lengths behind. Indeed it is going to be a race for the Arabs. 'But wait, no,' added the announcer, 'the giant black from Ireland has now passed the field and at a tremendous pace, overhauling the Arabs fast with only a furlong to go. Never seen this downhill five-furlong race run at such a fast pace by two-year-olds. Ebony is now up to the Arabs on the stand side. He is now beginning to leave the Arabs with only half a furlong to go.'

What a race for the Epsom historian! The crowd were

shouting with delight, so were the bookmakers, with two hot favourites. Indeed, they thought, what a rip-off – Ebony was fifty to one. 'The black,' said the announcer, was now half a length in front of the Arabs – all going at a fast pace.' Then one of the Arabs made a desperate last challenge and managed to hold Ebony by half a length to second place with the whip out. But Lydia passed the winning-post without whipping, just in time before there was a sharp crack rending the air. Ebony had split open its bit, so Lydia lost control and fell forward on the horse. The stewards and emergency attendants ran to the rescue just as Lydia slipped off the horse to the ground. The emergency flag went up and there was silence, until it was announced that Ebony was a clear winner – followed by cheers from the race crowd. A minute later the stewards announced that Ebony's rider had only suffered a sprained wrist after the collapse of the bit. Nevertheless, the enquiry flag remained and the public waited with impatience.

'Please be seated, Miss Lydia,' said one of the stewards. 'First of all, our congratulations. All we wish to know is the reason for the mechanical failure of the bit. If for example it had fractured a few yards before the winning-post, the public, although not many have placed bets on a fifty-to-one chance, might have been disappointed. That is why we are here, to mediate for the public. Will you therefore please ask the Buchanan stable to let me have a report why in their opinion the bit snapped at the critical moment.'

'Of course, sir.'

Afterwards, both Milligan and Isabelle interviewed Lydia in the emergency ward. She was a little shaken, although she had a tough constitution. Meanwhile the enquiry flag was lowered amid further cheers.

'So sorry, Miss, to end the race in such a dramatic fashion,' Lydia apologised.

Isabelle responded, 'Do not worry, Lydia, you ran an extraordinary well-gauged race, to become the hero of the afternoon, and what is the end result? Fame, to advance into the future with confidence.'

The official course doctor told Isabelle, 'Slight shock, Miss, and a sprained wrist. It will take a few weeks to remedy. That black is a giant – very strong. Do you believe, Miss Isabelle, it is reasonable for a young girl to race it under these highly competitive conditions?'

'Doctor, she volunteered to mount the stallion for this race – after considerable training time at the stud.'

'Do not worry, Doctor,' added Lydia with much enthusiasm, 'this is my vocation and that giant, as the announcer calls him, is so lovable. It was not his fault about the fracture of the bit – in fact Ebony did his best to balance me.'

'But why the wrist?' interrupted Isabelle.

'This happened, Miss during the first three furlongs, Ebony is so strong. It was about half-way when the pain started in my right wrist as I was trying to keep him in a straight line on that famous downhill straight of five furlongs. But the doctor has confirmed that, with treatment, there will be no more problems after the next few weeks. Ebony is such a friendly and intelligent stallion it would grieve me not to be his rider in the future.'

Isabelle then replied, 'Are you sure, Lydia, that you can manage him in future, because the racing public is doubtful. They blame me for encouraging you. But you have my blessing all the way if you can assure me that you can continue.'

'Bless you, Miss – there will be no problems in future, Indeed, the doctor has recommended strong straps for both wrists immediately.'

The next test race was at Newmarket, the Cambridgeshire Stakes for two-year-olds, late April. The Arabs had taken a beating at Epsom by only one Irish competitor over the five-furlong course, but now the distance was seven furlongs, in preparation for the Two Thousand Guineas classic at Newmarket the following year for three-year-old colts in May. But there were two other thoroughbreds in competition, according to Buchanan, one from France the other from Italy, both unbeaten two-year-olds.

After three weeks Lydia was able to remount Ebony in all the trials with success. It was during one evening in Mrs Milligan's kitchen, with Reverend Manning and Isabelle, when it was decided that Lydia was to be Ebony's rider at Newmarket for the Cambridgeshire Spring Stakes.

Mrs Milligan asked Lydia, 'Do you really feel up to the

challenge, Lydia? I know your family since it was my privilege to help bring you into this world. Your mother is a lifelong friend of mine, so it is reasonable for me to want to be assured about your future career in the racing world – particularly with that giant stallion.

Marshall told me yesterday he stands now at seventeen and a half hands!'

'Mrs Milligan, it is Miss Isabelle here to whom my recent success is due. She has taught me how to transmit love to Ebony. A little kindness instead of the whip goes a long way when an extra effort is needed fifty yards from the post under the great stress and excitement of the race.'

'Well said, young lady,' responded the vicar.

'But –' began George Marshall, the proprietor of the Marshall Racing Stables.

Milligan interrupted, 'Just a moment, George, the subject of love for a horse is comparatively new to me. Nevertheless, it is my fabulous experience to have witnessed it between Miss Isabelle and Hurry-On. Even now she goes every night to talk to Hurry-On, "the one they could never catch", and she gives him a few sugar lumps.'

George was mystified. 'So Milligan, you really believe this love business between these giant stallions and their young female riders is possible?'

'Without a doubt, George,' Milligan asserted.

'Well, that is quite a new dimension in my horse-training career.'

Milligan added, 'And it is my opinion also, George that young Lydia's love for that giant stallion, Ebony is reciprocated. Do not forget that racehorses are considered as the most intelligent of all animals – including Labrador dogs. A whip will never be required to urge on Ebony – he runs like the wind. Take for example his first race in public at Epsom recently. He was left at the post by five lengths, yet won by half a length. The bookmakers made a killing! Nevertheless, have no illusions, his price for the Newmarket Stakes is already five to one, compared with the Arab as favourites, according to Ladbrokes. Next time the race is over seven furlongs – that is, two furlongs more. Will Ebony be able to stay the distance? What do you think, George?'

'Difficult at this stage, Milligan to assess his limits, especially at that fast pace. The increase from five furlongs to seven is quite a stretch. However, within the next four weeks it will be possible for me to be more precise. Meanwhile, my faith is placed upon Isabelle's opinion.'

Isabelle responded, 'He is still so young, George – and so fast – it is difficult for me to imagine Ebony racing over more than five furlongs.'

As the weeks rolled by in the exquisite Berkshire village, the master, Leon and Richard were still all busy in Nigeria with the business of installing and commissioning industrial boiler plants. It is time, therefore, to consider the progress made by Ebony's twin Onward, another giant stallion. Onward was no sprinter, and not quite so violent as his sire at two years of age; in fact, now he was comparatively placid and easy to mount. In other words, as Milligan said – civilised!

'That is all very well, Milligan,' Isabelle protested, 'but has he the fiery spirit of Ebony or Hurry-On, also the energy to stay?'

'As you know, Miss, Onward has been lame for the last six months. The problems, however, have been resolved – although George does not advise racing him as a two-year-old. Meanwhile, Fred and his colleagues confirm that Onward has stamina and speed – as attested by trials recently on Marshall's track. So he has been entered for the Newmarket Spring Stakes over two and a half miles, late April next year, when he will be a three-year-old.'

During the remainder of the year Isabelle acquired a special affection for Onward. Often she was seen mounted on him racing through the fields and woods surrounding Oakfield Lodge early in the morning, sometimes for three or four miles – frequently at racing speeds.

Isabelle concluded eventually that Onward was a stayer of substance. Ginger, who likewise was trained to mount Onward, was also becoming intimately acquainted with him.

Isabelle was also a busy mother – supervising the welfare of the young twins, and also the training of Ebony and Onward.

*

Meanwhile the time for the Newmarket Cambridgeshire Spring Stakes for two-year-olds, over seven furlongs, approached. Ebony was in excellent form, but two new competitors had entered the field, from France and from Italy – both unbeaten so far as two-year-olds.

It was as usual in the famous kitchen of Mrs Milligan that prognostics were being made soon after Easter, when quite suddenly there was a knock at the door.

It was an important emissary from Monsieur Bussac, a well-known French racehorse owner.

'*Mes respects, madame,*' he addressed Mrs Milligan. '*Excusez-moi pour cette interuption de votre soirée.*'

Isabelle replied, 'No problem, sir.'

'Quite simply, *madame*, my master is keenly interested in your stallion Ebony, and is prepared to pay any reasonable price for an immediate sale – for example a quarter of a million pounds cash. Here is the card of Monsieur Bussac, madam.'

'Please give my compliment to Monsieur Bussac, *monsieur*, and thank him most cordially for his kind offer, but Ebony is not for sale.'

'Is that your final word, *madame?*'

Isabelle nodded, and he departed a little crestfallen.

'Well, Mrs Milligan, your kitchen has made history this evening,' Isabelle commented. 'Even as a young two-year-old the market price for Ebony is now a quarter of a million pounds! Yet only one win to his credit, and that first time out!'

Incredible, thought the vicar. 'You must be disappointed, George,' he told the owner of the Marshall Stables.

'No Reverend Manning, just surprised and puzzled. After all, such a sum is a dream for both breeder and trainer!'

Milligan responded, 'That is where the love element comes in, George. Miss Isabelle visits those two young stallions every night, whatever the weather or circumstances, and Hurry-On, who is never forgotten and still her favourite.'

152

'Do not worry George,' Isabelle added. 'We must plan our strategy for the future together, with the help of the vicar.'

George continued, 'Ebony is fast, Reverend Manning – never known a two-year-old so devastatingly fast as Ebony was in all my racing experience, but he has raced only over a short distance. Newmarket Two Thousand Guineas is a mile.'

'The next engagement,' said Milligan, 'is over seven furlongs, in the middle of May, the Newmarket Stakes. What news from Buchanan about competition?' he asked.

Both the Italian and French sprinters are not yet beaten, equally very fast, and both in a race at Longchamp at the end of April – with the Arabs,' replied Isabelle.

'Excellent,' responded the vicar. 'Now we shall all have a reasonable idea about competition, at the end of April.'

There was a huge crowd at Longchamp for this important race exclusively for thoroughbred two-year olds. Both Milligan and the vicar were present.

'Do you speak French, Milligan?' the vicar asked.

'No sir, but my army field-glasses will be sufficient for me during this seven-furlong race, so do not worry about the announcer and his comments in French,' He commenced, 'The Italian, French and Arab horses are all well to the front. At three furlongs, one of the Arabs together with the French and Italian horses, hold the lead. It is a fast pace,' observed Milligan.

The three were racing neck to neck up to three furlongs from the post, when the French horse known as Slimer began to leave the leaders. Slimer eventually won in record time for the seven-furlong race by two lengths. The Arabs dead-heated for second place.

'He is an exceptional young stallion, Reverend Manning. Our Ebony will have competition at Newmarket next month. Slimer is also well bred as a sprinter.'

This news was received at with surprise at Oakfield Lodge.

'And what about the Arabs?' Isabelle enquired.

'No, Miss Isabelle, they were left two lengths behind the "French wonder horse" as they referred to it in the newspaper this morning.'

'Good,' responded Isabelle. 'This is just the competition needed for Ebony at Newmarket.'

Meanwhile, there was another important race for two-year-olds at York, two weeks before the Newmarket Classic. Slimer, to the surprise of the racing world, was entered – evidently as a trial before the Newmarket event.

Slimer spread-eagled the field by ten lengths and was marked down as favourite for the Newmarket race in fourteen days' time. It was learned from the owner that he wanted Slimer to become acquainted with the English climate. Lydia had recovered and was ready for the event. A few days before the meeting Isabelle asked Lydia about her thoughts for the race.

'The eyes of the racing world, Lydia, will be interested in this two-year olds race as a prelude to the great classic for three-year-olds at Newmarket, Epsom and Royal Ascot, next year.'

'Ebony and me, Miss, we are kin – as the Red Indians say. All I know is simply that the French horse Slimer will have to be very fast to test Ebony.'

21

It was the end of May, just before the Newmarket event.

Slimer was a hot favourite at two to one. That night in Mrs Milligan's kitchen several people were discussing Ebony's prospects.

Milly entered the kitchen – just back from a four-week holiday with some French cousins at the small town of Lussac, near Bordeaux. She brought in a telegram from Buchanan addressed to Mrs Milligan. 'Expect me Thursday night Gorgeous. Please stock up with plenty of whisky and Boyo's' (his name for Milligan's old and crusty port wine). The race was to be run on Wednesday.

Mrs Milligan was happy to see Milly – her favourite. After a warm hug she remarked to Isabelle, 'Only the French, Miss, can show us grace and elegance in this modern world.'

'Especially the ones from Bordeaux, Mrs Milligan,' replied Isabelle after an affectionate embrace for Milly. 'Any conquests, Milly, during the last few weeks in Bordeaux?'

Milly blushed. 'Four to be exact, Isabelle.'

'Ca alors, Milly!'

'All a little outside my age group – between thirty and thirty-five, mostly engaged in wine production. However, they're was one young man, Michael Requier, whose family is engaged in trade with the Far East. The family is also breeding and racing thoroughbreds. In fact, Michael became keenly interested to know that you were breeding bloodstock from Hurry-On and Colleen. Your own name as the rider of Hurry-On is well known in the French racing world. However, the relevant information is simply that they have two entries, one a filly named Rachael entered for the Newmarket two-year-old stakes for fillies only on

Tuesday, and the other one the colt named Maestro in the same race as Ebony on Wednesday. Confidentially, Michael informed me that both are French-bred, and are fast, and that they expect to win the two events in spite of what they have heard of the competition.'

'Did you hear that, Milligan?'

'Yes, Miss. What is the breeding of Maestro?'

'The stables are near Bordeaux, the bloodstock is from Normandy,' Milly explained.

'Have they been raced yet as two-year-olds?' asked Milligan.

'Yes,' responded Milly. 'And won both events comfortably.'

'So Michael interests you, Milly?' Isabelle wanted to know.

'He says that I bewitch him. But he does not have the same effect on me.'

'Since then you have been sleeping with butterflies in your stomach!'

Milligan interrupted, addressing Isabelle. 'This is a serious turn of events, Miss. Just how fast is Maestro? That is now the question.'

'Milligan, we will have the answer to that question soon,'

'True,' added George. 'It will be as well to have my stopwatch experts alerted.'

Unfortunately, Ebony had to be withdrawn from the Newmarket contest, and the race was won comfortably by Maestro. The other race was won easily by Rachael.

22

Soon after breakfast Onward was saddled and with Isabelle up, after a few words with Milligan, horse and rider were racing through the meadows towards St Mary's Church. Onward was recovering from trouble with a retarded tendon formed late on the left hind leg. All winter he had been carefully nursed by Isabelle. It was a growth problem. Isabelle noticed, however, as the weeks passed that Onward was becoming, like his sire, a formidable stallion. Indeed, she prayed often and prepared for another stayer.

Eventually she arrived at the delightful cottage of Reverend Radcliff, the assistant to the vicar.

'Can it be Isabelle from Oakfield Lodge, but surely not Hurry-On – although an exact replica, black from nose to tail and what a height!'

'Seventeen and a half hands last week, John.'

'Is this wise, Isabelle, now you have started serious motherhood. For all our sakes do take care, and especially for the sake of your dear husband, who has given me immense pleasure by his interpretation of Chopin, Brahms and Haydn. Do come in for a cup of coffee and bring me up to date with the studies of your brother Roger,' John invited. 'We have a letter from Lucie at Girton College with a request.'

He handed Isabelle the letter and she read:

'Dear Vicar, Will you kindly send a message, by hand, to Mr Roger at Oakfield Lodge, inviting him to attend as my guest at a concert in hall. I will be playing two piano concertos by Chopin and Brahms. On 31 May at seven pm. Have no courage to write to him direct to the Lodge! Gratefully, dear Vicar, Lucie.'

'Well, well,' responded Isabelle. Wonders never cease. Why no courage, John?'

'You may not know that Mrs Arnold is her foster mother. Her family were liquidated by the fascists. They were landowners in northern Italy – engaged in the wine trade. There is a cousin, also in northern Italy. In the Church we have been informed, and have been requested to keep an eye on her development until she reaches the age of maturity. All costs are paid to us from an Italian bank every month to provide for all her needs – they are her trustees, entrusted with the administration of her inherited property, which is vast!'

Isabelle asked, 'And the cousin, John?'

'She is over eighty, and she wants Lucie to sign several documents about her succession to the title of £2.5 million, the estimated value of her estate in Florence.'

'Great Scot John! So this village girl is an heiress of Italian origin!'

John warned, 'This information, Isabelle, is strictly confidential. The devastation of warn-torn Europe has brought to light in its aftermath untold atrocities committed by the dictators in Italy and Germany. This incident is only one of many.'

'Presumably by maturity, the Italians have decreed an age?'

'Yes, it is twenty-one.'

'In about twelve months' time,' added Isabelle. 'Won't it come as an unpleasant shock, John?'

'Precisely, that is where we are counting upon you for help – for example it will mean breaking the news of her past parentage.'

'And what about Mrs Arnold?'

'That presents no problem. She has been aware of the position ever since the American missionary delivered the child to her cottage about eighteen years ago – soon after her own mother died in Italy.'

Isabelle was still puzzled. 'But why Winkfield?'

'This was at the request of the cousin, who wanted her kept out of harm's way, safe from fascists still keen to acquire the rights of the estate,' John explained. 'The cousin has requested Lucie's presence for a few nights only, at her Italian villa, when she reaches twenty-one. Will you be that chaperon?'

Isabelle was startled. 'Dear John, this is rather sudden.'

'All expenses paid, first-class to Florence. It will be only for about two nights.'

'My Italian is non-existent, John,' Isabelle objected.

'What an opportunity for a complete change, Isabelle.'

'You are quite right, John. When the time comes, I can make arrangements with Mrs Plant, about continuing the routine, especially for the twins and the offspring of Hurry-On.'

The same evening Roger was bewildered by the news from Isabelle. 'It is simply unbelievable, and why the secrecy by the Church all these years?'

'No known relatives, Roger except the cousin, evidently a shrewd woman, with eighty years' experience of violence in her country.'

'Agreed, she cannot be blamed. Nevertheless to withhold from the child a birthright secret for eighteen years is going to be devastating news for her,' responded Roger.

'Will you volunteer to be the carrier of this news to Lucie at Cambridge, in view of your association with her.'

'No problem, Isabelle.'

'Just how much do you know about Lucie, Roger?'

Roger was embarrassed. 'We have touched on this subject before, dear sister of mine.'

'True Roger, please fill me in.'

Roger propounded his views about Lucie. 'Dearest Isabelle, for me with my ignorance about the female sex, Lucie remains at enigma – beautiful in a youthful sense, literally beyond description. Spiritually, dear sister of mine, she remains a complete mystery.'

'How do you mean?'

'Take for example my random visits to the church during my evening walks with the dogs. As you know, the church door is always left open. So, after a few minutes' meditation, I suddenly notice Lucie is also there. This has happened three or four times in her vacations, but each time, dear Isabelle, her veil is wet with tears! She accepts my company to escort her back to their little cottage, because she knows that no question will be asked. In fact, she gives me a radiant smile – dear sister that smile at seven pm makes the sun re-shine. No word is spoken throughout, but the eyelashes are still wet with tears from an unknown emotion. No crude kiss goodnight, yet those eyes shine straight from the Italian heavens – as I now know. Sometimes Mrs Arnold invites me into her lovely little cottage, but Lucie remains generally reserved unless the subject is about classical music!'

'So, Roger, she is deeply religious, but why the tears on the veil?'

'Here, dear sister, is a grey area. With special delicacy, tact and understanding it has taxed all my faculties, mental physical and spiritual to contain her extremely sensitive nature, during those weeks back at her cottage. There is only one interesting observation, however. Upon arriving at the cottage each occasion, her conversation is always in Italian with her mother!'

'That is no surprise, Roger. It is her silence which puzzles me, and the tears. Has she a devotee or an admirer?'

'You can be assured, dear sister, that the tears are not due to any involvement with me, or any other known person.'

'Don't be silly, Roger – that was obvious long ago. Nevertheless, as you commented earlier, there is a mystery. Evidently she is a mystic – so what goes on in her head to cause the tears to flow into her veil in St Mary's church alone in the evenings? Something, somewhere, dear Roger is wrong. We must take the measure of this mystery, which may be due to a spiritual conflict! Do you know her intimately enough to ask a few questions?'

'No Isabelle – the situation at this stage is too delicate. Perhaps at Cambridge there may be light, although I have visited her there before, and things have been the same. The invitation gives hope, and you may leave the rest to my discreet understanding. There is indeed no question of love between us, Isabelle. Nevertheless, there is a strong protective instinct in me about Lucie. Yet so far little dialogue.'

'Let it rest at that, dear brother of mine. This young lady has deep foundations. It is her private emotional disturbances which interest me, especially at St Mary's.

There is a shrine in the church to the Holy Virgin Mary. Is this the area from which she appears at the moment of your departure?'

'Precisely, Isabelle.'

'It is possible that she has communications with the Holy Spirit world quite beyond us.'

Roger was too dazed to reply.

Roger, arrived in Cambridge with the legal papers from the church and those from the Italian cousin. He drove up in the two-seater Ford which belonged to Milligan, the following Monday.

In a large hall, Lucie was delivering an impromptu lecture upon how to transmit feeling and love on the piano to the works of Brahms, Chopin, Haydn and Mozart – instead of attaching so much wasted energy to the efficient rendering of the works. The young audience was keenly interested, and several were struggling to make themselves heard above the clamour with their questions, teachers and students alike. Eventually Lucie observed Roger. Her eyes lit up. There was a sudden silence when everyone noticed the senior sister, the female supervisor, and Roger at the entrance.

Lucie gave a deep curtsey to the sister, and a nod of reverence to the female supervisor. To Roger she quite simply held out both her hands. Roger kissed them and gave her a warm brotherly hug in front of all the gathering, which fully approved. Leave was granted for Roger to be allowed to spend one hour privately with Lucie together with the sister, in order to discuss in confidence the details of her inheritance.

The sister in charge opened the subject. 'Dear Lucie, we are granted one hour to explain to you an event which may change your thoughts about life on this Earth.'

'Why, dear Sister, is it a misdemeanour I have committed.'

The sister was fond of this young undergraduate and was tempted to hug her close. 'No, my child. This is a question of a vast fortune due to you when reaching the age of twenty-one.'

'Oh,' responded Lucie, 'but Sister, does it mean some

people will take me away from here where my life has only just begun to expand and to be so much enjoyed?'

'No, dear child, you may stay as long as you wish, but it is important for you to know the extent of the fortune to which you will be entitled in a few months from now. Money is a responsibility.'

'Is it enough, sister, to enable my mother in Winkfield to update our little cottage, and to provide for me a piano?

Roger was surprised at her reaction, when she was told the amount.

"It seems an awful lot, Sister, but are you sure that people will not take me away from here, or from my mother in our little cottage at Winkfield?' she said with tears in her eyes.

'Be assured, Lucie, no-one will ever interfere with your studies or your life,' prompted Roger. He thought, she is indeed a lovely child of God, without any interest in worldly values.

'And will Mr Roger always be my friend?'

Roger was momentarily baffled. 'Of course, dear Lucie, but with that commitment may we have the answer to a special question and the subject of a mystery to me and some others close to you, for example to your mother in Winkfield?'

She sat with her hands folded in her lap, looking down a picture of exquisite youthful beauty. She replied, 'One day your question was sure to come. You are too observant, Mr Roger. The answer is impossible to hide. You are about to ask the reason for the tears you saw in my veil on several evenings at St Mary's. Well then, the reason for the tears is quite simple. At my age, immature with still so much to learn, it has occurred often to me during the last eighteen months that the Holy Virgin Mary suffered equally with Christ on the Cross two thousand years ago, yet so little has ever been written about her ordeal and not a lot preached about the subject in this country, at least not that I have heard. Hence my intense grief for her and admiration for her courage to stand by her Son until all was finished.'

'But that all happened two thousand years ago, Lucie.'

'True, Mr Roger, but to me it is news, fabulous news.

The Holy Virgin, for me, is living because so many of my intercessions have been answered!'

'Did you know that Mrs Arnold is not your true mother?'

'Dear Mr Roger, long ago!'

'Now you have the answer to your question, Mr Roger.'

'Not quite, Lucie. For example, when did you first feel this intense emotion for the Holy Virgin Mary? When did it start?' asked Roger.

Lucie was a little embarrassed. 'About a year ago when walking through the corn fields of your father's estate, the sun was going down on a frosty evening late February. The sky was so clear and the sun was low on the horizon. It was by the big oak tree when my presence was disturbed by another being, perhaps from another world. The experience was new to me, the message was faint, the being was not visible. Then came the voice, slow, clear full of grace, "Do not worry, Lucie, we are watching over you". Hence now and for ever my complete faith in the Holy Virgin Mary.'

'Lucie, the message given at the oak tree has another meaning,' Roger added. 'Do you understand that sooner or later you will eventually be asked to undertake a particular task on this Earth by your new friend from above.'

She smiled as always with that understanding full of mystic silence and hidden thoughts, her hands crossed on her lap. What a picture she made, if only, thought Roger, the world would stand still. It was such a heavenly moment.

'My child,' interrupted the sister, 'it is late.'

'Lucie became suddenly alive. 'Dear Sister, promise me that no-one will take me away from you, in spite of all the inheritance problems.'

'Do not worry about that problem, Lucie. Mr Roger will confirm that you are under security here and no one will abduct you either legally or illegally.'

Roger nodded.

Before his departure, Roger, together with the sister in charge and the supervisor, held a meeting about Lucie.

'Thank you, Sister, for your interest in Lucie,' Roger began. 'She seems to be still completely immature about the physical world around her.'

'Possibly, Mr Roger, but Lucie is quite an experienced young girl about the spiritual facts of life, as you have witnessed. About her future we in the church remain confused, except that she is inspired from above without doubt.'

'In what way, Sister?'

'For example, the discussions about music you heard this afternoon. She is in demand already and her lectures, only at student level, are enlightening even to the music staff, indeed masterful. She is a strange child, Mr Roger. We do not know how she will develop in future. All we can say is that she has not only a first-class brain, but that she is stimulated with creative activity from a source beyond our comprehension, and seems to be so happy with the student community and the staff.'

The College concert later in the evening was a great success. Lucie excelled herself by her performance on the grand piano in the Chopin piano concerto. The music was executed with exceptional feeling and brilliantly played. At the conclusion the ovation was overwhelming. Lucie bowed low and gave a deep curtsey to the sister.

Roger congratulated her and promised to visit her again soon.

Before his return to Winkfield, Lucie whispered, 'Come again soon, Mr Roger.'

23

The next day Hurry-On was harnessed and Isabelle was up at six am. Milligan, engaged in the milking routine, was surprised to see her so early.

'Presumably, Miss Isabelle, after one hour through the woods with Hurry-On, you will be ready for your usual cup of coffee with the assistant at St Mary's.'

Isabelle smiled. 'John is interested to hear about Mr Roger's visit to Girton,' she explained.

While Isabelle was talking to John, a shadow passed by the window lit by the early sun.

'That was a horse and rider, Isabelle,' John remarked. 'It must be someone from the farm.'

At that moment Ginger appeared at the front door, and tethered at the gate post was Onward, now fast recovering from his setback earlier in the season. He jumped, whinnied and stamped with joy to see Isabelle, who had nursed him through his lame period.

'Careful, Isabelle, he seems to be spirited,' suggested John, who was surprised to see her run to Onward and give him a fond hug on his nose. Onward was so delighted, he lashed out with pleasure. Hurry-on looked on, perhaps a little jealous.

'What is the problem, Ginger?' Isabelle asked.

'A message from Milligan, Miss. Mr Roger collapsed at the front gate, just before his drive to the station. Dr Loretz was called immediately, and pronounced no specific problem, but that Roger must miss the next term at Faraday House, and repeat it later. He will write a medical certificate. Roger is now a little shattered. He is in his bedroom and asking for you, Miss Isabelle. According to Dr Loretz, his nervous system is in a state of partial exhaustion, after too much concentration on his studies.'

Ginger and Isabelle took their leave and departed, Isabelle riding Onward.

'What about a race, Ginger?' she suggested. It is about two miles to Oakfield Lodge and Ginger was thrilled to be mounted on such a renowned stayer as Hurry-On. Isabelle set a fast pace, over brooks, ditches and small hedges. Hurry-On followed close behind. It was then that Isabelle settled down to race. Both stallions went like the wind, yet Onward was only half a length away. The last mile Hurry-On was fully extended, but Onward remained only half a length away, no more trouble, evidently, with the lame leg. Another quarter of a mile from the farm and Hurry-On was urged for even more effort.

'Faster, my darling,' Ginger encouraged, the same words used by Isabelle for the Gold Cup the previous year. Onward, however, still held his position. At the end of the trial Isabelle was happy. Onward was ready for the racing world. They both arrived at the same time at the farm.

Milligan was surprised. 'They look full-blown, Miss.'

Isabelle was exhilarated. 'True, Milligan, but not Onward. He is going to be a stayer, he was urged with all my finesse, my muscles were in complete unison with his great strength.'

Isabelle entered the bedroom of Roger – her favourite brother.

Roger said immediately, 'Dad told me that even if it is a question of life or death, this Faraday House final must be passed.'

'Maybe Roger. Do not take this instruction too seriously. He regrets deeply his own lack of advanced education, hence his zeal for you to succeed with your studies.'

The next day John came to see Roger, who was still in a nervous state, and not eating.

'It frightens me, John, to hear someone ring the bell at the front door,' Roger explained.

'Why?' asked John.

'They say it is due to a shattered nervous system. The reason for the nervous collapse is difficult to explain because there is no explanation. No, this trouble is simply that my fellow students grasp so fast – not me. There is therefore a battle, all through every summer holiday to try and catch up. Dad is so generous with all expenses, books and extra lessons with my tutor. For Dad's sake it is most important for me to succeed.'

John replied, 'Good, in that case you have six months to recover and to revise your work for the next and final term in January, and above all learn to eat normally again. It is true that Handel wrote the *Messiah* during fourteen days on glasses of milk. But you are a struggling student. You must eat to survive.'

'Correct, John.'

'Then we can relax for a little while,' added John.

'And the first essential Roger is to encourage you to eat, the body must be fed. In this establishment you have every luxury and the wine cellar of your father, known in this village to equal the best in the country, and yet you never take a drop.'

'My brain operates on strychnine,' Roger explained, 'the medicine recommended by Dr Loretz.'

'Within the next few days we will forget about strychnine, and live normally,' John told him. 'You will still be able to continue your studies, even with your tutor, Mr Anido, in Earls Court three times per week, but in this case there will be no rush. You are now free from the tension, Roger. Your problem is only physical and biological, it may take two or three months to build up the nervous tissues so that you can absorb the contents of the lectures at the condensed rate at which they are delivered in class at the university. It is this which we have to prepare before the final three months.'

'So be it John, we start tomorrow.'

Roger slept for the next twenty hours.

Following upon the race back from the vicarage, Isabelle decided indeed Onward was now ready for the racing world after the setback with his lame leg.

Milligan and the vicar were keenly interested in the news, that evening, in Mrs Milligan's kitchen.

'In that case, we must arrange with Marshall for a public trial soon. It may be possible to enter Onward for the St Leger in late September next year, with a trial at Newbury beforehand this August.'

Ginger was excited. 'Miss, this programme will make my mark in the racing world.'

The Newbury race application was accepted, a little late. It was the first experience of a racecourse for Onward. There were twenty runners during the two and a half mile event. When the tapes went up, Onward was inquisitive, and in consequence a late starter by ten lengths!

Once in his stride, however, Onward went like a shark in the ocean. Nevertheless, ten lengths was a lot to catch up, especially as there were two entries from Ireland, also trained stayers, to be tried out before the St Leger. Ginger rode Onward fully extended and within a short time Ginger managed to catch up with the field. Onward seemed to enjoy the outing in spite of the rain. The other two trained stayers from Ireland were ten lengths in front of the field at the half-way distance. Ginger used the words often employed by Isabelle, 'Now my darling faster, faster.' Onward thrilled and exerted every effort. In fact at the one and a half mile post, Onward was only two lengths behind the two leaders. One furlong from the winning post, Onward made a supreme effort and just managed to catch the two fast-moving Irish challengers. The race crowd was frantic with excitement, and loud cheers greeted the Buchanan colours just as Onward managed to dead-heat with the leaders, which were priced at two to one, to Onward's fifty-to-one. The bookmakers were not happy, but they marked down the price of this unknown stallion Onward at much shorter odds in future. So the result was a dead heat for all three runners – most unusual.

There was quite a celebration in Mrs Milligan's that night.

'But why the late start, Isabelle?' asked the vicar.

'It was Onward's first time out on a racecourse, sir,' she explained. 'We expected anything to happen. However, his life as a two-year-old was ended with distinction as a potential stayer like his sire, Hurry-On. The bookmakers will be keenly interested to know what events Onward will be entered on the calendar next year as a three-year-old.'

'And what next events for Onward do you envisage, Isabelle?' asked Reverend Manning.

'Before Royal Ascot Reverend Manning, the Newbury

Cup and the Windburgh Stakes at Newmarket.'

'And what about Ebony the sprinter, his twin, Isabelle? He will be ready as a promising three-year-old next season.'

'The three Classics, Reverend Manning, in answer to your question. But Ebony will have to qualify first by a successful performance in the Two Thousand Guineas at Newmarket. However, the mile is just his distance.'

'No problem,' agreed George Marshall, who had just arrived from his splendid home and training stables next to Oakfield Lodge. 'The pace over a mile will be fast, but at least Ebony will have the experience of a Classic race. Do not forget also that his twin brother Onward has proved to be fast, even as a stayer. In fact, we are entering Ebony for the Two Thousand Guineas to win, sir.'

Reverend Manning was interested. 'So Ebony will be entered for the Classics as a sprinter, and Onward as the stayer.'

George replied, 'Indeed, Reverend Manning, simply to prove their respective merits.'

The discussion continued long into the night and was twelve thirty am when Isabelle arrived back at the Lodge – to find that Roger had retired long since, under sedatives prescribed by Dr Loretz. Nevertheless she ventured into his room, where the low table light was on, as he always requested. After his twelve hours of non-stop sleep, she was not surprised to find Roger awake.

'So you have come at last, sister,' he said.

'Are you well, Roger?'

'No problems after a complete day of rest, and to know that this current term at Faraday House can be repeated. This gives me almost three months to revise my work for the final term. It is such a relief, Isabelle. Already my nervous system is back to normal now to contemplate several fabulous months without rush, rush, rush and a temporary end to the intake of that ghastly strychnine.'

'Courage, Roger.' Isabelle replied. 'You have passed through a difficult four and a half years, and yet you remain industrious, just like your ancestors. You will always win through.'

'It must be so, Isabelle,' Roger agreed. 'Dad, pioneering in Nigeria, is so insistent I become an engineer. He is so generous, Isabelle, with the necessary purchase of technical literature, books, instruments and all expenses plus a generous cash allowance and the use of a small car. So long as this lovely home, with all its rich privileges and the tradition of dangerous adventure overseas, has a place in it for me, a struggling engineering student it is my duty to remain faithful to the high moral standards set by our father and mother and by Reverend Manning. For example, often it has been a temptation to accept hidden invitations from the village girls for a night of rapture. No Isabelle, my course is clear, to complete the course at Faraday House, and to conduct myself in an exemplary manner throughout. This was not always easy, in view of the temptation offered locally.'

Isabelle responded, 'Nevertheless, you were either inspired or urged to take that line, during those priceless formative years. However loss of health is a high price for success at your age.'

'So what is your course of action for the next few months, the Christmas term as you used to refer to it?'

'No problem, Isabelle. A steady no rush programme of revision in order to prepare for the last term for the finals. It is the degree which counts, and do not forget that during all my student days they have classified me as slow to grasp, and perhaps quick to develop later. In fact it is established now that "quick to grasp" is not my category.'

Roger's recovery was taking time. However, one day Lucie was announced!

'Dear Mr Roger, this is a surprise. Mummy told me about your collapse. The doctor is quite right to insist upon a reprieve.'

'So kind of you to come, Lucie. You look dazzling,' he told her.

She was indeed, especially with her smile.

'Presumably you have taken the music world in the college by storm?' he added.

Lucie blushed and replied, 'You may be interested to know, Mr Roger, that the Music Society in Cambridge which monitors up and coming young novices, has invited me to play Beethoven's Emperor Concerto early in December upon a superb grand piano. Will you be able to come?

Do hope so. If not, you will be interested to know that the BBC will relay the concert.'

'Of course, Lucie, and as before to give you moral support. So the BBC is interested?'

'Indeed Mr Roger, and you are so kind.' She gave him a kiss on his forehead.

'I am sorry to see you in this condition. Why is it?'

'The answer, dear Lucie, is simple. Unlike you, quick to grasp, hence your success at Girton, I am the reverse. It must be the peasant in me.'

Lucie laughed. 'Maybe, Mr Roger, but to drive yourself into the ground through this course of studies is most unreasonable, in my opinion. However, one day the Lord will have a special task for you to undertake.' (How true, years later in Nigeria.)

It was at that moment that John, the assistant to Reverend Manning was announced.

'Hello John, so good of you to come and see this wreck of a student,' Roger greeted him.

'How are you now, Roger?'

'Well enough at last to leave aside all further doses of strychnine. Do you know Lucie, who is on holiday from Cambridge?'

'*Enchanté*, Lucie. Are you the mystery young lady, always with a veil, often seen up to the end of last July and then vanished into the heavens!'

'Into Girton College, Cambridge,' explained Roger.

'So, Mr Roger, your friend John is from St Mary's Winkfield, the only link in England between me and my eighty-year-old cousin from Florence.'

John intervened. 'Please count upon me, Lucie, to guide or help you with any formalities needed by your cousin from Florence, whose business with you, we in the Church have been asked to monitor. Have you never seen your aged cousin, Lucie?'

'No, John. The Americans, according to recent reports, extricated my cousin, Countess Orlando, from the Italian predators, just in time to keep her safe.'

'And your future plans?' asked John.

'A modest income for life is all that I need. The capital may be disposed of amongst the peasants who worked the land, the rest to worthy Christian charities.'

'Or,' continued John, 'you may have creative ideas for the future after your years at Cambridge. For example, improvements of the wine estates and more modern equipment for the wine process.'

'It has not occurred to me, John. This life is so new and exciting.'

John responded, 'Before any decisions are made, listen carefully to what the Lord wishes you to do with this unexpected inheritance. Now, we must not impose any more on Roger, who is making a quick recovery, Meanwhile, it will be a pleasure to escort you to your cottage.'

'Bless you, Mr Roger. Remember that you are expected to attend the concert in December.'

'And you have accepted the invitation to play the concerto by the Music Society in Cambridge?' Roger asked.

'Lucie, will you do me a favour?' Roger asked.

'Yes, Mr Roger.'

'Good, from this moment onward, leave out the Mister before my name. When you were walking about the farm in bare feet, with Ginger and Lydia, not so long ago, and by helping dear Mrs Plant with dinner parties for the master when he was back from Lagos, it was necessary for the Lodge protocol. Now, Lucie, we are both young adults.'

Lucie smiled, and gave Roger another kiss before leaving.

It was later during the evening when Isabelle entered to establish the progress of the patient, her brother.

'Dearest sister, better now and what a let down – or is it let up – to leave off the strychnine. It will take a few days to adjust the nervous system. By the Lord's grace and Dad's cash it is possible for me to repeat this last term, the Christmas term, to restart in January.'

'Dr Loretz insists on three days in bed and nothing physical for a week.'

'No problem, Isabelle. It will give me time to plan a programme to be devoted to the ten different technical subjects.'

'Don't you think that with a little less planning, more golf and relaxation your health will return more quickly to normal?'

'You may be right, Isabelle. It is simply that the driving force in me keeps saying that time is not on my side even at my young age. In any case, during these first three days of physical rest the planning will be a stimulant.'

'You are incomprehensible, dear brother. What do you mean by this driving force? Evidently you are a driven man, as the psychologist would pronounce.'

'Never mind, Isabelle. It is not easy to explain. Perhaps one day.'

'Very well, but whither Lucie? Are you making progress?'

'Isabelle, you are out of touch. Lucie is an exquisite picture of Italian beauty. She has matured since her arrival at Girton. Far less shy now, in fact, much more articulate, and an accomplished pianist to boot. There is no question of love, Isabelle. My heart is set upon the affectionate Milly. Does that make sense?'

'Yes, Roger, it does indeed.'

24

We return now to the world of racing.

Onward was watched and nursed carefully by Isabelle during the winter in order to detect any recurrent weakness in the rear leg. But he became stronger as the months passed. One morning early in December, Isabelle decided to race Onward to the Vicarage, about two miles away, in order to visit John, the assistant to Reverend Manning.

'Hello, Isabelle, you are just in time for a French breakfast of coffee and bread,' he greeted her.

'Apologies, John, for this impromptu arrival. It was just an impulse to ascertain for myself whether Onward was making progress.'

John asked, 'And are you satisfied with the result?'

'He moves like a Rolls Royce, every muscle is in harmony like music, although as far as racing is concerned he will have to harmonise with Ginger, his future rider. Fortunately Ginger is an accomplished jockey, well trained with these stallions.'

'Coffee as usual, Isabelle?'

'So kind of you, John, to accommodate me without warning.'

'Your arrival is opportune, Isabelle. Lucie has captured my heart.'

Isabelle was startled. 'Just a minute, John, let me catch up!'

'First of all, Isabelle, it is important for me to know whether your brother is interested in Lucie.'

'The answer to that question, John, is simply that Roger's heart is set upon Milly, a charming companion for the last few years, so the field is free within this area – but what of Cambridge, John? There you will have to contend with competition from the undergraduates. According to Roger,

Lucie is much in demand, not only by the more mature students but also by the younger dons, as she becomes more and more alive to the outside world. Why not attend the next college concert on Friday, to which Roger was invited? It is not possible for him to go as his nervous system is still in need of repair. Roger, in fact, will be my department until he has satisfied me about his physical and mental health. He has had three months' grace to recover before the start of the Easter term on 5 January, after which hopefully he will be fighting fit. He has to be John – the diploma will be awarded at the end of the Easter term, if he's alive!'

'Why the last bit, Isabelle?'

'Because my brother, intimately known to me after our mother passed away ten years ago, nursed by me, is precious to me. For four and a half years he has torn his guts out in order to comply with the terminal exams, hell bent on obtaining the diploma at the end of the five and a half year course. He has one more term to go, John. He must be given every encouragement by me to pass. During this period he has insisted on work only, no girlfriends – except, Milly, for the last eighteen months – no relaxation, except golf at Sunningdale, no social life of any kind. He has been so determined to win through, his discipline is rigorous. Nevertheless, he is always relaxed in company with Milly, who has a degree from Oxford in engineering sciences. So, dear John, your proposed visit to Girton may bear fruit. Please let me know the outcome.'

'Most interesting Isabelle. So you believe there is a chance?'

'A slim chance, John,' Isabelle replied. 'You hardly know her. Nevertheless, an exceptional child, grown up in the strict Roman Catholic faith. Completely innocent until leaving for Girton last September. I'm sure you would be welcome to borrow Milligan's little Ford 8, if you decide to go.'

'Thank you very much, Isabelle, for your encouragement. Yes indeed, even as a modest parish priests' only salaried clerical assistant, I will begin to bid for her hand.'

Isabelle warned, 'The wooing may take time, John. She is such a stranger to this world. And, no doubt, she is still overwhelmed with all the attraction that Cambridge can offer to a well-educated but totally innocent Italian aristocrat.'

Isabelle galloped back to Oakfield Lodge with Ginger, who had arrived on Hurry-On just before her departure from the Vicarage.

'Any problems?' asked Isabelle.

'Milligan asked me to call you about Sun Flower, soon to receive her second calf. There are difficulties. Sun Flower is the best milker. He does not want to lose her.'

'Do not worry, Ginger. Ask Mrs Plant to let you have three bottles of my father's Dutch Amstel beer, and bring them to the stable where Sun Flower is installed.'

Soon afterwards Isabelle met Milligan. 'Have you the cord ready?' she asked.

'Yes, miss.'

'Is it a critical case?'

Milligan shook his head. 'No, Miss, the calf is there. It is simply coming out the wrong way.'

'In that case, we must do a little heaving after she is intoxicated with Amstel beer!'

It was a lovely calf, delivered without problems, and the mother survived, a little sore, but well enough.

'Were you satisfied with your run on Onward this morning?' Milligan enquired.

'No problems, Milligan. Onward may have missed racing as a two-year-old. As a three-year-old there will be no problems.'

The same night in Mrs Milligan's kitchen plans were confirmed for the two stallions, by Hurry-On, the one a potential sprinter, the other a potential stayer.

The Vicar asked Isabelle, 'At what race do you intend to introduce Onward?'

'George Marshall recommends the Newbury Cup, late March, over two and three-quarter miles, ought to be a reasonably quiet introduction to the racing world for stayers.'

'Sound reasoning,' responded the Vicar. 'Any information, Milligan about competition?'

'None, Reverend Manning. Most runners are so new to the season, especially those late three-year-olds for the first time out.'

*

It was a typical March day at Newbury. Onward had wintered well. He looked in spanking form on Thursday, the day of the race. There were twenty-four runners, several from the well-known stables. Onward was with many others priced at fifty to one for the Newbury Cup. The favourite was rated at seven to one revealing an open field. The racing year was young, in fact about to begin.

The Vicar watched the race with Milligan and Isabelle.

A gasp came from the crowd and the announcer explained that two horses had collided at the start. One was Onward, who had thrown Ginger, possibly due to course fright. However, Ginger, game and tough as ever, jumped on again. It caused quite a sensation. Isabelle, the vicar and Milligan were thrilled, as was the racing public. Some members re-read the race card. 'Sired by Hurry-On' – that made a difference. The bookmakers, always ready to sympathise with the public, uplifted the price to one hundred to one, but one bookmaker wiser than most also noticed bred by Hurry-On, 'the one they could never catch'. So instead of the uplifted price after the disastrous start, he reduced the price back to fifty to one. Meanwhile, Milligan, who had watched the sensational start, shouted, 'Taken fifty pounds at one hundred to one on Onward to win.' The nearby crowd in the stands were much intrigued.

'Name, sir?'

'Milligan, bailiff at local farm – Oakfield Lodge.'

'Was that wise, Milligan,' asked the vicar.

'Perhaps not, Reverend Manning, but my faith is in Ginger and Onward, who were left twenty-five lengths behind.'

Ginger and Onward settled down to the race of their lives. But as Ginger had rapidly reckoned, twenty-five lengths in a 2¾ mile race was not such a serious handicap for Onward.

'Now, my darling,' she urged, using the message initiated by Isabelle to all her stayers, 'my darling, faster, faster.' The giant stallion responded. Within a short time Onward was in touch with the last of the field. The leaders, mostly Arabs, were another twenty lengths in front of the field.

'Faster, my darling, faster.' Ginger felt every muscle in that giant responding to her intimate call. Onward was now in his element, as the rain came down in torrents, just as Onward became level with the field. Ginger was also in her element, mud flying in all directions. She felt the vibrating muscles of Onward exerting every effort to catch the three Arabs, now ten lengths in front of the field. 'Half a mile to go, my darling, please faster, faster.'

It was only two furlongs from the post when two of the Arabs made the challenge; the other one was exhausted, bottomed out.

'Now, my darling, all your Irish-bred effort, please, please.' Onward received the communication. The crowd was sympathetic and highly excited, and after the disastrous start, the mighty stallion responded to all the urging by Ginger. Through the mud and the rain and the race to the post, the race crowd watched with keen interest as the two leading Arab bred stallions were approaching the winning-post. Suddenly Onward made a final effort and just managed to draw level. In fact, the photo-finish revealed that Onward was half a neck in front of the two Arabs, although it was questioned several times, it proved Onward the winner. Screams of delight emerged from those in the race crowd who had backed the runner from the Buchanan stable at fifty to one.

In the paddock George gave a brief report to Isabelle and Milligan. 'It was the other runner, vicar which bumped into Ginger at the start.'

'Do not worry, Ginger,' interrupted Isabelle. 'You have distinguished yourself today before the racing public, and there is an official prize by the course authorities for you of two thousand pounds for your efforts in this important race. Your friend Lydia also will have soon her opportunity to race Ebony in the first of the classics.'

'Mum will be so happy, Miss Isabelle. With such a sum, she will be able to renovate the cottage.'

Meanwhile, the vicar congratulated Milligan upon his gamble. 'In one afternoon, Milligan you've acquired a fortune of five thousand pounds! What made you take such a risk? A hundred pounds is as precious as ever these days, when industry and the country are still recovering from the war.'

Milligan smiled. 'True, although the answer to your

question is difficult to express.'

'Why?'

'Because it was only a sudden instinct when Ginger remounted. It came to me that she must win through.'

'Remarkable,' responded Reverend Manning.

'At least, sir, Miss Isabelle will be provided with a cheque for the church before tomorrow morning as she sets off to the eight am communion service at St Mary's, in commemoration for this great day.'

'Thank you very much, Milligan.'

'Some, sir, used to refer to such an occasion as the "luck of the Irish" in the 1914 war.'

The same night, in Mrs Milligan's kitchen, with nine fine hams hanging from the rafters, several particularly well-covered hares and pheasants, the last of the season, many members of the village were present.

George the village policeman asked, 'Miss Isabelle what plans have you for my favourite Ebony?'

Isabelle smiled, 'Lydia will mount him, George. She has the stronger wrists. Ebony is fast but also rough. In fact, Ebony is the fastest sprinter yet known within my experience, he is also still wild, and strong enough to nearly break Lydia's wrist last year. His first race this year will be the Two Thousand Guineas late April.'

'Not before? It will be the first of the Classics?'

'No, George, we aim for the three Classics with Ebony, Lydia up, without other trials.'

George commented, 'This will keep the press and the racing public in suspense.'

'Precisely, and the starting prices will rise accordingly.'

'So, Miss Isabelle, you have confidence?'

At that moment, Mr Buchanan came in, this was a complete surprise. He addressed Milligan.

'Boyo, so sorry to arrive like this without prior notice. The car broke down at Liverpool. Is my little bedroom available?'

Mrs Milligan was delighted. 'Your bedroom is always ready, Mr Buchanan.'

'Mavoreen, you are more beautiful than ever with that lovely red hair.' He gave her an affectionate hug. 'Now to business, Isabelle. My warm congratulations for the

Newbury Stakes win, in particular for your skilful mount Ginger, a young lady of courage. What are your plans for Ebony, Isabelle?'

'The Two Thousand Guineas,' Isabelle repeated.

'Do you know that there are thirty-five runners and five of them from Italy and France, and several unbeaten? In fact, one runner from France, is Precipitation, said to be exceptional according to his performance as a two-year-old. Madame Faure is the owner. During the last three races in France the stallion has won by twenty lengths. The French believe that he is the horse of the century.'

'Dear Mr Buchanan, during the winter trials on the Marshall race track, our stallion has never impressed me so much. Ebony is so fast that the race crowd called him "that streak of ebony" last year.'

'Nevertheless, Isabelle, five unbeaten thoroughbreds.'

Isabelle smiled. 'Mr Buchanan, we had many problems with the training of Hurry-On, we were concerned about his ability to face the race crowd and to stay the course. He won through in spite of all odds, and our devoted nursing brought him to fame in the racing world. Ebony is a sprinter, Mr Buchanan. Lydia is an accomplished rider, now strong enough in the wrist to control him. There is spiritual intimacy between horse and jockey. In confidence, Mr Buchanan, between you and me, never was it possible for me to witness such a fast stallion as Ebony on the Marshall race track. Fred, George Marshall, the trainer and me, we have all watched as this mighty stallion completed his trials for the Two Thousand Guineas.'

'Dear Isabelle, you have made my day, although it is already eleven thirty! This calls for a special glass of old crusty port, Mavoreen.'

With the arrival of April speculation was rife about the Two Thousand Guineas race at Newmarket, worth about £250,000 in cash to the winner. The trials of Ebony were a guarded secret, although his performance as a two-year-old was not forgotten by the bookmakers. Since then Ebony had not appeared on a racecourse. Was he ill or lame? Yet now confirmed to run for the Two Thousand Guineas, the bookmakers were puzzled. So was Roger, returning from London as he read the racing events in the train. Apart from bookmakers, the racing public likewise were puzzled. On the other hand, there was a new challenger, well known in France but little known in England, an exceptional sprinter called Precipitation. In the Two Thousand Guineas at two to one, he was a clear favourite, based upon his performance in France: four successful wins as a two-year-old and two as a three-year-old. There were several other entries from Italy, Germany and America, yet not now with the outstanding history of the entry from France.

It was in the famous kitchen that the discussion took place later in the week about the Two Thousand Guineas and in particular about the sensational entry, Precipitation, from France.

Mr Buchanan asked, 'Have we no means of checking the times of his wins, Isabelle?'

'No Mr Buchanan, without an agent in France, all we know is that the condition was soft, after the heavy rains through Europe since September.'

At that moment a call came through from Mrs Plant at the Lodge. 'A lady, Miss Isabelle, calling from Paris, known to you apparently. The name is Madame Gabrielle Faure.'

'Thank you, Mrs Plant.'

Isabelle was thrilled; Gabrielle was her great friend and rival for the Gold Cup at royal Ascot and Longchamp, who shared the triple wedding.

'Please have the call put through to Mr Milligan.'

'Is that Isabelle of Oakfield Lodge?' Gabrielle asked.

'It is indeed, Gabrielle. How wonderful to hear your voice again. I haven't seen you since your marriage. Are you happy?'

'It is paradise, Isabelle, now two little ones. And you Isabelle?'

Isabelle replied, 'We have two gorgeous twins also.'

'Congratulations, Isabelle. Now, do you know that the owner of Precipitation is me, in France?'

'What!' Isabelle exploded, *'Cela me depasse!'*

'Calme-toi, ma chère. This is an extraordinary coincidence. My call is simply to establish once again our relations in the racing world, and to confirm that Precipitation is

invincible to date, at least.'

'That is what interests me in particular, apart from the news about your happy *foyer*.'

Gabrielle continued, 'Recently, however, my intelligence service revealed to me that my dear friend has a dark horse, known as Ebony, not even in action this year. Is he lame?'

'No Gabrielle, Ebony is not lame. He is now, like his sire Hurry-On a mighty stallion, and fast.'

'He will have to be very fast to catch Precipitation.'

'It will be such fun to be in competition again. When is Precipitation due for his first performance in England?'

'Nothing before the Two Thousand Guineas at Newmarket.' Gabrielle replied.

Isabelle protested, 'You give nothing away, Gabrielle.'

'Not with you, Isabelle. My objective is the Two Thousand Guineas, the Derby at Epsom and The Queen Mary Stakes, Royal Ascot and finally the Leger at Doncaster. My ambition after being beaten in the past against Hurry-On, the one they could never catch, is to settle the scores with Hurry-On's direct descendant, Ebony.'

'So far Precipitation is unbeaten so perhaps then he will emulate Hurry-On. Do not forget that your room is always ready, this time with a double bed.'

'So kind of you, Isabelle,' Gabrielle responded. Meanwhile, my trainer manager sitting next to me remains puzzled why Ebony has not yet run this season. He says, "Your young friend Miss Isabelle is a very dark horse and has fooled me so often in the past with Hurry-On". He adds that at last we know we have a serious competitor for the Two Thousand Guineas, the first of the season's great Classics.'

The early spring months which have been dry with the air arid,' Isabelle explained, 'Ebony has not made an appearance yet on a racecourse this flat season because the going must be soft for him. For the last ten days, however, the rain has tumbled out of the sky in southern England, and Ebony has responded.'

'This news may not be welcome to our trainer, Isabelle, because all our wins this year have been on firm ground.'

'As a suggestion, Gabrielle, it will be worth a hint if you ask the weatherman at Newmarket to give you a daily report. Do let me know a few days in advance when we can expect you and your husband for the Newmarket meeting. Sleep well.'

'Miss Isabelle,' encouraged George the trainer. 'It will surprise me to see any classic runner to outdistance Ebony in his present form this coming season. Not in my living memory has any stallion so fast ever been lodged in our stables.'

'Thank you, George.'

Milligan interrupted, 'George, what is the progress about Onward, the twin to Ebony?'

Isabelle smiled, for Onward was her favourite.

'A stayer, Milligan, class one, just like his sire Hurry-On. During his first race early this year at Newbury he dead-heated with two others on a $1^{1}/_{2}$ mile race after a late start left by 10 lengths. He is being trained now for the King George VI Stakes at Royal Ascot in June $3^{1}/_{4}$ miles and Longchamp at $3^{1}/_{2}$ miles late October. We may enter Onward for The Leger at Doncaster at $1^{3}/_{4}$ miles, but it may be too short a distance. However, his first race for the season, this time as a three-year-old will be at Newmarket, over two and a half miles in four weeks' time with Ginger up. Competition is unknown.'

Milligan looked at the programme. Two from Ireland and three from France, altogether thirty-four runners. Evidently a feeler against competition for the stayers.

Another call came through from the Lodge.

'Buchanan here. Is that my Mavoreen?'

'Just a moment, Mr Buchanan,' Isabelle answered.

'Bless you, my dear, it is you and George, in particular, to whom my news will be of interest. One of the great stayers owned by Madame Gabrielle and entered for the Newbury Stakes at Newmarket and for the King George VI Stakes at Royal Ascot. He is called Cat o' Nine Tails and he is, unbeaten over the distance.'

Isabelle nearly fainted. 'So it seems that once again we are in competition with my friend Gabrielle for both stayers and sprinters. Your flame Mrs Milligan wishes now to have a word with you.'

'Mavoreen,' was heard from the receiver.

The vicar was surprised. 'Tell me, Milligan, have we any

way of finding out the history of Cat o' Nine tails?'

'No problem, sir.'

After the call from Buchanan, Milligan put through a call to a friend working at Ladbrokes' on the night phone.

'Hello, Mr Milligan, what is the problem?'

'It is Cat o' Nine Tails. We want all the available racing history of this young stayer from France as soon as possible.'

'No problem, Milligan, give me twenty-four hours.'

'Splendid,' responded Isabelle. 'What a game, now competition for both stayers and sprinters and my dear friend knows nothing about Onward!'

Mrs Milligan commented, 'Do not forget, Miss, your old maxim. It is not whether you win or lose in this world, it is how you play the game that counts.'

'Bless you Mrs Milligan.

'How is Onward?' ventured the vicar.

Isabelle answered, 'As you know, sir, Onward has been under my care since his first race at Newbury late last year in which he impressed the public even after a late start, when he dead-heated with the winner. The Newbury Stakes, over the same distance at Newmarket, is in four weeks' time. It will settle whether he is a serious contender for the George VI Stakes at Royal Ascot in June. He will then have to compete with this new invader from France, Cat o Nine Tails, owned by my old racing competitor and friend in France, Gabrielle Faure.'

Another call came through from Mr Buchanan. 'A new development, Milligan, I learnt tonight that Cat o' Nine Tails has been withdrawn from Newmarket in favour of a race at St Cloud, France where he will be contending with all his French rivals over the same distance, two and a half miles, in three weeks time.'

'Excellent,' responded Isabelle. 'It will now be possible for me to assess the ability of Cat o' Nine Tails after his race at St Cloud and to make a comparison with Onward's performance at Newmarket a week later.'

Isabelle retired to the Lodge with Milly, who had recently returned fron another visit to Bordeaux and was now well established at the Piccadilly office of the master.

'How is Roger tonight, Milly?'

'He seems to be more confident than ever before and expects you tonight.'

Isabelle entered his room at midnight. He was fast asleep. As usual she said her prayers beside his bed. Always she felt that Roger was her first responsibility in this world of men descendants from a family of veterans who ventured out into equatorial Nigeria from 1908, a fever-ridden and a most inhospitable country in those days. The British, she thought are a dynamic and energetic race. They have an inherent force, partly spiritual, partly physical, probably both, yet always ready, to attempt the most impossible, for example the RAF in the Battle of Britain in 1940.

He opened his eyes slowly the bed light was dim. 'You, it must be late.'

'Not too late to have a little talk with my highest priority in this our lovely home at midnight. Are you well Roger?'

'My dear sister, after my forced retirement, my studies have become a pleasure instead of a desperate rush to catch up with the next lecture. No more strychnine to boost the brain, incredible to enjoy at dinner-time a glass of Château Margot 1949 from Dad's cellar, from time to time, and a game of golf at Sunningdale with George our village local policeman.'

'Roger, you do not know how much you are blessed.'

'What do you mean? For example, by being incapacitated from my inattendance at Faraday House for three months! Is that being blest?'

'No, dear Roger. You have driven yourself into the ground by sheer hard work with your studies, determined to win through during the last five years resulting in mental and physical collapse. This is well worthy, as Christ will have us believe. Please, please, therefore do not worry any more. You have now caught up with all your studies even enjoy them, and you are prepared, just like Napoleon, your favourite hero, to go into battle in future at your Marengo also! And physically, you are once more a fit man.'

Roger interrupted, 'In that case, dear sister of mine, why not a half bottle of Veuve Cliquot and a small piece of pâté de foie gras to send me off with dreams about Milly!'

'No problem, Roger, give me five minutes.'

Punctually Isabelle arrived with the half-bottle and the pâté.

'It never occurred to me that I could spoil my young brother to this extent.'

He was now wide awake. 'You have often explained to me, dear sister, the meaning of privilege is responsibility, nobless oblige. After five years of intense concentration, my privilege has arrived!'

'So it seems, dear Roger. Changing the subject. Your friendship with Milly, *Ca cole?*' (The French, dear reader, for is the relationship progressing happily).

'Yes, dear sister, in my dreams her lovely body is mine. It is tough this waiting period. It is also tantalising. But I take heed of that inspiring guide, often quoted by you in the past, "Honour thy father and mother so that thy days will be long and fruitful in the land which the Lord thy God giveth thee".'

Isabelle looked at Roger with wonder. 'So you remember that.'

'Of course, dear sister.'

'One day Roger, you will be a moral power in the land.'

'Moral power perhaps, dear Isabelle, but the night of our honeymoon will be an explosion from which my recovery will be long.'

Isabelle smiled. My dear brother, she thought evidently has strict standards, like Richard. They are leaders of men.'

His eyes started to close, all he could murmur was, 'God bless you dearest sister for the lovely *diner à deux avec le Veuve Cliquot à minuit.*

It was now one thirty. He was fast asleep as Isabelle cleared away the little side-table.

25

It was eleven am before Roger entered the dining-room the next morning. Mrs Plant was waiting for orders.

'So it is director's hours, now Mr Roger.'

He smiled and gave her a morning hug. He was now recovered and attending Faraday House once more. At that moment a visitor arrived, John the assistant vicar of St Mary's, and Isabelle returned from her morning gallop on Onward.

'Hello John, we were wondering about you, after your last visit with Lucie at Girton College,' Isabelle greeted him.

'That is the main reason for this visit, just as spring is about to burst forth. Isabelle, she is breathtaking in her innocence and beauty, at least to me. She has become less rigid, more informal, less shy. In other words, she is becoming daily more irresistible, and full of grace. Her smiles are far more frequent, and when they are provoked, the very sun shines from those black Italian eyes.'

'And the tears, do they continue?'

'Oh yes. Her thoughts are so private that it is too delicate for me to ask her questions, although the reason for the tears is clear after Roger's explanation.'

Roger smiled, 'It is true Isabelle, Lucie revealed her thoughts to me on this subject as you know several months ago. Briefly she grieves for the Holy Virgin and the terrible experience at the Crucifixion of the Lord. The world she claims has forgotten the Holy Virgin, and she wants our civilisation to know that she Lucie, is for ever with the Virgin Mary in thoughts about her agonizing experience two thousand years ago.'

Isabelle responded, 'Is she destined then Roger, for a life in the service of the Church?'

John interrupted, 'Surely not, Isabelle.'

'My dear John, you have a problem if you wish to win her hand. The Roman Catholic Church insists that the eventual children are brought up in that faith. Do you agree?'

John took time to respond. 'It is her vast fortune which is in the way, Isabelle. Me, a struggling curate, assistant to Reverend Manning – it seems incongruous, almost indecent, to aspire to her hand.'

'How wrong you are, John,' said Isabelle. 'Love is all powerful, if it is mutual, whatever the difficulties!'

'That is the problem, Isabelle. Is it mutual?'

'Well, you ought to know.'

'Agreed, but she is still too young and new to the outside world, and so innocent to grasp what we know of life even at our young age.'

'The solution to that problem,' responded Isabelle 'is simple. The English have a word for it – "courting", plenty of visits to Girton College during the coming spring in order to excite interest in you and what you have to offer.'

The Newmarket meeting was approaching. One night at the kitchen meeting with Mrs Milligan a message came through from Buchanan in Ireland via Mrs Plant, and Isabelle took the call.

'How are you, dear partner?' he began. 'Are you ready for a shock. Today, Cat o' Nine Tails spread-eagled the field at St Cloud and won by sixteen lengths, from all his rivals in France, Germany and Italy. The winner is now set to settle the score with the Hurry-On family at Newmarket early next month at the Windsor Castle Stakes. Onward will have to be exceptional to keep up, because the going was soft to good at St Cloud.'

'Mr Buchanan, all through the winter months Onward has been ridden and carefully nursed by me over the three miles after his set-back as a two-year-old. He performs like a true thoroughbred from his sire. It will be an education for me if Cat o' Nine Tails can keep up.'

Buchanan laughed. 'Never known anyone like you, dear Isabelle, for optimism. Nevertheless, at least you are aware of the strength of the competition. As far as Ebony is concerned, the Aga Khan has three unbeaten three-year-old fast sprinters, Arab stock, all unbeaten as two-year-olds, also the Italian horse who won by three lengths at Newmarket last year when a hot favourite. Finally, your friend Gabrielle has Precipitation entered also for the Two Thousand Guineas, although there are seven others from France, without known records or history. Precipitation is running at Longchamp in the French Classics for three- year-olds over the mile, the Prix de Paris, with forty runners. As a two-year-old he had a brilliant career – unbeaten. My informants advise me that Precipitation is the fastest three-year-old ever trained at the St Cloud stables. I will report again after the race.'

Isabelle smiled. 'Well, Mr Buchanan, this is serious news indeed. So dear Gabrielle intends to compete with us for both stayers and sprinter. Evidently she has ambitions for the Two Thousand Guineas, the Derby and the St Leger – even the triple crown! Mr Buchanan, she is a foe man worthy of my steel.'

'So you are not unduly alarmed?'

'No, Mr Buchanan. This is life. It is a stimulating challenge. As the vicar will insist, it is not whether you win or lose in this world, it is how you play the game that counts.'

'How right, Isabelle. Is my Mavoreen again available?'

'Of course, Mr Buchanan.' She handed over the receiver. 'Well, Milligan, so once again we have competition from my friend with both stayers and sprinters.'

'Not to worry, Miss. *Courage*, as they say in France.'

Roger and John, now a regular visitor, were in deep discussion about Lucie. Milly had long since retired in order to depart the next morning at seven-thirty for the Piccadilly office.

'Good evening, dear sister, John is interestsed to understand the meaning of your expression yesterday, when you remarked about the humdrum practical world, "Where true love is to be found". Did you really mean it?'

'Of course, John, that is the only area where you will find sincere love in the market-place of the working world. You may not be sufficiently experienced to understand that yet, but you will be after a few more visits to

Cambridge, especially during the social events with Lucie, and later on in the outside world. John, "shelter and retreat may safeguard innocence, but virtue does not begin until wrong has been met and mastered" – is that clear?'

'Well, Isabelle, it is clear, but a lot to digest all at once. By that you mean as applied to Lucie, of course.'

'What progress, John, during your last visit to Cambridge?'

'Only for a two-night stay, Isabelle. It was apparent that Lucie is much in demand, especially for music and for her views about the Holy Virgin Mary.'

'In what way about the Holy Virgin Mary?'

'You are aware already about the reason for the tears in the veil at St Mary's Church in Winkfield.'

'Go on.'

'Lucie remains still most emotional internally, even with the student life, and glamour around her in Cambridge. Always introspective, with so many questions about the persecution of the spirit of the Holy Virgin Mary in England during the Reformation.'

'And your response, John, as a member of the Church of England?'

'Indeed, Isabelle, often an embarrassing moment for me. We were brought up even at public school to not exactly abhor the Jews and Roman Catholics, who were excused for not attending certain semi-religious parades. However, since those days of the early twenties, quite a lot has been discovered by researchers into the subject. Fortunately Civil War in England was avoided at the time of the Reformation due perhaps to the tolerance of the Catholics in England then, who were strong in numbers, especially in the North. Only once or twice at Cambridge after the Sunday early morning communion was her veil seen to be wet at the end of the service before leaving. With a few choking sobs as she arose, an embarrassing moment, but two other undergraduates, male and female, turned in commiseration. "Can we help your friend"? they asked. With finger on my lips, silence was admonished. The two students were spellbound after Lucie cleared the tears from those black eyes. The boy murmured, "What an incredible beauty". The girl asked, "Was it a bereavement"?

Lucie smiled. Yes, it happened about two thousand years ago"! The boy responded, "So sorry to intrude upon such secret thoughts". It was then that Lucie gave a quick flash of smile, nothing more, and the very sun shone from those black Italian eyes! The strangers were rewarded for their kindness.'

The next day, John continued: 'Meanwhile, it is my impression that Lucie enjoys my company. She is relaxed and we talk about the peaceful and quiet life of Winkfield. She has selected finally to enter the medical profession, which means a seven-year course.'

The next Saturday Isabelle received a call from Ireland.
'Hello, Mr Buchanan.'
'Are you still fighting fit, my dear.'
'Always, Mr Buchanan.'
'You will need to be, because your friend from France, Gabrielle, is a shrewd player. In fact, her entry bred from the Cobler known as Cat o' Nine Tails, still remains unbeaten in France, indeed an exceptional stayer.'

It was a cold day at Newmarket, with a north-easter blowing. Yet Onward seemed to be intrigued with his surroundings as he walked around the ring. In fact, he attracted a lot of attention in the paddock. The trainer of the favourite, Invincible, told his jockey, 'Try to keep as close as possible to Onward. Remember his performance in the Newbury Cup. As a man full of years, Joe, remember this, rarely has it been my pleasure to see such a magnificent stallion in all my life. Your only chance is to go flat out from the start in the hope that Onward will once again be a late starter.'

The runners were now reduced to thirty-five for the three-mile race, considered a trial for the King George VI Stakes at Royal Ascot later in June.

As the horses cantered down to the post, the vicar remarked, 'There are so many runners. Do you really believe that Onward will be able to manage?

'It is my impression, Reverend Manning, that you will witness today a phenomenon rarely equalled in the racing world.'

They cantered down to the tapes. Onward was in the pink of condition, as were several other stayers for this three-mile race, including Invincible. There was a considerable attendance, in spite of the weather.

As the tapes went up, there was a gasp of surprise.

'Three runners collided at take-off. One with the Buchanan colours – Onward,' came the loudspeaker announcement. 'He has rejoined the race, but is twenty-five lengths behind. He must be considered as a write-off for this race!'

The vicar looked at Milligan. 'What a shame. And George's wife has lost her one-pound bet.'

'Courage, sir. Let me study the situation with these army field-glasses. But it was thought Milligan, a tricky situation. Isabelle was by his side. 'Have you faith Miss Isabelle, in your jockey Ginger?'

'Of course, Milligan, but how goes the battle front?'

After one mile Onward is now only ten lengths behind the field!'

'Remarkable!' exclaimed the vicar. The crowd began to buzz with excitement. But Invincible was by now ten lengths in front of the field, and Joe set to win by a handsome margin.

Ginger settled down to a battle of attrition. To Onward she urged, 'Now, my darling, all you have please, faster faster.' The mighty stallion felt the call and every muscle and sinew, every ounce of bodily strength and spirit vibrated to her call.

Isabelle was anxious. 'Well, Milligan?'

'No problems, Miss. Indeed a late start, you know Onward.'

It was a desperate situation. At the two-mile post Onward was now leading the pack most of the field, but Invincible was still ten lengths in front of him with another stayer. 'My darling, faster, faster, one more mile.' Onward again responded. Ginger felt those mighty muscles again working overtime. Little by little the gap with Invincible began to close, but what an incredible effort by Onward, now in spite of the snowflakes which began to fall out of the leaden grey sky, the excitement rose among the race crowd.

Isabelle tugged at Milligan's sleeve. 'How goes Ginger?' Milligan replied after a careful analysis through his well-worn army field-glasses.

'Tricky, Miss Isabelle, 'Half a mile to go. Onward is now four lengths in front of the pack, but Invincible still ten lengths in advance with the other stayer, possibly his stable companion. The pace is indeed fast for a three-mile race. It surprises me to witness such a fast finish. Only slowly is Onward overtaking the two leaders. Wait! Both leaders show signs now of exhaustion; whips are out. Yet Onward has not slowed down. He's now only three lengths behind the leaders. It is indeed an exciting finish, Miss, only one furlong to go.'

'Please, please, my darling, faster, faster,' urged Ginger.

Onward knew what was needed. That mighty stallion responded valiantly to the desperate call from his jockey. The race crowd was ecstatic with emotion. The gap was reduced to one length behind the two leaders only half a furlong from the post. Yet Onward remained in fighting trim, as the other two leaders were urged on by the whips. It was a photo finish. But to Milligan's experienced eye there was no doubt.

'Congratulations, Miss.'

True enough, within a few minutes the winner was announced as Onward, by a short head.

Joe was making a verbal report to the trainer of Invincible, near Milligan.

'Instructions were carried out to the letter, sir, but in the end we were driven into the ground. Invincible was completely blown.'

'Do not worry, Joe, you were up against one of the wonder stallions of the century, a true first son of Hurry-On "the one they could never catch".'

'In that case, sir, my conscience is eased. It is our first defeat.'

The trainer added, 'What you do not know, Joe, is that Invincible had a 25-length start on Onward, who was delayed at the tapes.'

'In that case, sir, Onward really must be a wonder horse! And it has been a privilege for me to have come second today.'

A week later on Sunday in the Milligan's kitchen there was

a discussion about the programme for the sprinter that streak of Ebony. In fact Ebony has wintered well. At that moment a call came through from Ireland. Buchanan in Ireland.

'Hello, Boyo,' he said to Milligan. 'News about competitors. Since Precipitation won the Prix de Paris by five lengths over the one mile, Ladbrokes has marked him down as favourite for the Two Thousand Guineas race on 26 April at four to one.

Milligan replied, 'Ebony has no engagement before the meeting, and we remain confident. His performance as a two-year-old is sufficient.'

Buchanan continued, 'Also, Cat o' Nine Tails spread-eagled a field of thirty-eight in the Grand Prix de L'Arc de Triomphe at Longchamps against all competitors from France, Italy and Germany won by ten lengths. Our friend Gabrielle is now ready for Royal Ascot, Newmarket and Epsom. Ladbrokes informs me that Cat o' Nine Tails is now favourite for the King George VI Stakes at Royal Ascot for three-year-olds, at five to one. Evidently they have not yet priced Onward for the same race after his impressive performance last week!'

Milligan smiled. 'That does not surprise me.'

There was much discussion in the kitchen after the call.

Milligan explained the news from Buchanan. 'It seems, my friends, that Miss Gabrielle is intending an invasion. The triple crown with Precipitation, the Two Thousand Guineas, the Derby and the St Leger at Doncaster. Also for the stayers at Royal Ascot, the King George VI Stakes over three and a half miles, with Cat o' Nine Tails.'

The vicar asked Isabelle. 'Do you seriously believe, dear Isabelle, that Ginger on Onward and Lydia on Ebony can contain this intense French competition with highly professional riders?'

Isabelle smiled. 'Dear Reverend Manning, you were witness at Newmarket, how Ginger distinguished herself on Onward, in front of a large interested race crowd. Left at the post by twenty-five lengths with that stallion Onward to win by a neck. What more proof, sir?'

'Very well, Isabelle, your enthusiasm is infectious. Nevertheless Cat o' Nine Tails is still unbeaten over three and a half miles, likewise Precipitation remains unbeaten over the one mile and both owned by Gabrielle!'

'It seems to me,' Milligan added, 'that both stayers and sprinters are well matched. It will depend more upon the riders, and after Newmarket, young Ginger will carry my shilling anywhere!'

'Very well then. Meanwhile what about the sprinter, Ebony?" asked the vicar.

'Precipitation, Reverend Manning, seems to be the wonder sprinter of the year we have to compete against,' replied Isabelle.

'So is Ebony, my dear,' responded Marshall. 'We must not forget how Lydia handled Ebony, as a two-year-old at Epsom last year, and sprained her wrist trying to control that giant flyer. Precipitation may be exceptional in France. Nevertheless, my claim stands; never have we seen on my training ground such a fast stallion over the seven furlongs as Ebony when he won the Epsom Stakes.' The discussion about the coming invasion from Gabrielle went on long into the night by the large wood fire in the famous kitchen. George Marshall summarized the prospects. 'Precipitation may be exceptional in France, Milligan, but Ebony remains for me and for my staff at the Marshall Stables a wonder stallion, as a three-year-old over the mile distance at this moment in time. Whether he will be able as a three-year-old to extend his strength to one and a half miles for the Derby is not yet clear to me. For Onward, however, there are no doubts, at two miles or over, just like his sire. Cat o' Nine Tails may yet be unbeaten but Royal Ascot in June will decided which is the better stayer, at the King George VI Stakes.'

Reverend Manning concluded, 'This has been a most instructive evening my friends. As you say, Isabelle, your friend is a foe worthy of your steel!'

Milligan laughed. 'It seems to me, sir, that their competition both for stayers and sprinters will have to be quite exceptional to catch Ebony and Onward.'

It was twelve-thirty am when Isabelle arrived back at the Lodge with Milly. They both went to see Roger fast asleep, a privilege for Milly. He was a picture of complete innocence, with the dull red lamp by the bedside. He had left a note:

Sister, please ask Milly to give me a kiss goodnight when you return from your meeting with Milligan tonight. A kiss from you also, do not forget!'

His instructions were carried out. Isabelle noticed a tear, they went to the kitchen for a cup of hot chocolate. 'Nothing wrong, Milly?' she asked.

'No Isabelle, except that Roger is all my humble world. My love for him is overflowing.'

'Good, in that case, since he is now approaching the last of his studies at Faraday House, perhaps he may be induced to make a declaration.'

Milly smiled, 'So you agree?'

'Of course, Milly. Have you thought about future prospects in Nigeria, and in that oven heat, Lagos?'

'Indeed yes Isabelle, and other problems. For example Lagos, future trade problems, financial problems, health problems, responsibilities during his absence in Lagos, and a host of unforeseen situations. Nevertheless, my faith in true love is not limited. My love for your dear brother knows no bounds, and our mutual faith will carry us through.'

'Careful Milly, he stirs, we must make our quiet exit.' They did.

Before eventually retiring Isabelle invited Milly to accompany her with a cup of hot chocolate.

'A good idea, Isabelle, after the emotion of the day.'

'Has he said anything at all, Milly?'

'Not officially, Isabelle, but he made the situation clear at Abingdon.'

'No competition from Lucie?'

Milly responded, 'It is not my impression.'

'In that case, my congratulations.'

'Before that, Isabelle, perhaps we ought to await the result of the Faraday House finals in June.'

Isabelle agreed, and after that they retired, both happy at the future prospects for love.

The quiet private telephone rang by Iabelle's bedside.

'My darling. So sorry to wake you up.'

'No matter, dearest Richard, I've only just retired.'

'Only just? Who was the boy-friend?' he teased.

'Hurry-On as usual, in his stables.'
'Ah! My only competition.'
Isabelle smiled.
'Are you still there?' enquired Richard.
'Yes, darling. Dreaming about you and hearing your breathing!'
'Good. Expect me tomorrow, early. Do not wake up. No one will hear me. I have a key, and it is my wish to ravish you!' And with that he rang off.
Isabelle slept with butterflies in her stomach.

26

Just before the international meeting at Newmarket for the Two Thousand Guineas, there was a race meeting at Newbury for three-year-olds. This included a one-mile race generally accepted as the trial race for the Two Thousand Guineas, known as the Newbury Spring Stakes. Several international owners entered their colts for this race in order to accustom them to the wet English climate and in particular to the going. It was for this race that Gabrielle managed to enter Precipitation, just before the closing date. The manoeuvre took the racing world by surprise. The Newbury authorities were delighted, hotel booking and demands for any kind of local accommodation became active overnight.

Buchanan's friends at Ladbrokes in London were, soon after this surprise entry, quietly in touch with the Irishman.

'At what are you pricing Precipitation Jimmy?' Buchanan asked.

'The price established five minutes ago, Mr Buchanan is two to one on.'

'Great scot, is there no competition from Europe?'

'Oh yes, three unbeaten colts from Italy and France, although it is not yet sure whether they will be trying. Precipitation is a famous name all over the racing world in Europe.'

At ten pm the following Monday evening this news was transmitted to Milligan, George Marshall, Isabelle and the vicar, who were all in the Milligan's kitchen.

'Most interesting, Milligan,' responded George, 'that is in ten days from now, it is the Newbury Spring Stakes.'

'Will you be able to accompany me, Milligan?' the vicar asked. 'It ought to be an instructive experience.'

George added, 'It will give me an indication also of the

performance of the wonder horse from France – the race time and conditions, established during the event by my scouts.'

They all agreed to attend the Newbury meeting.

There were twenty-seven runners, a lot for this less-known meeting. The press, however, built up the event and the attendance was a record, evidently attracted by the French wonder horse, Precipitation.

Just before the race, during the parade in the paddock, the French stallion commanded a lot of admiration and attention from the public.

'Without doubt,' Milligan commented to the vicar, a well-built and powerful stallion.'

'They're off,' came the announcement over the speaker. 'Seven runners are in the lead. It is a fast-run race. The favourite was left two lengths at the start, but it is making up ground fast. However, an outsider from Italy is now five lengths in front of the field at the half-mile post. The favourite from France is at present boxed in by the field – now he has extricated himself and is on the outside, overhauling the field at a rare pace. Precipitation has now passed the field in impressive style. Two furlongs from the post, Precipitation is now in the lead and performing sensationally. In spite of late challenges from the Italian and the other unbeaten stallion from France, a furlong from the post Precipitation was level with the Italian outsider. It was then that the race crowd witnessed a wonder of thoroughbred breeding and training. Precipitation made a dramatic effort and passed the post fifteen lengths in front of the Italian challenger!'

In spite of its odds-on-price the crowd responded to the result, but the bookies were not happy, and Precipitation was then priced at two to one on for the Two Thousand Guineas. At the same time the first call over Ebony was fifteen to one.

'Gorgeous,' exclaimed Milligan, after the reaction of the market.

'Why, Milligan, you must be over optimistic!' the vicar laughed.

'Because it is my humble opinion that Ebony will win!'

The press highlighted the event.

'Left at the start of the field including, international unbeaten stallions from Italy, and France, Precipitation the unbeaten French wonder horse spread-eagled the field at Newbury yesterday in front of a record crowd. The stallion is now a clear favourite for the first of the great Classics, the Two Thousand Guineas in fourteen days. The time over the one mile at Newbury was a record for the course, the going was good to fair,' read one report.

That night in the kitchen there was much deliberation and George suggested that Ebony ought to be withdrawn. 'To be second or third in the Two Thousand Guineas will reduce the stud fees radically,' he explained.

'True, George,' responded Isabelle. 'But suppose he wins? It is still my belief,' she insisted, 'that Ebony is a match for Precipitation, after those winter trials with Lydia up at the Marshall training track.

And so Ebony trained for the first Classic event.

An immense race crowd assembled at Newmarket to witness the Two Thousand Guineas, in fact worth about £250,000 for the owner today. Altogether thirty-seven runners from all over Europe assembled for this important event exclusively for three-year-old thoroughbred colts.

As the horses entered the parade ring, Milligan whispered to Isabelle, 'Courage, Miss. Lydia is well and ready. Ebony is still at fifteen to one, against the favourite Precipitation at three to one on.'

The parade was most impressive. Many important international personalities were present, directors of large companies in the UK and overseas, Arab rulers, and leading owners from Europe.

Isabelle then met Gabrielle. She was elegantly dressed in *haute couture*.

'Darling, you look gorgeous. How are the twins?' enquired Isabelle.

'They are lovely, Isabelle. And yours?'

'Indeed yes. They love to climb on the back of Hurry-On, during their Sunday morning romp.'

Gabrielle smiled. 'Dear Isabelle, this afternoon we are both to witness the effective value of the bloodlines from Hurry-On and the Cobler, both rivals from past years.

Once again we are competitors, and yet we can continue as good friends. Soon we will both go to the paddock to compare notes. My experts are surprised that Ebony has not run yet this year, so the market reflects its doubts. Yet Ebony won in great style as a two-year-old, first time out, with your well-known jockey Lydia. Maybe you have a special reason for not running him yet?'

'No, Gabrielle, it is simply to prepare Ebony for the two years of the great Classics as a three-and four-year-old. The process needs careful nursing, not too many events simply to bring in the cash. We believe that Ebony is now at racing pitch. This afternoon will reveal whether we are right.'

'But are you aware that during the past twelve months, no three-year-old has come within five lengths of Precipitation? He has raced against horses from all over the Continent, even from the USA.'

'Of course, dear Gabrielle, my friends are well aware of the repeated successes of Precipitation known now as, the French wonder horse. In fact my trainer has even asked me to withdraw Ebony from the race, in order not to upset our relations.'

'*Cela c'est vraiment gentille*, Isabelle. *Eh bien?*'

'*Non, chère* Gabrielle.'

'In that case, Isabelle the race this afternoon will decide which one of us is the owner of the fastest miler this year here and now at Newmarket.'

Both Precipitation and Ebony were the subject of immense admiration in the paddock. The trainer of Precipitation, observing Ebony, was heard to remark, 'What a fabulous stallion, at seventeen and a half hands, jet black all over, what breadth of shoulder. We may well have problems this time. Miss Gabrielle, it is my belief that we have at last a competitor, so far not encountered in our racing experiences in France. Why no record since a two-year-old?'

Gabrielle responded. 'We do not know. Isabelle plays her cards always close to her breast!'

As Lydia led Ebony around, Isabelle asked her how she felt herself.

'Thrilled, Miss Isabelle, like never before,' replied Lydia.

'And the wrists?'

'No problems, Miss. Doctor Loretz has supplied me with these double straps.'

'And you remain confident?'

Lydia nodded. 'Precipitation may be a world beater, Miss, but so far he has never run against Ebony!'

'Good luck, Lydia,' Isabelle said with a kiss, 'and bless you.'

The signal for mounting was established and thirty-seven thoroughbreds began to canter down to the starting tapes. What a lovely sunny afternoon, mused Isabelle, with the vicar, Milligan and Ginger at the top of the stands. Isabelle observed there must be at least 150,000 race-goers there this spring afternoon, to witness the first of the Classics, for a prize of £250,000 to the winning owner. For some strange reason Isabelle was not concerned with the cash prize, it was the event which was of paramount interest. After her nursing and training supervision of those two twin wonder stallions bred from Hurry-On, one of them was now on trial.

'They're off,' came the announcement from the loudspeaker. Then a gasp from the large crowd.

The loudspeaker continued, 'Evidently an accident has occurred as the thirty-seven lined-up. It seems that a collision has taken place amongst the runners at the extreme east end of the line. 'Unfortunately,' continued the announcer, 'the favourite Precipitation was involved on the course side, and another horse with unidentified colours was delayed on the stands side. Both the other runner and Precipitation therefore were left fifteen lengths at the start of the race.'

The market reacted fast. Precipitation quoted one bookmaker immediately at ten to one. Then, said the trainer of Precipitation, one hundred pounds to win. It was a fighting gesture.

'Well, Milligan,' asked Isabelle. 'How goes the front line, now?'

'Desperate, Miss. We are most unlikely to win, likewise the favourite. Both Precipitation and the other runner were left at the post by about fifteen lengths due to two collisions at each end of the starting line. The stewards ought to limit the number of entries next time, Miss.'

'Milligan, I have never known you to be a pessimist.'

'Because, Miss, the runner at the other end of the line so far not identified may be Ebony.'

The announcer continued, 'Both Precipitation and the other horse are making superhuman efforts to catch the field, although three unbeaten thoroughbreds from Italy and Germany are now two lengths in front.'

'So you see, Miss, the other horse may be Ebony.'

Then the announcer continued.

'After a disastrous start,' reported the commentator, the favourite and the outsider, now identified as Buchanan's Ebony, running at opposite sides of the course, are making up lost ground very fast indeed.'

Lydia whispered to Ebony, 'My darling, we are in a spot, as the Americans say. Faster, faster.' Her anxiety was transmitted to Ebony. She felt his exertion in response through all that fabulous mountain of bone and muscle.

Both Precipitation and Ebony were soon level with the leaders of the field, the unbeaten runners from Italy and France.

The announcer continued, 'Ebony on the stand side is now level with Precipitation.' Again, a loud cheer greeted this news.

'The three leaders are still clear by two lengths from the two late starters, but they are catching up fast, both on opposite sides of the course with the three leaders in the middle.'

As the runners approached the one furlong from home post, the announcer confirmed that all five front runners were level. The race crowd was in uproar. What a race! Precipitation was never more extended in all his career, as afterwards confirmed by his trainer. During the last furlong Lydia made every last effort, physical and spiritual. Indeed she was surprised to see through the corner of her eye that Ebony still had a challenger on the left. The cheek of it, she thought. If it was not for that trouble at the start....

'Now, my darling, one last bound, please, please.'

Ebony won by half a length. Precipitation had met his master at last.

Lydia was completely exhausted as she nearly fell from Ebony in the enclosure.

'Congratulations, my dear Lydia,' came from Isabelle.

The enquiry flag was raised. The crowd awaited the result as George and Isabelle went before the stewards.

'Good afternoon, Lady Cameron. We wished simply to know why Ebony was not run earlier in the season.'

'We feared he might develop the same laming condition as his twin Onward, who has now recovered. Here are the medical certificates.'

'Thank you Lady Cameron, and our congratulations.'

Gabrielle greeted her immediately after the meeting with the stewards.

'My darling, you have beaten us by half a length, the first time ever for Precipitation.'

'Dearest Gabrielle,' responded Isabelle, 'It is difficult for me to express my emotions....'

'Do you remember at Longchamp, after Hurry-On beat my Cobler in the Arc de Triomphe that you said it is not whether you win or lose, it is how you play the game which counts?'

'Yes, indeed it is true throughout life, but, why, Gabrielle, do you now refer to this subject?'

'Simply because, my pride has taken a deep dive. The whole of the racing world of France was counting upon me to show those English thoroughbreds that we also can produce equally good stallions from Normandy.'

'Gabrielle, soon, very soon, you will receive an excellent opportunity to illustrate to your critics that Precipitation is still a wonder horse, even on the English turf.' Isabelle explained. 'You have entered Precipitation for the Derby. Keep him in full training and he will win.'

Gabrielle was puzzled. Isabelle, it is difficult for me to understand.'

'You do not have to. You will learn much within the next week or two!' Isabelle promised.

It was late when they departed their separate ways. On the way back to Dover by car, Gabrielle still pondered her conversation with Isabelle.

One week later Gabrielle received devastating news from Paris TSF that Ebony had to be scratched from the list of

Derby entries, due to suspected lameness in one of his hind legs.

'*Desolé, chère Isabelle,*' Gabrielle commiserated on the telephone to Oakfield Lodge.

'It is not quite so serious. Nevertheless, the vet people have advised caution if our aim is long term, so we decided to take no risks. Indeed Ebony may have won at great cost against your Precipitation, fully extended, as the Americans put it. So we decided that his next race will be the Queen Mary Stakes at Royal Ascot in June, with all the Derby runners, yours included.'

'So be it, Isabelle. Hopefully Precipitation will be able to give a good account of himself against Ebony at Royal Ascot, which will be out next greatest challenge within the near future.'

'Meanwhile, it seems to me that the Derby is open for you, Gabrielle. In fact, you will see me there. Good luck. This is incidentally what was meant by my reminder that it is not whether you win or lose in this world, it is how you play the game that counts!'

'Dearest Isabelle, you are wonderful, how right you are.'

27

Lucie stayed the night at Oakfield Lodge before leaving with Isabelle for Florence in order to meet the eighty-year- old cousin in the grand villa.

Countess Orlando was a large, imperious woman and welcomed the travellers with affection. Indeed, thought Isabelle, this establishment needs many hands to run it.

'You are most welcome, Lady Cameron. Or may I call you Miss Isabelle, like Lucie? The Roman Catholic Church has kept me informed about your village Winkfield, and in particular about the care for Lucie which you and your friends have bestowed upon her during the last twenty years. It is not easy for me to express my appreciation. Lucie has grown up to be a lovely young girl now a student at Cambridge University. Presumably, Miss Isabelle, it is an approved institution for young and inexperienced young ladies of high-born elegance.'

'Undoubtedly Contessa.' Isabelle smiled about the words 'approved institution' for Cambridge. 'Indeed, Contessa, it is renowned throughout England as having amongst the highest standards of learning and culture, but not perhaps of the elegance of the Sorbonne.

'Most happy to hear you confirm that Miss Isabelle. Marcos, my personal assistant, will give you both a conducted tour of the town's attractions.'

This lasted until late that evening. Isabelle and Lucie were impressed. Lucie, in fact, was revered for her charm and position by several of the managers of the estate. Her knowledge of Italian seemed now to flow like a waterfall and Isabelle was happy for her.

The next day, after the many signatures were appended to all the documents supplied by the bank and the lawyers, Lucie, upon reaching the age of twenty-one, was to become the proprietor of the estate, valued at £2.75 million. She was introduced to the general manager of the estate, who urged her to visit the vineyards at least once every three months, with her special friend Isabelle.

'It must have taken a long time to develop such a fruitful area for the vines, Contessa.'

'True, but we need another half a million pounds to extend further. This represents the profit from the last year's crop tax paid. In fact, the yield was a record due to exceptional weather conditions.'

'Well?'

'We need the signature of Lucie to implement it.'

'Not to worry, Contessa. If you have the documents ready tomorrow before our departure, together with the approval of the Italian legal advisers of Lucie's. There will be no problem.'

All the necessary signatures were appended that night.

The next day Lucie and Isabelle departed for London, with the valuable document which established that Lucie was the sole owner of the estate.

They arrived back at Oakfield Lodge at six. Lucie was urged to stay, but she insisted that her mother would be upset not to see her for a little while before the dinner reception, specially prepared by Mrs Plant for her, in company with Reverend Manning, Roger, John and Milly, under Isabelle's direction.

The vicar was full of warmth. 'Although Roman Catholic, you will always be welcome to our humble services at St Mary's, dear Lucie.'

'Thank you very much, Reverend Manning. St Mary's will always be my private place of worship, since the nearest Roman Catholic church is seven miles away in Windsor.

Only one regret Reverend Manning.' Lucie blushed and hesitated.

'Well, my child.'

Lucie continued. 'It is difficult for me not to be indiscreet.'

'Try to tell me your problem in simple terms.'

Isabelle asked whether she preferred the subject to be revealed in private.

'Oh no Isabelle, you are all so kind. It will make me

happy to reveal my request to everyone, in order to establish whether as a Roman Catholic there is any objection.'

'Please continue, Lucie,' urged Reverend Manning.

Lucie blushed. 'Do hope no one will be offended sir.'

'Well?' encouraged Isabelle.

'It is a question simply of the Lady chapel at St Mary's. With my new income from the inheritance in Italy, together with guidance from Reverend Manning, will it be possible to make the Lady chapel a truly lovely place of worship for all denominations without upsetting the ecclesiastical requirements of the Church of England, and provide all the capital expenditure and funds for its indefinite upkeep?'

'A lovely gesture,' responded Reverend Manning. 'There will be no problem, but I will send a note of recommendation to the ecclesiastic authorities in the local diocese, with a request for their urgent confirmation. Bless you, this calls for celebration,' he added.

'How right, Reverend Manning,' responded Roger. 'Fortunately a few bottles of Veuve Clicquot have already been placed in readiness for this occasion.'

Trust Roger, thought Isabelle.

A splendid welcome-back home dinner party took place.

Lucie was so pleased and had explained to her mother that she would be a little late as she had been invited to dine at the lodge, with Reverend Manning in attendance. Her mother requested, 'In that case my darling, give me five minutes.'

Mrs Arnold returned with a jewelled tiara for Lucie's lovely Italian head of black curly hair and a diamond necklace. With her new frock bought in Cambridge she looked fully qualified to be seated with the vicar at the Lodge, her mother thought.

When she returned to the Lodge, after a deep curtsey to Isabelle and Reverend Manning, Lucie explained, 'My mother asked me to wear these old family jewels in honour of your kind invitation.'

Isabelle was surprised and moved. 'Lucie, they are fabulous – real diamonds, presumably, true old-Italian style.' She gave a warm hug to Lucie.

'You surprise me, Isabelle. At the cottage we always thought that they were glass imitations.'

Reverend Manning examined the necklace. 'Do explain to your mother, that this jewellery is worth a fortune. It ought to be kept in a bank.'

'Yes, sir. My mother simply thought that it was such a good occasion to show them.'

'Quite right, Lucie,' added Roger.

Milly added, 'They are gorgeous. This is the first time I have set my eyes on real diamonds.'

'It is the same for me. My mother only unearthed them for me tonight. She said that this was the occasion to display them.'

Later during the evening the vicar revealed to Isabelle their value. 'It is important to explain to Mrs Arnold that these jewels are valuable, my estimate is a quarter of a million pounds!'

Isabelle was thunderstruck. 'Surely, Reverend Manning, Lucie thought that they were only ornaments to be worn at a party.'

'Believe me, my knowledge of diamonds is not elementary. These are fine-cut Amsterdam stones of long ago – evidently emanating from an ancient family in Italy.'

'So what do you advise?'

'Into the bank tomorrow, as soon as possible. Indeed, in spite of losing her parents during the war, she is a well-blessed child. A brilliant intellect plus a rich inheritance is a base from which she is well endowed.'

The Derby season approached. It was the second week of May. There had been no rain since the Two Thousand Guineas mid-April, and the chalky surface of the well-worn Epsom track was becoming hard, in fact the weathermen prophesied clear sunny periods for the following ten days, and firm to hard going on the course.

The night before the Derby acceptance date, a meeting took place, in Mrs Milligan's famous kitchen, between Isabelle, her trainer George Marshall the Vicar and Milligan.

'So, you agree, Isabelle, that we ought to cancel Ebony in view of the going,' Marshall began.

'Indeed yes, George,' Isabelle agreed. 'Ebony must be ready for Royal Ascot and the Ledger at Doncaster, together with the Arc de Triomphe at Longchamp in August, subject to going conditions.'

Milligan remonstrated. 'That means forgoing a possible cash prize for the Derby.'

'True, Milligan – at the risk of possible harm to his sinews, limbs and tendons on the hard ground, and consequent failure to compete at Royal Ascot Longchamp and Doncaster. With far greater prize money, quite apart from the stud fees.'

The Derby cancellation caused a sensation in the racing press of Europe on the Thursday.

From Paris, Gabrielle called. 'Isabelle, my dear, the racing world of Paris is convinced that "les Anglais" have cold feet and do not wish to compete with my Precipitation in the Derby in ten days' time.'

'It is true, dear Gabrielle, the consensus of opinion chez moi in London is in agreement with your friends in Paris, but for reasons not quite understood either in Paris nor in London.'

'You puzzle me. Is it a question of an Irish bomb?'

'No, Gabrielle, it is a question of the weather.'

'Is the ground too muddy at Epsom?'

'On the contrary it would encourage me if it was.'

'Well, then, Isabelle dear, the reason?'

'You seem to have forgotten the remarks made by your trainer quite recently about the unknown factors in the past, during the competition between your thoroughbred the Cobler and my Hurry-On,' Isabelle responded. 'The reason is simply that the going is at present too hard for Ebony. We need good to soft going for the ideal conditions.'

'*Cela me dépasse,* chère Isabelle.'

'Nevertheless, Gabrielle, our decision ought to give you and your friends in Paris a lot of encouragement.'

'Still, what a pity, we cannot measure ourselves in this important contest, so often rivals in the past,' Gabrielle added. Hopefully our next contest will be the Queen Mary Stakes at Royal Ascot, where the course is regularly watered, in any case.

In fact the following day the ante-post price for Precipitation dropped to evens, in an anticipated field of thirty-five runners, three of whom were unbeaten.

As usual Gabrielle was invited with her husband to stay at Oakfield Lodge for the Epsom event.

She arrived with her twins plus nanny on the Monday of Epsom week. The BMW with Hunt met them at Heathrow. At six pm that evening there was pandemonium in the nursery, with two sets of twins claiming attention from all and sundry at their feeding time. And there was a merry nursery party before the little ones were safely ensconced in four beds, next to one another. Isabelle looked preoccupied, her eyes were moist.

'*Qu'est-ce qu'il se passe,* Isabelle?'

'It is simply that, as you say in France, *Les années passent trop vite.*'

Gabrielle gave her an affectionate hug.

'What a lovely picture to see all the four little ones sleeping, content with their day's lot,' Isabelle commented, as, they settled down to an evening talk with Veuve Clicquot before the arrival of Milly and Roger from London. Gabrielle's husband was not due to arrive until Tuesday night, the day before the Derby.

Both Roger and Milly gave an affectionate welcome to Gabrielle, who congratulated them upon their engagement.

Gabrielle asked Milly, 'You are prepared to consider several months of absence from your future husband, when he is in Nigeria?'

'They say that absence makes the heart grow fonder,' Milly answered.

How right she was, thought Isabelle, Daddy even at eighty-five, spends eight months each year in that Lagos oven, soon her brother and now Richard her husband would too.

Milly continued, 'Perhaps it will be more of a question of what the Lord asks of us. Engineering expertise is still at a premium in Nigeria, and it is quite evident to me, only recently a resident in this lovely home, that privilege is indeed responsibility, noblesse oblige. For example, not long ago it came to my ears how Leon solved three local

Nigerian boiler factory problems from his bed in the Hospital for Tropical Diseases in London after arriving from Lagos, seriously ill with malignant tertian malaria, a killer disease responsible for half a million deaths in Nigeria annually. His chief Nigerian assistant Shegu, a six foot six Yoruba man, came from Lagos to London and two weeks later as Leon's fever came under control by intensive care Shegu was met by Isabelle and Roger. They went straight to his hospital bed, where the engineering problems were all resolved.'

'Richard was there also,' added Isabelle. All within the half-hour permitted by the sister in charge of the intensive care unit.'

'Later,' continued Milly, 'Shegu was pressed hard by us all to stay the night at the Lodge. His answer was simple and to the point, to Isabelle he said "Mistress Isabelle, our work is in the Lord's time in Nigeria. Our expatriates like Leon are so precious. He left for Heathrow airport – after not even twelve hours in London".'

Isabelle dabbed her eyes. She was overflowing with emotion for Leon her brother and also for that gallant Yoruba, Shegu! No wonder Daddy loves his Nigerian,' she thought.

'It is true,' added Isabelle, 'they were dramatic moments. Three factories in Nigeria had boiler problems. NTC (Zaria, North Nigeria, BAT group), Lever Brothers at Agbara, South West Nigeria, and Cadburys, Lagos. It surprised me after his setbacks that Leon ever wanted to return to that fever-infested equatorial part of West Africa. That night Shegu arrived back at Lagos Airport with all his technical answers, as confirmed a few weeks later by Telex from the Lagos office.'

'What a dynamic family Isabelle, with such a responsible overseas connection in Black Africa,' Gabrielle commented.

'Hence, the reason for Milly's remarks about privilege being responsibility.'

'And how right,' responded Roger, who had been listening throughout.

Derby day arrived with a cold, dry north wind. The going

remained firm to hard. At seven-thirty, as usual, Milly and Roger left for Datchet in the little two-seater Ford, to catch the fast local train to Paddington. They noticed excitement in the air everywhere about the Derby; in fact, hundreds of Londoners in coaches, hired lorries, ancient private cars fifty years old, and dozens of London trains displaying the notice EPSOM.

As Hunt, the Oakfield Lodge chauffeur drove Isabelle, Gabrielle and Daniel in the BMW, Gabrielle remarked, 'Everyone seems to be going our way.'

'*Sporting Life* estimate at least 150,000 visitors today,' Isabelle said. 'The course will be bathed in full sunshine, in spite of the chill north wind which is stimulating, to say the least.'

As they passed through the security barriers Gabrielle who was dressed for the occasion in true Parisian style appropriately, caused quite a stir. 'The owner of the favourite, and what a lovely woman!' Indeed, both Isabelle and Gabrielle were both in their prime, beautiful women, even as mothers.

She turned to Isabelle, 'Please be my guide during all circumstances, win or lose, as you say in English.'

'Do not worry,' Isabelle reassured her. 'First of all we will enjoy a glass of champagne with Daniel and your trainer, Monsieur Dupont.'

It was in the paddock where they met Milligan, 'Delighted to meet you again Monsieur Milligan. Since your unbeaten Ebony will not be competing, are you able to give me some course hints about Precipitation?'

'Indeed yes, monsieur, Ask your jockey to keep on the outside, especially before Tattenham Corner, the mile post of this one and a half mile race. He will then win monsieur by twenty lengths!'

'This is most encouraging advice. Bless you.'

Indeed Precipitation attracted much notice in the paddock during the parade. Both Milligan and Isabelle were impressed by its size and width of shoulder.

A fine Normandy thoroughbred, Madame,' her trainer remarked to Isabelle.

'At least, Miss Isabelle, the course at Royal Ascot will be watered,' commented Milligan.

The runners, now thirty-four, cantered down to the tapes, up on the hill. Two unbeaten Italian entries were included.

Both Milligan and the vicar were invited to join Isabelle in her box.

'This is a great pleasure, Gabrielle, to see you and Daniel again,' responded the vicar. 'And my congratulations about the arrival of the twins, it seems a boy and a girl, identical ages to those born to Isabelle. How blessed you are!'

'So kind of you, Reverend Manning, to still think of us in your lovely village of Winkfield.'

Then the race began.

At least fifteen runners are all in the lead at the half-mile post including the favourite, Precipitation,' said the commentator. As they approach Tattenham Corner the favourite on the inside risks being boxed in by several runners in front of him unless he makes his challenge now.'

How very true, Gabrielle thought, observing that Milligan's advice had not been taken. Now luck was necessary. It meant slowing down Precipitation to emerge from behind the field and then crossing to the outside, at least two lengths' loss of distance during this fast pace – a serious penalty for not heeding advice given. Hope was lost in the stands. Gabrielle sought Isabelle's hand with a tear in her eyes. 'We have lost, Isabelle, boxed in as you say in English!'

'Not quite,' Isabelle responded. '*Courage*, as you say in French. Look, Precipitation has extricated himself from the box and is now racing for his life.'

There was half a mile to go. Precipitation excelled himself in front of a vast audience. Little by little he gained on the field then it was a question of the two Italian leaders five lengths ahead. Half a furlong to go and he was half a length behind the Italians and fully extended. The pace was still very fast as three runners approached the winning-post. The result was a photo finish. After a short interval Precipitation was announced as the winner by a short head. Gabrielle fainted but she recovered soon, however, with the help of Reverend Manning's smelling salts.

'Gabrielle, you have won, this is no time to faint,' Isabelle encouraged her. 'As owner you will be requested to lead in Precipitation at the paddock as the Derby winner in front of all the reporters and photographers.'

'Will you come with me?' Gabrielle asked.

'Of course, leave the press to me.' So with Daniel, Reverend Manning, Milligan, Isabelle led her friend to the paddock.

The trainer was most apologetic. 'Very sorry madame, our rider, an able young French jockey, misunderstood the instructions kindly offered by my friend Milligan, your bailiff at the Lodge.'

'Nevertheless,' interrupted the vicar, 'the win must have been convincing because the off-course betting price for the Queen Mary Stakes at Royal Ascot on 20 June has just been quoted at two to one with Ebony second favourite at seven to one!'

A great cheer went up as Gabrielle led in Precipitation. The chief steward of the course, Sir James Monkton, was the first to receive Gabrielle.

'*Felicitations*, madame, It was a close result. May you continue to grace our English race course. We enjoy competition. Your friend Lady Cameron is a competitor, it seems, and yet evidently you are intimate friends.' Turning to Isabelle, he added, 'It is always a thrill for the public, Lady Cameron, to see those Irish colours of yours at Royal Ascot. Presumably you will each be competing in the Queen Mary Stakes?'

'Yes indeed, Sir James.'

'How very right, Lady Cameron, as it should be a friendly international competition it is often also a great opportunity to resolve mutual political problems. To conclude, Lady Cameron, when may we see again your husband Sir Richard at the Albert Hall?'

'He will be back from Lagos in October, Sir James, perhaps in time for action at the Albert Hall.'

The press was then allowed to take over, and to ask questions, and after a merry half-hour Gabrielle was introduced to dozens of race-goers. Several members of the press asked Gabrielle the name of her tailor or haute couturier, for she was dressed with typical French elegance and style. Isabelle interrupted, 'The answer to that question, gentlemen, is left to your imagination. As you know, it is indiscreet for my friend to reveal in public the answers to your question on that subject.'

Just before Gabrielle and Daniel Faure retired to their room at the Lodge after dining that night, Gabrielle took Isabelle aside.

'Just a quiet thought,' she said. 'My jockey told our trainer that in his opinion the going was not so hard as he was led to expect; in fact, it seemed in some places quite yielding.'

'Really?' responded Isabelle. 'During Royal Ascot, at least it will be good to yielding.' Then she added with a special smile, 'You won, my dear, and that is what counts. Are you happy?'

'Of course,'

Isabelle gave her an affectionate good night kiss.

Back in Mrs Milligan's kitchen, many questions were asked.

'Did you record the time?' Mr Marshall asked Milligan.

'Very fast for the Derby. Remember, however, that the ground was estimated as firm to hard.'

The vicar interupted, 'So now, Isabelle – she had just arrived from the Lodge – 'how do you rate your chance with Ebony for the Queen Mary Stakes in three weeks' time?'

'Precipitation is fast, sir, beautifully built, a true thoroughbred roan from Normandy. It was not handled to advantage around Tattenham Corner, otherwise he would have won by twenty lengths. He is in a class by himself, Reverend Manning.'

'So is Ebony, Isabelle,' interrupted George Marshall the trainer. 'Indeed, it will be a fascinating contest. The Queen Mary Stakes is over the same distance as the Derby, with all the Derby runners, as usual, included.'

Isabelle retired late that night to the Lodge. The visitors were in bed fast asleep. Her prayers, as usual, were said next to the bed of her brother Roger at midnight. He did not wake up. She sat by his window, and thought about the emotions of the day. The news from Richard in Lagos that he would be back for Royal Ascot. The two sets of twins happy in their innocence. It had been a happy dinner-party and Gabrielle had won the Derby. She continued to sit with so many thoughts, on the open window ledge. What a fabulous world, she thought, yet there seems to be so little time for it to stop turning even just to savour the presence of these lovely moments, for example, Richard the bread-winner in Lagos, Roger my charge since Mummy passed away, Milly, with wonderful prospects for Roger, and Daddy still going strong at eighty-six in Lagos, the master. No, thought Isabelle time does not stop for those blissful moments, but at least they can be treasured and remembered.

With that she left Roger's room and went to say goodnight to Milly, who was reading in bed.

'After your long day at Epsom with your friends, Isabelle, don't you think that it is time for sleep?'

'True, but what a wonderful summer night. Expectancy is all around in the farm, the garden and the fields. The wind has changed, soft warm with a much higher humidity, from the south. No longer the harsh north-easter of Epsom. Growth is the order of the day, rain is in the air. Hurry-On in the stables was stamping his feet ten minutes ago, a sure sign of warm rain to come soon after this six weeks of the dry wind. Is all still well with that brother of mine?'

'Indeed. Tonight on the way home in the train to Datchet he asked me to think of an appropriate day for the announcement of our engagement.'

'Dearest Milly, that is wonderful news.' She gave Milly a warm hug. 'In that case you ought to be asleep by now.'

'That is just the point, sleep will not come. Someone once told me that marriage is a serious business.'

'Good, in that case the solution to the problem is simple. We will celebrate the occasion with half a bottle of Veuve Clicquot now. Do you agree?'

'Yes indeed, that should settle my emotions and my mind.'

'Why the mind?'

'Because, dear Isabelle, the male body at my twenty-three years of age is totally unknown to me.'

'Dear Milly, such a lovely young maiden still a virgin in this wide world. That is gorgeous and indeed deserve a midnight celebration,' thought Isabelle. 'Give me ten minutes,' she said aloud.

Ten minutes later Isabelle arrived with the half bottle and two slices of pâté de foie-gras and brown bread.

'Dearest Milly, I'm so very pleased for you. But without a father or mother, upon whom are you counting for marital advice?'

'Give me your hand, Isabelle. The answer to that question is you! My only hope left to me under the circumstances.'

'Bless you, Milly you may count upon me one hundred percent.'

Milly's eyes were full of tears.

'No problem?' Isabelle asked.

'Perhaps it is the champagne, or perhaps simply to express my gratitude for your great kindness to me. Your house if my fabulous gift from God in Heaven after the death of my dear parents in the air crash ten years ago.'

'So, from now no more worries. If there are, refer them all, repeat all, to me. They will be resolved one time – as they say in Lagos!'

With that encouragement Milly was soon asleep as Isabelle with a heart full of song left the bedroom with the tray for the kitchen.

28

Isabelle never slept long. It was very early morning, five am. The air was coming in her bedroom window soft and warm. The urge was strong, so clad only in her nightdress, she mounted Hurry-On, who was stamping his feet with impatience. Her hair flowed behind her like, a true Amazon warrior, she thought.

Indeed, she was in another world on Hurry-On, racing fast through the lovely sleepy countryside on this June morning. She felt completely elated as the trees, brooks, hedgerows, and the gorgeous misty early dawn unfolded. Darling Richard, she murmured, my body needs you, do come home soon. Hurry-On raced on at speed. He knew that his mistress was troubled in spirit, so he raced like the wind. On and on they raced. 'Faster, my darling.' Hurry-On had loved that call from his mistress for more speed ever since winning the Gold Cup at Royal Ascot. They arrived at the point of no return, John's Cottage. He happened to be up in the garden, an early starter, and she was about to return to the Lodge.

'Isabelle,' he ejaculated. 'Don't you think that this is tempting providence, mounted on that giant stallion in your nightdress like a goddess from the woods?'

'You are right. Early this morning it was the passion in me. Last night Milly and Roger made known that they are to be formally engaged. So straight from bed in the soft dawn air, in my nightdress, the urge was so strong to mount Hurry-On, who was waiting for me with impatience. He is now satisfied, because he has been ridden hard for the last twenty minutes and all is well in the world of nature and in Heaven.'

'At this time in the morning, don't you think that you are taking a great risk attracting undesirable attention, as a young mother with twins?'

'No, John, to feel the soft wind going through my body on this giant stallion was like Heaven, as we raced through the falling dew and the awakening countryside, with all its fabulous wild-flower scents. Not inviting providence but experiencing a little of nature's delight; God-given from Heaven with His angels close by!'

'John asked, 'Can you be persuaded to descend from that giant stallion, accept a large cup of milk and coffee, and become earthbound for perhaps five minutes with me on the veranda – with my best dressing-gown to cover your prominent contours!'

The coffee and milk were soon forthcoming.

'Is it not a wonderful moment, so early in the morning, with the advent of summer to share a cup of coffee in all innocence from the outside world, in this lovely garden!' Isabelle enthused.

'Perhaps, but suppose the Bishop appears at any moment,' John smiled. 'Nevertheless, will you promise me to be prudent in future? After all a lady in her nightdress on a giant stallion is an explosive attraction to the most worthy Christian! Even a bishop.'

'No problem John. It takes lovable friends like you to bring me back to Earth, especially during this exquisite moment, early dawn, as the birds begin their June-time chorus.'

John looked at his watch. 'It is not easy for me to break this enchanting spell, but before the early communion service, your counsel is invited upon my problem about Lucie. There is competition, as expected. Lucie is not only a brilliant pianist, she attracts attention also from both young dons and undergraduates in particular by those who struggle with their studies in music and Italian. Whatever the problem, the sister in charge confirms that Lucie remains full of charm and grace, always so anxious to help and advise the less fortunate.'

'Well, that is indeed most commendable. So what is your immediate strategy in order to win the hand of this Italian goddess?' Isabelle asked.

'A good question. Every two weeks, Roger lends me the little car in order to take messages and parcels of home-made cakes for Lucie. This gives me a passport to Lucie and her activities.'

'So, you make progress.'

'True, Isabelle, but now we have to be prudent. The Bishop is staying with Reverend Manning and from this veranda we have only a hundred yards of road to warn us of any approach.'

Isabelle was enjoying herself. 'Do not worry, John. If they unfrock you, they will have to extract me from the railings at Downing Street. So, the next problem.'

'Dear Isabelle, this is confidential and intimate. May it be so between us?'

'Of course, John.'

'Good. Lucie is a Roman Catholic. I am Senior Assistant to Reverend Manning, a strict Church of England Priest. How will it be possible for me to reconcile my love for Lucie with the problems between the Roman Catholics in Rome and my church, the Church of England.'

'Do not worry, John. My response must be given later, for there is activity a hundred yards from your door.'

Hurry-On was summoned. The silk dressing-gown was returned to John. Isabelle gave him a warm and an affectionate kiss.

When she arrived back at the farm, Milligan was not surprised to see Isabelle scantily dressed.

'Good morning, Miss. Fortunately a dry morning for your early venture.'

She smiled. 'Milligan, it was a fabulous venture racing with Hurry-On through the Heaven-sent summer at dawn, with all its abundant life blooming in the woods and lanes of Winkfield.'

'Perhaps, Miss, next time you may wish to leave a note on the gate of the lower field, just in case of accidents. My Labrador dog will soon trace you and the stallion.'

'Splendid idea, Milligan. You are always so helpful.'

'Meanwhile, Miss, the nightdress may perhaps prove to be irresistible to the young farm hands due soon for the milking period.'

'Of course, dear Milligan. Bless you.' With that she left for her room at the Lodge.

Life was gorgeous she thought, but she was concerned

for John, in particular for his anxiety about the conflicts in his mind over the prospect of union with Lucie, a Roman Catholic. What nonsense, she thought. Where there is true love, this subject ought to present no problems. She decided to make a rendez-vous the following morning at the same time by telephone.

'John Radcliff here. Who is speaking?'

'Isabelle here, John. Will be with you at the same time tomorrow in order to give you my opinion about your personal problem, as promised, properly dressed!'

'But dear Isabelle –'

'Must rush, John. The four twins are screaming for their breakfast. Bless you. Six am tomorrow with Hurry-On. Bye-bye.'

John thought, What a lass, as they say in Yorkshire.

That evening Reverend Manning came to dinner. Roger and Milly wanted to discuss their marriage plans. They had just returned from London and were still upstairs changing when the vicar arrived.

'It seems, Isabelle, you thrive on motherhood. How is Richard?'

'Very well, thank you, Reverend Manning. He is due back in December for three months and may accept another invitation to perform at the Albert Hall.'

'Hopefully you will invite me, in the event.'

'Of course. Before the others join us, may I ask your opinion upon a clerical issue? Suppose a Church of England curate falls in love with a Roman Catholic, a profound believer. In the event of converting upon marriage, would the curate be able to continue his practice?'

'There is no prospect for a curate converted to Rome continuing to practice under Church of England licence, this is the rule of the establishment where there must be rules. Nevertheless as a convert to Rome, for convenience to marriage, the curate would be able to find a situation within the local church in the UK, without problems, but not as a Church of England priest.'

'Sufficient, Reverend Manning, to support himself and his family?'

'There would be no problem about work, but whether enough money to support a family, it is not possible to say.'

'Thank you so much, Reverend Manning, for your advice.'

'Perhaps a useful service may be performed in order to establish the date and place where the young lady was baptised, which is usually undertaken during the christening.'

Isabelle then excused herself for about an hour during which Milly and Roger discussed engagement plans with the vicar.

Meanwhile from her bedroom she made a telephone call to Countess Orlando.

'So sorry to trouble you, Contessa. It is Isabelle speaking from Winkfield, England.'

'My dear Isabelle, it is always a pleasure to hear from you. What is the problem?'

'Have you any papers concerning the faith in which Lucie was baptised, or christened. Was there a formal ceremony?'

'I am afraid no such papers exist. Lucie was smuggled out of Florence in a wooden box covered with a blanket when she was a few months old on top of which was a cartload of potatoes. The cart was driven by me, pulled by a donkey. She was only a baby. Her birth certificate was written by the Italian doctor before we had to flee the Fascists when fighting in the streets was intense. Lucie's mother died at the age of twenty-eight, soon after Lucie was born, from pneumonia. Mrs Arnold who is well known to that incredible organization, the intelligence service of the Royal Navy. At that time little notice was taken of me dressed as a peasant driving a cart full of precious potatoes!'

'Thank you so much, Contessa. You have resolved my problem. Goodnight.'

Well, well, thought Isabelle. So Lucie has been reared as Roman Catholic in Windsor, still not yet baptised with any denomination. John will be interested. He was, at five-thirty am the next morning by appointment on the veranda with Isabelle in his new borrowed dressing gown, clad in her nightdress as before and her hair loose to her shoulders, at the assistant curate's cottage.

'Really Isabelle. You are always welcome, but your

presence scantily clad on this giant stallion is surely overdoing unconventionality and married with little twins to boot!'

'Agreed, John, but my news about Lucie is important. Besides a woman knows when she is safe! It seems dear John that your course of action is clear. You must win her hand, after that the clerical problems vanish.'

John was silent for a moment. 'This is most encouraging news. With the loan of Milligan's car, Lucie will see me again on Saturday. Bless you, dear Isabelle.'

After a hot bowl of coffee, Isabelle departed for the Lodge.

This was Heaven, she thought. Indeed she was tempted even to take off her nightdress, and did so, during the half-hour return to the Lodge, so soft was the wind through her breasts and body and so uplifting, and local nature was so stimulating. It was like magic, she felt exultant as if in another spirit life, enclosed within the world of nature; even the birds and the bees joined in – and Hurry-On was in his element. Fortunately prudence prevailed and she re-robed, as she noticed one of the farm men in the upper meadow. Milligan as usual was watching out for her.

'Hurry-On seems to be happy, Miss. Evidently he has been exercised, fully extended.'

Isabelle smiled. 'Right Milligan, we raced home. It was gorgeous. Do excuse me for my informal attire but that outing was unforgettable. Heaven sent!'

'Dear Miss Isabelle, you are known to me from a tiny tot in bare feet on the farm. But please take care. My Labrador has been alerted in case of problems during these early rides, scantily attired!'

'Bless you Milligan.'

Soon after breakfast Isabelle made tracks to Mrs Arnold's cottage. Isabelle wasted no time in asking if Lucie had been baptised a Roman Catholic.

'No, Miss Isabelle,' Mrs Arnold replied. 'Soon after her mother's death, without other relatives her cousin applied to me to be her foster-mother – all expenses paid until the age of twenty-one. She went to the local village school until the age of nine. The cousin followed her progress closely and asked me to apply to Windsor High School, to which already she had written concerning Lucie. Naturally Lucie was accepted unconditionally. As time passed, however, I noticed that Lucie had acquired various prints of the Holy Virgin Mary. She was also keen on the Lady chapel of St Mary's. It seems therefore, Miss Isabelle, that the subject of denomination has never been raised. Is it important?'

Isabelle was embarrassed. 'Not immediately, Mrs Arnold, but perhaps later. Please do not worry Mrs Arnold. What about this suggestion. Let me drive you to see her at Cambridge. We can go to church together, after inspecting the College, and then return.'

Mrs Arnold took both Isabelle's hands. 'That would make my life wonderful, Miss Isabelle. Lucie is all my love in this world.'

John was also invited on the expedition. It was a memorable occasion, and a great success.

Mrs Arnold was intrigued with Lucie's domestic welfare at Girton. 'What a fabulous institution – all owing to the care given by the Royal Navy!' she exclaimed.

As Royal Ascot approached Mrs Milligan's kitchen hummed with excitement. Trainers, jockeys and even a few bookies were always welcome, especially about the Marshall stable. Nothing was ever given away. Indeed it was not necessary, except that several enquiries were made about the entries from Ireland, from the Buchanan stable, the notorious blue and green colours on the course.

One of the visitors was George, the local policeman.

'Mrs Milligan,' he began, it says in the *Sporting Life* that your friend Mr Buchanan has three entries for the Royal Ascot meeting.'

'Well, George, what is the problem?' responded Mrs Milligan.

'For example, in the Coventry Stakes for two-year-olds, he has an entry, Catch Me, which has never been out, not even run in the Epsom Downs Stakes for two-year-olds. Also,' continued George, 'at the same meeting in the Wokingham Stakes, our friend's entry Thunder is not run since a three-year-old, when he had an impressive record of wins. Finally, his famous stallion Hurricane, now a six-year-old, who dead-heated for second place with the

Cobler when your Hurry-On was the Gold Cup winner, is entered now for the Hunt Cup, claimed to be the fastest seven-furlong race in Europe. Hurricane is the two to one favourite. Why the low price when he has not run this year and with forty-one runners to boot?'

'Evidently you study the market,' Mrs Milligan responded. 'When Paddy Buchanan arrives next week, you will be invited to attend the discussion here.'

When Isabelle returned to the Lodge she sat by the open window. Richard's Labrador somehow had managed to find his way in and was seated quietly by her side.

'Dante, you are gorgeous, but be very quiet please,' she told him. He was, and as usual most affectionate.

What a wonderful world, she thought, in spite of all its man-made problems.

Royal Ascot was approaching. It was not just a race meeting, it was a fabulous gathering for race-goers from all over the world.

Before retiring she went to see Hurry-On and Onward in the stables this warm June night. Onward was restless, sensing the damp wind. Isabelle, clad only in her nightdress felt tiny spots of rain. Likewise Hurry-On stamped his feet. Isabelle felt the moist air. Gabrielle, she thought, will be worried about Precipitation and competition from Ebony for the Queen Mary Stakes.

As she sat on the lower part of the stable door, some strange thoughts seemed to flow through her sensitive spirit, as the tiny spots of cool rain touched her cheeks, driven by a high humid wind from the south. The scent from the flowers in the garden was intoxicating, the moon was bright as the light weight clouds raced across it, and she allowed her motherly thoughts to rip without control as the wind fanned her lovely breasts and body. Isabelle was at all times spiritually aware and profoundly responsive to the strange moods, such as the one now into which she seemed to be drifting.

During the following week there was much excitement about Royal Ascot. Sunday night late there was the usual meeting in Mrs Milligan's kitchen. Many friends were present including George Waldron. Mrs Milligan was on the phone to Mr Buchanan in Ireland.

'It seems Mavoreen that you are well informed. Firstly my compliments to George. In due course he will know all the answers after the final trials at the stud farm here in Ireland. Meanwhile, Lydia has proved her ability to master our giant stallion sprinters.'

The steady rain had set in, day after day, since Isabelle had visited Hurry-On at one am in his stable last week.

Reverend Manning addressed George Marshall, the local trainers, 'The turn of the weather must make a difference to the form for the race programme at Royal Ascot, George.'

'It does indeed, sir. It is reflected also in the ante-post prices of the bookmakers. For example Precipitation, Hot favourite for the Queen Mary Stakes at two to one after his win in the Derby, has gone down now to four to one, still favourite, and Ebony on the other hand was quoted today by the famous bookmakers, Pickersgrill, at five to one from ten to one a week ago.'

'Why George,' responded Reverend Manning, 'Ebony has not run since the Two Thousand Guineas race at Newmarket in April.'

'True, Reverend Manning, but what a performance! The bookmakers are shrewd fellows! Then the going was good, not hard.'

A week later Isabelle received news that Richard was unable to return to the UK for the Royal Ascot meeting, due to exceptional developments for the installation of industrial boiler plants with the Nigeria National Petroleum Corporation in Port Harcourt, Southern Nigeria. The Ascot weekend arrived at last and the wife of George the local policeman was most anxious to visit Mrs Milligan's kitchen, where she was sure to receive a few hints about the Buchanan stable.

It was Saturday evening and many were gathered therein. Milligan addressed the vicar.

'It seems, sir, that the confirmation notice from the Buchanan stable must have missed the *Sporting Life* late news yesterday. However, a call from Ireland at midnight confirmed that all entrants had been accepted the same day for Royal Ascot to start Tuesday next week.'

A shout of approval greeted this intelligence. 'This is good news, Miligan,' responded the vicar. 'Have you an indication of his programme?'

'Yes sir it is highly confidential at this stage, for the bookmakers are completely in the dark, and most anxious to learn which entries are only trying or really out to win.'

'Except,' retorted Mrs Milligan 'the whole racing world is well aware that the Buchanan stable never sends a contender to Royal Ascot without it has a good chance to win.'

'Bless him,' said George's wife.

'To be serious,' interrupted George Marshall director of the local stable at Winkfield. 'Do you know how many stallions Mr Buchanan will require me to lodge during the meeting?'

'Yes, four at least,' responded Milligan.

'Splendid. Which events do you feel he will be trying?'

The bailiff hesitated. 'The answer to that question is not yet clear, Mr Marshall. However, take the Tuesday event the six furlong spring for two year-olds, the Coventry Stakes. His entry, Catch Me has never been out. We know nothing of its early history or the home trials. Secondly, he has an entry known as Thunder for the Wokingham Stakes, another six-furlong race, a handicap for all ages. Thunder has not run since a three-year-old when he never lost a race throughout the season before going lame, that was two years ago. Then his stallion Hurricane, entered for the Hunt Cup, a seven-furlong race for all ages – as you will remember he was second to Hurry-On for the Gold Cup, now trained to compete at a much shorter distance. Finally there is another entry Mickey Mouse for the King Stand Stakes on the Friday, a six-year-old not run for two years, exceptional sprinter as a three-year-old, never run since. Why? Nobody knows.'

George's wife interrupted. 'Thank you so much, Milligan, how very like him. Mickey Mouse was quoted at fifty to one yesterday.'

'How true,' said Mrs Marshall. 'He was fifty to one today also.'

Mrs Milligan commented, 'It will surprise me, Miss

Isabelle, if they do not lock him up after this meeting.'

'Do not worry, Mrs Milligan, our partner is a particularly shrewd Irish trainer, a specialist for producing long-priced winners at Royal Ascot, always bidding against the challengers of the racing world, and to please the ladies!'

The happy gathering began to break up and the rains never ceased. As the French visitors often remarked, 'Came the rains, at Royal Ascot!'

It was Sunday night, late, Roger her brother was fast asleep after a busy day at Faraday House as Isabelle was sitting on the window frame of Roger's bedroom, after another convivial gathering at the kitchen of Mrs Milligan, where she learned that Mr Buchanan was due to arrive, possibly on Monday night for the Royal Ascot meeting.

Her thoughts were inspired. Gabrielle was due to arrive, also with the twins and her husband, tomorrow evening from Paris. The little cots for the twins were already installed next to the cots of her own twins in the intervening room between her bedroom and that to be occupied by Gabrielle and her husband Daniel.

Suddenly the red alarm showed upon Roger's desk, indicating a muted telephone outside call. Isabelle left for her own room to answer the call. It was eleven-thirty pm.

'So sorry to disturb you,' apologised John from his cottage, 'at this late hour. Is it possible for me to see you early tomorrow morning here at my cottage? Tuesday is the start of Royal Ascot and a small problem has developed which you may be able to resolve before the festivities.'

'Willingly, John, and in view of the fine warm rain you will find me suitably clad this time for the occasion.'

John smiled as he remembered when she arrived on Hurry-On only in her nightdress! 'Bless you Isabelle, good night.'

It must be a problem about Lucie, she thought on the way to her bedroom.

After a gorgeous sleep from which the alarm clock deprived her of further bliss dreaming about Richard, she mounted Hurry-On at six am. The fine rain continued as she raced through the meadows and the country paths across the fields. She loved the rain and the warm wind, just like Hurry-On, who was in his element. John was waiting for her with a hot pot of coffee on the veranda, sheltered from the rain, as Hurry-On arrived, ridden fast from Oakfield Lodge, steaming all over.

'So kind of you to call, Isabelle. My mind needs a lot of unloading from the uncertainties about my future course through this life. Without sister, mother, sister-in-law or others my instincts have gravitated towards you for guidance.'

'Well John, what is the principal problem? Is it Lucie?'

'Lucie is only a part of my problem, the second part.'

'And the first?'

'This is the difficult part, Isabelle. My soul seems to be on fire. There are many conflicts within my mind about our institutionalized church systems. It is not responding to the needs of the day, or perhaps it's me who is at fault, like so many ordinary people who seem to be searching or craving for guidance. I remain at a kind of spiritual standstill or bewilderment at the current mismanagement of Church funds. Of course, it is neccessary to have an established Church in England – no problem there. After all, the law of the land is based upon the establishment. Isabelle, it is my intention if possible to go further, but it is difficult to know in what direction in order to be able to visit the sick, the handicapped, the old and the less privileged or distressed.'

'Commendable indeed, John. Why not?'

'Cash, Isabelle, is one of the principal problems, in consequence lack of independence for action.'

'One day, dear John our Lord will have a special assignment for you,' Isabelle encouraged him. 'Let us turn to the most practical issue of Lucie. Now for some news, John. Lucie has never been baptised. The formality has been overlooked. She was brought up in the Catholic school close to Windsor and it was assumed that she was a Roman Catholic. This news may interest her during your next visit to Cambridge.'

'Are you sure of this, Isabelle?'

'It was confirmed to me by Mrs Arnold. It was all due to her hurried escape from northern Italy as a child.'

'Thank you, Isabelle. This is news indeed.'

Soon afterwards Isabelle was racing back to Oakfield Lodge in fine rain.

The Royal Ascot meeting was to commence next day, and the informal meeting in the kitchen was attended by several members of the village, keenly interested to meet Paddy Buchanan, due about ten thirty pm from Northern Ireland.

Mrs Milligan explained,'It appears that he has five potential winners at the Royal Ascot meeting to start tommorrow. Lydia, who has been trained to mount his leading young sprinters entered for the Royal Ascot meeting, will be returning with him.'

Isabelle pondered the prospects. She had great affection for both her entries. Ebony for the Queen Mary Stakes – at which all the Derby entries were entered, including Precipitation the Derby winner, owned by her dear friend Gabrielle – and Onward, direct son of Hurry-On, entered for the King George VI Stakes, on the Thursday.

As usual she entered the kitchen of Mrs Milligan to find many local friends.

The door bell rang and a deep Irish ascent was heard throughout the hall 'Boyo!' This was the name which Mr Buchanan always gave to Milligan. Everyone knew it was the Irishman, but they did not expect to see Lydia looking a picture of health coming first into the kitchen.

'My child you have grown. Your mum will be happy to see you back at home,' said Mrs Milligan.

Then Buchanan gave an affectionate hug to Mrs Milligan, and the merry gathering continued.

Likewise Isabelle gave an affectionate hug to Lydia.

'Oh, Miss, what an experience!'

'My friends,' boomed Buchanan. 'First of all, your Lydia has been commissioned by me to mount my three entries at Royal Ascot in the races described as follows: The Coventry Stakes, five furlongs for two-year-olds, my entry is Catch Me. The Wokingham Stakes, six furlongs, all ages, my entry is Thunder. The Kingstand Stakes, five furlongs, considered by my French friends as the fastest five-furlong race for all ages, in the racing world, my entry is Mickey Mouse.

Lydia is well acquainted with all three runners, having

trained with them during the last four weeks in Northern Ireland. Lydia, my dear friends, has excelled herself, as a first-class mount for these giant stallions.'

Everyone clapped.

'Well done, Lydia,' said Isabelle with a fond kiss. 'Tomorrow you must renew your acquaintance with Ebony, who will be your mount for the Queen Mary Stakes on Wednesday.'

'Thank you, Miss, so much for your encouragement. Ebony is my only concern. So much has been heard of Precipitation, the Derby winner, it makes me a little anxious. He must be very fast.'

'My dear child,' urged Buchanan, 'so is Ebony.'

Every week from the Marshall Stables the reports about Ebony are the same, the fastest animal on four legs ever known over the $1^{1}/_{2}$ miles distance from this stable.' You have three days before the Queen Mary Stakes on Wednesday to reacquaint yourself with Ebony, to be raced fully extended on the local Marshall track, the result must be top secret.'

'Thank you, sir.' Milligan interrupted. 'How are you, George?' addressing George Marshall.

'Do not worry, Milligan, the guard dogs will be particularly vigilant this week.'

'Do you mean, Buchanan, that you are making a serious bid for all three races?'

'George,' interrupted Mrs Milligan, 'they will lock him up with bread and water before the end of the meeting!'

Buchanan continued, 'Isn't she gorgeous,' addressing her husband. 'With a lovely red-head like that, Boyo, it is a wonder that you ever go to sleep at night!'

Everyone laughed.

The vicar asked, 'Do you mean your chances are good for all three entries from Ireland, quite apart from the two from this stable, Mr Buchanan?'

'It is in my bones, Reverend Manning, they may win by a whisker, but they will win!'

'Incredible, Buchanan. How can you be so certain?'

'We had a little farm in North Ireland. As a boy it was my job to catch and break in the wild stallions from the moors. It was a fascination, sir, to catch and train those giant stallions. Then we started to breed them and to race them at point-to-points locally. It was a great success. Eventually we started to enter the more promising colts at the Royal Ascot meetings for high stakes, but all at high entry fees! We studied form. It paid off. We knew our stallions and they won high-valued prizes. The bookmakers were happy and so were the punters at Royal Ascot as the years went by.'

'Interesting, Mr Buchanan. In that case, your prospects and predictions will be followed by me with assiduous care.'

Isabelle was about to retire from the happy gathering.

'Are you well Miss?' Milligan asked Isabelle.

'Oh yes thank you, Milligan. A little sleepy after the early morning ride. It seems that your friend Buchanan is about to invade Royal Ascot.' He did.

29

With Tuesday came the Coventry Stakes. The build-up of smart cars, coaches, and elegant horse-drawn hansoms around Winkfield and Ascot at eleven am was dense. Racegoers from all over Europe converged on this famous international racing arena. As usual the traffic police excelled themselves.

Isabelle was always impressed by the Royal Ascot authorities and she marvelled at the thousands of visitors arriving in well-provided parking facilities on the grass with huge trees to shelter them from the sunlight or fine rain during picnics. Although the slight rain today was intermittent it was warm. Isabelle and Milly arranged a picnic near the car for her guests, instead of an inside restaurant. Large umbrellas were organized by Hunt the chauffeur. Gabrielle and Daniel Faure, the vicar, George, Milly, Isabelle and Roger all enjoyed the occasion as they exchanged notes with other picnic parties, in spite of the light rain.

Milly was thrilled as they passed through the entrance to the paddock. So many elegantly attired young ladies attracted her attention. Then in the paddock she met Catch Me, the two year old.

'Roger what a beauty,' she exclaimed.

Isabelle joined them, with Lydia.

'Isabelle, the combination of Lydia and Catch Me is irresistible and a part of my next week's salary will be invested on them today,' Milly added.

As the runners galloped down to the starting tapes, thirty-five entries in all, Reverend Manning remarked, 'Milligan, Catch Me is forty-five to one at Tattersalls. Why?'

'Because sir, he has not yet run on a racecourse, so typical of Buchanan. Not even to compete with the two-year-olds at the Epsom Stand Stakes last month. It is important to remember that the five-furlong Coventry Stakes at Royal Ascot is the first great Classic for two-year-olds – after all the introductions at Epsom and Newmarket. This race always gives a pointer to next year's Derby winner.'

'So you believe Buchanan is trying in spite of the first three from the French Bussac Stable, all quoted at four to one as favourites,' Milligan smiled. 'This is normal. These two-year-olds are all unpredictable.'

'They're off,' came the announcement over the loudspeaker. 'A fast run race from the start. Five runners are in the lead, three prominent colours from the French Bussac Stable – wait, one near the stand side in the colours of the Irish Buchanan Stable.' Shrieks of joy from the ladies were received with this news. 'Five all running neck to neck at the half-way line,' continued the commentary. 'Two with Bussac colours are starting to leave the field behind, but the lone runner on the stand side is holding them close to the lead. It is an exceptionally fast-run race.'

The ladies by now were crazy with delight; no wonder, at forty-five to one prospect!

'What do you think, Milligan?' asked the vicar.

'That lass Lydia has been well schooled at the Irish stable, sir. Horse and jockey are both fully extended.'

'One furlong to go,' continued the speaker, 'both riders on the Bussac stallions are pressing with the whips out, but Catch Me, the runner from the Buchanan Stable on the stand side is still holding level with the Bussac runners as they approach the post. Indeed a terrific race, two co-favourites and a rank outsider at forty-five to one, first time out. It is a photo finish,'

Lydia was so exhausted she nearly fell off the two-year-old as Isabelle caught her.

"Well done, Lydia. Buchanan has just been requested at the stewards' office. He assured me it was simply a question of the birth certificate papers for Catch Me.'

At that moment Catch Me was declared the winner by a short head, confirmed by a photo.

'Congratulations, my dear,' said Isabelle, with a warm hug and a kiss for Lydia. 'What a sensation! George's wife will not sleep tonight, with her housekeeping on at forty-five to one.'

A few minutes later Buchanan returned.

Congratulations, Lydia. The stewards were satisfied with the birth certificate, and my reason for not running Catch Me earlier in the season due to the hard going at Epsom.'

'But why the objection?' interposed Lydia.'

Buchanan replied, 'Your nearest rival complained that you were too close at the off and claimed that you hindered his start. However, since his mount was nearly last, there was no valid complaint.'

Indeed it was an eventful evening in Mrs Milligan's. Half the village was there.

'My dear friends,' boomed Buchanan, 'let us drink to the success of this remarkable young lady, Lydia, our rider today, the winner of the Coventry Stakes, Royal Ascot, at forty-five to one. We all wish her another success tomorrow in the Queen Mary Stakes on Ebony, who will meet the unbeaten Precipitation in company with all the classic Derby horses. Today Ebony was quoted at ten to one against Precipitation two to one favourite after so many successes in France plus the Epsom Derby winner over the same distance. Indeed it is a privilege to have with us the owner of Precipitation, Madame Gabrielle Faure.'

The company gave her a warm welcome.

'Thank you my friends. It is true that in France, and even at the Derby this year, Precipitation remains unbeaten. But once again my stable is up against the famous Hurry-On breed created by my dear friend Isabelle. Her stallion missed the Derby, a mystery to us in France but equally remains unbeaten after his sensational Two Thousand Guineas performance. It will be therefore a race of the giants. As you say in England, may the best horse win.'

A loud cheer greeted this expression of good will. Isabelle then returned to the Lodge. The night was warm and fine rain continued as she sat on a window seat, with her thoughts about this wonderful world, her adorable twins, the engagement of Milly and Roger, and her husband Richard working with her brother Leon in the steaming heat of the rain forests in Southern Nigeria and unable to return for the Royal Ascot meeting. What men! Just like her father and Uncle Bill, pioneers of West

African trade, men they used to refer to as 'those who went down to the sea in ships.' She shed a tear. Dear Mummy brought us up when Daddy was absent for ten months every year in the rain forests or in Kano and the Northern Desert areas, she thought. No wonder they say privilege is responsibility, the days when men were men! Her thoughts continued to roam. Perhaps it was true that all men were in need of forgiveness from the womenfolk responsible for their welfare. Yet how close and affectionate were their relations in spite of the separations. The home-comings were heavenly and unforgettable, then the departures at three thirty am, always on the Sunday morning after Royal Ascot, when the master together with his guests from Lagos left for Liverpool, Hunt driving, to catch the MV Apapa, the passenger boat to Lagos. Those were moving times – most of the farm hands and even Belsher the gardener turned out for the departure of the master.

As she passed Milly's bedroom, the light was on. So she knocked and was admitted. As usual Milly was reading late.

'What a lovely day at Royal Ascot,' Milly said. 'Thank you very much for your kind invitation. Roger was thrilled to see the Coventry Stakes. What a race at the end, it will be hardly possible for me to sleep tonight. Meanwhile my best wishes for tomorrow in the Queen Mary Stakes with Ebony.'

'But surely Miss Evans has let you off to see Ebony compete?'

'I am afraid, your brother has sent in a long report from the Calabar Province and my presence will be essential. However, Miss Evans indicated that it may be possible for me to attend the King George VI Stakes on Thursday to see your Onward and Gabrielle's Cat o' Nine Tails compete.'

Isabelle told her, 'Tomorrow Miss Evans will be requested to let you free for Thursday.'

'No, no, Isabelle,' Milly protested. 'Let me examine the mail from Lagos first. It would not be right to abandon my responsibility in case of a heavy work-load for Miss Evans.'

'How right you are, Milly, and of course Roger will be

starting his finals tomorrow. Perhaps you will both be able to see the performance of Onward in the King George VI Stakes on Thursday? Subject to dear Miss Evans, and Faraday House.'

Isabelle retired to her room. It was one am. Tomorrow was the great day for her Ebony, the giant black sprinter only run once this year, with distinction in the Two Thousand Guineas race at Newmarket, and now in direct competition with Precipitation, the unbeaten wonder of Europe, owned by her dear friend Gabrielle, sleeping next door!

As usual Isabelle was up early on Wednesday, a beautiful June dawn, no wind and Hurry-On stamping his feet with impatience for a short run through the country paths and local dew-filled woods. John was on his veranda preparing the sermon for next Sunday, because Reverend Manning would be on a lecture tour.

'Good morning, Isabelle,' he called. 'There seems to be some sympathy between us this morning because a double pot of hot coffee and milk is on the table waiting your arrival.'

'Bless you, after the ceremonies in the kitchen last night, this is indeed a joyous welcome.'

John commented, 'This is a critical day for your racing fortunes, is it not?'

'Yes, this is the day that Ebony, son of that lovely black behind us, is going to compete with Gabrielle's Precipitation.'

'And what about his other son, Onward?'

'Onward will race tomorrow, against Cat o' Nine Tails, also owned by Gabrielle.'

'Lucie arrives tonight at her cottage, her mother confirmed it last night.'

Isabelle responded, 'Well, why not come to Royal Ascot with Lucie to see Onward perform in the King George VI Stakes as my guests?'

'That will be a dream for us both. Thank you. A message will be sent to the cottage tonight. Lucie will need a little time for preparations.'

Several of the farm men were always invited to attend

the Wednesday and Thursday at Royal Ascot. This was a tradition established by the master over the last forty years and he paid for seats in the public stand.

The usual picnic champagne lunch was prepared for the guests and supervised by Isabelle before their departure for the course. It was a splendid cloudless day, no wind. The course was in excellent condition after two days of the fine rain called *Crachin* in Brittany.

Gabrielle and her husband were thrilled with the car-park lunch gathering under the oak trees, and many French neighbours also picnicking came to exchange notes with Isabelle's party.

After the first two events were completed, the parade commenced for the runners entered for the Queen Mary Stakes. The prize money attracted all the runners of the Classic races such as the Derby. Precipitation was standing by Louis his rider from France, and Gabrielle was talking to her husband Daniel, before the invitation was given over the radio system to prepare to mount for the parade.

Daniel asked, 'Are you clear about your instructions, Louis?'

'No problem, sir, never beaten yet and never will be.'

Indeed, Daniel was impressed. Precipitation was a picture of fitness.

Jim Mercer, the trainer, approached.

'Are you as sanguine, as your young rider?' David asked him.

'Indeed yes, sir, although as Precipitation has never run against Ebony.'

'How do you mean, Jim?'

'Consider the records, sir. It is my opinion that we can contain all the opposition, as in the Derby. Even the market reflects my view, Precipitation now a four to one favourite with thirty-seven runners. The joker in the pack is simply that Precipitation has never run against Ebony, supremely bred by Hurry-On, "the one they could never catch", yet Ebony at ten to one as we entered the course an hour ago, has run only once this year, but over the Two Thousand Guineas he won in such impressive style, only one mile. The Queen Mary Stakes, the same distance as the Derby, one and a half miles presents a different picture for Ebony, and we have won three races in France over that distance since early April, sir. Hence my sanguine sentiments about our Precipitation.'

'Splendid, Jim. My wife will be encouraged.'

At that moment the thin warm fine rain started to fall, as predicted in the *Sporting Life* the same morning.

Soon afterwards Gabrielle, Isabelle, the vicar and George Marshall all joined the group.

George then asked Isabelle, 'My dear, do you ever have a heavy bet on your entries?'

'No George. Isabelle has never been known to bet on her entries,' the vicar answered for Isabelle.

George continued, 'Jim has just informed me that Ebony's odds fell from ten to one to seven to one suddenly about five minutes ago.'

Everyone looked at Isabelle.

'My dear friends, no one gambles in the family to alter the price of our entries so suddenly by a third,' she confirmed. 'Surely it would take a large unexpected investment to upset the market so quickly.'

There was silence, then Gabrielle suddenly recollected. 'Isabelle, don't you remember? It may be because the fine rain just started. Just as before with Hurry-On, we were outwitted by the going, as you call it in England.'

'It is only one hour before the race, so it is not going to affect the surface of the course during that time.'

'Very well then, why the short price for Ebony, cut by thirty percent in five minutes when the rain started?'

'My dear Gabrielle, it is not possible for me to answer that question. The bookmakers are shrewd people.'

The rain now started in earnest, just as the parade commenced. For the first time Jim Mercer saw Ebony. He was surprised, to say the least!

'Madame,' he addressed Gabrielle, 'what a depth of chest, and the height. He must be equal to Precipitation.'

'The same height, Jim, nevertheless agreed a magnificent stallion, like all those from the Hurry-On stable.'

'My instructions, madame, with your approval, will be simple, "flat out from the very start".'

'No problem, Jim, except to remember that for the first time we are up against the unknown in spite of our record as the Derby winner. Nevertheless, my dear friend Isabelle attaches importance to the winner of the Queen Mary Stakes for breeding fees, apart from the immediate prize-money. Also other leading stallions who missed the Derby are competing.'

As the race began, Gabrielle was elated, 'Once again we go into battle against this incredible breed from the Hurry- On stable, just like Napoleon at Marengo!'

'The favourite is prominent with three greys from the Aga Khan stable, but only after a mix-up at the tapes,' said the announcer. 'Three runners at the start were boxed in, including both Precipitation and Ebony, so there was only room for one to emerge from the confusion, either Ebony or Precipitation. It was noted from the stands that either Ebony was not fast enough, or allowed Precipitation to enter the narrow gap between the two adjacent runners.' explained the announcer, adding, 'that with such large fields, this situation was inevitable.' He continued, 'The Arabs are now two lengths in front of the field, indeed a fast-run race, although the misty rain makes it difficult to detect the relative position of the favourite and Ebony.' Silence from the race-goers. 'The favourite has now extricated itself from the field and is now two lengths behind the Arabs. Meanwhile Ebony was obliged to fall back and steer clear towards the stand side of the course in order to emerge with two other mounts immediately towards the front.' Seconds later the announcer continued, 'At last Ebony is now clear of the entanglement and closing in on the field, who are going fast, endeavouring to reduce the gap of four lengths between them and the Arab leaders, now with Precipitation half a length behind.'

'Well, Milligan?' asked the vicar.

'A proper mix-up, sir, at the start. However, only a quarter of a mile from the start the situation is serious but not critical. Fortunately, my military field-glasses can detect the position in spite of the mist of fine rain.'

The announcer continued, 'Ebony is now edging foward towards the Arabs and the field. Precipitation is half a length behind the leaders, still holding his position. Now, seven furlongs to go just before the Ascot straight.'

'Lydia has edged towards the left, the stand side, slightly

uphill from the course side. She is determined to be free from further problems,' concluded Milligan.

'The favourite is closing in now on the Arabs,' the announcer continued, 'and all are running together. However, on the stand side, Ebony in the Buchanan colours is making up the interval fast, now only one length behind the leaders.'

This encouraging news was received with shrieks of joy all over Royal Ascot. The rain was now tumbling out of the sky.

'Well, Milligan, what now?' asked the vicar.

'Tricky, sir, only two furlongs to go, but wait. Lydia evidently is determined to have no more involvement. She has still kept to the stand side.'

The loudspeaker continued, 'The favourite is now challenging the Arabs for supremacy, and is holding on, in fact now half a length behind. Wait, another challenger on the stand side, not possible to see the colours in this downpour, yes it is Ebony, now almost level with the leaders.' More shrieks of delight. 'Only one furlong to go. Precipitation now is leaving the Arabs, but closely followed by Ebony, who is apparently in his element with the rain. Only a furlong from the post.'

Gabrielle sought Isabelle's hand.

'Precipitation is now making his final challenge two lengths in front of the Arabs' the announcer continued, 'but Ebony has also emerged to confront the leader at a rare pace not often seen at this stage of such an important contest. They are now neck to neck at the post. It may be a photo finish,' concluded the announcer.

The result officially established Ebony as the winner by a short head. This was declared as the green flag was hoisted. Then the red flag for an enquiry.

Lydia entered the Jockey Club office.

'Congratulations, Lydia, a remarkable effort. All we wish to know is the reason for your delay at the start. You are invited to give your own impressions.'

'The gap was narrow, either it was Precipitation or me on Ebony but not both at this early stage.'

'Well?'

'My charge, Ebony, was restrained.'

'And you let your principal rival Precipitation take precedence during this urgent and tricky situation?'

'Yes sir, for two reasons. A collision was inevitable, secondly sir, my mistress Isabelle, Lady Cameron, insists that it is not whether you win or lose in this world, it is how you play the game that counts!'

This remark was received with wonder and surprise by the committee. 'Thank you, Lydia. This assembly is satisfied with your explanation and in particular with the exemplary way in which you had to judge so quickly the appropriate solution at the tapes. Please convey my compliments to your mistress, and add that she will soon receive a communication from me about her father's expected arrival from Lagos.'

Soon after her departure, one of the committee members observed, 'You know, colonel, that remark about win or lose can be applied to many of our financial institutions in the City!'

'How right you are William.'

As the red flag was lowered, more shrieks of delight were in evidence all over the course. Even the bookmakers joined in the emotional chorus.

30

After the successful result of the Queen Mary Stakes there was much activity in the Milligan's kitchen.

'A bit close my friend, a short head,' Milligan observed to Buchanan.

'Boyo, how right you are. Nevertheless, with a field of thirty-seven, and a frustrating start, and against an unbeaten favourite, my respect and congratulation go first to the rider, Lydia.'

Everyone clapped. Isabelle gave her an affectionate hug.

'It is true, Lydia,' she said. 'You perfomed with distinction. Your mum will be happy tonight.'

'She is very happy, Miss, and asked me to give you tonight this diamond brooch, an heirloom, worn all her life by my Italian great-grandmother, for all your kindness to me.'

Isabelle gave her another hug. 'Are you related to Lucie?'

'Yes, Miss, distantly.'

That explains a lot, thought Isabelle.

'Now,' concluded Buchanan, 'we are about to contest the next big race within our family circle, the King George VI Stakes, over three and a half miles for three-year-olds. Our Onward – favourite of your Miss Isabelle, is to compete against Cat o' Nine Tails, whose owner is with us tonight. Once again we must remember that Madame Faure's entry, Cat o' Nine Tails, has never lost a race throughout Europe, and two years ago she presented us with a formidable adversary in the Cobler, who was the only stallion in the racing world ever to come within one length from beating Hurry-On in the Gold Cup, then a four-year-old, during his long history as the one they could never catch. Onward was born with a slight impediment so that it was not possible to race him as a two-year-old. In fact he has only raced once in his life, trained under the infinite care of Miss

Isabelle. Onward's performance at Newbury was so impressive that it was decided to enter him for the King George VI Stakes tomorrow, price tonight at fifteen to one, against the favourite at eight to one. Cat o' Nine Tails, owned by our friend and competitor with us tonight, Miss Gabrielle.'

Everyone clapped.

Gabrielle responded, 'Seven times, dear friends, my three-year-old roan, Cat o' Nine Tails, has won 2½ miles contests throughout Europe, always by a comfortable five lengths. But my respect for the Irish-bred stallions is far higher than for any other racing blood throughout the world. So, even if we can give a good account of our challenge to your stable, all honours will be satisfied.'

Considerable applause greeted this magnanimous speech – in French-accented English.

As the party broke up to prepare for the great race the next day, the vicar approached Isabelle, who was exchanging notes with Milligan and Ginger, Onward's jockey.

'Permit me to see the lovely brooch given to you this evening,' the vicar requested.

Isabelle unbuckled it and gave it to Reverend Manning.

'You see, Milligan, a beautiful cut stone of long ago, evidently from Amsterdam. Look after it, my dear, it is worth a small fortune!'

Isabelle was speechless. Evidently Lydia, like Lucie, had a history.

The party dispersed, but before entering the Lodge Isabelle went to say goodnight to Hurry-On with Gabrielle, armed with a few sugar lumps from Mrs Milligan's kitchen.

'Even in retirement, he is still a massive stallion,' commented Gabrielle.

Peace settled over the house as Isabelle completed her evening prayer for Roger – fast asleep long ago. The bright light from Milly's room revealed that she was still awake. Even as she knocked Milly invited her to enter.

'So how is my dear brother coping with the beginning of finals?' she asked.

'Encouraging signs,' Milly responded. 'It is my belief that he will make it, but what an imposition: two and a half weeks including six-hour papers. It is a lot to ask of these students.'

'True, Milly, although all we need is a humble pass, a third. At least then they have learned how to learn. Afterwards their studies begin – as the Principal explained to Roger's class last week. The Principal also added, "From now on, my friends, we can refer to you as gentlemen"!'

Milly laughed.

'No problems with his health, Milly, for the next two weeks?'

'Count upon me to cover that front.'

Isabelle gave her an affectionate good night kiss.

At six am next morning, attired only in her nightdress, for it was a beautiful warm sunny morning with a dew-filled atmosphere, she mounted Hurry-On, who was as eager as ever for a race across the meadows to John's cottage. This was King George VI Stakes day, and John was waiting on the veranda with the large coffee pot.

'Two minutes late Isabelle!' he greeted her. 'Here is my dressing-gown in case of interruptions.'

'These are magic days. Isn't life simply gorgeous! Your lovely cultivated garden this June morning is a credit to all the work behind the scenes.'

'Work yes, Isabelle, but for me a fascination to tend and care for each plant in my humble plot.'

As he hesitated, Isabelle interrupted, 'Well, John?'

'Let me be honest Isabelle, Lucie is an heiress.'

'So are you, John – an heir to the greatest treasure on Earth, an intimate knowledge of the Holy Scriptures. Do you think that it would be possible for me to mount Hurry-On, in my nightie and to race through the woods and meadows of Winkfield to arrive at your cottage at six thirty am and not to feel completely safe, without my feminine and spiritual intuitions and a mother to boot, to give you all possible encouragement for your future prospects.'

'True, Isabelle, although that is the least of my problems, except that it may be a little awkward if the Bishop decided also to arrive early in order to enjoy the delights of my plot, your hidden curves, and the vicar's garden!'

Isabelle smiled and continued to enquire, 'Apart from Lucie's exalted station, do you seriously feel a basic and strong emotion of love for her hand in marriage – to live with her until death do you part. Is the passion in you truly disturbed for her care and welfare on this Earth – you, a comparative stranger in her life. Marriage, John is a serious business.'

'My dear Isabelle, she is a creature from another world. It is not easy for me to respond to your question. At Girton College she is as ever in demand, surrounded by so many undergraduates, males as well as females, even dons, principally for her ability in classical music, and delivery of interpretation, very much like your dear husband Richard."

'So you feel that the situation is hopeless, in so far as she does not respond to your apparent overtures?'

'That describes my predicament.'

'Again, don't you feel that it is a little presumptuous to expect Lucie, not yet twenty-one years old, sheltered and guarded by a foster-mother and the Roman Catholics in Windsor most of her life, to take an intimate interest in you, at this early stage? Perhaps Royal Ascot may introduce the element of a different experience in her life. This is King George VI Stakes, and you are both included in my party. Tell Lucie that today she will be amongst the elite of the land in the Enclosure, and must be dressed for the part.'

She was!

'Bless you, Isabelle, We will arrive at the Lodge as agreed in time for the departure of your party for our first visit to Royal Ascot about twelve thirty pm, in preparation for the champagne lunch under the oak trees in the No. 3 car park.'

Gold Cup day was a convivial occasion. Gabrielle, Isabelle, Milly and Lucie all dressed in style, attracted a lot of attention from the neighbouring picnic parties, mostly French and a few Italians. Daniel, husband of Gabrielle, expressed his thought to the vicar.

'This can happen only in England, sir, when my countrymen from France open their hearts to one another in this fabulous open-air picnic at Royal Ascot with the sunshine just trying to stream in through the oak trees and this rare soft air. For example, several captains of French industry and even ministers are here today, exchanging notes with one another, and the ladies are always active talking about domestic problems and prospects for their offspring. Truly, vicar, this is quite an occasion, and probably the last of the meetings when difficult problems are resolved quietly and privately amongst leaders of industry, and perhaps some clarity of thought introduced amongst the international political leaders.'

'Well, Daniel, as a French national you are most welcome to attend the service at St Mary's church on Sunday.'

'Reverend Manning, during my stay at the Lodge last evening it was decided to take a walk with the farm dogs and visit several of the local inns, which always warmly welcome me and echo the heart of England. Long into the night sometimes, even after closing time, my discussions with the local village people and the innkeepers have been fascinating. Not only about racing because they know that my wife Gabrielle is the owner of Cat o' Nine Tails to run against Onward this afternoon, but also about the more important facts of life. The local people, dear vicar, are shrewd and are well aware of the international problems of Europe. It was one am before my return to the Lodge, and Gabrielle was fast asleep!'

Lucie and John were both active and helpful to Isabelle during the picnic and contributed to ensure harmony between the adjacent parties of French and Italian visitors. In fact, Isabelle was surprised at Lucie's fluency in the Italian language.

Eventually their party gravitated towards the entrance of Royal Ascot and settled down to observe the elegance around them in the paddock.

Upon arriving at the parade ground just before the first race, they received their first surprise, this time from Isabelle. The betting had already opened for the big race, the third event of the meeting, and the second favourite was an entry known already to Gabrielle, Maestro owner Mr J Requier. In fact, Maestro had given Cat o' Nine Tails a serious challenge last month at Longchamp, when he was late from the starting-gage. But he made up fifteen lengths to come second to Cat o' Nine Tails. Maestro was now quoted second favourite at seven to one.

Her trainer met Gabrielle in the paddock. 'It was a last

minute entry, madame,' he explained. 'Whether Maestro will be able to stay the distance with the going soft is doubtful in my opinion.'

'Yet, Jim, to have overhauled the field and to challenge us within five lengths over a three-mile race, from a late start of fifteen lengths' handicap at Longchamp last month, this is a new factor for us to consider.'

Both Isabellle and Milligan were made aware of the new element for the competition. 'This will be his first race in the UK, Miss, because Maestro was cancelled for the Newmarket contest,' said the bailiff.

At three fifteen pm they were all present at the parade.

'Ginger is waiting for instructions, Miss,' Milligan reported.

'What do you think? The race is half a mile longer than the race in France.'

'Let them make the pace, Miss,' Milligan suggested. 'They are both competitors in France where they like to go all out from the start.'

Ginger was standing by. 'Did you hear that advice?' Isabelle asked, 'And do you feel confident?'

'Oh yes, Miss. Onward is one of our favourites at the Lodge. He understands our mutual language.'

Isabelle added, 'The main problem is our inexperience of the two mighty stallions, both roans, bred in Normandy from the best bloodstock in France.'

'They have not yet met the wild Irish blacks!' Ginger replied.

'Well said, Ginger,' responded the vicar, who had just joined Isabelle and Milligan.

As the parade proceeded, the betting altered dramatically. Maestro and Cat o' Nine Tails were suddenly quoted co-favourites at five to one and Onward went out at sixteen to one.

Both Milligan and the vicar smiled, and Isabelle asked Milligan for the reason.

'According to talk on the rails, it is cash from Paris. They seem to have forgotten the Hurry-On breed. It seems to me that a lot of lessons are going to be learnt today.'

Indeed, Gabrielle was already nervous. 'In France, they think it will be a two-horse race, with forty entries. The market does not seem to remember that Onward is a direct descendant of Hurry-On. And now comes the rain.' Gabrielle looked at Isabelle. 'How is it possible for me to predict the result with this independent variable you refer to as the going. It is impossible. There seems to be so many variables to cope with on the English turf.'

'Courage, Madame Gabrielle, isn't that the great challenge of the English turf,' said a new voice next to Isabelle, as they were about to move away from the paddock after the signal to mount was given. Then in French the voice continued, 'In France, dear *Madame*, we are competitors, but here at Royal Ascot we are allies, for there is one stallion which causes us concern in Bordeaux. It is the Hurry-On bred Onward; our stable lost heavily to Hurry-On, and now we have to contend with his first-born, Onward, against which my father instructed me to wage a small fortune. So, no more anxiety, dear *Madame*, today Onward and the rest will be relegated to the "also-rans" – cut to size by our own runners, the finest bloodstock in France.'

Gabrielle recovered her wits. 'Of course, you are the son of Monsieur Requier. Your enthusiasm is infectious, *Monsieur*.'

'*Enchanté, Madame*. Michael is the name.'

He continued, full of enthusiasm, in French. 'If we don't speculate, *Madame*, we will never accumulate. After the events today the Irish competition will never again venture near our shores!'

Gabrielle was amused, 'How inspiring, to hear your youthful prediction.'

Isabelle who was quite fluent in French, pondered this discussion.

'The only way we can beat Onward is to run him into the ground, by going flat out from the start,' Michael continued, in English.

Milligan responded, 'My only hope for your investment, *Monsieur* is that it is an each way wager.' Gabrielle interrupted.

'Michael, these are my friends, the owners of Onward.'

Michael coloured with embarrassment, but Milly came to his rescue. 'Remember me, Michael?'

With great relief Michael gave Milly an affectionate hug.

'As you say in English, it appears that my remarks about Onward were ill-judged.'

Milly then introduced Isabelle. 'Lady Cameron is the owner of Onward, Michael.'

'*Madame, mes compliments et mes excuses.*'

'Your observations about Onward, Michael, will be judged only by the result of the next race. After all your father may be the winner. Your intended strategy for Maestro will then be justified, honours satisfied.'

'Lady Cameron, thank you for the grace given to extricate me from my excessive enthusiasm.'

'That is only natural, Michael. Without enthusiasm where would the younger generation be today in this competitive society. Incidentally, where are you staying, in London? You will be welcome to my home any time.'

'Yes, in London, only for one night. Nevertheless, thank you very much for your kind invitation.'

The jockeys prepared to leave the paddock with their stallions. Milly and Lucie were fascinated with the grace and potential power of the runners. This was to be a long race, three and a half miles. Ginger threw them a kiss as she passed by the barrier to the course.

'Very best wishes, Ginger, from us all,' saluted Isabelle as she returned the kiss.

As they walked to their boxes in the stands Michael remarked to Milly, 'What a friendly intimate introduction to the owner, jockey and the trainer of the Hurry-On stable.'

'Well, next time you visit Royal Ascot, remember the invitation from Lady Cameron.'

'Indeed the invitation is already recorded.'

The fine rain continued as the runners cantered towards the starting tapes.

Isabelle pressed Gabrielle's hand. 'Cat o' Nine tails is a true aristocrat among thoroughbreds. Today he looks invincible.'

As Gabrielle looked up at the sky and the rain started to tumble down, she added, 'Courage, Gabrielle.'

As Ginger lined up for the starter's orders, Isabelle smiled. Thank God for the rain.

'They're off,' came the call from the loudspeakers on

the stands. 'After two furlongs all runners seem to be in line. Only Onward, in Buchanan colours, has got off to a slow start after being boxed in. Amongst the seven leaders as they pass the stands are the two favourites, Cat o' Nine Tails and Maestro, both challengers from France, amongst five Arab greys, followed by the field, behind them is Onward, who does not seem to be in any hurry. No wait, Onward has woken up, he is now approaching a bunch of about twenty runners, about four lengths behind.

Milligan smiled, but the vicar was worried. 'Ginger does not seem to be in any hurry, Milligan.'

'Still three miles to go as they approach the far side of the course, sir, from where it will be difficult to follow them in this thin misty rain,

The announcer continued, 'The Buchanan runner Onward has now caught up with the field and is going well. The five leaders are fifteen lengths clear. Cat o' Nine Tails and Maestro are still contending for the lead. However, there is still two and a half miles to go. The rain is too heavy and visibility is difficult on the far side of the course, but my colleagues in the country report that, at the two mile post Maestro and Cat o' Nine Tails are still racing neck and neck about five lengths in front of the five Arab greys. This first group is now fifteen lengths in front of the main field. There was no mention of Onward.

'At the one and a half mile post the two leaders Maestro and Cat o' Nine Tails are now six lengths in front of the Arabs, still racing neck and neck. The leading bunch of Arabs is now fifteen lengths in front of the main group of runners, still no news of Onward,' the announcer continued. However a sudden perturbation has occurred in the betting. The reason is inexplicable. The price of the late starter from the Buchanan stable has been reduced suddenly after passing the one and a half mile post, from seventeen to one to eight to one. No reason is yet discernible from the stands. In fact the leaders are just becoming visible through this deluge.'

In the stands the vicar was worried. 'Why, Milligan, the sudden change in the market?'

The bailiff removed his military field-glasses and smiled. 'Difficult to ascertain the local situation from here sir, but my confidence in the tick-tack communication system has never yet failed. Excuse me for five minutes now, sir. Even at eight to one a few pounds will be placed before it comes down to four to one.

'Milligan....'

But he had disappeared to the course only just in time. After he placed £100 at eight to one, seconds later the market closed. Upon returning to his seat next to the vicar he heard the announcer.

'The leaders here have just passed the mile post and are at last visible,' reported the announcer. Maestro and Cat o' Nine Tails still in the lead, now seven lengths in front of the Arabs, ten lengths from the field, still no news about the late starter. But now wait, there is a lone runner on the outside. All we can distinguish from here is that the stallion is jet black and the rider's cap may be white. It is Onward on the far side, now levelling with the Arabs.'

Indeed Ginger at last was in action. 'Come, my darling,' she urged. 'It seems that we have left it a bit late in this rain. Faster, faster, faster!'

The mighty stallion responded and Ginger felt those mighty muscles ripple to her intimate call for every effort. Now the leaders approached the famous Ascot straight of five furlongs. Yet Onward still needed ten lengths to catch the two leaders. She smiled, so did Milligan – so did the bookmakers! 'Faster, my darling,' Ginger, still on the outside, was well placed on the slightly higher ground on the stand side of the course.

But the Arabs also were making up ground, now only one length behind the two leaders at the three-furlong post.

At the two-furlong post the two leaders and three of the Arabs were all racing in line, fully extended. The announcer continued, 'Less than two furlongs to go, a very open race with the two favourite and the Arab-bred runners, all in line. One of the Arabs and Cat o' Nine Tails are now both making a final challenge. But Onward is making an impressive challenge against Cat o' Nine Tails for the last furlong. Maestro also is making a valiant effort to hold his position.'

'Still faster, faster, my darling,' murmured Ginger, as

Onward responded half a furlong from the post, now level with Cat o' Nine Tails, at last. However, Onward still had reserves after the slow start and responded with every effort to Ginger's cry for help, and just managed to reach the post a clear length in front of Cat o' Nine Tails, with Maestro and two of the Arabs contending for third place. The public, especially the ladies, were frantic with praise for Onward, like the bookmakers!

Gabrielle fell into Isabelle's arms. 'Once again the Irish breeding has beaten my string of unbeaten winners. What is the answer?'

Isabelle stroked her lovely head hard. 'Come now, it has been a fair contest,' Isabelle comforted her. 'Cat o' Nine Tails has done wonders in appalling weather conditions.'

But Gabrielle, who was very feminine and lovable, was still not able to contain her tears.

Meanwhile there was great excitement at the enclosure as the winner was led in. Ginger, covered completely with mud, received a royal reception as Isabelle gave her a warm hug and kisses.

'Congratulations.'

'Careful, Miss you will be muddied!'

'No problem, Ginger, it will be honest and worthy mud. It was a magnificent effort.

'However, the enquiry flag has been hoisted, would you like me to come with you?'

'Oh yes please, Miss. My nervous energy may not last out before the stewards.' As they entered the courtroom the Chairman, well known to Isabelle, gave them a warm welcome.

'Firstly, our congratulations, Lady Cameron upon the result of the race and to Miss Ginger, the jockey,' said the Chairman. 'We have only one question for Miss Ginger. Why the delay with your challenge? We believe that you were in a position to make your challenge even before the five furlong straight, because it was evident at the end that Onward, even after the three and half miles, was far from exhausted.'

'True sir, for two reasons. Onward, as you observed, was still not fully extended. Indeed I realised this when I urged him to race with every effort at the start to the five furlong straight. However, the main reason, sir, is that as a two year old Onward was lame in the rear legs. In consequence, sir, it was incumbent upon me not to over-race him at this stage.

'Secondly sir, the visibility through the misty rain confused me about our position – so much so that I did not notice the leaders in front of the Arabs until the five furlong straight. From that moment every demand was made upon Onward. He responded, a bit late it is true, but like never before, with immense energy and grace. Somehow he knew we were in trouble – our very spirits seemed to be in unison. Indeed, it was an unforgettable experience to feel those mighty muscles working overtime, especially after my alarm at the sight of the two leaders in front of the Arabs. Whether we could catch the two leaders was clearly debatable, in view of the distance which I calculated to be at least fifteen lengths. Once again I selected the "high road" of the course, the stand side, in view of the shocking conditions – although my mistress, Lady Cameron, has often told me in the past to avoid it, as it is not encouraged by the stewards.'

The Colonel smiled. 'True, except under difficult weather conditions. Pray continue, Miss Ginger.'

'With a handicap of fifteen lengths, to compete with the unbeaten French stayers over the five-furlong Ascot straight seemed an impossible situation. However, there were two surprises. The turf on the high road was more firm. Secondly, within a short space of time it was evident that Onward was rapidly overhauling the front runners, who had been competing for the lead throughout the race and were now nearing exhaustion, as I learned afterwards.'

So ended her verbal report.

Isabelle pressed her hand.

'Miss Ginger, we are all grateful to you for your detailed report. Our only observation is simply that next time during such an important race, mounted on such a powerful stallion, endeavour to keep up with the leaders from the start,' said the Chairman.

'Yes, sir.'

'Any other questions, gentlemen? Splendid,' Then instructions were given to withdraw the enquiry notice.

There was pandemonium on the Course. Somewhere someone was overheard to shout, 'Another one they could never catch.'

'Once again Lady Cameron your entry seems to have captured the affections of the public,' the Chairman remarked. 'Please convey my compliments to your dear father upon his arrival back from Nigeria in December.'

31

Ginger was driven back to her cottage, where her mother greeted her with open arms.

'It was all on the radio, my precious. Congratulations, you must be exhausted.'

'No, Mummy, tired yes, but so happy for Miss Isabelle, the winning owner. She has been so kind to me over the years. Indeed there were several male jockeys expecting to be given my assignment this afternoon. Yet several weeks ago the mistress selected me. It is so important, dear Mummy, to be wanted in this world.'

Her mother then encouraged, 'Then, now for a hot bath, after all that rain and mud, a quick change and a light supper.'

Ginger was soon asleep in bed, too tired to attend the celebration party in the Milligan's kitchen.

Indeed it was not until the following day that Ginger woke up to see a note in the tea tray her mother had just delivered to her bedside.

'Dear Ginger. So sorry not to see you last night at the celebrations in Mrs Milligan's. You must have been exhausted after your splendid effort. However, good news. As the jockey you are qualified to receive £2,000 for winning the King George VI Stakes. Congratulations, my dear, and bless you. Affectionately, Isabelle Cameron.'

PS Last night Madame Faure and young Monsieur Requier, owner of Cat o' Nine Tails and Maestro, persuaded me to enter Onward for the Prix d'Arc de Triomphe race at Longchamp near Paris late October. Will you be the jockey. Do you speak French?

At that moment her mother returned.

'So at last you are awake. Your pot of tea will be cold, so here is a fresh one. Never known you to sleep so long. Even the early birds of June failed to wake you!'

'Mummy, a warm hug first of all.'

'Do you know, that you are news in all the papers? So many well-wishers and callers from the village, it was necessary to erect a notice. "Ginger is fast asleep. Please not to disturb" – and the telephone receiver had to be left off.'

'Dearest Mummy, another hug please.' Then her mother read the newspaper account of her efforts during the great race:

'The jockey known as Ginger rode a remarkable race against the French challengers, and handled that giant stallion Onward with such consummate grace from the five-furlong straight that it was a privilege to witness it in such difficult weather conditions....'

'So, my dear child, you have become famous overnight.'

'Mummy, this publicity frightens me. It is only you that counts for me.'

Her mother thought, she is still only a lovely child even at twenty years of age. 'Come, Ginger,' she said aloud. 'You must return soon to the land of the living, the racing world. Remember Mr Marshall wants you to attend a meeting at 11.45 about the race result and to discuss your next assignment.'

'Yes, the Prix de l'Arc de Triomphe in October, near Paris. I read about it in the note from Miss Isabelle.'

Her mother was duly impressed when she read the note from Isabelle, as Ginger dressed.

'This sum of money must be put into safe keeping in a bank.'

'Oh no. It is going to be spent upon fitting our little cottage with every convenience – plus central heating. No more cold winter evenings with our modest wood fire. We will have proper radiators, plus hot water.'

'You must be mad, child.'

'Just you wait until after the race for the Prix de l'Arc

de Triomphe....' Can you keep a top secret, Mummy?'

'Of course, Ginger darling.'

'Well, at Longchamp in October. Those two competitors Cat o' Nine Tails and Maestro are going to receive a shock. Because next time Onward is going to be raced faster from the start, as requested by the Royal Ascot Stewards, We will win not by one length, it will be more like twenty lengths!'

'Ginger, that is what Reverend Manning refers to as over confidence resulting in tears,' warned her mother.

'Confidence is bursting inside me. With that mighty stallion not yet fully extended, it makes me so impatient to show the racing world what we can achieve together.'

'Do take care, my little one...'

At that moment there was a knock at the door. The Marshall van was waiting to take her to the meeting.

'Goodbye, Mummy. See you this evening.'

Her mother pondered a long time over the events of yesterday and also the letter from Isabelle. Bless the child, a little baby not so long ago! Then she noticed a note addressed to her on the kitchen table.

> 'Dearest Mummy. May be a little late this evening because it is St Peter's Day, and the communion service will not finish until seven thirty. All my love. Ginger.'

'Without doubt,' her mother murmured, 'my little one is a child of God.'

Several members of both stables were present at the meeting in the Marshall room.

'Congratulations, Ginger' echoed as she entered just in time, from several of those present.

Buchanan was there. 'My dear, it was a splendid effort. Nevertheless, perhaps the Colonel had a point – next time, do not worry too much about the history of Onward as a two year old. His lameness has vanished. So today, my friends,' he continued – Isabelle the vicar, Milligan, Lydia, Ginger, Daniel Faure (also a shareholder) and the auditors, together with legal advisers were all present – 'we have to discuss our future programme.'

'First of all, the St Leger Stakes at Doncaster, late

September. Are you confident, Lydia, that Ebony can cope satisfactorily against Precipitation with the extra quarter of a mile?'

Lydia responded, 'May it be possible, sir, to give you my opinion within the next few weeks?'

'Of course, Lydia. 'Second, Longchamp. Ginger, how do you feel about this challenge?'

'I have complete confidence sir,' responded Ginger with a winning smile.

'Really, in spite of meeting the French on their home ground?'

Ginger smiled again. 'It will surprise me, sir, if there are problems.'

'In spite of today's list of forty five entries for one of the most coveted prizes in Europe, and competition also from Italy, Germany and Spain?'

Ginger thought of her mum and the heating, and smiled again. 'It will be a privilege for me to compete, sir. At this stage it will interest me to hear about the current competition,'

'You will be briefed fully in due course,' Buchanan told her.

'Now, my friends, we are all agreed, presumably, that Onward is to be entered next year for the Gold Cup over two and three quarter miles at Royal Ascot in June. Good, no problems. And Ebony depending upon his performance in the St Leger, this year, will be trained for the Stewards Cup late July at Goodwood next year, run over one and three quarter miles. Good, no problems.'

The meeting broke up with satisfaction on all sides. Buchanan reminded everyone that his stable in Ireland had a runner in the King Stand Stakes that afternoon, the last day of Royal Ascot.

Milligan commented, 'He is priced at fifty to one, and there are forty one runners.'

'True, Boyo. He is five years old, not run for nearly two years due to coughing and now fit.'

'The King Stand Stakes is meant to be the fastest five furlong race in Europe, for all ages,' Milligan observed.

'True, Boyo, and Foray is very fast over the five-furlong straight. It is a great pity Thunder had to be cancelled for the Wokingham Stakes, due to coughing early this week. Lydia will be the jockey for Foray. Boyo, never have we seen in my ground in North Ireland such a powerful sprinter at his age over the five furlongs as Foray.'

Milligan warned. 'But the stewards will ask questions if he wins.'

'At five years old, Boyo, questions are rarely serious, the Classic stage is when questions are asked.'

The fine warm rain, slight today, continued. Once again it was a convivial picnic lunch.

On the way to the paddock after lunch, as the party arrived at the parade ring, Ginger accidentally bumped into young Michael Requier.

'*Excusez-moi, mademoiselle,*' he began. 'Are you the Onward jockey by chance, who trounced my Maestro in the King George VI Stakes yesterday?'

'It seems so *monsieur.*'

'Great God – whoever let you out –'

'From where, *monsieur?*'

'From the devil, mademoiselle. Our stable lost a fortune yesterday.'

'Perhaps it is within my power to repair the damage done, sir.'

'What do you mean, young lady?'

'The Prix de l'Arc de Triomphe, sir.'

'Oh yes. Why only a few minutes ago it was announced that your Onward was entered. 'Let me assure you, young lady, that you will receive the biggest trouncing of your life, so much so that you will never again attempt to compete at Longchamp.'

Ginger smiled. 'But sir, that is just the challenge we like to receive in England, from France.'

'You English are incomprehensible, *mademoiselle.*'

'To conclude sir, you may be able to recoup some of your losses today by a modest wager on Foray in the King Stand Stakes.'

What a hell of a cheek, thought Michael. Aloud, he said, 'So you believe that your colleague Lydia really has a chance, a woman against forty aggressive male jockeys? The confidence of the English is beyond comprehension!'

As Ginger went in search of her friend Lydia, she met Isabelle.

'So you had another meeting with Monsieur Requier, Ginger?'

'Yes, Miss – not a happy one.'

'He is bitter about their loss over the King George VI Stakes, so I gave him some encouragement about the King Stand Stakes today. It made him even more resentful. He asked me who let me out! From where, I asked. He replied – from Hell!'

Isabelle smiled. 'Do not worry too much about this incident. When the next opportunity occurs, young Michael will recieve a piece of my mind! Here is Lydia.

Ginger was happy to meet her friend just before the last race of the meeting.

As the forty one runners lined up behind the tapes Milligan noticed that Lydia was drawn up on the stand side – slighty higher ground, a good precaution in this fine rain.

'It does not seem right Milligan, that Lydia is the only female amongst all those experienced riders,' commented Reverend Manning.

Isabelle responded, 'That is the least of my concerns, sir. Lydia has proved herself to the racing world both at the Two Thousand Guineas and at the Queen Mary Stakes here on Wednesday. True, she has had little time to become closely united with Foray. Soon, however, we will judge her ability on a comparatively strange stallion.'

There were so many runners together in the lead it was not easy to identify the leaders in the short five-furlong race for sprinters. At the four furlong post from home the three favourites, all at fifteen to one – it was an open market in such a large field – were all in the lead about one length clear of the field. Another horse on the stand side was holding them for the lead – an Irish black with white feet, in Buchanan colours. Two of the leaders, now two furlongs from home, were making their challenge, but Foray was also challenging. At one furlong to go all three were making every effort for the winning-post. It was indeed a fast run race.'

'My darling,' urged Lydia, 'faster, faster. We were only strangers together a few days ago, but now we are friends.

In spirit we are together now. Faster, faster.'

The response from Foray surprised the public!

It was a photo finish. There was silence until the result was heard. Foray had won by a short head from the two French entries of the Bussac stables. Ginger rushed to the winners' enclosure to be first to congratulate her friend, but Lydia's face revealed pain.

'Thank God you are here, Ginger. It is the wrist again. Can you take charge of Foray?' The medical team arrived quickly and Lydia was attended to without delay. Isabelle and Milligan were surprised to see Ginger mounted on Foray as he was led in. The announcer quickly made it clear that Lydia was under medical attention, so Isabelle and Milligan went to the clinic, where Lydia was just recovering from a faint due to the pain.

'So sorry, to end the race in this condition,' she murmured.

'Do not worry, Lydia,' Isabelle replied. 'This is my department. A doctor and a nurse will accompany you to your cottage – upon my instructions – unless it is necessary to go to the Windsor Hospital.'

After a brief examination, the doctor asked, 'Has this happened before, Lydia?'

'Yes, Doctor, but on the other wrist.'

'Good, in that case do not worry young Lady. It is just a bad sprain. You will have to be subjected to two to three weeks' treatment. That means wearing straps and making daily visits to Windsor Hospital. How do you feel now? No more pain?'

'Oh no, Doctor, it is such a relief.'

'Good. Meanwhile, no pressure of any kind must be put on this left wrist until we meet at Windsor Hospital tomorrow morning.'

The doctor gave instructions to Isabelle about the right treatment. 'She must have endured great pain, Lady Cameron, during the later part of that race. Please ensure that she is looked after tonight. Here are some temporary pain-killing tablets – they may not be necessary after the injection I have just administered. The swelling must go down before the straps can be used.'

Isabelle hugged Lydia. 'Now we can congratulate you

upon a magnificent performance, under those difficult conditions. Indeed the public is already asking who was the jockey on Foray.'

'It will not prevent me, from continuing to ride?' Lydia asked anxiously.

'Of course not, Lydia, but the Stewards Cup at Goodwood may not be possible. However, should you be fit again for the St Leger in September against Precipitation.'

'That will be my dream, Miss. As she was placed in the ambulance with Milligan, she went fast asleep.

Isabelle and Milligan returned to the winners enclosure. 'If that jockey Lydia wants a position in our stable, one of the best-known in France, she will be more than welcome. There is a permanent place for that lass, based upon the magnificent horsemanship we witnssed today as she exerted every ounce of effort from Foray to win from my unbeaten Samson.'

'I will tell her, sir. What name shall I say?' asked Milligan.

'Bussac. Here is my card – *Director-General Bussac Stable, Paris, France*. Let me sign it,' he said, writing, *Felicitations, young lady, we will meet again happily, J Bussac.*

'Miss Lydia will receive your card, tonight, sir,' Milligan assured him.

'Who was that?' asked the vicar.

Milligan replied, 'Monsieur J Bussac is head of the Bussac Stable near Paris. Lydia has won an admirer – a Frenchman! Oh la la!'

'You mean, Milligan, that they want her for a jockey?'

'Exactly, sir.'

'In other words, Milligan, Lydia is now in demand as a free-lance.'

As the party was leaving the paddock, Jim, Gabrielle's trainer, approached Isabelle. 'Excuse me, Miss, is it true that you will not run Ebony at Sandown for the Stewards Cup next month?'

'Correct, Jim. Ebony recommenced slight coughing last night after his efforts during the Queen Mary Stakes on Wednesday.'

'And the St Leger, at Doncaster?'

'Not yet certain, Jim, but still on the list of entries.'

Gabrielle looked quizzically at Isabelle. 'Yesterday Ebony

was two to one favourite. Now Precipitation is a three to one favourite.' Isabelle pressed her hand. 'So you have scratched off Ebony for the Stewards Cup?'

'Yes.'

'So Ebony is indeed coughing?'

'Why the inflexion, dear Gabrielle?'

'It is only because of your lovely expression earlier this year about the Derby: It is not whether you win or lose in this world, it is how you play the game that counts!'

As one woman to another, let us sleep on it.'

'Isabelle, *tu es extraordinaire.*'

It was then that Milligan came over. 'Excuse me, Miss he said to Isabelle, 'Ladbrokes have requested me to ask about your intention for Ebony in the St Leger this September.'

'Tell them that Ebony will run!'

Gabrielle added, 'It is all beginning to make sense.'

The next day Ebony was favourite for the St Leger at three to one.

32

The Ascot party broke up and high summer commenced at Oakfield Lodge – warm and sunny days when Roger relaxed at Sunningdale with Smithers, the assistant professional, waiting for the final result of his degree course. Every evening Milly returned from the London office, often with the news from Leon and Richard in Lagos. Just before her departure for a holiday with her cousin in Bordeaux, a letter from Faraday House arrived. Roger was awarded the degree, not honours or even a first, but at least it was pass. Isabelle was thrilled and arranged a celebration dinner at the Lodge with Reverend Manning, Milly, Lucie and John.

'So Roger, as your Principal says, your studies are about to begin,' observed John.

'True, but with one exception, a cardinal issue during the last years, is no longer the desperate factor in my daily life at Faraday House. Now, as to the elements of the thirteen subjects such as hydraulics, steam generation, steam distribution, combustion, boiler water treatment chemistry, boiler plant installation, friction (a vital subject for car accidents), electronic traction, railway engineering, transmission and distribution of electrical energy, principals of radio communication and introduction to process plants, it will give me pleasure in future to consider each subject with time on my side, for a change.'

'In other words, no more doses of strychnine.'

The vicar interrupted, 'Presumably, without a tutor, this happy result would not have been possible.'

'No sir. Often during our Saturday afternoons you have underlined that students are either quick to grasp or slow to develop. With me it was the latter. Yet it was always a fascination for me to witness the ability of those students from Cambridge who, previous to entering Faraday House, had taken honours degrees in the classics.'

Reverend Manning smiled. 'Throughout your life as an engineer, my boy, you will observe that the top leading engineering analysts have stemmed from the classics as their first line of university studies.'

In late September Gabrielle returned to the Lodge with Daniel and the twins for a few days during the Doncaster St Leger which is the most popular event in the northern racing world, and always well attended because of its international status. As it is located close to the big manufacturing cities of Lancashire and Yorkshire, the race-goers came mostly from the engineering works and the manufacturing companies, as Isabelle explained to Gabrielle. Isabelle always found the Doncaster race crowd full of fun and the joy of life. In particular Isabelle loved the local Yorkshire accent, with which she was well acquainted from her early youth near York. In fact to her amusement Hunt the chauffeur was unable to understand the petrol station attendant, who thought he was a local man.

'Te cum from te mill lad?' he asked. Hunt was puzzled. 'Is it French, Miss?'

Isabelle was enraptured and replied in a broad Yorkshire accent, to the delight of the attendant. It was then that a wayfarer from the country passed the BMW limousine still in the service station.

'Owt to eat lass, skint?'

'No problem, lad. To the surprise of Gabrielle and the guests, she emptied her purse, notes and coins, into his two hands.

'The Lord bless thee, lass,' he thanked her.

'But why?' asked Gabrielle.

'He is an old man. One of the two medals on his heart was inscribed *Ypres salient, 1916.* Whether true or not, the very name of Ypres is a reminder of – Daddy, and Uncle Bill and Uncle Tommy was gassed at the battle of Ypres!' This was said with a tear in her eye, as the car approached the famous racecourse.

Jim greeted the party at the paddock. Gabrielle asked

in French after his charge.

'No problem, *Madame,* except.... It is Ebony, now in the parade ring. He has attracted just as much attention from the visitors, even those from overseas, as our Precipitation. The massive stallion is the same height and build as our own.'

Gabrielle responded, 'Splendid, Jim. Then don't you see that the contest rests in the hands of the jockeys. Is ours the equal of their Lydia?'

'A difficult question to answer, *madame.* Lydia is a young woman, already famous. We must have faith.'

At that moment Milligan arrived and Gabrielle asked, 'Is the going what you refer to as good, Milligan?'

'Good to fair, madam. No mud today.'

Gabrielle made a prayer of thanks. Those Irish! she thought.

'Any news of the betting?' asked the vicar.

The bailiff replied, 'Yes sir, the number of confirmed runners has been reduced to thirty five for the St Leger. After his win by sixteen lengths at Goodwood, Precipitation is now a clear favourite. You will recollect, sir, that Ebony after his impressive win at Royal Ascot in the Queen Mary Stakes has not run since. So he is third favourite at ten to one. Precipitation is hot at five to one.'

Gabrielle asked, 'Who is the second favourite?'

'There are two, *Madame,* both from the Bussac stable. So far unbeaten, but out only once this year. They are fine Normandy stallions known as Marengo and Friedland.'

'Evidently Monsieur Bussac is a student of Napoleon,' responded Isabelle.

'But their performance over this distance?' asked Gabrielle.

'Fast, *Madame,* according to my friend in Pickersgill the international bookmakers. They raced at St Cloud during June and July, and both won by a distance in excess of twenty lengths!'

Isabelle commented. 'It seems that both of us have competition this afternoon.'

'And their price, Milligan?' asked Gabrielle.

'Ten minutes ago they were both quoted at six to one joint second favourites.'

'*Ca alors!*' expostulated Gabrielle. 'Monsieur Bussac is serious.'

Jim the trainer intervened. 'He is known, *Madame*, to wager heavily when trying. The wagers are made from Paris, according to the bookmakers.'

'Evidently he is trying this afternoon, with two second favourites, in addition the prize money is in excess of £200,000!'

All this was said in French in the paddock during the parade of the stallions in company with their owners and their trainers. The discussion was observed by a large, cigar-smoking Frenchman close to Isabelle.

'*Excusez-moi, madame,*' he addressed Gabrielle. 'My name is Bussac. I am delighted to meet the celebrated Madame Faure, a bastion in the field against the English.'

'Clearly, *monsieur*, likewise you have equal courage to venture this far north with your two stallions, Marengo and Friedland. Like Bonaparte at Arcola and Lodi!'

'They are both well tried and my trainer insists that they ought to be introduced at top level to the English competition. We have about two hundred stallions in training, and these two show promise for this particular distance.'

At that moment Isabelle appeared and was introduced.

'*Chère madame*, this meeting has made my day, as they say in America. Whether win or lose today, my friends in Paris will know that at last we have met!'

'Was there a problem, *monsieur*?'

'Indeed there was *madame*. Your horses from Hurry-On have carved us up, as they say in banking circles, and we do not yet know the secret. But we have a clue to be proved this afternoon.'

'And that *monsieur*?'

'After the race, chère madame, you will know my intimate thoughts about the subject.'

Milligan observed to Isabelle, 'Never known so many French flags, Miss, red white and blue. Quite an invasion.'

'And the betting, Milligan?'

'No change yet, except that the price of Precipitation has hardened to nine to two.'

Ebony was last to enter the parade ring. A whistle of surprise greeted his arrival.

'What a fabulous stallion,' came a murmur from the crowd.

'How do you feel, Lydia,' asked Isabelle.

'Elated, Miss. The unknowns from France are Marengo and Friedland. Perhaps we ought to rename Ebony, Waterloo!'

'So you really feel confident at this international gathering with 150,000 spectators from all over Europe?'

'Confident, Miss, like never before, and this time no rain and no mud, more room, wide starting-gate to prevent being boxed in, everyone so full of fun. My competitors are even trying to teach me some French!'

Indeed, thought Isabelle, Lydia is fast becoming an attraction.

The Bussac stallions also caused quite a sensation as they left the paddock. It seemed that all the racecourse was fluttering flags of red, white and blue and cries of 'Vive la France' echoed from all quarters.

'It seems, sir, Milligan addressed the vicar, 'that amongst the fancied runners we are now in the minority at four to one against the French, including an outsider at eight to one, two from the Bussac stable and Madame Gabrielle.'

Lydia was the last to mount after last-minute directions from George Marshall trainer and milligan.

'In this case, Lydia the instructions are simple, 'fast from the start. It is probably the fastest one and three-quarter mile race in Europe. Huge fees for breeding depend on the outcome.'

Isabelle added, 'Good luck,' and gave her a kiss.

Lydia had never seen so many French flags. Where are are our flags? she thought.

The runners lined up. Then they were off.

'No accidents from the start,' began the commentary. 'The going is firm. The setting pace is fast for this distance. Two furlongs from the start all the outsiders are in line, about nine in all. Three furlongs out and the Bussac entries are just in front by one length, closely followed by Precipitation, the favourite. Ebony, on the other side of the course, is also holding the leaders.'

Shouts of delight rang through the stands as one wit called out, 'Rule, Britannia.'

'Evidently, Milligan, your friend Buchanan is popular even in the North,' the vicar observed.

The bailiff smiled, and replied, 'Even in France, sir! As you will observe at Longchamp in October.'

The announcer continued, 'At the half-way post, the pace is still very fast, thanks to the Bussac entries. Only three runners are now able to keep up. The field is already ten lengths behind. Precipitation and Ebony are only a length behind the leaders, together with one other outsider from France. The leaders are now approaching the famous six-furlong straight before the winning-post. The favourite, Precipitation, has now moved up to join the Bussac leaders.' A few seconds later the announcer added, 'Ebony on the outside has also joined the leaders now all in line three furlongs from the post, fully extended.' The crowd were cheering. 'There are now five runners all together, only two furlongs from the post, all making their challenge. The French outsider has now fallen behind, but all the other four race together. It is an outstanding contest, three French challengers contesting against the Irish-bred Ebony.' Emotions were high, one furlong from home.

Lydia murmured to Ebony, 'Come, my darling, it is a tough race. One more last effort please, now, now!' Ebony responded, just as the French Precipitation also made his final challenge. The two raced together very closely, followed by the Bussac runners. The crowd was truly mad with excitement as the two French and one English contenders approached the winning-post.

'More, more, please,' Lydia urged Ebony, who responded with every effort in answer to his mistress. The result was clear, Ebony passed the post half a length in front of Precipitation. Once again the excitement was too much for Gabrielle. She collapsed into Isabelle's arms. Within a few minutes, however, she recovered, with the help of the smelling salts from the vicar.

'Forgive me, Isabelle. It is inexcusable of me to react in this way.'

'*Calme-toi*, dear Gabrielle. Precipitation ran a great race. The Bussac challenger was two lengths behind him. His reputation in France is therefore unimpeachable!'

'You are so kind, Isabelle, but it seems that my only hope

for the future of our Normandy bloodstock is to invest in the wild Irish strain, as Jim my trainer suggested last night.'

'Permit me, *chère madame*.' The big, cigar-smoking Monsieur Bussac re-introduced himself. 'First of all, courage, *madame, et mes excuses, chère Madame* Isabelle, but it distresses me to see one of our illustrious supporters of the French turf upset. Firstly, it is my firm opinion that our Normandy breed is equal to that of the Irish. Today it has been my pleasure to witness an unforgettable contest between the French and the Irish thoroughbreds. But who really won it? With my powerful field-glasses the answer was simple. If you had the advantage of my detailed observation, *madame* you would have witnessed that the real winner of that race was Lydia, that young jockey my trainer described as the young witch of the Irish!'

Isabelle was amused. 'You are too kind, *monsieur*. Lydia will be delighted to know that she has become a witch!'

'Truly Lydia is a mistress of the art. So courage, Madame Gabrielle, it was not the Normandy bloodstock that failed this memorable day, it was the witch of the Irish who beat us both! Madame Isabelle, is it possible for me to ask a favour of you? You have an exceptional rider in Lydia, without whom Gabrielle would have been the winner of the St Leger today. Well, as you may know my stable near Paris contains two hundred thoroughbreds. Now, this may sound to you a fairy tale from an old-timer like me. No one in my stable dare mount my latest young virile stallion, a two-year-old. He is so violent, he has thrown all my best riders! His name is Volcan, because he is indeed explosive. In English the name means volcano. My proposal is simply that during the October meeting at Longchamp, may we have Lydia to mount Volcan for the President Stakes at the meeting? The race is for two-year-olds.'

'Have you asked, Lydia, *monsieur*?'

'Oh yes, *madame*. Her eyes lit up when she discovered that Volcan was fully Irish bred, and added, "but my mistress must approve".'

Isabelle smiled. 'You work fast, Monsieur Bussac. Lydia will need at least eight days with Volcan by way of introduction, to judge whether she can race.'

'Splendid, Madame Isabelle. May we agree then to a visit

from Lydia early next month, say on the first of October?'

'Of course, *monsieur*. In fact, her great friend Ginger is my rider for Onward, entered in the Arc de Triomphe at the same meeting.'

'Well, well, *Madame,* an invasion from the Irish for a change! You can be assured of a popular reception.'

Isabelle smiled. 'So Monsieur Bussac, you may expect Lydia on the first of October, *chez vous,* near Paris.'

'Leave all the arrangement to me, *madame.*'

'Since the Longchamp meeting is to start on 10 October, do you mind if Ginger accompanies her? They are both very young and do not speak French.'

'A splendid suggestion, *madame,* there is plenty of room at my château, where they will be under the care of my wife.'

'Thank you, *monsieur,* your suggestion relieves me of anxiety for they are both under twenty-one and do not speak French.'

'Be assured Madame Isabelle, *tout sera en regle,* and my household speak fluent English.'

On the way back to the Lodge from Doncaster, both Gabrielle and Isabelle slept in the BMW, driven by Hunt, after an excellent early dinner given by Monsieur Bussac in one of the well-known inns in Doncaster. It was one am when Isabelle was able to see Roger, fast asleep, and to say her prayers for the blessings of the day by his bedside. It was a warm late September evening, she sat on the window seat fitted to a large window specially requested by Roger long ago. Dear God, she thought, if only time would stop sometimes. My dear brother soon to be married to a lovely young girl. I will miss my nightly vigil over his sleeping, and my prayers, more than my heart can sustain, in the absence of my Richard in Nigeria. Yet what a lovely girl Milly is, spiritually and physically, she thought.

33

Eventually the great day for the Longchamp meeting arrived. The party from the Lodge travelled by car. The young riders Lydia and Ginger caused much laughter as they exchanged notes about their elementary studies in French.

'But Milligan, this book bought last week in Smith's in Windsor says it guarantees I will understand French in three days,' Lydia protested.

'The operative word is understand. It depends upon your interpretation of it,' Ginger argued.

'So you believe that the book is a rip-off?'

'Not necessarily. Since your strange powers with racing stallions have intrigued the French public, you may need that little book for many years to come.'

It had been a lovely early sunny morning when Lydia first approached the open pen enclosing the young Irish two-year-old. Early October is perhaps the most attractive season in Paris.

With a loud clang an attendant shut the main gate, which was fixed with the notice *attention dangereux*. At the same time Volcan lashed out with his hind legs evidently glad to be rid of the attendant.

Lydia approached the barrier and started to hum 'Sur le pont d'Avignon', the only French song she knew. Volcan was interested. The wild Irish eyes began to relax, the hind legs became less taut. Who was this creature with a singsong voice? Volcan became inquisitive. He sniffed and approached the barrier. Lydia, as taught by Isabelle, offered a hand with a sugar lump. Volcan was puzzled and dived at the proffered hand, then consumed the sugar with relish, lashing out with all fours. He returned for more, this time two lumps. But Lydia insisted on more civilised behaviour, she withdrew her hand as he dived for it.

'Patience, *mon petit*.' Good expression that, thought Lydia from the book!

Next time he was less aggressive. This exercise went on for one hour, by which time Volcan and Lydia became formally acquainted. Eventually she sat on the steel rail of the fence. Volcan remained intrigued and allowed her to stroke the side of his neck, without interrupting the tune of 'Sur le pont....' It was then that the general manager of the stud arrived. In excellent English Monsieur Becot introduced himself.

'*Bon jour, monsieur*.' Lydia responded. 'Will you please attach this halter to Volcan, since it is my intention to walk him around.'

'It is too dangerous, Miss. He is not yet broken in.'

'Precisely, *monsieur*, and it is my intention to do just that.'

'Let me call two of our experienced riders, Miss, for he is still wild and stubborn.'

'Please, *monsieur*!' With that, Lydia was over the fence. Slipping the halter on Volcan she started to walk him in a circle within the pen, gently singing all the time. And Volcan began to take an interest in this young lady.

Meanwhile, Monsieur Becot was almost lost for words. 'It is dangerous, Miss to handle an unbroken colt.'

'That is why it is such a privilege for me to contribute to the job of breaking in Volcan. Now, *monsieur*, please let me have the halter and the reins.'

'You mean Miss, that you wish to lead him out for a little walk around? My most experienced stable boys have tried, with disastrous results.'

'*Cher monsieur*, my position in England is not that of a stableboy.'

'True, Miss, but you are my responsibility and only a young lady.'

'Please, *monsieur*, just see how quiet he is with me walking with him in this tiny circle within his pen.'

'Very well, Miss just for half an hour exercise in the stable yard.'

'At the same time *monsieur*, do not forget the saddle and stirrups, needed just to mount him for a few seconds.'

'Very well, miss, the ambulance service will be alerted in case of a throw.'

Lydia smiled. Evidently Frenchmen have little faith in female riders, she thought. It may be necessary for me to introduce them to equal rights!

The harness soon arrived and replaced the halter supplied previously from the stable.

Volcan was surprised to feel the leather saddle, and looked at Lydia, his new friend, for explanation.

She kept breathing, 'Sur le pont', and his eyes returned to normal.

Eventually, in the yard next to his stable, Lydia, a highly experienced rider, mounted in front of several stable-hands with open mouths.

'Open the race track, please *monsieur*,' Lydia requested. And after protesting in vain, the general manager opened the gate.

'But Miss....'

'Please, *cher monsieur*, so far all is well.'

'Yes, but....'

'Quick, or Volcan will jump the gate!'

'*Ouvrez vite*,' came the command.

Lydia was happy at last; so was Volcan. She felt the ripple of those pent-up muscles, and away he went at a terrific pace on the private race track, with several stableboys mounted on the practice sprinters. They never caught Volcan. At last he was in his element. It was only after three miles that she felt he had been sufficiently exercised to let off all the pent-up steam of the last few weeks. The last quarter of a mile was concluded in heavy rain. Good, thought Lydia.

Upon her arrival back at the stud, Monsieur Becot was full of praise. 'No wonder they call you the "witch of the Irish"!' Three of my boys will rub him down.'

'No *monsieur*, this first time, it will be my job. The action will cement intimacy. It may take two hours, but it is so necessary,' Lydia insisted. 'Also will you kindly arrange for me to have a camp-bed here just for the night, and a low-voltage lamp. A night with Volcan will then complete the treatment. The stable door may be left open at the top.'

Becot began, 'But, Miss –'

'Do not worry, *monsieur*. This procedure is common practice when breaking in highly sensitive young stallions. Once he settles down tonight I will return to my room at the house.'

Volcan was delighted with the rub-down by Lydia and to observe that she was going to settle down in the stable, apparently for the night.

It was about midnight when Lydia returned to the house. The room was luxuriant with so many lamps and mirrors. After the English-speaking housekeeper departed, she knelt by her bedside for short prayer of thanks given for the happy day and the lovely bedroom.

Early the next morning at the stableyard, she was asked by Monsieur Becot whether she wished for a trial run soon after breakfast with some of the local practice stallions.

'No, *monsieur*, let the trials take place with a few of your fastest two-year-olds,' Lydia told him.

'Yet Volcan has never seen a racecourse. His first appearance is to be only an introduction to the public.'

'True, but in three days' time, it will be more than an introduction. Volcan will be out to win! All that is asked is a little faith in the "witch from Ireland"!'

Monsieur Becot smiled. 'Very well, young lady, we have two unbeaten two-year-olds, only ran once this year. We will match them against Volcan this morning. It will surprise me if Volcan can come within twenty lengths of these on the six furlong straight.'

The request from Lydia to Monsieur Becot, the patron, who was away on business, caused a stir among the staff. Kicking his heels with glee, Volcan was happy to be led out of his stable by Lydia. Her French was limited to *Calme-toi*, Volcan – and he was excited which made it difficult for her to control him, especially when he observed the other two-year-olds lined up with him and ready to race.

Monsieur Becot signalled for the start flag to be raised. Lydia was thrilled '*Chèri*' she murmured, '*Sois sage.*' The flag went down. They were off.

Volcan seemed to understand. He nearly wrenched Lydia off the saddle. What power, she thought. Nevertheless, he was a late starter by at least one length. Then Lydia settled down to a battle with these Frenchmen and their unbeaten two-year-olds. Indeed, she was in her element. We will soon show Monsieur Becot, she thought, whether this wild, impossible Irish newcomer to the French racing world is to be degraded as horsemeat. How stupid people can be.

The race was on. Lydia, a highly experienced jockey, gauged rapidly the extent of the competition. The two unbeaten two-year-olds were now two lengths in advance after one furlong.

'Now, *chéri*,' she murmured, '*plus*, more, *plus*, more, speed!'

Volcan responded, to the great surprise of the onlookers. It gave her such a thrill to feel this mighty young stallion responding to her cry for help. Even to her surprise, he soon passed the unbeaten leaders before the halfway line of the trial run!

Monsieur Becot in the main stand was almost speechless. 'Never seen anything like it on this test track in forty years for a two-year-old trial.'

As the race progressed, Volcan increased his speed until finally he ended twenty lengths in front. Pandemonium broke out amongst the onlookers. As Volcan passed the final post he gave Lydia a sharp surprise. Either the other runners were below standard, or else Volcan was exceptionally fast. It was rare for Lydia to be nearly launched out of the saddle. In fact, there was a similarity with Ebony as a two-year-old.

Monsieur Becot, approached beaming with pleasure. 'No wonder they refer to you as the Irish Witch. Congratulations.'

'Was the time impressive, *monsieur*?'

'Not only impressive, it was a record for the rest run for two-year-olds. Monsieur Bussac, when he phones tonight from New York, will be most happy to know that he has a reasonable chance in the big race the day after tomorrow at Longchamp.'

'Two requests, Monsieur Becot,' Lydia asked. 'First, this trial race today must be kept top secret.'

'You have seen the security and alarm systems surrounding the estate.' Monsieur Becot asured her.

'Yes, but in England we have a saying – "Walls have ears,

and ears have toes, that's the way the message goes"! The result this morning may become dynamite in the betting circles, if it ever becomes known outside this estate. Volcan was priced at fifty to one, by the leading bookmakers in London yesterday.'

Monsieur Becot put a call through to the house, to alert all the guards to be extra vigilant.

'The second request, Monsieur Becot; can you obtain for me a list of the more promising competitors, their immediate history and country of origin?' Lydia added.

'That presents no problem, Miss. As two-year-olds, most of them have no history. At present there are four favourites in a field of thirty-five, three from Italy, one from Germany. All unbeaten with impressive times. In fact, you are our only hope, and we could do with a winner. This is one of the largest stables in France and we have had plenty of seconds this year but no winners. The prize for the race, a major event for France is £300,000.'

'Do not worry, Monsieur Becot. Rarely has it been my pleasure to mount such a dynamic two-year-old as Volcan after two years as a rider for my mistress, Lady Cameron. In fact, you may confirm tonight to Monsieur Bussac, when he phones from New York, that he has acquired an exceptional thoroughbred in Volcan, in great confidence. It would be most unwise for Monsieur Bussac to reveal this news to any of his *copines* or *copans* in New York!'

'You really are an Irish witch, Miss.'

'Not really, *monsieur*, just a young village girl from Winkfield in England, with plenty of horse-sense.'

'Now it is possible for me to understand, Miss, what is known in France by the English under statement.'

'You are most kind, monsieur Becot.'

Before the great day, Lydia regularly exercised Volcan, often with an admiring audience. However, the evening before the race, Monsieur Bussac telephoned from the USA.

'Hello, Lydia. So your new name is the Witch of Ireland. How gorgeous!' He continued, 'You are confident, that our stable has a chance tomorrow?'

'More than a chance, a fighting chance Monsieur Bussac. Confidentially it is my opinion that your Volcan is exceptional and that in my experience as a jockey on Irish thoroughbreds which goes back to seven years ago, from the age of thirteen. Your Volcan will take a lot of catching tomorrow.'

'So Lydia, even with four favourites from Italy and Germany at three to one in a field of thirty five, you feel that we have a chance?'

'More than a chance, *monsieur*, a fighting chance!'

Monsieur Bussac smiled into his telephone, 'In that case, you may count upon my presence at Longchamp tomorrow.'

It was eleven pm when the security from the main gate telephoned Lydia in English. 'Excuse me, Miss, a young lady, apparently a friend of yours from England, Miss Ginger, wishes to stay with you for a few nights.'

'Oh yes, please allow her to come in, and explain to the house-keeper she may share my room.'

The two famous jockeys threw themselves into one another's arms to the relief of the housekeeper, Maria, a Portuguese.

'Maria, Ginger is my colleague at the stud in England.'

'In that case she will be Santa Maria to me!' cried Ginger.

Maria was overwhelmed with emotion. '*Merci beaucoup*, Miss Ginger.'

They talked and talked far into the night, like two sparrows.

'So Ginger, it seems that we are both equally in demand at Longchamp.'

'With an embarrassing difference, Lydia. You are by far in the most enviable position, a fifty to one chance, a complete outsider, never run before. What a gift form Heaven – if Volcan is the stallion you describe. My responsibility is weighty, hence my request to be here with you.'

'Why?' Lydia asked.

'Because Onward was quoted in London at evens. In other words, the bookmakers stand to lose millions if Onward wins the race the day after tomorrow. Nevertheless, there is a little score to be settled between me and the Colonel at Royal Ascot.'

'Personal?' Lydia wanted to know.

'If you like, yes. He reminded me that, in the interests

of the public, the runners must perform flat out from the start, that is not necessarily my view, but this time the Colonel may not be disappointed.'

'Why?'

'You shall judge for yourself dear Lydia after three thirty tomorrow.'

Lydia remarked, 'You are still a little sore about their observations, then. Ginger, that would be the least of my problems. You performed miraculously through all that rain and mud in the King George VI at Royal Ascot.'

'That is why his comments stung me.'

'Mountains out of molehills,' Lydia asserted. 'The racing world would know the truth. Why do you think that the bookmakers have priced Onward and you at evens, in the European race with perhaps the greatest value for the calendar year, and you are concerned about the observation made by the Colonel. Really, you make me laugh.'

Ginger smiled. 'Perhaps you are right Lydia. She changed the subject, 'What about your prospects tomorrow?'

'Not a tenth of your responsibility, at fifty to one, nevertheless not without its features, as Holmes would say to Watson. A much shorter race, six furlongs for two-year-olds, the most coveted prize for their age group in Europe – rather like our Coventry Stakes at Royal Ascot – but the prize money is far higher, as always in France. However, the stable needs to win, so in spite of the intense competition from Italy and Germany, four favourites all at three to one, my instructions have been flat out from the start. Nevertheless Monsieur Bussac had conveyed to me that the stable is hoping for a miracle, they need to win, the first hopefully this year!'

With the riders settled down for the night at one am. Maria came at nine am. They were both fast asleep. She tried again at ten am, this time they stirred.

'Ladies, in ten minutes you will be served in bed with a French breakfast with coffee and hot milk.'

'Gorgeous, Maria!' they both echoed, 'Croissants and fruit juice, please.'

After a clean-up in the bathroom they were back in bed just in time for the arrival of Maria, who seemed to have adopted them.

'*Alors, mes enfants.*' Have you everything you need?'

'One question, Maria.

'Yes, my child.'

'In the lovely bathroom next to this exquisite bedroom there is a tiny bath. Is it for babies?'

Maria, a true mother, replied, 'No, my children, it is called a bidet.'

Its functions were gracefully explained and they both enjoyed a laugh about their ignorance.

Ginger ventured, 'No one has a bidet in our village, Maria.'

Lydia added, 'My mum will have one on our list of improvements after this next race!'

Maria was in fits of laughter after their revelations as she entered the kitchen, full of gladness. Yet, when fully armed security guards entered for their cup of coffee, she thought, those young girls, highly qualified as professional riders, are today responsible for winning or losing, high stakes in case, at the end of the day!

'Is all well, Maria?' asked the security guard.

'No problems, sir,' she responded.

'Will you please ask them to be ready for Monsieur Becot to take them to Longchamp at two pm. The master has asked me to escort them.'

'Indeed sir, no problem,' replied Maria.

Before leaving the compound Lydia escorted Ginger on a tour of the stables.

34

Upon arrival at Longchamp Lydia and Ginger met Isabelle, the vicar and Milligan.

'Well children,' asked Milligan, 'Did you both sleep well in the luxurious home of Monsieur Bussac?'

Ginger gave him a hug. 'Mr Milligan, we both discovered something quite new, it is called a bidet.'

'Quiet, Ginger, this subject is not appropriate at present,' Milligan responded.

Isabelle laughed.

Eventually at three thirty the entries for the six furlong race for two-year-old sprinters were requested to prepare to depart for the parade ground. Volcan was looking superb.

Isabelle gave a kiss to Lydia 'Keep very calm, judge each situation as you experienced in the Queen Mary Stakes at Royal Ascot. Good luck.'

As the race started, Monsieur Bussac arrived in the same box as Isabelle, Reverend Manning, Milligan and George Marshall.

'Madame Isabelle, *milles excuses* for the interruption, just arrived from New York, simply had to see the race!'

Isabelle welcomed him. 'Your entry was still fifty to one at the close of the betting, a minute ago.

Monsieur Bussac smiled. 'So much now depends on your lovely Lydia.'

After one furlong ten of the thirty-five runners were all in line. A few seconds later, the three Italians the German, were in the lead. Volcan on the outside, was moving at a great pace to challenge the leaders. It was a short race, very fast. Two furlongs from the post, the whips were out for the four leaders, but Volcan was gaining ground, with no whip! One furlong from home. Volcan was edging forward, now level with the German contender. Half a furlong to go and Volcan was without doubt making splendid effort.

'My darling, just a little more,' Lydia murmured to Volcan, 'please faster, faster.'

Volcan heard the call from his mistress from spirit to body. He knew that he had to be in front for this sprint race against the Italian and German stallions. He exerted every ounce of his young powerful muscles. He went past the post almost in line with four other contestants. The race crowd was moved with emotion as the result was announced. Lydia on Volcan had won by a very short head – perhaps by a whisker, thought Isabelle.

The bookmakers and the ladies were ecstatic with joy a winner at fifty to one!

Several of the ladies kissed the bookmakers, who referred to Lydia as the witch! 'It is not fair, English witch must not be allowed,' several Italian and German race-goers complained.

Monsieur Bussac was overwhelmed with the result, 'Madame Isabelle – perhaps it should be Lady Cameron.'

'Just call me Isabelle,' she smiled. 'We are race-goers together.'

'Bless you, Isabelle, then refer to me please as Jacques.'

'Good, in that case Jacques, we may both learn something by listening to Lydia's report.'

'How right, Isabelle. Let us go now before the press invade her.'

'Bless you, Lydia,' Isabelle said with a kiss.

'So sorry it was such a near win,' Lydia apologised. 'My conclusion is simply that Volcan is made for a longer distance, the mile for example. He was far from blown at the end, whereas the Italian favourites all had their whips out to the end. In other words, over seven furlongs or even a mile Volcan would have won by several lengths.'

'Very interesting,' interrupted Monsieur Bussac. 'First of all, young lady, my congratulations and grateful thanks for mounting Volcan, apparently so diffcult at the start when he arrived from Ireland. No one was able to mount him without being thrown. You will be hearing from me, via your mistress, in due course.'

Lydia was saluted as a heroine in the winning enclosure, with many cries of '*Sorcière Anglaise!*'

As Monsieur Bussac walked away from the enclosure with Isabelle he remarked, 'That win, Isabelle, has put my stable, without a win this year, on its feet, a prize of £450,000, and a gamble of £10,000 to win at fifty to one that is nearly half a million pounds to keep in training 200 thoroughbreds. It will be a successful year for the stable.'

'Congratulations, Jacques. But what a risk at fifty to one and by a whisker to boot!'

'True, but, Napoleon always skated on a low factor of safety. Take the bridge at Lodi, for example. Three times the flag was shot down, until he took it personally with bullets flying around him and led the renewed attack in person. He won two vital bridges of the campaign.'

Isabelle smiled, 'A student of Bonaparte, Jacques?'

'As always. Now, the subject of breeding. It is my wish to have a business accommodation with you about my mares to be serviced by your Hurry-On.'

'No problem Jacques. It will be expensive!' Isabelle warned.

That night, in single beds pushed together, Lydia and Ginger discussed the day's adventure in the most luxurious bedroom they had ever shared together.

'Ginger, did you know that there are twenty-four lamps in this bedroom?'

'No,' replied Ginger, preoccupied with studying the report supplied by her mistress about competition from the thirty-five runners in the Arc de Triomphe Stakes to be run at three thirty at Longchamp.

There was a knock at the door. The head housekeeper Maria entered. It was eleven pm.

'Now young children, before the night closes is there anything you need?'

'Yes, there is,' Lydia responded. 'Something very special, Santa Maria.'

'A cup of something, *mes enfants?*' she enquired.

'*Non merci*, Santa Maria, simply a kiss good night!'

Maria could hardly suppress a tear. What wonderful children, she thought, and what an incredible responsibility when the high stakes are considered in the racing world.

No wonder the security service was dumbfounded this week, by the addition of double guards, and special dogs throughout.

Before retiring, Ginger enquired of Lydia, who was going to sleep, 'Don't you think you left it a little late? They said you won by a whisker!'

'Believe me, I tried everything, including a prayer. The competition was a group of sprinters. As I explained to Monsieur Bussac and to our mistress, Volcan will be far better over the seven furlongs or even over the mile. How do you feel about tomorrow, Ginger?' asked her friend.

'A few debts to pay off, including that arrogant Monsieur Michael Requier. Yesterday, in fact, he informed me to be prepared for the thrashing of my life, by his Mistral, recent winner of two events over three and a half miles by five lengths.'

'You mean also the Colonel at Royal Ascot? Really, Ginger, it was all well meant.'

'Maybe. However, after the studying of the information supplied by our Miss Isabelle about the competition, Longchamp will be surprised tomorrow. Bless you, Lydia. Good night, and again my congratulations upon the result today.'

It was a fabulous October morning, sharp but sunshine blessed. A short walk in the lovely garden with Santa Maria, as they called the housekeeper, before breakfast fascinated Lydia and Ginger. There were so many sub-tropical plants.

'Santa Maria, you must have a wonderful gardener,' Ginger exclaimed.

Maria smiled. 'There are seven of them. Apparently Monsieur Bussac remained in his Paris flat last night, otherwise he would be pleased to show you around.'

Soon after one thirty Milligan arrived with his team of boys to ensure that Onward was well groomed after his morning exercise with Ginger, in company with Lydia and Monsieur Becot.

Becot told Milligan, 'Rarely have we seen here such a powerful, massive stallion *monsieur*. My best wishes for your success today with Ginger up.'

'*Merci, monsieur*,' replied Milligan. 'It will interest me to learn the name of the stallion which can compete with Onward today.'

The Arc de Trimphe was the great race of the meeting and of the year. Onward remained a strong market favourite at two to one. Gabrielle, beautifully turned out for this fashionable event, was not optimistic, even after two successful wins over the three-mile distance with Cat o' Nine Tails recently, each by five lengths! He was priced at five to one, second favourite. Maestro was third favourite at six to one, also with recent wins over this distance.

'We have learned too many lessons in the past whenever competing with the Hurry-On breed over this distance,' Gabrielle told the press. Indeed Onward, with Ginger up, commanded much attention.

Isabelle asked Ginger, 'Is all well now that you are ready for the challenge?'

'Never felt more confident Miss, especially after reading your reports last night,'

Isabelle smiled, 'The Colonel at Ascot?'

'Precisely, Miss. This is the first occasion when it is hoped he will be more happy with my tactics than at Royal Ascot in the King George VI Stakes.'

'You must forget his observations, Ginger. It was his duty to record the facts.'

The bell sounded.

'Bless you and good luck, Ginger.' Isabelle began.

Lydia interrupted, 'No whiskers please!'

'Of that you can be certain,' Ginger replied and away she cantered.

'What did Ginger mean by that remark?' Isabelle wanted to know.

'You will soon see, Miss.'

What a fabulous day, she thought, as the thirty-five runners took up their position before the start. Both her rivals, Cat o' Nine Tails and the Maestro, were at the opposite end of the line. Ginger was relaxed. This time her strategy was clear.

Longchamp was not to forget this event for many years to come. The pace was fast from the start. Ginger was up with the leaders this time. For the first quarter mile the leaders were all in a bunch of fifteen according to the announcer.

'How is Ginger doing?' asked the vicar.

'No problems, sir,' Milligan responded. 'This time out in front with the leaders, and three miles to go.'

'That's a change, Milligan.'

The announcer continued, in both French and English, as a graceful gesture to the visitors. Milligan was impressed, and with his powerful field-glasses continued to follow the commentary.

'They are approaching the mile post. Maestro and Cat o' Nine Tails are both in front, closely followed by the favourite Onward and three Italian unbeaten stayers.' Then the race situation stabilised until the two-mile post. The Italian leaders were urged forward and led by two lengths. 'Still a mile and a half to go. Both Cat o' Nine Tails and Maestro are being urged forward to maintain the challenge,' the announcer continued.

Ginger murmured to Onward, 'Now, my darling, this is where we begin to leave the field.' At the last mile post the three Italian stayers, together with Maestro and Cat o' Nine Tails, were beginning to fight for the lead. Onward was still close behind, much to the surprise and disgust of Michael Requier. 'The favourite Onward is now moving up to the leaders,' they heard over the loudspeaker. The leaders noticed the challenge. Whips are out half a mile from home. Too early, thought Milly. The Italian contenders were unable to meet the challenge. Then half a mile from the post Onward started to race. The public had rarely witnessed such a sensational conclusion to the famous event valued at £300,000 prize money. A quarter of a mile from home, Onward was in front of all competitors and at the post Onward won by five lengths. A loud cheer was heard from all quarters of the course. At the reception a special cry was heard, often repeated, "the ghost of Hurry-On". Isabelle was deeply moved.

'Are you well?' ventured Gabrielle.

Isabelle smiled, however not before a tear or two managed to trickle down her cheeks.

'Are you sure?' She was a little embarrassed with her emotion. 'But you have won. My dear, why the...?'

'Do not worry, Gabrielle. The spirit takes me like this sometimes without warning. It was just a fleeting memory of long ago, my first encounter with Hurry-On, frightened, badly treated, neglected, mud everywhere half starved, ready to be sold for horsemeat in Italy, straight from the wild moors of Ireland, with a large notice outside his pen "Dangerous". This was the moment when we first met and after one hour alone together, with the wind and rain blowing, we became intimate friends. Today his first born has won a highly coveted prize in Europe, the Arc de Triomphe, of immense value to our little stable in Winkfield.'

'But now you are expected to lead him in,' Gabrielle reminded her.

'Dearest Gabrielle, please lend me your mirror. It would not do to be seen tearful at moments like this.'

The racing circle of France gave an impressive reception to Isabelle as Monsieur Bussac accompanied her to the leading-in ceremony.

'Congratulations, my dear, and also to that splendid rider Ginger, evidently another witch! The timing was perfect. But the bookmakers have marked him down already to evens for the Gold Cup at Royal Ascot next year!'

'You are so kind, Jacques. Hopefully we will meet again next year at Royal Ascot.'

They did – but that is another story.

Meanwhile the same evening in London as Milly was leaving the Piccadilly office, the news vendor was active, 'Read all about it, son of Hurry-On, the one they could never catch spread-eagles the field at Longchamp.' An extract from that paper was sent to Isabelle, who kept it in her bedroom until her last days.

Milly murmured a prayer of thanks and added, 'Bless you, Ginger.'

35

As the lovely months of July and August slipped by, Roger relaxed and was set to work on a few jobs on the farm. His marriage with Milly and eventual entry into the Nigerian engineering business, were planned for December, with the return of the master.

Early in October, after Doncaster and Longchamp, during a walk through the cattle paths of the fields adjacent to the Lodge, Louis, (the assistant to the vicar at St Mary's) Roger and John heard a low-flying plane and felt that something was wrong. John observed that it was a modern military plane. It seemed to be gliding slowly to land in the fields, yet there was little room between the oak trees.

Roger remarked, 'He is in trouble. Quick, Louis, race back to the Lodge. First, telephone the police, then ask Milligan to bring help with any fire-fighting cylinders available, and alert Isabelle to stand by to direct the necessary help from the police.'

The plane was now close to the land. It travelled just overhead – the pilot could be seen trying to extricate himself. The plane was marked with the Nato sign; in brackets the German cross was seen, indicating the Luftwaffe. Evidently a German, thought Roger. Probably lost his way. Then came the crash as the plane landed in the soft undergrowth of the local woodland, hardly a hundred yards away. John and Roger raced to free the pilot as the first yellow tongues of flame were seen emerging from one of the two aero gas turbine engines. The pilot seemed to have lost consciousness, thought John. Indeed Roger thought he was dead as they struggled to free him from the cockpit. The flames travelled fast.

'Roger, take care,' John called as he smashed his way through the window part of the door. Fortunately the pilot recovered sufficiently to open the door, then fell back as the flames started to lick around the nose of the plane.

'Quickly, John. He is too heavy for me. Together we can do it.' They did, and dragged the pilot, now unconscious, fifty yards away. Part of Roger's clothing was on fire. John pushed Roger into a running stream about four feet deep to dampen the fire, then came the explosion and the plane went up in flames. Fortunately, they were all insulated by the trees and shrubs from the flying debris. It was at this stage that Roger, badly burned, also passed out. So John had two wounded on his hands. However, the local police, with Roger's friend George the constable, and the ambulance all arrived – together with the German Doctor Loretz, friend of the family. Quickly Dr Loretz analysed the situation.

'A lucky escape for all concerned, Isabelle. Both unconscious men to bed at once. You have sufficient facilities at the Lodge? Good. Expect me back in half an hour with all the necessary aid, plus a qualified nurse who may need to stay with you for about one week. Meanwhile, I will report the situation to the Military HQ at Reading. You may receive a few security officers late in the afternoon. Remember this is October, sleepy England, and Sunday to boot...!'

Isabelle enquired, 'But Roger, Doctor?'

'Do not worry, my dear, he will wake up in about an hour. By then the nurse will have dealt with the burns to his arms and neck. Those two boys acted with courage and deserve full praise for their precipitate rush to help rescue the pilot. The German remains a mystery. Physically he seems unhurt, it is his mind which seems to have collapsed! More later.'

John was exhausted, but well, and was able to fill in the details for Isabelle as both the two wounded soldiers were put to bed.

The capable nurse soon took over with medical authority and worked on the burns sustained by Roger, with success.

Eventually Roger awoke to find that his arms were immobile with bandages and was about to curse and swear until he was aware of Isabelle and the nurse.

'So, dear sister, it seems there is life in me yet!'

Isabelle smiled. 'More than that, you are a hero, having saved the life of the German with your friend John, who remains unhurt and will come to see you after the nurse has completed the initial therapy.'

'After which at least four doubles of Ballantine whisky will go down well.'

'Not after pain-killers, dear brother of mine. Try to understand that for the rest of the day you are a wounded soldier.'

Roger pulled a face. 'It is easier now to understand how those heroes felt who managed to survive Second Ypres, April first gas attack at St Julien four miles north of Ypres – Uncle Bill's favourite topic.' He closed his eyes.

The nurse nodded to Isabelle, who closed the curtains of the wide-open window, as Roger always liked it, to shade the room from the late afternoon sunlight. Isabelle gazed a few minutes upon the relaxed features of her charge in this world, especially upon those long eyelashes just like a young girl's. As John knocked and entered, she motioned silence. She kissed Roger on the forehead and they both left the room.

'You both did a splendid job, John.'

'Your brother was the first to enter that inferno and deserves the fullest praise.'

Isabelle insisted, 'Without you, however, both Roger and the German would be burnt alive. Bless you.' She gave him a kiss.

It was then that the military from Reading asked to see Isabelle. The commanding officer, known to Isabelle after the experience with Richard a few years ago, remembered their acquaintance.

'So, once again, Lady Cameron, we are indebted to you for your timely action. How is your brother?'

'Thank you, officer. He must be recovering fast, because just before passing out he asked for four doubles of Ballantine!'

'Splendid.' The other two officers were both highly amused. 'A true grandson of the soldiers of Mons, Ypres and the Somme, Lady Cameron!'

'Indeed his first baptism of fire, officer. We are all proud of him this day, together with his friend John, the assistant vicar to St Mary's local church.'

The introduction was made, and the officer told John, 'Delighted to meet you, sir.' Then he turned to Isabelle. 'Lady Cameron, may we keep you for five minutes about the subject of the German?'

'Of course, officer. Let us go to the study. Meanwhile, John, do not forget dinner with us tonight, including Milly, Lucie and Reverend Manning.'

'This German is giving International Security some headaches. His name is Heinz Gallard, a brilliant engineer, in life taciturn, no time for fools, inclined to arrogance – typically German.'

Isabelle added, 'Typically English also, officer!'

'True, Lady Cameron, but to continue. He is highly respected in Germany as one of the leading brains on the subject of aero gas turbines and rocket propulsion. The Federal Government of Germany requests that he be preserved at all costs, and brought back to normal health with care. I remember the delicacy you exercised as you brought your husband back to health a few years ago.' The officer paused.

'Has he a girl-friend, officer?'

'A good question.'

'Intelligence are currently making enquiries. You will hear from me on that subject in due course. Meanwhile are you prepared to accept the challenge to bring him back to health, mentally in particular, for it appears according to our medical experts that it is his memory that is damaged? All expenses defrayed by the German government, which attaches extreme importance to his recovery, in special care.'

'Willingly, officer. It will be a challenge to us all here, and fun,' responded Isabelle.

'Splendid. In that case that concludes my brief for today. The nurse will be in residence for as long as you feel it is necessary.'

A few hours later Heinz was still asleep with the nurse close by.

Isabelle noticed several textbooks on the subject of aero gas turbines placed by his bedside, together with the New Testament in German and a few books on applied mathematics, and thought, it seems Roger may be interested in our invalid.

A few days later Heinz was able to venture into the farm and to the stables, where he met Ginger cleaning down Onward after an early morning exercise. Heinz loved horses. He was an accomplished rider and able to appreciate the principal features of showjumpers, but of thoroughbreds for racing he was ignorant.

'A racer?' he enquired.

'More than that sir, a winner last week at Longchamp, Paris,' Ginger proudly told him.

Vaguely Heinz remembered reading about the event. Indeed, he envied those who were able to mount racehorses.

It was a woman apparently, Miss, who rode that stallion to victory. His name was Onward according to the press. It would interest me to meet such a female. They do not exist in Germany. And so this is the wonder stallion which spread-eagled the field at Longchamp. You have made my day, Miss, as the Americans say.'

'Incidentally sir, the woman at Longchamp last week was me.'

Heinz was thunderstruck. 'Impossible, Miss. Excuse me! Indeed, it is a privilege to meet you. The press refers to you as "Ginger the witch from Ireland".'

They shook hands. 'In fact, sir, there are two witches according to the French, for my friend Lydia also won at Longchamp on Volcan.'

'Incredible,' he remarked.

'Do you mind describing to me your thoughts during that great event, in particular how you were able to gauge the potential of the enemy during the event?'

How very German, she thought, then said aloud, 'It was not so difficult. Competition had been studied with care, and after my previous mistakes at Royal Ascot in difficult weather conditions, and after a reprimand by the stewards in The King George VI Stakes, I learned my lesson. The unknown were the Bussac entries, who challenged too early.'

'Then you urged on to the post with a whip?'

'A whip is never carried by me, sir.'

'Impossible, Miss. How then do you urge on your runner?'

'In the event of an emergency, by prayer! Hence the reason for our labels in France as witches.'

'Who is the other one?'

'My friend Lydia, winner of the St Leger at Doncaster a few weeks ago, together with the Queen Mary Stakes at Royal Ascot in June.'

'*Ca alors* – as they say in France. Do you speak French, Miss?'

'No, sir.'

'My French is better than my English.'

Lydia came over to meet Heinz. She was slightly older, a little more sophisticated, and at the same time fast becoming an attractive young woman, but rather aggressive and emotional.

'You must be Heinz, sir, crashing into our peaceful countryside, frightening our rabbits, our cattle, our chickens, our cows – now with reduced milk yield – and upsetting our valuable thoroughbreds.'

'My sincere apologies, Miss. There is no excuse, except that as you say in England, it was an act of God!'

Lydia stamped her foot, still full of passion. 'God, what a race,' she said aloud.

'Why, thought Ginger, is Lydia so disturbed with this stranger?

Heinz was on his guard. Here was a woman of passion, evidently anti-German.

'Act of God, my foot,' Lydia continued. 'My father went down in our battleship the *Hood*, with a note in his diary, "Eighteen-inch shells are all around us, a hundred yards off, from a distance of twenty-seven miles". His last note! It was the *Bismarck*!'

Heinz replied, 'A strange coincidence, Miss. My father went down in the *Bismarck* – with the note, "The gnats described by our navy in their records were in fact the Swordfish aircraft of Coastal Command, which dropped a bomb into the propeller systems of the most powerful battleship ever known, disintegrating the rudder mechanism and causing her to move only in a circle. The British Navy then, with four battleships, pounded her to pieces, yet she went down fighting to the end[?].'

'My uncle, sir, was one of the pilots of those Swordfish aircraft, the gnats, said by German naval reports to be tied together with string.'

Heinz bowed with great respect. 'Miss, it seems that we have something in common!'

Lydia continued, 'Ten of the Swordfish aircraft all carried the bomb. The aircraft which released the critical bomb is a matter for Coast Command. It may have been my uncle.'

'Permit me to repeat, Miss, my gracious respects and sympathy.'

It was then that the nurse arrived. 'Hello, Heinz, treatment time upstairs, in accordance with medical instructions from Reading.'

A note from Isabelle was on his table. *'You are invited to attend a family dinner-party tonight, subject to the approval of the nurses from Reading. Both Ginger and Lydia are included in the party.'*

'Well, nurse?'

'The pulse is high, Heinz. Why?'

Lydia and Ginger were left alone together in Ebony's stable.

'Don't you think, Lydia, that you were somewhat abrupt with this German stranger, an enforced guest under our roof to boot!' Ginger continued, 'We have been brought up together, since babes in our cots, within the confines of Winkfield, we went together to the village school then the high school at Bracknell. The close association, you will agree, surely give me licence to comment on your unwarranted antipathy towards this stranger.'

'Go on.'

'Perhaps a short note expressing your regret, at the same time an apology for the emotional outburst this evening about the war?'

'Ginger, only you in all this world could persuade me to undertake such an action. Very well, will you help me to write it? Those bloody Germans. Sorry to impose on you like this. Perhaps the races have drained my nervous energy.' There was a tear in her eyes. 'Maybe, Ginger, or perhaps it is my daddy who is needed in times like these.'

'Come now, let us get ready for the dinner-party at the Lodge, in company with the enemy!'

Lydia smiled. 'Dear Ginger, you are always so calm, no wonder you spread-eagled the field at Longchamp last week in company with the finest thoroughbreds in Europe. No question of a win by a whisker or a short head. You must help me through this early life, by giving me advice. Nevertheless, it is tough. Those bloody Germans!' She repeated.

They both retired to their respective cottages to dress for dinner.

It was a merry occasion, the vicar and Milly, recently returned from Bordeaux, together with Isabelle, Lydia, Ginger and the German Heinz. Not Roger, he was still in bed.

The vicar was most interested to meet Heinz, and asked about the crash.

'It was a technical problem, sir,' Heinz answered, 'being analysed by our engineers from Duisburg.'

'But you, Heinz, the military in Germany are keen that you remain with us for the season.'

'True, sir, for reasons still not quite clear to me.'

'Do you like it here?' the vicar enquired.

'It is paradise, sir. My only concern is for having frightened the farm animals during the crash landing, especially the chickens and the milk cows!'

Lydia looked down at her plate, Ginger smiled, and only Isabelle responded.

'But the egg production has been exceptional since then.'

Milly added, 'Excellent, it was high time to move those lazy hens into action. Only the excitement of the crash made it possible.'

This comment caused mirth from everyone, except Lydia.

Finally, Isabelle added that even the milk yields that morning were up.'

Splendid, in that case you will be able to attend our little church on Sunday,' said the vicar. 'Perhaps you ought to know, Heinz, that my responsibilities here do not end with the church. In fact the Colonel of the Military in Duisburg has been in communication with me about the accident. He had been assured by Dr Loretz, our local German doctor, that you are making a rapid recovery. It appears also that you are working on some new designs for rocket propulsions.'

Heinz was startled. 'It is meant to be top secret, sir.'

'The military authorities in Duisburg have made that clear to me, so much so that your latest drawings and designs will be delivered to me tomorrow by special messenger from the factory in Germany.'

Good, thought Heinz, the Germans still work fast when it is necessary. 'Thank you very much for your kindness,' he said aloud.

The vicar continued, 'Secondly, the medical authorities in Duisburg have urged a four to six week relaxation, here if desired, where you can continue your engineering studies at leisure. Finally, the authorities there explained to me that, after the passing away of your parents during the war, you have pursued a course of advanced technical studies, with brilliant papers written on physics and on chemistry ever since leaving university, without any social life whatsoever. Your German friends even pray that you may find a suitable girl-friend in England to calm you down, or they will send you one from Germany!'

Heinz smiled. 'You may inform my friends in Duisburg, sir, that indeed a young lady has at last come into my life who strikes cords in my heart, as they say in romantic tales. But she is unaware of my passion for her at this present moment in time. She may be in Duisburg, Paris or even in England.'

Isabelle commented, 'Dear Heinz, what a tantalising response.'

The vicar continued, 'Evidently you have lived a quiet and rather lonely life since leaving university.'

'Not lonely, sir. The Holy Virgin Mary is always present in my evening prayers, also in the early morning prayers. Her daily guidance has given me great confidence in the pursuit of my scientific studies and now in my humble life's work at the research department in Duisburg.'

'So you are a deeply religious believer?'

'Yes, sir, at least as far as it is possible for me to

understand. But my hardship has been quite simply no one with whom to discuss my thoughts about spiritual life and what our Lord wishes from me in his world – my Germany,' Heinz explained.

Lydia was greatly moved. Her eyes were misty, as Ginger noticed.

The vicar asked, 'So why is it that in Duisburg they are more concerned with your mental state than with the crash, which must have just missed the chickens?'

Everyone laughed except Lydia.

'This is true, sir. Previous test crashes hardened me to these sort of incidents. If the Lord wishes me out of his world, so be it! The crash was exceptional in that the door release mechanism was jammed, and Roger fortunately saved my life, by the use of his strong arm! He is not here tonight, otherwise it would give me great pleasure to thank him for his courage in breaking through the door and braving the flames with such fearless unconcern for his safety, so typical of the young English fighter-pilots much respected by my countrymen during the war.'

Milly was thrilled – a special kiss tonight for her betrothed.

'Perhaps tomorrow you will be able to meet my brother,' Isabelle said. 'He is recovering upstairs from first-degree burns.'

'Your brother,' ejaculated Heinz. 'No one told me. It touches me deeply, Miss, to know that my saviour from that inferno is your brother, assisted by John his friend from the local church. What an incredible race, to produce the young men like your brother and to make them the only fighter pilots ever to trounce the Luftwaffe, not forgetting in particular those brave young men who piloted the gnats which sank the *Bismarck*!'

Lydia was unable to contain her tears, which flowed quietly. Suddenly Heinz noticed them, and jumped up and went to her side with his white silk handkerchief to stop the tears. A gallant gesture, thought the vicar. Everyone was surprised that not a word was spoken by Lydia or Heinz.

Heinz addressed Isabelle, 'Please excuse me, Miss, but Lydia revealed to me this afternoon that her father and his co-pilots were responsible for the bomb that sank the *Bismarck*. We had a small confrontation about the chickens after the crash.'

Lydia responded, 'Please forgive me, Miss for this emotion. Heinz has not told you that his father went down in the *Bismarck*, like my father who went down in the *Hood*, and my uncle was a member of Coastal Command responsible for dropping the fatal bomb on the rudder of the *Bismarck*.'

'How very interesting,' observed the vicar.

Isabelle responded, 'Lydia, do you feel relaxed enough to continue the evening?'

'Oh yes, Miss. So sorry again for the emotions. In future it will be my aim to behave like an adult.'

'Not too soon, Lydia. You are such a lovely young girl at present, even with the tears!' responded Isabelle.

The vicar smiled. What lovable people, he thought.

This remark caused merriment.

Ginger pressed her hand. 'Dear Lydia, you never cease to surprise me. Take those sensational wins, for example at Royal Ascot, by a short head, by a short neck, and at Longchamp by a whisker, at fifty to one for Monsieur Jacques Bussac – what a rip-off for the bookmakers, as Milligan expressed it. Indeed it was a boon from Heaven as underlined by Monsieur Becot, the Bussac stud manager, after his stud finances had seen ten months of no winners, like the lean years of no corn as in Egypt thousands of years ago, as he told Milligan before returning to London.

Lydia smiled for the first time in the evening.

Heinz was elated. 'Are we friends now, Lydia?'

Lydia swallowed, looked up, then responded. 'Yes, Heinz,' she smiled.

Splendid, thought Isabelle.

The vicar continued, 'Then why are they concerned in Duisburg for your mental health and anxious for you to relax here?'

Heinz smiled. 'As indicated earlier, sir, it is not easy to explain, even in Duisburg they do not understand or they are bone-headed!'

There was a respectful silence.

'Reverend Manning, my physical, mental and spiritul make-up is one hundred percent, in perfect order. Indeed it will be paradise to work on the rocket propulsion plans during the next few weeks in the lovely rose garden I noticed this evening.'

Isabelle made a note.

Heinz went on, 'To you vicar, my emotional problem may seem to be a storm in a teacup, as you say in English, 'but to me it is sometimes a nightmare. Lydia tonight confirmed my thoughts about my country and my countrymen. It worries me far more than my engineering problems in Duisburg or my next crash on a test flight with a defective gas turbine engine. Twice in this century Germany has made a bid to conquer the world by force. Bismarck always advised never to go to war with England. Why, vicar, did this have to happen? As Lydia revealed to me earlier today, the battleship *Bismarck* was able to drop eighteen-inch shells a few hundred yards from the *Hood*, twenty-seven miles away, indeed an engineering feat never known before the war, yet my admiration for the German engineers was overshadowed by the way Lydia referred to her grief for the loss of her father. Why is it not possible for highly industrial countries to co-exist instead of fighting one another? These simple thoughts alarm my friends in Duisburg, so they brand me as a mental case, presumably.'

'Not quite, Heinz,' replied the vicar. 'They have so much respect for your ability and technical leadership, they simply want you to become more sociable.'

Isabelle interrupted, 'Do not worry, Heinz, we will all help you to relax here on the farm.'

The evening broke at eleven pm. Heinz and Milly offered to accompany Lydia and Ginger home. The October evening was mild as they laughed and talked on the country road to the village of Winkfield. At the gate of her cottage, Heinz asked Lydia, 'Will you grant me one request?'

'If it is possible.'

'No more tears from now?' He held out his hand to say good night.

She did not reply – instead she stood on tip toe to kiss

him good night on his cheek and murmured, 'No more tears, Heinz,' and rushed to her cottage front door with Ginger, who was staying the night.

'Well,' said Milly, 'it seems that Lydia is happy at last.'

Heinz did not reply immediately. He took her arm to walk back to the Lodge.

Meanwhile, Ginger and Lydia went to their bedroom in the cottage. Her mother was asleep in another room.

'Did you really mean to kiss the enemy?' Ginger asked.

'It has been an emotional night,' Lydia responded. 'It was difficult for me to understand my instincts and thoughts. Perhaps my gesture made me look foolish, but he seemed so kind.'

'Your gesture was well-timed Lydia, that young man has much to think about tonight.'

'What do you mean?'

'Because, he has become fond of you!'

'How do you know?' Lydia asked, but Ginger did not reply.

36

Early the next morning Heinz was already enjoying a walk in the fields at six-thirty am when he met Isabelle on Hurry-On, returning from John's cottage. Heinz seemed to be walking in a daze as if deeply preoccupied with some obscure thoughts.

'Good morning, Miss Isabelle. It is a pleasure to see how you handle that giant black – what a beauty.'

'He is known as the one they could never catch.' Isabelle told him. 'Did you sleep well Heinz?'

'No, Miss Isabelle, I had strange disturbances of an emotional nature, which I wish to discuss with Reverend Manning.'

'Will you be able to see my brother this morning, soon after breakfast?' Isabelle asked.

The nurse was with Roger as they entered his bedroom. Roger was propped up on pillows surrounded with bandages. Heinz went straight to his bedside, knelt down and with a simple prayer, adding, 'Bless you, Roger, for your gallant action.'

At that moment Milly entered and was moved with the impromptu ceremony.

'Thank you, Heinz,' Roger responded. 'This is my betrothed, Milly.'

'Indeed we have met already. My congratulations, Milly. Within the next few weeks will you both be my guests during a short visit to Duisburg to see Farben Industries, the place where my research work is conducted. A private plane will collect us at a small aerodrome for test engineers near here and take you both to my HQ. You will be interested also, Roger, as a future engineer, in the development of our boiler and combustion division, we are building rocket propulsion engines with a take-off thrust of forty miles a second into space!'

Roger was keenly interested, but the nurse intervened.

'It seems, Miss Isabelle, that the visit will be enough for this morning. His pulse is too high.'

'No problem, nurse, time only for love talk. But when will it be possible to enjoy the next meeting with my new friend from Germany, so that we can talk about rocket propulsion to Mars?'

Roger asked Milly, as the others left. 'Heinz is just the engineer that interests me, building rocket propulsion engines to cope with the great heat transfer to withstand 2000 degrees centigrade to the shell at take-off. This is engineering, Milly, nothing like the Germans when it comes to rocketry.'

Addressing Roger, Milly added, 'Now, my darling, perhaps it is time to sleep.'

'Milly, when will we marry?'

'Soon after your father returns from Lagos in December. It is only reasonable.'

'And where to live, my darling?'

'In heaven, precious!'

Roger smiled, '*Tu es adorable!*'

He went to sleep immediately, after all the excitement. Milly drew the curtains.

Later in the evening Heinz discussed his problems with Isabelle as they were walking around the well-tended garden.

'Miss Isabelle, what is to be said is embarrassing,' he began.

'Continue....'

'Before precipitating myself into your lovely farmland, the medical experts at the factory in Duisburg cautioned me to be less intense at my work and at thirty years of age to try and find a social outlet. In fact, they accused me of being anti-social simply because of no outside friends, even up to my age no interest in the feminine sex.'

'Why?' interrupted Isabelle.

'A relevant question, Miss Isabelle. I was born in the most industrial part of Germany, the Ruhr. My father and grandfather revealed to me in detail the devastation caused by the Allies during the war against Hitler, as they advanced into Western Germany, where my grandfather survived miraculously and where hardly a building remained upright after the raids of Bomber Command.

'As a sensitive human I am very proud of my German birthright, but the country was devastated by war – the result of spiritual inexperience, political ineptitude and military mismanagement. My nature became introverted and arrogant, simply because I could resolve technical problems, however involved in far less time than my contemporaries, and because of my distress at the decisions of our past leaders since 1900 to embark on two world wars for domination of the world, I felt that to shun society was the safer course for my brittle nature. Miss Isabelle, the fabric of your family society in England has remained intact for over a thousand years of tradition. Our traditions have been smashed by the Kaiser and Hitler. We are now trying to rebuild, but it is heavy, unrewarding work.'

Isabelle replied, 'Our cities also were devastated. Coventry was flattened, and the London dockland fire raged non-stop for days. Liverpool and others took a beating.'

He held his head a moment. 'Dear Miss Isabelle, all this I know and it grieves me. However, arriving here in this heavenly part of England, my mind, body and spirit have received a bombshell. Not physically from the crash it was of no consequence to me if my life on this Earth ended, having crashed on four previous test flights – but from meeting your jockey, Lydia!'

'A dangerous occupation, Heinz.'

'True, Miss Isabelle, but since my arrival here my mind has received a jolt. It is my desire now to live, and live abundantly.'

'Why the sudden change?'

'A good question, as they say in your country. In my quiet moments, away from the activity of heavy engineering in the workshops of Farben Industries in Duisburg, where there is a splendid view from my bedroom window of many factories all working night shifts in the heart of the Ruhr, the power-plant area of Germany. As a young man spiritually aware all my life, living alone in my well-appointed luxury flat on a little hill in the town, it has grieved me so often to dwell upon the lost opportunities of Germany this century. My knowledge of religious history in Europe and England is deep, my chief relaxation away from the test beds. Indeed, the subject of the dissolution of the monasteries in England is quite a passion for me to study – Henry VIII was indeed a wicked man.'

Isabelle smiled.

'Miss Isabelle, so very sorry to importune you with my personal experience since arriving here, but my first shock, after the crash was the meeting with your jockey Lydia. Indeed, it was a confrontation. She revealed to me a note, sent to her from the Admiralty with a last message from her father – "Eighteen-inch shells all around us within a few hundred yards, twenty-seven miles away from the *Bismarck*. The *Hood* blew up", she added. She cursed the Germans and all their race, Miss Isabelle, me included, stamping her feet on the ground because my crash had disturbed her chickens! Tears falling fast from her lovely eyes. It was an embarrassing situation until it was explained that my father went down in the *Bismarck*, then she calmed down a little. We parted. The next day we met with her friend Ginger. Once again my apologies were discreet, with especial respect for her loss, and she responded for her lack of control about the Germans. This surprised me. Even more, yesterday evening, as Milly and I said good night at her cottage door, it seemed to me a kind gesture to express that hopefully there were no more tears. She surprised me also with a silent kiss on both cheeks and rushed into her cottage!'

Isabelle smiled, 'So like her passionate nature, Heinz.'

'It was then that unusual and strange feelings were beginning to flow through my body. We shared a sympathy about the loss of our respective fathers in battle. Now, Miss Isabelle, it is my impression that Lydia no longer considers me a cursed German. Now to the point, Miss Isabelle. May it be possible for me to see Lydia socially during the four-week holiday given to me by Farben Industries, now that we have both found mutual sympathy?'

Isabelle was interested. 'Of course, Heinz, no problem, except that in England we ask that all intentions are honourable, and if the friendship develops, it is essential that you meet her mother.'

'Miss Isabelle, be assured they will be honourable and discreet, with such a sensitive nature, to which Lydia will hopefully respond.'

'Do not forget, Heinz, that Lydia is about to embark on the racing events of her life next year at Royal Ascot, Epsom, Newmarket, the St Ledger and Longchamp. In other words, Heinz, Lydia may already have many other suitors. The best of luck, nevertheless.'

To encourage the association, Isabelle often invited Lydia for dinner, especially after Roger was able to walk about and spend time listening to Heinz talking about combustion and gas-firing practice in Duisburg.

Lydia enjoyed those evenings, especially the walk back to her cottage with Heinz and Milly as chaperon – insisted upon by Isabelle.

One night there seemed to be balm in the air as Lydia on tiptoe reached to kiss Heinz on his cheek. Heinz gently put his arms round to support her. Lydia felt the soft pressure on her breasts and with delicacy turned her lips to him. Heinz folded her to his body. What a heavenly moment he experienced! He released her gently, and she ran into her cottage without another word, breathing hard.

Her mother was worried. 'Where is Heinz, my darling?' Lydia smiled and said nothing. She went straight to her statue of the Holy Virgin Mary and murmured, 'Holy Virgin Mary, why are you so gracious to me? Thank you!'

The friendship ripened as the last October days drifted into November. One day Lydia was walking arm in arm with Heinz through the field paths and glades around Oakfield Lodge. They talked and talked, until they arrived at Ebony's stable.

'Heinz, give me twenty minutes,' Lydia requested. 'He is asking for a run over the mile stretch.' He noticed that when Lydia spoke to Ebony, his ears pricked, working forward and backward.

'It will give me immense pleasure to see you in action,' Heinz told her.

Finally Lydia mounted and Heinz marvelled at the consummate ease with which she handled the giant stallion. Lydia and Ebony went like the wind over that mile.

'Faster, my darling,' she whispered. Eventually she

arrived, happy and exhausted, yet insisted on rubbing down Ebony before retiring.

'So now, dear Lydia, all passions are satisfied?'

She smiled, 'For today, yes, Heinz.'

'And...?'

'Tomorrow night in the Lady chapel of St Mary's in the village, built by my friend Lucie, a Roman Catholic, it is necessary for me to attend a special meeting with an interlocutor who has promised to advise me about our future. You are invited to attend.'

'Indeed it will be a privilege. Is the person a man or woman?'

'Neither, Heinz.'

Heinz was puzzled, to say the least, for at least one hour afterwards during his walk around the village square.

At that moment Isabelle arrived to explain that Reverend Manning had the technical documentation and four top-level engineers from Farben Industries wished to meet Heinz for about one and a half hours tomorrow here at Oakfield Lodge in order to resolve two problems. One was on heat limitations to a newly produced metal alloy used recently on failed American rocket tests, the other concerned calculations for improving thrust on newly developed German gas turbines for rockets.

'Mrs Plant has prepared the study which is fitted with a long oak table suitable for such an important meeting, and Roger will be thrilled to attend the discussion if he is permitted.'

'Do tell Roger he will be most welcome, although most of the technical discussion will be in German.' Heinz added. 'May it be possible for Lydia also to attend, just in case a glass of water may be necessary without delay?'

'Of course, dear Heinz, no problem.' Isabelle smiled. So did Lydia, who heard the message.

'It may be strange to you, Miss Isabelle to ask for the presence of Lydia during a higly technical discussion.'

'Go on.'

'It is not easy to explain because the reason is beyond me. During the last few weeks Lydia has often been with me, either in the study or in the kitchen, or in the kitchen garden, when my homework has been done about this meeting tomorrow, involving calculations in applied mathematics in particular involving non-linear differential equations and the logarithmic derivative of the gamma function.'

'The fact remains Miss Isabelle, that during her tactful presence my brain seems to work at depth and with concentration I rarely experienced in Germany, and also at incredible speed, so that at the meeting my mind will be ready with the answers to their questions. Why the presence of Lydia has contributed so much to my solutions is beyond me. No doubt you as the spiritual head of this lovely family will be able to explain.'

'No, Heinz, it is not possible for me to explain, although it does happen in some exceptional cases. Nevertheless, this sympathy between you both is essential for this meeting tomorrow. That is obvious, so be it, Heinz.' She turned to Lydia. 'How do you feel about this meeting? The racing world does not want to lose you just yet.'

'You have my complete assurance, Miss that in no way does this affect my commitment to those fabulous stallions. Nevertheless, it does intrigue me to know how, simply why with my presence it is possible for Heinz to be inspired.'

'Mutual sympathy, dear Lydia is rare. Treasure it, but is not unknown.'

'How interesting,' responded Lydia, 'because often during the last few weeks, sometimes on a gate-post in the fields or especially in the kitchen garden by the sundial or by the remote oak trees next to St Mary's near the upper fields, Heinz will work an hour at a time on his calculations with his miniature slide-rule, steam tables, trig and log tables, as he called them, in fact no time for love talk…!'

'Dear Lydia, what a fabulous opportunity for you.'

'How, Miss?'

'Because you have found a young man of substance, quite apart from the fact that he has proved himself as an affectionate young man who needs love. Dear Lydia, you cannot miss. You are indeed blessed!'

The next day, direct from London Airport, the German engineers arrived at ten thirty am with Reverend Manning to mediate where necessary. The vicar was fluent in

German, due to his regular association with Dr Loretz. The visitors profusely praised Roger for rescuing Heinz from the burning plane, and confirmed that he would be most welcome at the factory at Duisburg with his friends Milly and Lydia.

During the meeting, as Milly related to Isabelle later in the day, Heinz never ceased to explain and emphasise all his own solutions to the technical queries raised by the engineering team from the factory in Duisburg, all in German, whilst she and Lydia served the company with coffee and biscuits, and water for Heinz. Indeed, Milly observed how Heinz responded immediately to their technical questions in a firm and confident military tone, as they liked it in German industry – but with concern, after the effects of the crash and the warning from the nurse about the pulse rate. In fact, there was only one instant at a critical moment in the discussion when Heinz turned to Lydia and asked for blank paper. Heinz made a sketch to illustrate his point about the value of the critical heat which must not be exceeded in the metal during the gas-fired rocket tests.

'Otherwise, during my test,' Heinz underlined in English 'there will be an explosion, and my new English friend Lydia will not be happy!'

Everybody laughed and Lydia blushed deep red!

'Gentlemen,' observed Milly, 'it is one pm, lunch is ready, and the flight time to Frankfurt is three thirty pm which leaves plenty of time to arrive at London Airport and have lunch without rush.'

Milly was relieved that the gathering continued in complete harmony.

'Miss Milly, you are an angel,' expressed one of the Germans in excellent English, 'indeed my energy would have soon collapsed without some sustenance after a four am start.'

It was a particularly merry occasion, with the vicar and Isabelle as hosts. Herr Gallard, Heinz's uncle, was most interested to discuss with Isabelle the progress Heinz had made since the crash.

'He seems to be very happy here, sir, and he is welcome to stay as long as he wishes.'

'You are most kind, Lady Cameron, especially as Heinz seems to have blossomed out in mind and body. There must be a reason for this change.'

'Perhaps that is because of his attachment to, Lydia, sir. My advice is simply to let their association mature a little longer. It may ripen into a creative conclusion!'

Outside as Hunt departed with the Germans, it was teeming with rain. Heinz went to the airport with his new friend Lydia, to see off his Uncle Gallard a former Luftwaffe pilot. Addressing Lydia in confidence, he said:

'My dear, you have made Heinz a new man, mentally and physically. He used to be an able mathematician and also a first-class physicist. Now he is back to normal and has put us all on the right track during this discussion this morning. The answers flowed just like the master of old as he used to be a year ago. This experience for me, my dear, is simply miraculous. Here is my card, please count upon me in case of personal problems, he is most precious to us in Germany, and to me in particular.'

They said goodbye at the reception. Lydia and Milly read the card: *Director General, Farben Industries, Duisburg, Germany.*

'So, Lydia,' remarked Milly, 'you have a precious cargo on your hands, to nurse back to normal health.'

'And you, dear Milly, with Roger after the crash and rescue.'

'No problem on that front, Lydia, he improves daily.'

37

The same evening the vicar was invited to stay for dinner. Indeed, it was a most animated gathering with Roger, Heinz, Milly, Lydia and Isabelle as hostess. Lucie and John also dropped in unexpectedly.

Lucie smiled, 'We are planning now for marriage. Do you think that it is too early?'

'Of course not, dear Lucie. Indeed my congratulations,' she said with a warm hug. 'And what about my early morning call, John, mounted on Hurry-On for my pot of coffee on your veranda?'

'You will always be welcome, even at six am in the morning,' John told her.

Isabelle turned to Heinz, 'You will be able to witness Lydia in action on our local training ground at the Marshall Stables, against some of the unbeaten high-flyers from Europe, the roan stallions from the famous Bussac stable in Normandy – who will reside here during the winter months for breeding.'

'You never cease to surprise me,' he said to Lydia. What a responsibility, he thought.

'It is a privilege, sir,' Heinz ventured, addressing Reverend Manning, 'to meet you here tonight in this less formal situation and to thank you cordially for your intervention on our behalf with the police and immigration authorities, which it seems are particularly strict here in England.'

'Not at all, Heinz. After what we witnessed this morning with your friends from Germany, our first priority evidently is to see you again fit and well. Incidentally are you a Roman Catholic?'

'No sir, a Protestant, as most of us in Germany.'

'Splendid, a denomination close to our English Church.

In which case our local service on Sunday does not present any problem.'

'No sir, the service is a pleasure to attend. In fact, my spiritual problems are not confined to the Church either in Germany or England.'

'Problems?' prompted the vicar.

'Well yes, sir, the pursuit of a full and happy life. For example, opportunity. Is the Lord really working his purpose out, as they tell us in the hymn books? Also for example, from whence comes that interaction between rider and horse, apparently a spiritual gift possessed by Lydia, Ginger and Mistress Isabelle? Even in French racing circles they refer to Lydia and Ginger as "*Sorcière Anglaises*".'

Isabelle encouraged the vicar, 'Do not worry sir, we are all interested in this challenge thrown up by our German visitor.'

The vicar responded, 'Well, Heinz, take your principal question first about the Lord working his purpose out. Try to imagine first of all, with your knowledge of planetary science, that the solar system was not forgotten during the creation of the universe. It has taken millions of years to create His Earth, to be filled with people also of His creation, given freedom of thought. Our creator selects with care officers who He believes will be capable of promoting His interests on His Earth from the Pharaohs of Egypt to Christ His Son and our leaders of the present day. If you follow the history of the world you will agree surely after some of the events even in this century, that His purpose is evident everywhere. Sometimes young enthusiasts ask me, "Does God ever sleep"? My reply is simple, "How can He ever rest"? The officers He has placed into responsible positions in the past, for example, Gladstone, Napoleon and Caesar all die off eventually and must be replaced, even from the days of Joseph and the Pharaohs. His angels are seeking consistently for officers the world over – yes, even today – to be placed into positions of responsibility, in every profession and trade known to man. Believe me, Heinz, whether a minor office boy, a director general, a successful self-made man, doctor, engineer or scientist, your adult livelihood will be selected for you by the Lord, based upon your ability, spiritual integrity, your attitude to life and well-being. You will be judged on your merit, depending on your stewardship of the job allotted to your initial activity, whether a simple road-sweeper or the aspiring managing director of a large industrial conglomerate like Farben Industries in Germany or ICI in England. So, in answer to the question by the young enthusiast, the answer is no, the Lord never sleeps!

'Your next problem, Heinz: opportunity. It is my experience that there never will be equality of ability or opportunity in this world. Take for example our dear friend Roger, bottom of every class for eight years at Abingdon, and for five and a half years at London University Engineering Faculty, to emerge with only a third-class degree even after the immense drive and energy devoted to his studies during those years. Sooner or later he will find his feet in this world. Opportunity, Heinz is in the very exclusive hands of God in Heaven, no-one else!

'Thirdly, Heinz, your observations about the intimacy between the riders here with us tonight and the massive stallions, is a subject quite beyond me. My advice is simply to accept the phenomenon, evidently the reason why in France they are referred to as witches! This subject is not for me to comment on, it is not within my knowledge or experience.

'Finally, the pursuit of a full and happy life – your first question. The answer to this question is simple. There is no reason why life throughout its span cannot be stimulating and happy every day, every hour, providing that the strictest attention is given to prayer daily, morning and evening. After all, it is well known that prayer is the breath of the spirit. Does that answer you?'

'My grateful thanks, Reverend Manning especially for the solution offered to my current problems. It has been quite a revelation. Shame on me for not knowing anyone like you in Duisburg, sir!'

Lydia pressed his hand

'That is easy for me to understand, Heinz, from what we have gleaned about you, especially after the visit of the technical experts from your factory in Duisburg. For example, so far in your young life the passion has been physics, chemistry, mathematics and with that brain, plus the unusual imagination to resolve intricate technical problems in heavy engineering, you have blasted your way to the top, to hold now the respect of the entire technical management of the German factory employing a quarter of a million people. Understandable, Heinz. However, perhaps it is possible for me to give you a little guidance in order to bring a smile to your face more often, and reveal to you a simple fact.'

Unfortunately, the telephone interrupted this discussion. The vicar answered it.

'Is it possible to speak with Mr Heinz Gallard? This is George Manfield, managing director of Monnouth Industries, Manchester. We have just received a translation of his paper on heat transmission during combustion to special metals from our agent in Cologne, with a note that Mr Gallard is staying at Oakfield Lodge.'

'What you say is quite correct, Mr Manfield,' the vicar replied, 'but Mr Gallard is still under doctor's orders and convalescing after his plane accident. I suggest you send him a letter at this address and he will respond in due course.'

'Plane accident, I do hope he is well.'

'Improving rapidly, Mr Manfield,' the vicar assured the caller. As he put down the receiver, the vicar continued, 'So you see, Heinz, you are now in demand in England.'

'And your final guidance, vicar, after this unfortunate interruption?'

'Quite simple, Heinz – beware of the barrenness of a busy life. In other words, if and when you find a simple treasure, such as a painting, an attractive garden attached to a simple cottage or an old cathedral of historic fame, or perhaps the blessing, more important than any others, a devoted future partner in life' – this time Heinz squeezed Lydia's hand so hard she nearly uttered a cry – 'then treasure it and pursue it with your vast mental ability and nervous energy.'

'Thank you so much, sir.'

'It seems to me that you have driven yourself through most of your early life. Now presumably it is simply to rise to an exalted position in the company, at the expense of excluding all social contact with society, given at the start with an exceptional brain for mathematics, physics and apparently a sound knowledge of the Scriptures.'

Heinz's face assumed sadness. 'No sir, it would be a wrong analysis. The true reason for excluding myself from society is twofold, based upon my thought about Germany during my maturing years. The first, the unredeemable failure of the leaders of my country to prevent so much distress in two world wars. Their logic for me is totally inconceivable as it is seen today as reprehensible and, so with death of my parents my life grew inward and was devoted to intricate design work as an engineer, for it was evident to me that my natural gift in this world was physics and mathematics – late into the night seven days a week my passion continued, not to be top of the technical team, vicar (in spite of my German arrogance and impatience with my lot in this world), that passed long ago, but to work for the redemption of my country, which is loved by me in spite of the blot it has left on this Earth. How it will ever be possible for me to reconcile my thoughts and shame for those leaders of 1914 and 1939 remains for me unknown to date.

'Secondly, it is fortunate that, parallel with my intensity for work is my equal enthusiasm for the Holy Scriptures. From the Old Testament through to the New, my studies have rarely ceased and have remained a constant wonder to me, especially with the spiritual conflict generated by the recent advent of planetary science. My donations to the cathedral at Duisburg are generous, but my social activity there is zero in spite of strong encouragement from the priests, where there are no problems so long as my place at the early morning Sunday Communion service is not occupied! So vicar to continue, we come now to the unexpected event of the crash, when Roger saved my life. The incident unhinged my thinking for several hours. Gas-turbine tests are routine for me and crashes often happen, but certain safety precautions in this case failed. It occurs to me it was a message for me from the unknown, and it came with a shock a few days later walking slowly through the farm. A young girl called Lydia indicted me, together with all the German race, for nearly killing her chickens with fright during the crash. This was quite a surprise. It was necessary to keep calm and try to establish a link between the crash and the chickens. She gave me such a broadside from her verbal guns about Germany and its arrogant people that it took me several moments to collect my wits. My apologies were offered immediately without much effect, yet in my quiet moments soon afterwards it occurred to me that some strange spiritual force had interrupted my rigid life-style, to crash through my normal and rigorous routine. For example, it was not easy for me to imagine that, as a proud and arrogant German in my present position at the factory, it was possible to be reduced to size by this attractive young English girl. So, with much meditation, it was necessary to re-think my life and examine with care the accusations levelled at me by Lydia. My position now is that of a chastenend man. But at least a dear young friend has come into my lonely life; perhaps the angels have arranged it.'

Lydia was shedding some tears, Isabelle was comforting her.

'You are a very lucky young lass, Lydia, so dry those lovely eyes, now!'

'A very interesting account, Heinz,' responded the vicar. 'Hopefully your friendship with Lydia will mature.'

At that moment Mrs Plant arrived with a telegram for Isabelle from Hamburg.

> We understand Heinz Gallard is still recovering at your home. Is it possible to visit him on Monday to discuss a metal fatigue problem on our boiler plant now under test for Japan?' Most gratefully and apologies, Hans Suriff, Farben Factory, Hamburg.

This was read aloud by Isabelle. She added, 'It seems that you are popular tonight Heinz. Have we your permission to accept on your behalf?'

'You are most understanding, Mistress Isabelle. Their problem can be settled in one hour. So very sorry to impose on your kindness with these talks.'

'Not at all. It is life for this home, the coming and the going. The house then vibrates with energy. It is a big establishment and it must be filled to be productive and full of life!'

Then Mrs Plant informed Isabelle that a small parcel had just arrived by hand from Germany for Heinz. Inside was a tiny box with a note.

The vicar remarked 'A little early for Christmas, don't you think!'

Heinz translated the note from his factory. 'From Chief Analyst to Heinz in England. Herewith sample of fine metal dust found in the special metal fuel pipes of the aerogas turbines of your plane, hence the reason for the crash. Top-level technical investigation underway.' There was a postscript: 'There must have been an angel near where you pancaked! Some like it hot! Take care.' It was signed by the Munster technical director, Farben Industries. A few more tears flowed from the lovely eyes of Lydia. Isabelle pressed her hand.

That night after dinner Heinz accompanied Lydia to her cottage, this time without Milly her chaperone, a walk of twenty minutes. He held her close, as they continued their walk in the starlight for another hour.

'My darling, a heavenly night. Until tomorrow,' she said at last.

Heinz held her warm responsive body close as they embraced. What an exquisite kiss, he thought. So soft, so full of fire and passion, and vibrating with love.

'My trouble, Lydia, is simply that the love of a young girl is unknown to me, hence my lack of practice!'

Lydia responded, 'That is precisely what is so wonderful for me, my darling.'

He was introduced to her mother.

'You are most welcome, Heinz. The village knows all about you, and your miraculous escape. But the real sensation is simply that a tall German has come into our lives. Some of the older ones are frightened and even ask me whether the Germans still manufacture Zeppelins to bomb London, as they claim to have seen in 1917. However, it has been a delight for me to dispel those ideas and to assure them that all is peace now on the western front.'

'You are most gracious, Mrs Alton. Please assure them that in future the English and the Germans will work together during any future conflagrations.'

'Lydia never ceases to tell me about you. Can you assure me that your feelings are mutual.'

'You have my confirmation, Mrs Alton, spiritually and physically.'

After a cup of coffee and a discussion about his activities, Heinz departed, full of happiness in heart – so much so that he took the long road back to Oakfield Lodge, an hour's walk on a black and windy night, accompanied by Richard's dogs Dante and Lupe. Zeppelins, indeed. So even today the older folk remember the 1914 war, he thought. Later, walking past the tiny cenotaph next to St Mary's, he observed with his small pocket lamp the words *To those who fell, 1914-1918*. For several moments he remained there in reverence to the British dead, filled with admiration for their historic and miraculous victories. What wonderful people, Heinz reflected, as he knelt down on the damp stones to give thanks for his precipitate arrival in this tiny village, peopled with such spiritually aware inhabitants, then added, But when is my country going to grow up spiritually and forget about Aryan Man? Heinz then reflected for half an hour on his knees on the wet stone by the small village memorial, as the fine warm rain fell.

Dear Germany when are you ever going to put an end to thoughts about conquests of the world? Bismarck insisted before he passed away during the early days of this century 'Never go to war with Great Britain'. It is in all the European history books. Indeed, it was a shock to Kaiser Wilhelm II after the invasion of Belgium in August 1914, when England declared war on Germany, followed immediately by France. Yet the Kaiser was ready and planned for a quick result – one and a half million veteran troops of the Prussian Guard crossed the Rhine during the first fourteen days of that terrible venture. Even history books are written about the atrocities committed by the storm troops as they marched through Belgium. Then came the node to the venture or the hard tumour on the joint decision made by the German High Command led by General von Moltke. The first setback to the advance he recollected from history came as a surprise to the High Command, Names unknown hitherto appeared in the news – Mons, Arles, the Marne, that immortal French endeavour to halt the Prussian armies, where, it is said, angels were seen to encourage the French First Reserve, and eventually of the first battle, Ypres. And then an extraordinary event – 250,000 women from every class in the United Kingdom between ages seventeen and thirty-five, volunteered and even forced their way to the battle zone in northern France to help and nurse their beloved wounded soldiers. Nowhere, thought Heinz, has the female population of any country responded with such heroism to the help of their menfolk. How the British and French armies ever managed to contain the initial German onslaught still remains obscure to us in Germany. The German back-up supplies problem apparently was one of the causes. They were unable to keep up.

Then Heinz recollected, Moltke was soon replaced by General von Falkenheim and eventually the four-years war of attrition ended in 1918. What an incredible waste, thought Heinz.

Then from a nearby cottage window on that wet warm night came the sounds of the Haydn String Quartet No. 3, the Emperor, the old Imperial German national anthem. Heinz was taken by surprise, nevertheless he came to attention until the end and murmured, 'May God help Germany.'

His thoughts continued, Hitler, the able obssesive leader and one-time soldier from the western front, within fifteen years was master of Germany. During those twenty years from 1918 to 1939 Germany became the military power in Europe. Unemployment in Germany was down to zero, every factory was placed upon a war footing. Even after the years of the Great Depression 1919-1934, industry in Germany prospered, the Luftwaffe became the most formidable air force in the world. The German naval force likewise expanded rapidly – in spite of the limit of 10,000 tons for German pocket battleships, imposed by the Allies. The *Bismarck*, the largest battleship ever conceived, was completed at 75,000 tons in 1939! There were others, like the *Graf Spee,* sunk in the South Atlantic, at 10,000 tons. All this, thought Heinz, in twenty years – what a race, perhaps the most dynamic the world has ever known. But incorrectly inspired, by both the Kaiser and Hitler. It is vital now – without any delay that modern Germany works her passage back to normality and Christian standards, he concluded.

The reasons for the rise of Hitler had been unclear to Heinz until a few years ago. The blockade of all German ports until the armistice 1918 was extended for another twelve months at the insistence of the French. During that time one million German babies died, starved through lack of food for the mothers. The German soldiers, returning from the western front, never forgot that tragedy, Heinz recalled that the German army of 1918 never surrendered, it was the folk starving at home that caused the German collapse.

Naturally, Hitler, an able and obsessive man, caught on to the spirit of this tragic situation and the might of modern Germany was born from those front-line Germans in the 1914-1918 war who never surrendered.

But, he reflected. where do we go from here? Can Germany ever become a truly great nation, great as the English, who are so well acquainted with the past world and its growing-up problems – especially those of the developing areas of Africa and India, where English rulers excelled for over four hundred years to educate those primitive, least civilised races, just as the Romans governed Spain, France and England two thousand years earlier.

During his visits to Cologne soon after settling down at Oxford, Heinz was told by the older members of the family group that early this century there existed a custom practised by some spiritually advanced high schools in Germany to lead those students who had finished their eight-year course, to the gate of the town, in order to wish them God speed on their way through life by singing Psalm 37 (Psalm of David). Did this mean, pondered Heinz, that at one time early this century the German people and their leaders were spiritually aware? Why was it then that Imperial Germany advocated that 'might was right', and that the methods of the mailed fist never failed, eventually leading to their collapse? Is so whatever happened to the divine spirit that prompted the choral celebration of the Psalm 37 sung by those young men and girls at the end of their last year, the last day as they left the establishment where they had passed their formative years before 1914?

As his thoughts continued to race and the light soft rain continued to drop around the war memorial next to St Mary's church, Heinz recalled that the German armies in November 1918 surrendered, not because they were beaten in battle, Their armies were starved into surrender. Many of those dynamic soldiers who had attended as youngsters those early schools of learning must have been desperately disillusioned. Indeed, as they returned to Christian existence it was evidently a comparatively simple matter for Hitler to persuade them to join the ranks of National Socialism, where discipline and sense of order became an attraction after the chaos of 1919 in Germany.

Heinz continued to develop his thoughts, and recalled that the new political leaders of Germany had no time for Communism nor democratic government. Indeed, they enrolled the youth of the nation into production for the state, rigorously orientated. The German mind always disliked disorder. From ten million unemployed in 1926, there was little unemployed anywhere in Germany by 1936. The whole of industrial Germany, the most powerful nation in Europe at the time, was then engaged upon the production of armaments and fully intent on war – for example the most powerful battleships were constructed, the *Bismarck*, the *Tirpitz* and the *Graf Spee*, also a formidable air force – alas, with hindsight to where did it lead? Where now, thought Heinz, was the spirit of Psalm 37? Surely there must have been many Germans alive then who were aggrieved at the totalitarianism of the Reich at the time, especially older ones who were spiritually aware under one-time imperial Germany.

Heinz continued with his thoughts in the light rain on that warm summer night, now well past midnight, with Dante the labrador urging him to return home to his warm straw bed. Is it posible, he wondered, that a few of those German students of long ago, now old men, still remember the Psalm 37 of their youth. What must be their thoughts! Can the spirit of present Germany rise to the spiritual challenge of the present age? What an opportunity! No, thought Heinz, the leaders of Germany have always been moribund, totally inexperienced and far from a settled state of mind. The French are even in a worse condition – governed by a democratic dictatorship represented by the president, no flow of constructive discussion in parliament as for example in the British government, where there is a healthy balance of discussion from their back-benchers quite unknown in European parliaments.

On his way home in the dark to Oakfield Lodge his thoughts turned to history. It became known soon after 1919 that in the event of victory it was the intention of Imperial Germany to take over the management of the British Empire. The dark races were to become slaves indefinitely. Evidently, thought Heinz, our Creator thought differently. After all, the world and its people were his creation. Then, thought Heinz, why Hitler? Again the answer flowed, basically to combat Communism! What now then for Europe? The thoughts continued to flow. Europe has suffered much this century. Now it must settle down to help those desperate people in Africa everywhere by self-sacrifice for the help of others, all over the world. With these thoughts Heinz walked back to his warm bed at Oakfield Lodge at 1.30 am, soaked through. He slept late next day!

38

It was the last week of October when Isabelle received a message from Monsieur Jacques Bussac.

'My dear Isabelle, there is trouble at my stable with my favourite young two year old, Volcan, soon to become a three year old in December. As you kindly suggested, every morning I visit Volcan soon after breakfast. We are friends, but he is far from friendly with my riding staff. Volcan seems to enjoy throwing my best riders. The Prix de L'Etoile, the final race of the season for two-year-olds in France is on 2 November, All Souls' Day. The race is one mile, intended as a trial run for the famous Two Thousand Guineas classic at Newmarket in April next year in England for three-year-olds.
   The equivalent prize money of £300,000.
   Monsieur Becot, my trainer-manager, insists that the only person in all this world who can manage Volcan for this major event is your rider Lydia. There are forty runners, four are unbeaten, Italian, American, French and German all co-favourites at four to one. Volcan is sixteen to one in spite of his splendid earlier performance in August. It seems that the racing public know of his wild behaviour locally. Domestic news travels fast, in France!
In consequence, dear Iabelle, *je suis coincé*. Can you help me by sending your lovely Lydia to mount Volcan once again? Is she available soon to become re- acquainted with that wild Irish young stallion?'

Isabelle was thrilled, so was Lydia. She replied:

'No problem, Jacques. Her friend Ginger wishes to

accompany her. You will remember Ginger was the witch who won the Arc de Triomphe on Onward. Also, Lydia will need a brief history in English of the competition.'

'Most grateful for your response to my crisis. Both youngsters are booked first-class, Air France on 30 October, and will be met at Orly by my chauffeur Persival upon arrival.

Dear Isabelle, cannot thank you enough. Lydia will have detailed history of all four favourites ready in her bedroom upon arrival. The housekeeper Santa Maria is most happy to know that "her children" are coming again!'

Upon the arrival of Lydia and Ginger at the outer yard of Volcan's stable there was pandemonium. Volcan went mad. He raced around in circles, lashed out at everyone and indeed looked dangerous. Only Lydia noticed his eyes were relaxed and full of affection.

Lydia was about to jump the stile when a strong arm caught her.

'Monsieur Becot, you are now going to witness a scene you will not forget.'

Volcan continued lashing out in all directions, he was so full of love for Lydia and needed to express it. After a few seconds Lydia sat on the steel fence.

'*Chéri, calme-toi.*'

Volcan pressed his nose into her breast, lifted her off the fence into mid air and let her down gently!

Monsieur Becot was dumbfounded, likewise all his twenty staff, as some of them commented, 'a real witch from Ireland!' Volcan, however, was hardly able to contain his emotions.

'Monsieur Becot, please saddle him up. He needs to be extended on your mile training track without delay and with your best competitors.'

Ginger was delighted to see both rider and horse so at one in a company with two powerful two-year-old Normandy stallions from the Bussac stable.

'Faster *chéri*,' Lydia murmured to Volcan as they raced.

Little did they know that Monsieur Becot was timing the

mile run, and the end of which he said simply, 'Fabulous.'

Ginger responded, 'So you are happy, Monsieur Becot.

Volcan has outclassed our best this afternoon!' he replied.

'Which ever runner can beat that time on our track will be a winner any where in Europe.'

However, the public soon found out that Lydia had arrived from England to mount Volcan, and his price went down overnight from ten to one to five to one.

Santa Maria was delighted to see 'her children' again, especially after the sensational trial this afternoon. Monsieur Bussac and Isabelle telephoned to establish that they were happy once again in their new home.

The next morning, Milligan and the vicar, also invited to the meeting by Monsieur Bussac, called to collect the riders at twelve for a light lunch at the course; the famous two-year-old stakes was scheduled for two pm.

'Well, Lydia,' the vicar enquired, 'how do you feel to be in this international racing limelight again this afternoon. Nervous?'

'Oh no, sir, simply elated. My dear mum is so happy in Winkfield, win or lose.'

After lunch, Lydia was preparing for the parade with the help of Ginger, when she met Monsieur Bussac.

'Well, my dear, are you disturbed about so much international focus on you this afternoon?'

'Oh no sir, it is all so stimulating. Our little village of Winkfield is thrilled! And your stallion Volcan is so loveable. He remembers me.'

'So it seems,' responded Monsieur Bussac thoughtfully – as he remembered the account given by Monsieur Becot about the wild reintroduction at the stables yesterday between Volcan and Lydia.

During the parade Volcan was the subject of general comparison with the Italian, German and French competition. What a fabulous two-year-old, remarked many of the visitors.

As the bell for the line-up was sounded, Monsieur Bussac was heard to say in English, 'Bless you, child, good luck.' Ginger threw kisses to Lydia, with similar encouraging words.

Lydia marked the colours of the competition,: the Italian was green, French was red and the German was black.

The speakers announced suddenly, 'They're off.' But within a few seconds a murmur was detected from the stands, followed by the announcer explaining that there was a minor collision at the start. Both the French and the German runners on the stand side had collided, and on the course side two outsiders had wedged in Volcan, who forced himself free of the wedge with his immense thrust.

'A near miss, my darling,' Lydia murmured in her best French.

These incidents resulted in a two-length late start for all three. Meanwhile the Italian co-favourite was leading the field by two lengths, going at a rare pace. The announcer continued, 'After a quarter of a mile the two co-favourites have caught up with the field, together with the witch on Volcan, but the Italian wonder stallion is now three lengths in front. At the half mile post the co-favourite, together with the witch are now one length in front of the field of thirty-six runners.'

'Now *chéri, plus vite*' breathed Lydia.

Volcan knew the cry for help; he edged in front of the two co-favourites. The announcer noticed and confirmed that the witch had overtaken the co-favourites and was moving at a fast pace in pursuit of the Italian contender, still two lengths in front with only a quarter of a mile before the post. '*Chéri, plus vite, plus vite.*' Again Volcan heard that cry and began to race like never before, every muscle in perfect unison with Lydia's body. The race crowd watched spell-bound as this mighty young two-year-old stallion started to close the distance with the Italian still racing flat out, now only half a length behind. The Italian jockey started to use his whip. Lydia bent low, close to Volcan's mane, and again urged him on with a whisper. A hundred yards from the post Volcan started to lead at last by a short head from the Italian, and from the German and French runners. Finally at the end Volcan passed the post half a length in front of the three co-favourites, amidst a great cheer from the French racing public. But the enquiry flag was raised. The jockeys of the two outsiders who had wedged in Lydia were under question by the stewards.

Lydia was there also at the invitation of the officials of the enquiry, accompanied by Milligan and Monsieur Becot.

The President of the assembly addressed the court. 'From the television records, gentlemen, it would appear that both jockeys on the outside attemped to wedge in Volcan. May we have your confirmation that this was not intentional under oath?'

Confirmation was given and it was explained that it was an accident due to the full number of runners for the race.

Lydia was asked, 'Are you satisfied with this response, *mademoiselle?*'

'Thank you sir, perfectly satisfied. My mistress often tells us, "It is not whether you win or lose in this world, it is how you play the game which counts".'

The assembly, after the translation smiled. But Lydia was surprised when both French jockeys approached her and requested her hand, which they kissed, with the words, '*Milles excuses, mademoiselle.*'

Indeed gallant Frenchmen, Milligan thought.

Upon re-entering the enclosure after weighing in, a considerable cheer was raised for Lydia. Monsieur Bussac gave her a kiss on both cheeks. Monsieur Becot was ecstatic with praise. After a warm hug from Ginger, Milligan informed Monsieur Bussac that the London bookmakers had just quoted Volcan as favourite, at evens, for both the Newmarket Two Thousand Guineas and the Derby next year.

Monsieur Bussac replied, 'This is encouraging news, *Monsieur*, but Volcan has not yet been entered for either event.'

Indeed, Lydia had become quite a favourite with the French public, even the French press next morning gave full vent to the successful combination of the English witch and the French stallion against competitors from the Italian and German runners.

At Heathrow the following afternoon at the reception, Lydia was the first to notice Heinz, and rushed straight into his outstretched arms.

A few weeks after the win by Volcan at Longchamp and the happy reunion between Heinz and Lydia, a letter arrived for Roger from the Principal of Faraday House, together with an elaborate document – a parchment with many signatories. It was the engineering science degree, after five and a half years of concentration and devotion to his studies. It was not an honours degree, it was not a first or even a second. It was a third, which for the rest of his life Roger was determined to ask in Heaven, if fortunate enough to ever arrive there, why not better than a third – only a simple pass after all that effort. At least it was the degree, established and respected by all future engineers in Nigeria as time revealed eventually. In fact, he confided his disappointment to Isabelle with a tear in his eye.

'Dear Roger, sometimes you seem to be blind about the facts. This letter which accompanied the degree already states that "this student has experienced a struggle to achieve this happy conclusion to his efforts – we have several certificates from the medical profession indicating just how hard this student has tried to secure the degree. This is the sort of student in our experience who will go a long way to success. Only the future will tell. We wish him every success along his lonely road"! You ought to be very proud indeed. So let us now have no more nonsense on this subject.'

The master was delighted. Next day in his office he expounded, 'No young student, however successful, will ever enter the working world successfully without a working knowledge of French. On Monday morning Miss Evans will have prepared for you a six-month programme at the Sorbonne, Paris, to commence July. Then 5 January the next year you will depart for a twelve months' working tour of Western Africa for our London company. This will give you three months to relax after your efforts. Then a few months in our Piccadilly office studying reports, particularly about Nigeria, in order to understand how our overseas reports are prepared. Is that clear Roger?'

'Yes, sir.'

'Meanwhile, your expense account will be doubled, plus any additional holidays which you select.'

Poor Roger, all he wanted was peace to roam the fields and woods of Oakfield Lodge with the lovely dogs, and to start some studies from a fifth-form French grammar book. Also to commune with his Creator, ever close to Roger, especially in the Old Testamant and the Psalms.

Time passed. Paris – what a fabulous experience at the division of the Sorbonne known as Institute Britannique, where only French was spoken during tea time! Some French students also attended who wanted to hear English spoken. It was then that Roger became acquainted with Annie, a law student, incredibly beautiful and full of grace. Every evening from September until late December he walked back with her to Place Pasteur, her parents' home, often in fine warm rain. Fabulous, those days, thought Roger, years afterwards. Annie was training for the legal profession at the bar in Paris. Every morning from Place Pasteur to Boule Mich, several fellow students accompanied Annie and Roger in the No. 32 Paris local bus to the Sorbonne.

It was early November when Roger received news that Milly was coming to spend ten days in Paris for a holiday from the London office.

'Well, well, thought Isabelle, and wondered about Annie, his new friend in Paris.

Roger, however, was delighted to see Milly, attractive as ever and full of grace. It was late November when Milly left for London, and during a final dinner occasion before departure for London at the Viel restaurant in Boulevard Magdeline, Roger was able to discuss their prospect for their future.

'Upon my return to Winkfield, Milly, it is my intention to announce our engagement, before the master confirms my date of departure for Lagos early January.'

'Roger, this is news, but the subject has never been discussed between us!'

'True, Milly. My feelings for you have always been so strong, especially after the care and attention you gave me during the last five difficult years at Faraday House, that it seemed to me as the years passed that it was going to be difficult for me to live without you. Before my return to Winkfield, therefore, on 15 December, will you be able to give the subject some thought? Meanwhile, Milly, *mille excuses*, as the French say, for my arrogance by taking so much for granted. Due perhaps to inexperience.'

Milly smiled. 'Of course, Roger, much thought will be given to such an important declaration. My answer will be given on 15 December, when we are both back at Oakfield Lodge.'

'Not before, Milly?'

'No, Roger. Marriage is a serious subject. It must be well planned to be a successful operation in this present world.'

Roger considered. 'You are right, dear Milly, but at least my proposal is clear.'

'Quite clear, Roger. My two distant cousins in Bordeaux have made similar proposals. In fact before returning to the London office in ten days' time, I have accepted invitations to stay with each of the two French families in turn.'

Roger nearly exploded!

'One invitation,' continued Milly, 'is from the Requier family. You may remember that one of their members, a young man, was not very polite to Ginger, our rider on Onward at Longchamp and at Royal Ascot. She floored him by a comfortable win in both events. He was so cross that he referred to Ginger as "that witch" in the French press the next day. Ginger was so proud to be mentioned in the *Figaro* as a witch she framed it for all to see in their cottage at Winkfield!'

'This is news to me, Milly, yet it explains your visits to Bordeaux during the last few years. Dear Milly, you have brought me back to mother earth in my growing-up stage. It does not surprise me that these two different French families were interested in your visits. You will have to bear with me, Milly, in my complete lack of wooing experience after those five and a half years of concentration at Faraday House. At what time do you leave for Bordeaux?'

'Eight thirty am tomorrow from Gare de Lyons.'

'Count on me to be there to see you off.'

'Thank you, dear Roger.'

He was more than thoughtful on the way back to his hotel in Place Pasteur from Boulevard Magdeline, about thirty-five minutes' walk. Milly was beautifully built, full of grace and French élégance, and très avisée. It never occurred to him that others were after the hand of Milly!

Fortunately at the station next morning, there was time for half an hour's discussion.

'You look gorgeous, Milly.'

'Did you sleep well, Roger?'

'Not at all.'

'Why?'

'Thinking of you going off into another world without me.'

Milly smiled. 'There is a French word for it, *courage*.'

Yes, thought Roger.

'Tell me, Roger, do you believe in marital relations before marriage?'

'Definitely *not* Milly, the New Testament makes this clear,' Roger responded; he felt on his own ground.

'That is what it is important to me to know. You have made my day. Bless you, dear Roger.' She gave him a warm kiss as the train left.

Once back at Oakfield Lodge, there was one further problem for Roger and Milly: in order to cement the engagement, the date of the marriage had to be established. In fact, Roger insisted that the marriage must take place after his working tour of Western Africa, as already instructed by the master earlier, in order to prove to himself of sufficient worth to accept all the responsibilities of married life. This was accepted by Milly on condition that there was to be no official engagement announcement, which left Milly free from formal commitments. Roger had to accept this condition, which was only fair on Milly, and it made sense.

39

After several visits to Cambridge during the summer and autumn terms to see Lucie at Girton College, John became encouraged also to press his hand for engagement to marriage. Lucie made several visits to her cousin in Florence, who underlined her responsibilities for the estate as the sole owner.

'My plan is simple, dear cousin. The proposal is to make ten per cent of the shares over to each of the ten overseers but not to split the estate. My position will remain as the principal shareholder and adviser at our Annual General Meeting. Does that make sense?'

'Admirable, my dear, so long as your offspring benefit likewise and provision on that subject is made clear in your will and testament. Next, the subject of marriage, my child. Presumably, without baptism in the Roman Catholic faith, you will be content to be married under the jurisdiction of the Church of England. In view of the fact that your future husband is a minister of that Christian faith, you have my blessing on the subject. The location of the union presumably will be in England, at the Winkfield church.'

'Thank you dear cousin, very much. However, there is an alternative proposal, namely to be married here in Florence in a Roman Catholic church. My fiancé John does not mind, apart from which he knows that it will give you great pleasure.'

'A splendid suggestion, Lucie. Will you leave all arrangements to me, including all costs? The ten managers and their wives will be overwhelmed with joy.

'Most willingly, dear cousin, and guidance about the wedding dress also.'

'It makes me feel young again.'

Upon returning to Winkfield Lucie issued invitations to

Isabelle and all available members of the family. Roger and Milly also were able to attend. The agreed date was 7 June, a few weeks before the departure of Roger for his six-month studies at the Sorbonne. Dispensation was granted to Lucie for the weeks of absence from her studies at Girton. Isabelle and Milly were keenly interested in all the activity and sometimes accompanied Lucie to Florence as advisers on all feminine matters.

Eventually the marriage took place in the Cathedral in Florence, and indeed it was a most impressive religious ceremony; to Isabelle it seemed that half the town turned out. Signora, the old cousin, was well known for kindness and generosity to many local worshippers in Florence. The ten managers of the estate and all their cousins came to support the occasion and to partake in the feasting and revelry, which went from the end of the church service at one pm until midnight. The bride and groom departed for a hidden cottage on the north coast of Italy, all organised by the cousin at about three pm, in true Italian style, where selected Italian domestic helpers from the villa in Florence were able to provide the desired intimacy.

John never forgot the exquisite beauty of Lucie as she walked down the aisle in the grace of the occasion to the altar on that June day. The complete silence in that highly packed cathedral was full of heavenly grace as the marriage vows were exchanged. What a contrast a little later from the choir and string orchestra as the ceremony continued after the blessings. A memorable wedding, which was not forgotten in Florence for a long time afterwards – nor at Winkfield by Isabelle, Roger and Milly, as they recounted in detail to all the local village members the great pageant of the spectacular event.

A few weeks later, after Lucie and John had settled into their newly built home near the Winkfield vicarage, Lucie decided that she wished to teach locally in the village, instructing young children in the Christian faith. Her studies at Girton College continued, in which she continued to excel. However, she became fond of her part-time devotion to activities in the school for children. attached to the village church of Reverend Manning. Attendance grew, for Lucie had a gift of transmitting the spirit of love to these local rustics. The children loved their lessons and they came from miles around. In fact, twice weekly the attendance was about thirty-four children. The vicar was approached.

'Perhaps we can extend the programme to three times a week, sir.'

'No problem, Lucie. After all, you founded this little addition to the Winkfield church activities, together with the improvements and adornment to our Lady Chapel. The government inspectors are due next week in order to establish in class that the teaching is in accord with patterns laid down.'

'Thank you, sir, very much.'

This way of life continued into the late summer, and one Sunday morning at nine am Lucie noticed a little stranger, a boy of about eight years old, sitting in the last row of the classroom. She knelt down by the small desk.

'Who are you? Where do you come from? What is your name? Are your parents known to me?'

The little boy looked up – a little frightened. 'If my presence is not right, Miss, my departure will take place now. My father insisted that there must be no trouble with my presence in your new school.'

'Do not worry, little boy, but who are you – your name?'

The little boy looked down on the floor, 'Miss, I am a Jew born and bred. Now you will want to turn me out.' He started to gather a little parcel by his side.

'No, child, please do not leave us, but please let me know the reasons for your visit to this Christian chapel.'

The little boy hesitated, 'My name is Levi, Miss.' Lucie was thrilled with the name of her favourite character in the New Testament, a smuggler to evade payment of custom duty, a man of the underworld selected by Christ two thousand years ago to help Him to bring in the sinners and loafers of Jerusalem to the great feast.

'Very well, Levi, then why come to this remote little convent early on this lovely June morning, as a Jew, to attend my class on Christianity?'

The little boy looked up, again a little frightened. Because, Miss, little Jesus died for me.'

Lucie nearly collapsed. She struggled to gain control,

handkerchief to her eyes. 'My dear child, you will be always most welcome to these classes.'

The boy observed her distress. 'Are you well, Miss? Are you perhaps upset with my presence?' She noticed his perfect English, spoken by someone so young. She hugged him close; he smiled, a lovely young face so full of innocence.

'Do not worry, Levi, we are now close friends. Who are your parents?'

'My mother passed away five years ago. My home is on the Asher Estate, close by.'

'Does your father approve of this meeting?'

Lucie knew of it, a vast place of 10,000 acres, the occupants of which were unknown by the village.

'Oh yes, Miss, he wants to see you soon! My young friends in the village school at Winkfield asked to come to this church gathering on Sunday for young people. So today my father gave me permission, and asked me to tell you to come and see him one evening before his departure for Lagos in December.'

Well, well, thought Lucie, A Jewish family!

A few days later Lucie ventured forth to meet his father, a French Jew, Monsieur de Moncret, a fine tall courteous man keenly interested to meet Lucie.

The introduction was brief, evidently he was a man whose time is valuable.

'So you are Lucie. Please excuse the familiarity, *madame*, but time is short before my return to Nigeria.'

'Will you take your little boy with you?'

'That is quite impossible, Lucie. Hence my keen interest to meet you this evening.'

At that moment a uniformed steward entered. 'Two urgent calls from Lagos, *monsieur*.'

'Please ask them to phone back in one hour from now.'

'No problem, *monsieur*.'

'The boy has now no mother, Lucie. In fact, there is no mother, wife, sister or mistress who can be counted on to welcome the interests of Levi. Can you help me with this problem, all costs for my account. His governess is due any moment to bid me good night with Levi.'

'Are you sure that you wish your child to be brought up

in the Christian Faith? Levi will have to be baptised.'

'In fact, it is my great desire.'

'In that case, sir, there ought to be no problem. My address for the present is given on this card for all future communications.'

At that moment the governess entered with Levi, who was so pleased to see Lucie that he ran immediately to her chair and settled himself under her arm.

'You see what is needed, Lucie – a little motherly care and love, that priceless commodity, so rare to find in this world!'

'You may count upon me one hundred per cent. When he has kissed you good night, will you kindly ask the governess to accompany me to his bedroom, where a short prayer will be said with me by his bedside, before my departure.'

'Thank you so much, Lucie. The estate manager and bailiff will be intructed to ensure that you and your selected children at the Sunday School from now will have the rights of entry at all times to the farms and the park. Please, meanwhile, each month let me have a short note about the progress made with Levi's entry into the Christian faith.'

Lucie settled down happily to her new teaching vocation at the vicarage, and John commenced to edit books on practical Christian codes of conduct. Meanwhile, Levi prospered under their care.

Soon after Richard's return from Lagos, Isabelle received a letter from Jacqueline in Paris, confirming that Richard had been officially recommended to perform concertos by Brahms, Haydn, Chopin and Mozart at the Conservatoire de Paris in late October. This news came as a surprise to Richard, who responded without delay.

'Impossible, my darling. It gives me only from August until the end of October to acquire the perfection well known and desired by the Conservatoire de Paris.'

Isabelle was crestfallen. 'Surely, Richard, with the dogs once again for company in Inverness, and those twenty-mile tramps through the windswept forests of the Highlands and with a lunch-time rest at the crofters' cottages, where you will want to share your lamb sandwich and a wee dram with their inmates, you would be well equipped after a few weeks to confront the Conservatoire authorities. Sir William is an understanding conductor.'

'Your request is demanding, Isabelle. Please give me a few hours to work out the parameters. Meanwhile, please telephone Miss Glenfield and ask whether the grand piano remains in excellent order.'

It was next morning, at 5.30 am when Isabelle awoke to find that Richard's place in their double bed was cold and that he had left the room fully dressed for an early morning stroll. It was high summer, so perhaps he had gone for a long walk. Yet upon arriving downstairs she discovered that the dogs also had likewise disappeared from their open kennels, close to the kitchen door. There was a note by an empty coffee cup: 'The earth is the Lords and the fullness thereof. Blessed be the name of the Lord. *Bonne route.*

What can he mean by these words, thought Isabelle. The morning was warm, the sun was up, Hurry-On was stamping his feet! Isabelle was in her nightdress. The men were in the shed milking a pedigree herd of forty-eight shorthorns. Isabelle adjusted the bridle and her soft saddle and mounted Hurry-On, who was full of joy to find his mistress up so early and ready for a gallop into the early morning mists. Away they went at speed as Milligan read the note fixed to the gatepost as usual – 'Back in one hour. Gone to John's!'

'Well,' thought Milligan, Hurry-On deserves a run on such a lovely morning with such a lovely rider.

Lucie, already up, was delighted to see Isabelle. 'Your dear husband left half an hour ago after his large cup of French coffee, but he left behind these rough musical scores on Haydn and Brahms. Please therefore do sit down and enjoy a cup of coffee also. I'm in my new dressing gown from Florence – just in case the Bishop appears. He is staying next door with Reverend Manning as usual. Our own house will be completed soon, quite close by.'

'So married life suits you, Lucie?'

'Oh yes, Isabelle, and John is impatient for babies!'

'How very right. Since we are such close neighbours, do please let me know whenever you may need help from me, now I'm a mature mother of twins.'

'Several musical scores were left on the garden table. Your dear husband wanted to be alone for half an hour, as he explained, to imbibe the early light and nature's awakening sounds, which encourage inspiration,' she continued. 'Before leaving, he kept saying, "Brahms is OK, Hadyn likewise, even Mozart, but Chopin *no*". Is it possible for me to help, Richard?' I asked.

' "Yes indeed, Lucie, a gorgeous kiss from those full young lips," he replied. 'Perhaps it was wrong of me, Isabelle, but I granted his request, even in my *robe de chambre*. My whole body vibrated to his kiss. He seemed to be worked up with intense passion – indeed my body was a little breathless. Just before his departure he looked at me like a man on fire. "Is there something wrong Richard"? I asked." No, dear Lucie, your spiritual world, so well known in the village, has revealed to me this morning that the Chopin piece will be the great success of the concert at the Conservatoire de Paris. No wonder they refer to you in Cambridge as an angel", he said. "It seems to me that our spirits have met together this morning – to help me with this latest request from Paris to perform. If successful, Lucie, the Chopin will be dedicated to you, my inspiration in this little garden on a lovely summer morning, with you in a lovely *robe de chambre*"! Then he left, but not without another warm intimate kiss once again, which made my body vibrate for at least a minute after his departure.'

Isabelle noticed that all the scores except those sketched for Chopin were left on the table. So, thought Isabelle, my dear husband is a passionate man. May the Lord bless him.

Richard did not arrive until noon. The dogs were exhausted. After removing his muddy shoes, he noticed her in their kitchen.

'Darling you win,' he remarked, 'but it cost me a spiritual battle – Chopin was the problem. The answer to your request is Yes!'

She reached up to him on tiptoe to kiss him. 'So it was Lucie who helped you to make up your mind.'

'Yes, without doubt, a remarkable young, sympathetic spirit from another world! She was left with two warmhearted kisses for the inspiration.'

'Hopefully you did not frighten her with your burst of passion.'

'Lucie is far too deeply immersed in the spirit world to be disturbed by my affectionate address. In fact, dear Isabelle, she was irresistible in that dawn sunlit mist, with her long curly tresses falling over her unadorned shoulders and her innocent inviting full lips – it was just that fleeting vision of her beauty that gave me the key link to the exquisite harmony and grace needed for the Piano Concerto No. 2 by Chopin, Indeed, it is possible for me to tell you now that, yes, you and your friend Jacqueline will not be disappointed at the Paris Consevatoire late October. Meanwhile please ensure that everything in Inverness is in perfect order ready for Monday, plus two extra blankets for my bed – necessary after the great heat of Lagos.'

Isabelle remained a little subdued.

'What is the problem, my darling?'

She smiled, but remained silent. He lifted her on to the couch and with all his passion kissed her.

'You are disturbed about my classical inspiration with Lucie this morning.'

'No, it is not that.'

'Well?'

She looked uncertain, a little shy. He became concerned. She continued, 'It seems that you have two adorables now!'

'*Ca alor,*' he ejaculated. '*Tu es la seule adorable*! Dearest Isabelle, you must try to understand – not having seen a white woman in Nigeria for the last three months, the brains in my head have become restless upon arriving back into circulation, especially after the vision seen this morning.'

She was reassured when he started to explore her lovely breasts. Unfortunately, Mrs Plant was knocking at the door.

Isabelle quickly readjusted her dress, as Richard cursed his luck.

'Do not worry, my darling, you will be ravished tonight and filled with delight and exquisite pleasure, in order to assure you that there is only one adorable in my life.'

Later in the day Isabelle pondered Richard's experience with Lucie. Indeed it was well known that inexplicable sympathy existed between complete strangers sometimes suddenly, for no given reason, especially between people under stress, or people devoted to music, art, literature and wth spiritual experience.

Richard kept his word, she was in ecstasy in his arms all night, and rather late morning for breakfast ... noted by Mrs Plant!

Once back in the Highlands, Richard's energy burst forth as the August wind and early autumn rains approached from the west. This was the life, those twenty-mile tramps through the glens, in the teeming warm rain, mile after mile including a stop occasionally at a crofter's hut, where a few rapid notes were made to the rough blank paper, which served as a temporary score for Chopin. The three dogs Dante, Boozer and Lupa were tired, and often came to search and sniff at his pockets for the bones, full of meat, prepared by the housekeeper beforehand.

One of the crofters, well known to Richard since he was a boy of ten years old, asked him, 'So, Master Richard, may we expect to hear your performance from Paris on the radio in late October?'

'You may indeed, Jock.'

'Bless you, lad,' Jock replied.

It was then that the dogs came to ask for their food, at the same time Richard loved to share his delicious lamb sandwich with the three crofters and their more modest fare in their hillside home, with two wee bairns he noticed – fast asleep indeed adorable babies.

'Jock, any problems?'

'No lad, except that the game laws are a bit stiff.'

'Leave that to me. You and our friends may continue without problems. Let it be culling, putting it down to excess production of game.'

'Thank thee master.'

Miss Glenfield was overwhelmed when Richard returned at seven pm – soaked through for the rain had never stopped all day!

'Please rub down the dogs, Miss Glenfield, before they retire to their fresh straw-filled kennels. Is the water for my bath hot?'

'Very hot, Richard, as you used to like it twenty years ago!'

Fully refreshed, and changed and with a light meal, to the distress of Miss Glenfield, Richard started to work on his scores for Chopin, Brahms, Haydn and Mozart until two am at the grand piano. All was asleep when he left the study. The old castle was happy to have him once again in its spirit, as he knelt down and gave thanks by the lovely statue of the Holy Virgin, installed by his mother many years ago. The dogs were fast asleep as he went to inspect their abode, and Miss Glenfield left a note 'Do not hesitate to press the bell, in case of need.'

The dear soul, thought Richard. What a privilege to be looked after by these lovely people.

He slept in ecstasy, remembering last night with his wife, and that fabulous kiss in the morning mist with Lucie, and that phantom music of the Highland glens and the forests' winds and rain through which he had tramped for several hours with the dogs all day.

Miss Glenfield ventured to accost him at ten am, but he was still asleep. She tried again at eleven, this time with success, and with a large bowl of strong Darjeeling tea.

'Dear Richard, are you well?'

'Not until you give me a kiss.'

'No problem, Richard, but so many phone calls, telegrams and letters, it seems so important for you to give a few answers soon.'

'The most important action for the moment, Miss Glenfield, is another large pot of Darjeeling tea.'

Bless the boy, she thought as she retired from his room.

Richard continued to work on the piano at several scores, with the dogs around him all morning. The rain had eased off, so after a light lunch sandwich and a pint of home-brewed beer, he set off with the dogs once again in another direction through sunlit glades. After a while he sat on a tree-log to write. It was a beautiful early autumn evening, about five pm, when the Highland colours everywhere seemed to be playing tricks with his imagination. He stopped writing. The cloud layers, sun-rays and the autumn colours all appeared as (seen just as in the early morning mists of last weekend) to create in the evening sky that exquisite face of Lucie, full red inviting lips and dazzling dark tresses just covering her breasts and shoulders, in her nightdress! Little wonder, he thought, that he was precipitated at that time into ... another world, a passionate kiss, which was not returned. In fact Lucie simply expressed mild surprise with a very slight smile; no word was spoken.

Most wrong of me, thought Richard. Yet just now that strange vision ... will she be at the concert in Paris? He must try to take more control of these feelings. Yet his work continued at a furious pace, no paper was left and the sun was low, and he felt cold. In fact the dogs urged him to move. Yet that vision, what did it mean? At least now he was enthusiastic and confident he would be able to render a work to remember at the Conservatoire. And he did.

During the gathering and reunion with Jacqueline, her friends, her husband Sir William, the conductor, and Gaston, their French friend. Isabelle had the impression that Richard was looking for someone. Meanwhile, Isabelle had never seen in London such elegance and exquisite taste, the colours of the gowns in harmony with the natural beauty of the French female complexion.

The concert commenced with piano concertos by Mozart and Brahms, which were applauded loudly by the audience. After the interval music by Haydn then followed, and eventually the well-known works by Chopin, the Concerto No. 2 and Polonaise Op. 13. Richard's hand seemed to race across the keyboard with infinite grace, effortless, and with the consummate ease of a master player, to produce such harmony, as Gaston had remarked the previous year, he had rarely experienced before in his lifetime. The audience remained spellbound until the end. It was only then that Richard seemed to awake from another world. Indeed it was the applause that brought him back to reality, and the affectionate embrace from the conductor, Sir William. The standing ovation continued for two minutes, and he gave a graceful bow to the assembly.

The evening party, a private affair, was arranged at one of the well-known restaurants in Rue Royale.

Isabelle noticed a note on the plate prepared for Richard. 'Perhaps it is from the President, Richard?'

The note was opened, it read quite simply: *Félicitations, L*
Well, thought Isabelle.
'More important, my darling. It was from an angel!'
Just before they went to sleep in a large double bed, Isabelle asked, 'Did it have real wings?'
He replied, as he hugged her close, '*Tu es adorable,*' and they slept close until eleven am the next morning!
The French press gave a glowing account of the performance.